FAR AWAY FROM NOWHERE

Far Away from Nowhere

STORIES

Matthew McConkey

Also by Matthew McConkey

Home Again
Scarecrows and Shadows
Maple Lane
Everything Fades In Time
Summerland

Table of Contents

For Tinker

WALTISMS

Bill Breaman and his wife, Amy, sat in the crowded church amongst people he didn't even know– save the two adult children of his best friend. Walt Wickham was the man in the casket on display at the front of the church, just under the podium the preacher used for his Sunday sermons. Bill was seventy now and had just celebrated a birthday with his family when the news came about his only real friend. Walt made it to seventy-one. His death hit Bill close to home in more ways than one. Not only were they like brothers, but the age at which Walt died was close to Bill's. Both of those elements caused Bill to call into question his mortality.

The news of Walt's death shouldn't have hit him as hard as it did. He and Walt had discussed death not too long ago—especially after Lucy, his wife—died a year back. The two of them talked about how many years they may have left. This conversation took place on Walt's front porch that evening. Bill had taken his evening stroll down Nap Street where he lived and turned down Owl Lane where his best friend for over sixty years lived.

Walt was the only true friend he ever had– the only one that stayed around him. Not that Bill was a bad guy; it was just the other friends in their group had broken connections with them during high school, moved off, or died. When it came down to it, Bill and Walt were the only ones left. Somehow Bill figured this would be how it ended, with just the two of them.

***

They were sitting on Walt's front porch as Walt waved at cars that traveled slowly down his street. Walt knew everyone– it seemed to Bill. That particular day, the two got to talking about what they always talked about: the old days. That seemed like the only thing of interest anymore. Both being retired with nothing much else to do, the good old days always put the two of them in a good mood– no matter what was going on in their lives behind closed doors.

Death came up oftentimes, too. Walt was preoccupied with the subject, and Bill wondered if Walt knew something that he didn't. Like did he get some bad news at the doctor? Bill never asked because one thing that he learned a long time ago about his best friend was that he was a private person. He found out how Walt was doing via his wife, Lucy, who loved to talk and gossip. Walt? Never. He wasn't wired that way. But Bill remembered Walt's daddy, and he was the same way when they were growing up. You just can't beat your DNA.

"What do you think it'll be like when one of us dies?" Walt asked.

"It'll be strange, Walt. Very strange." Bill replied to this question, one he had answered before—many times—with careful consideration. Most of that was for show. He wanted to show Walt that he was thinking about it.

"I mean to tell you," Walt said, spitting tobacco out of his mouth across the front porch and into the hedges. "Me and you have been together longer than me and Lucy have been married, and that's a long time."

"Since we were ten years old," Bill said.

"That's a damn lifetime– you know it?"

Bill nodded, "It is, Walt. Goes by fast, doesn't it?"

"Sure as hell does. Remember back when Daddy used to tell us to appreciate our youth? He wasn't lying. That man knew what was coming. What eventually comes for us all...old age."

"Yup. If we're lucky. Hell, we could've ended up like Tommy Tillburton and died right before high school graduation. Remember that?"

Walt nodded slowly, "Yup. He was a good one though, wasn't he?"

Bill nodded, rocking slowly in the rocking chair beside his pal. "Yup. He was a good one."

"Grandpa Anderson lived to be a hundred and four. Think about that for a second. We're still thirty-four years away from him right now."

"Crazy to think about, ain't it?" Bill said passively.

"Yup. He used to tell me– this was back when me and Lucy first got married– he said, 'Walter,' he always called me Walter, you see, he said, 'Walter. Living long is a curse. Don't let people tell you any different.' He was fifty when me and Lucy got married. Thereabouts, I reckon. He was younger than we are now."

Bill shook his head, "Crazy."

Walt leaned over in his rocking chair and spat another mouthful of tobacco across the porch and into the hedges. "Yup, it is. Crazy."

***

Lucy had died a year after that front porch conversation, leaving Walt to shuffle around his house all by himself. It was okay, Walt had told him.

"I still feel her here. So I'm not lonely really. The kids and grandkids come by on Sundays. And I got you and Amy. It's just different, is all."

Again, that was Walt, private Walt. Bill knew better though. He knew that his friend was heartbroken, devastated by his wife's passing. Who wouldn't be? He'd be lost if something happened to Amy. He shuddered to think about that reality and hoped he would go first. He knew that was selfish thinking, but he didn't care. Bill could never bear to see his wife die. He wasn't as strong as Walt. No way.

But a year and some change after Lucy's death, there was Bill again at the same church mourning his best friend of sixty years. Amy squeezed Bill's hand as the preacher got up to begin the service for the man in the box. As the preacher reached the podium and cleared his throat, he started to speak. A hush rolled over those in attendance. It was quiet there except for the man at the podium who talked about God and His promises, taking the words from the Bible.

As the preacher spoke about death not being the true end of life, and about how Walt Wickham was with his wife, Bill sat back on the pew and his mind began to drift—as it often did—and thought about another conversation he and Walt had a few months ago on his front porch. It was about a guy who lived in between them, Dale Derrick.

Dale was around sixty-five, had retired, and did nothing but sit all day and night. He had no family, no pets, no hobbies. The man just sat either in his house or on his front porch. If you saw Dale, he was always sitting. He once told people that he stood on concrete all his life and that sitting down was a gift from God. When the news came down that Dale died in his sleep and was found by the guy who cuts his yard, it was the topic of conversation between Bill and Walt.

"He sat down too damn much," Walt said, spitting his tobacco across his front porch and into the hedges that evening.

Bill rocked slowly in his rocking chair and nodded. "Yup."

"You won't catch me just sitting around getting fat, no sir. I still get out and take my walks around the neighborhood, mow my own yard–hell, I still do as much as I can."

"Me too," Bill said. "Dale fell into that trap of getting old. He stopped going. I told him several times when I was on my way over here, and I'd see him sitting on his front porch that he needed to get some exercise."

"And what did you tell you?"

"He got plenty when he was young," Bill replied.

"Yeah, well, apparently not enough, I reckon. Now look at him."

"I don't want to fully retire. I don't. I don't want to end up like Dale. And it's easy to do that, easy to just sit down and never get up," Bill said.

"Hell yes, I know what you mean. If I didn't work three days a week at the plant, I'd go out of my mind around here. I've got hobbies, but sometimes you just need out of the house. Since Lucy's gone, I'm glad I never fully retired."

"Same here. I still might not be the fastest Pepsi vendor on the route, but I do my job when I'm there. Three days is plenty," Bill said. "But I tell you what though– I can start to feel my age now. Getting up from stocking those bottom shelves with those twenty-four packs is getting harder. I suspect when I can't do it anymore, I'll know when I have to have help getting up."

"Yup. That's when you'll finally reach the age of knowing when you just can't do it anymore. But, we still got most of our hair and all our original teeth, so that's something ain't it? Won't matter if we can't get up– we still doing better than most in those departments," Walt laughed and spit tobacco across the front porch into the hedges.

"Yup," Bill replied.

***

Bill was jarred out of his trance by his wife softly pushing him. He looked at her and then around. She nodded up to the preacher and when Bill turned his eyes to the man up at the podium, the man was looking back at him, waiting. Bill knew what he was waiting for. He was waiting for Bill to get up and walk past his friend in the box, up the three stairs, and to the podium. From there he would talk about his best friend to those in attendance.

How did he get that honor? Walt's children had asked if he would say some words about their dad. Bill was happy to do it and didn't see any dread in it. But he was nervous about it, to say the least. Not because he was afraid of talking before large crowds but rather how odd and out of place he felt to be talking about someone—a best friend who was like a brother—while they weren't around to hear any of it. This was going to be the final time Bill and Walt would be in the same place together.

In that moment of thought, tears formed in his eyes just for a second before he blinked them away. Bill cleared his throat and looked at his wife, who nodded her head in a "you can do this" kind of way. Bill had a eulogy written– numerous pages he had written earlier. But when he read the speech again, it felt robotic, rehearsed. He didn't like that and thought Walt wouldn't like it, either. So he was going to wing it. He hadn't told this to Amy, of course, because if he had, then she would have freaked out. She thought what he had written was really touching. He looked over at Walt's children and grandchildren, and they were smiling up at him. Bill nodded to them.

With all eyes on him—which was over a thousand because the place was packed—Bill cleared his throat yet again and started...

"We're here today to mourn the passing of Walt Wickham. He was a good man. An honest man. He was a beloved husband and father. He was my best friend. But that's too shallow of a description of our relationship. He was a brother to me. We had more time together than we had with our families. And that's crazy when you stop to think about it. For sixty years, he and I were in each other's lives.

"We met when we were ten years old in the fifth grade. Back in 1990, this was. A long time ago. It's a long time ago only if you think of it in terms of years. Walt didn't change very much from then until he got to be an old man."

People in the audience chuckled, even his kids because they knew Walt was pretty much the same dad they had known from start to finish. Bill was relieved that the subtle joke landed in this time of grief. He smiled and began to feel more at ease up at the podium.

"I can't count the number of conversations me and Walt had over the years. We talked about everything: kids, family, work, politics, sports, women— you name it, we talked about it. We had been through a lot together. I'm going to miss him terribly. I know that. But Walt always had these things he said to me throughout our time together as friends and as brothers. They were quotes he had made up, well before you could Google quotes about life. Walt was good at that. He was good at dispensing words of wisdom. I'm sure you kids know all about that. Trust me, he did the same for me."

Again, chuckles from the audience and his kids.

"Those quotes of his always stuck with me, and they still do even today. I had written this long eulogy about Walt. But I decided to just toss it and wing it. I don't think I'll ever be able to sum up the man's life that meant so much to me and to all of you. So I'm not going to try. But what I am going to do is talk about how Walt was always there to help me.

"I remember back when we were young married men—just married for about I'd say, maybe a year and a half—he and I were sitting on my front porch. We'd built that porch back in 2001. It was several days before 9/11 happened. Me and Walt were sitting on the edge of the front porch, down on the floor because I hadn't bought any chairs yet— couldn't afford to. Barely had enough money for the wood for the porch. Back then, me and Walt were struggling to pay bills because when you're starting out newly married with kids on the way, it was hard on us.

"So anyways, we're sitting there talking about the future, and our current job situation as it was, and Walt said to me one of the things I'll never forget. It was one of those "Waltisms." He said, 'You gotta work with what you got.' Something about that saying of his really resonated with me. I used it just the other day when I told my son about an issue that he was having. It's a universal saying because it fits every situation. Walt always knew the right time to pull those out.

"Another one of those Waltisms was when me and my wife, Amy, first started talking before we got married. We had met at the store I serviced because I was their potato chip vendor at the time. I saw her, thought she was pretty, and I still think that. She and I would flirt back and forth for months. I was nineteen at the time, and I was up in Walt's bedroom at his parents' house, rambling on and on about Amy. I wasn't sure if she was interested at all. So, I asked Walt what he thought about it, based on everything I had told him.

"He was playing on his Nintendo 64– Mario Brothers, I'm pretty sure– when he paused the game and looked over at me. 'If she's interested, she'll talk. If she's not, then she won't. But it sounds like she's interested, Billy.' That's how I knew that Amy was interested. I applied that same Waltism to my own kids when they weren't sure if someone they liked, liked them back. I just told them what Walt had told me. They thought I was a genius, but it was Walt that was the smart guy, not me.

"Another time, one of these Waltisms came when he was having issues down at the factory he worked in. He was telling me a story about a dust-up between him and his supervisor. I can't really remember exactly what it was about. But when Walt finished telling me his story about the issues between them, I felt he was right. I knew that he wasn't going to back down. That wasn't the kind of man he was. If he felt he was right, he just dug in his heels even more. I will say the man was more right than wrong by leaps and bounds. But I'm sure if Lucy was here, she'd argue about that.

"There was a strong chance that he was going to be fired; and if he got fired, what was that going to mean not only for him, but for his young family? But he said something after everything eventually settled down. He said, 'You have to teach people how to treat you'. What he meant by that was if you allow people to walk all over you, they'll think you're okay with it. I've applied that to my life as well and have also told my kids that Waltism along with the rest of them.

"Walt had another one of those sayings. It was back when he got skipped for a big job promotion down at the factory. Man, he really wanted that job too. Getting it would have made it so Lucy didn't have to work ever again. That was the goal when their kids were young. It didn't happen, of course. But I remember me and him were out to eat over at Junction Cafe one evening. It was our thing that we did every other Wednesday: just go in and order something small. Usually a hamburger or chicken strips. We had gone to that place since we were kids and saw the ownership change hands at least five times. But the constant thing was me and Walt. They knew us by name there and usually, they brought out what they thought we'd order. Most of the time, they were right on the money. Very few times they weren't, but it was okay; we'd go ahead and eat anyway because we liked everything there. Walt sometimes liked it a little too much.

"So me and Walt were talking the night he got told he didn't get the promotion. They went in favor of this hot-shot college graduate. I asked Walt if he was upset. He said that he was, and we talked about it. But he told me that 'one of the keys to life is how you react to things.' He was right about that. Another one of those Waltisms I've applied to my life as well as my kids.

"I'll tell this one story at the risk of my wife cutting me when we get home. Ah, we've been together for so long, it probably won't matter anyway. So back when me and Amy first got married, we had a fight. I can't remember what it was about. If you think about it—study a bit— most fights you can't remember throughout a marriage, especially if they're long like ours. Anyway, I remember slamming the front door and going for a walk out in the neighborhood. I was probably around thirty at the time, I reckon.

"I found myself over at Walt and Lucy's house, and he was outside in the yard on his John Deere rider, cutting grass. He saw me and stopped, and we talked for a bit. I finally got around to saying what it was I was doing out that way right around sunset. I told him what was going on: about the fight me and Amy had. I remember he wiped his sweaty face with a rag from his back pocket, and he looked at me. He said he understood where I was coming from because Lucy was the same way. Then he spoke one of his Waltisms that hit home with me, as they all did.

"He says, 'Marriages are all about trade-offs. Meaning: what are you willing to put up with—trade—in order to keep the peace with the person you love'? He was right. I'm sure Amy has made a LOT of trade-offs being married to me for as long as she has been. But Walt was right about that. He was right about more than he was wrong. One of the smartest men I ever knew.

"There was a girl I dated in high school. I was crazy about her. She was a cheerleader, and I was a basketball player. We dated off and on, and then we decided that we were just going to be exclusive. Well, that didn't last long as most high school romances don't. Forever to a teenager is about a month. So me and Kelly dated, and then it ended and ended really bad—like, everyone in school knew about it, and they all took sides. It was very messy.

"So, me and Walt are out riding around one night in his Malibu Classic, and we were talking about how off the rails things had gone with me and Kelly. We're sitting at a stop light, and Walt looks over at me and says, 'If relationships didn't go bad, then everyone would still be with the first person they said yes to.' You can't argue with that logic. I never tried when Walt gave me insights. He seemed to have his finger always on the button. He knew what to say and when to say it. If he was quiet, that meant he was thinking. Which was often. He wasn't a talker for all the years I knew him; and trust me, that was a lot of years.

"I'm going to miss him greatly, as will his family. He was family to me. More than a friend—a twin flame. I don't know what being in this world without him really feels like since we met all those decades ago. I do know that it will be an adjustment for me. As it will for you guys. Sometimes you get lucky as a human. Someone comes into your life, and you get to keep them for as long as I was able to know Walt. We used to talk about what it was going to be like when one of us died. And I'm sure if Walt was here, he'd have one of his Waltisims to say that'd make it somehow make sense."

AT THE STARS

It was a gloomy, rainy afternoon at the graveside service for Matthew Morgan. He was the man in the box that sat atop the freshly dug grave, and the one that they all came to see off one final time. His death was a shock– unexpected to say the least. He was not sick. He was pretty healthy, by all accounts. But what could have ended his life? Most in attendance thought the culprit was a massive stroke or a heart attack. Maybe a brain aneurysm. Honestly, it was none of the three. What happened to Matthew Morgan was something so simple, so silly– that when it happened, it was nothing. At least, that was how Matthew perceived it.

On the day he died, Matthew had gotten out of the shower like he had done a million times before in his life. This time was different. When he got out of the shower, he placed his right foot on the tile floor and when he began to place his left leg out of the tub, his right foot slipped out from underneath him. He went sprawling, hitting his head against the wall of the tub, and then he rolled onto the floor of the bathroom in a heap.

"Honey! You okay in there?!" Carrie asked from the other side of the locked bathroom door after hearing him fall.

"Yeah, I'm okay," Matthew said, laying there wet and naked on the floor. "I'm good. Just slipped and fell is all. But I'm okay."

"Do you need help getting up?" she asked, twisting the locked doorknob.

Matthew lay there and felt a terrible pain radiate throughout his head. It seemed that his head had taken the brunt of the fall. He felt dizzy, woozy.

"No," he replied. "I'm good. Just give me a second and I'll be fine."

Matthew laid on the floor for a bit, then rolled over to his side and picked himself off the floor. He stood and looked himself over for any blood or cuts. All was good. But the pain in his head, especially the back of it, was more prominent. *I might have a concussion though*, he thought, as he reached for a towel to dry off.

At some point in the night, Matthew died in his sleep alongside his wife. When she woke up, she lay there, listening to her phone go off. It was time to get up and get ready for work. She threw the covers off and got out of bed, shutting her phone's alarm off. She walked out of the bedroom and down the hall for her early morning shower. After the shower was over, she dried off, got dressed for work, and out the front door she went to start her day– an hour and a half after the alarm woke her. Matthew was in the bed– dead from the blow to the head when he slipped while getting out of the shower. What people didn't know– how could they– was that when Matthew fell and hit his head against the wall of the shower, his brain began to bleed.

As the morning went on, Carrie hadn't heard from her husband. Which was weird because she usually did at some point in the morning before he went off to work. She waited an hour before his usual good morning text. The hour came and went, and she texted him to see if he had overslept. She waited another forty-five minutes and texted again. Nothing back. Getting worried, she called his phone. After several rings, it went to his voicemail. That's when she got scared. She told her boss that she needed to go home to see about her husband. The whole time driving, she was calling his phone.

Carrie finally pulled into the driveway and saw that Matthew's truck was still sitting there. That's when her heart fell into her stomach. Seeing that truck, she knew that something terrible had happened to him. Call it her wife's intuition, but she knew that what awaited her beyond that front door was life-changing. She sat in the driveway, thinking a million thoughts at once, not wanting to get out of that car and go inside.

She thought about calling the police and giving them the key to go inside to see about Matthew. And she nearly went that route, had the 9-1-1 number dialed, ready to hit send on her phone. Then she shut the screen off. This was her job, and hers to do alone. Carrie, drawing in a deep breath and exhaling as loudly as she could, opened the driver's side car door and stepped out into the drizzle of the cold November morning.

***

The graveside service was exactly what Matthew wanted. "No viewing whatsoever," he had told Carrie one night. "People got more important things to do than to come see me in a box."

Matthew, of course, thought his death was decades down the road, not a mere six months later after he spoke those last wishes to his wife. It was a small, quick service performed by the Reverend Peter Johnson, a man of faith that Matthew had known as a wild kid while in high school. Carrie, and their two boys, Dylan and Raylan, stood, flanking their mother. There were a few cousins, an aunt and uncle, and his four best friends: Danielle, Dusty, Travis, and Corky. Out of all the friends, Travis was the one that had stayed behind. Well, sort of. Travis, after high school, had gone into the Air Force and did that for a while. Once his time was up, he decided not to reenlist. Instead, he went back to school, finished his college degree, and became a history teacher at the same high school where they all graduated. He and Matthew maintained a friendship the entire time. Travis, standing at the grave of his best friend, had tears in his eyes.

Danielle, who was close to Matthew back in the day, was the closest of his friends. The two of them had dated during their freshman year of high school. After having sex with each other, both their firsts, things had gotten awkward around the rest of the guys. Eventually, Matthew and Danielle decided that it would be best to just stay friends. And that's what they did: they stayed best friends throughout. Danielle ended up leaving the year after they all graduated high school to go to college at Auburn University. She never made it back to live in Tennessee although she promised them all, especially Matthew, that she was coming back. He took it hard, and the guys knew that he would. He still loved her, even though they had called their relationship off to keep the friendship. He was never the same after she moved away.

Corky moved away, too, but not as far as Danielle did. He moved to middle Tennessee where he got a job in a boat factory at entry level. It was good money, and not long after that, he met his wife. Six months after that, they got married. All of the friends were there, even Danielle had driven up from Alabama to attend the wedding. It was the last time the five of them were together in the same place. That memory had not been lost on any of them as they stood at the graveside of their dead friend. Corky knew this was the first time since his wedding he had seen them. They looked different. Corky remembered them as they were back in high school, and seeing them at the graveside shocked him because they were all still the same, but not. It was weird to him.

Dusty stayed around the area, actually in the same town they all grew up in. He went to college, got a nice job as an insurance salesman, and eventually opened up his own office with State Farm. His mug was plastered on several billboards around the county and if you ever needed insured—home or auto—call him, and he'd hook you up. He had taken care of Matthew's House and Auto fifteen years ago. That was the last time that Dusty had seen his friend. He remembered that day while standing there at the grave. Matthew had come down, and the two of them talked and Dusty got Matthew's information down in the computer system. After the paperwork was finished, Dusty took him out for lunch where the two of them sat for the better part of two hours, laughing and talking about old times. That was the last time he had spoken to his best friend...fifteen years ago, and he lived six blocks away from him.

When Reverend Johnson spoke his final words of scripture, the small crowd around Matthew's casket began to slowly break away. Dusty and Corky had walked away together, slowly across the graveyard towards the street where the cars were parked.

"You good?" Dusty asked.

Corky shrugged his shoulders, "I guess so. Just...just weird that one of us is gone now. You never know how you're going to feel when the first one dies, but I feel pretty low right now."

Dusty nodded, "Yeah me, too. I can't believe that Danielle showed; didn't expect that one."

"Me either. The last time I saw her was at my wedding."

Dusty smiled, "Same."

"She still looks good. Travis has put on some weight, huh?"

"We ain't exactly GQ models over here, my friend." Dusty stopped and looked at Travis and Danielle who were trailing behind. "I think we should talk to them." Travis and Danielle slowly caught up to Corky and Dusty. "It's been a long time guys." Dusty leaned over and bear hugged the two of them. Everyone was all smiles.

Corky got his hugs in as well, and the four stood back and looked at the other– at what time had done over the last couple of decades. To each of them, they still saw the other in the same light as they were in their youths. It was weird but true. Danielle stood there and saw that youthful glow still hanging around Dusty's face, that smile from Corky that was ever present, and Travis's hair that looked as it did the day of Corky's wedding when she last saw them. They had changed, she thought, but not changed.

"Sucky day," Corky said, remarking about what had brought them all together.

"Yeah. Do we know what he died of? I didn't want to ask his wife," Danielle asked the guys.

"We don't know. Most likely a heart attack or stroke. At least that's what my money is on. Was he healthy?" Travis asked, looking at Dusty.

"How would I know?"

"Well, you lived only six blocks from him and was his insurance agent...I just assumed that the two of you were still close."

Dusty shook his head, "No. I guess we just never had the time– I don't know. We did have lunch together."

"Oh yeah?" Corky asked. "How long ago was that?"

Dusty kind of halfhearted chuckled, "Fifteen years ago when I signed him to an insurance policy for his home and auto."

"It's a shame that we never got to know his wife and kids over there. Hell, for that matter, he never knew our families," Travis reflected on that sobering thought.

"What do we know about each other anymore?" Danielle asked, looking at her old friends from the way back. "Probably not much of anything, I bet," Danielle said truthfully.

The four of them stood silently, thinking thoughts about the past that somehow involved much younger, much more innocent versions than the ones standing there, watching people slowly walk to their vehicles. Corky turned his head and gave Matthew's graveside another look. He saw his wife and two children standing there speaking with the reverend. For some reason, a thought of something they all did a long time ago rattled his brain. It was a promise made many years ago in a drugstore.

"Do you guys remember the time capsule?" he asked, turning to his three friends and awaiting their answers.

"I think so," Danielle said. "Didn't we bury it in your backyard back in the summer of 1992?"

Dusty shook his head, "No, it was July of 1991, and it was in Travis's backyard."

"I remember that," Travis said to the group, "I remember Matt making us take our most prized possessions, and put them in this metal box, and then had us in case it in concrete so it wouldn't ruin."

"You think it's still there?" Danielle asked.

"Should be, I guess. But my mom doesn't live there anymore; hasn't since twenty years ago, I reckon."

"So it's been in the ground, what, thirty-five plus years? You guys think it's intact?" Corky asked.

"It was in concrete. Me and Matt put some in the hole we dug, put the box with the stuff in it, poured some concrete over that, and then covered it up with dirt," Dusty recalled.

"I don't remember what I put in there," Danielle said, trying to journey back to that day in question.

"Me either," Corky said.

Travis shook his head, "No clue. Hell, I can barely remember yesterday."

The group fell silent and thought about the metal box that was buried from a long time ago, back when they were children, back when things were much simpler.

"Well, remember, we all agreed that when one of us dies, the rest of us were to go get it. We'll take it to the cabin and see what all is in there," Dusty suggested.

The cabin that he was referencing was the very last time the five of them were together as teens. It was their high school graduation, and Dusty had talked his parents into letting him and his friends go to the cabin by the lake his parents owned to hang out to celebrate. Everyone looked at the other and thought about Dusty's suggestion and then about what they had going on in their personal lives. Turns out, not much.

"I can be available for several hours," Corky said. "I just got to tell Dana what's going on."

"I'm in. Stacy is with her mom until Monday anyways," Travis told them.

Danielle was the harder sell. She needed to get back to Alabama, back home. There were things there that needed her attention. Coming back home was hard enough, but staying longer than she had planned? She would have to think about it some.

"I don't know, boys. I've really got to get back home. I've got a five-hour drive ahead of me."

Dusty was about to open his mouth and try to talk her out of going home...at least put it off for a few hours. Maybe back when they were kids he could've done that, but as an adult? Dusty felt as he stood there he didn't really know her. Hell, did he know any of them anymore? Back then, they were his best friends, and at that point in time, he didn't think he could live without them. But he had, for over twenty years now, had done great, and had a great life. So if Danielle didn't want to stay, it wasn't his place, nor the others, to say a word. The guys nodded their heads.

"Well it was good seeing all of you, really it was. And good luck with that time capsule. Message me on Facebook, and let me know what I had in there, would you?" Danielle told them as she broke away from the boys.

That was that; she walked across the cemetery towards her SUV without looking back. Too much time had passed by, too many days and years to be precise, for them to be upset. When the news broke about Matthew's death, it was Corky who rounded up the group on Facebook and broke the news to them. Danielle showing up, which he never thought was a possibility, was a bonus; why push for anything else? If she wanted to honor Matthew's memory, she already did more than was required. She showed up. None of them spoke a bad word towards Danielle after she walked away. They just watched her go, out of their lives, probably for the very last time.

"I'll drive to my old house and see if they'll let us dig in their yard," Travis said, laughing at the idea.

"I'll go get my shovel," Corky said.

"Right behind you," Dusty said to Corky, playfully pushing him as they walked across the cemetery.

***

Danielle was heading south on I-75 back home in her SUV– back to where nothing was waiting on her anymore but a nearly empty apartment and a career. She thought about seeing the boys for the final time out at the cemetery. They had changed– there was no mistaking that. But she still felt that connection with them; it was undeniable after all the years that had rolled by like fog in the night. She felt ashamed for not staying behind and going to unearth the time capsule that Matthew had suggested way back when. Danielle was hurting and needed to get back home, away from Claxton and her friends, and especially Matthew. Some miles would be exactly what the doctor ordered. Maybe once she got home she could begin to process everything; process the future that never was going to be.

Matthew's death had hit her hard, and she was surprised at herself that she could come to see him one final time. Danielle considered not coming to the service and nearly didn't. She had talked herself out of coming to Claxton and decided that he would've understood because Matthew was a very understanding man. However, there was that nagging piece of her that knew she had to come. Her soul would not be at peace unless she did. The entire way there, she drove on what seemed to be autopilot. Her thoughts as she traveled north to Tennessee, back to her hometown, were of Matthew and their group of best friends. It was the five of them: "The Fab Five," as they were called in high school.

Heading south back home, Danielle smiled to herself driving on that lonely stretch of interstate, lost in thought, about that particular point in time when Matthew first brought up the time capsule. It was a hot July in 1991. Danielle thought maybe it was certainly past the Fourth, but how far, she had no clue. They were all sitting inside Wilson's

Drugstore in the booth seats where people sometimes sat to read the paper or drink their Cokes. Most of the time, the gang of five would sit in there reading comic books the boys had just bought while Danielle sipped her Coke through a straw.

"You know what would be cool," Matthew spoke, absently turning the pages of his Batman comic.

"Having sex with your mom?" Corky said, holding up his hand for a high five. Of course, no one gave him one.

"No...if we all put something in a time capsule."

"You mean putting stuff in it and, like, digging it up years from now? That kind of thing?" Dusty asked.

Matthew nodded, "Yeah, exactly. I think that would be cool; go back years later, like when we're older, and dig it up and see if what we put in there still has meaning or whatever."

Danielle looked over at Matthew while his eyes were still down on the comic book. She had a crush on him and was thinking about telling him before the summer was over– before they all started high school in late August. She was pretty sure that he liked her too. They were friends, best friends, all five of them were, but she had a connection to Matthew that was profound.

Many nights she lay in her bed thinking about him, much like girls her age did the boys they liked. Sitting and listening to him talk about the time capsule made her heart jump. He was always thinking, always looking for something to give meaning to his life at such a young age. At his core, Matthew was a romantic, a dreamer, someone she could fall in love with. If she was being honest with herself, she already was.

"So when do you want to do this time capsule?" Danielle asked.

Matthew looked up at her. Their eyes met, as they often did that summer, and he smiled a little. There was always that unspoken thing between them, it seemed to him. "Whenever, I guess."

"We could bury it in my backyard if you guys want to," Travis suggested.

"We could do that. What would you guys put in it?" Matthew asked everyone at the booth they were sitting in.

All of them sat in silence thinking about what their contributions would be, what items of personal significance would be locked away for years. The talk amongst them for a bit went about all sorts of stuff that they would put in.

Corky joked that he would put a box of condoms in to which Travis said, "You might as well because you ain't going to need them." They all laughed, even Corky, at that burn.

"Seriously though, let's all think about it," Matthew said.

"When do you want to dig it up? Twenty years? Thirty?" Dusty asked.

Matthew sat back and looked around the drugstore, "What about when one of us dies?" That suggestion was morbid and took the group by surprise. And as silence fell over them, the idea of digging it up when one of them died seemed to be the right thing to do.

"It'll be like an honor thing. Like that person is still with us in a way.," Matthew said, pushing the idea a little more. Eventually, they settled on that, as macabre as it sounded. They took a vote, as they often did when group things were involved, and it was unanimous.

Driving her SUV home, Danielle felt low. She had gone back on her promise made there in the drugstore on that hot July day. The boys were fulfilling their end, so why wasn't she? If she wasn't going to see the promise through, then why even come to the funeral? Danielle ran her fingers through her hair and looked around at the nearly deserted interstate.

Going back home, away from the guys and the promise of that time capsule, was her turning her back on them for good. But hadn't she already done that by leaving and not staying in touch, aside from the occasional Like on their Facebook posts? She wasn't that kid anymore when it was her and the guys growing up. She was different now, by leaps and bounds. She snuck a look at herself in the rearview mirror and caught a glimpse of the woman she now was, and what she saw looking back at her wasn't what she liked. Even the mirrors back home in Alabama showed the same thing.

Thoughts of Matthew clung to her as miles put more distance between her and Claxton. She loved him at one point in time. Did she ever stop? Even after it ended, did she ever stop? They had remained best friends after the breakup, but that was more of her than it was him. Seeing his casket at the graveside service had rattled her immensely. The last image of him, the one that she always thought about from time to time was of a younger Matthew, one that was tanned riding his bicycle alongside hers down empty streets in the summer wearing that Braves hat that he always wore. That was her go-to image in her head when times got bad, and there were many of those throughout her life.

Seeing that casket and knowing that he was inside it, too young to die, the image of youth was now transplanted with the mental image of an older man, dressed in a blue suit with graying hair. No matter how hard she tried to bring the image of him back in the day into her mind—when the summer days were long and the nights short, back when they used to make out behind her daddy's barn, back when it was something to be a girl in love—the image of the man in the box haunted her. Perhaps that was why she decided to head for home; maybe she was trying to escape any more memories that seemed to be sticking to her like glue. She had made a promise, not just to Matthew, but to the rest of her friends. It was a promise that she had intended not to keep. "It's best to keep going," she told herself. "Just keep going."

***

Travis pulled into the driveway of his old house. He hadn't been there in twenty years, and that was when he helped his mother move out into the condo she's in now. A new family was occupying the house now. Who they were, Travis had no idea, but he was about to meet them for the first time. He was too old for being nervous, at least that's what he thought. Those nerves came out in full force when he parked his car and got out, making his way across the walkway and up the front porch steps.

He ran the doorbell, a new feature on the side of the front door, and stood idle on the front porch. He pressed the doorbell again, and suddenly the front door opened. Through the full glass storm door, a woman much younger than him answered, "How can I help you?" Travis could tell that she was nervous, so he flashed her a smile and put his hands down to his sides.

"Hi, My name is Travis Booker, and this used to be my house when I was a kid."

"Okay?" the lady behind the glass replied.

"Yeah, so I have a crazy question to ask you."

The nerves were growing ever more present inside Travis' body now, causing him to stammer in his words a little. "A long time ago, when I lived here, me and my best friends buried a time capsule in the backyard. We weren't supposed to dig it up until one of us died. Well, Matthew Morgan, died a few days ago…"

"We know Matthew, great guy," the woman behind the glass said. "Shame to hear about him. He coached little league baseball last summer. Taught our son how to play first base. He was just a phenomenal man."

"Yeah, he was," Travis said, feeling a bit easier now about this business. "But what I was getting to: since Matt's dead, we all said back when we were little that whoever died first, we'd get the time capsule. I was wondering if me and my friends could go in your backyard and dig it up."

Without hesitation, the woman behind the glass smiled and said, "That is so cool! Sure, no problem. Do you remember where ya'll buried it?"

"I think so, yeah. Is the willow tree still standing?"

"Oh yeah."

"Good. It's twenty paces east of it. At least, I think it's twenty paces," Travis chuckled.

***

Matthew, Corky, Danielle, Dusty, and Travis all stood in Travis's backyard, looking around for a good place to bury the metal box. The metal box, a medium-sized stainless steel box with two silver latches connected to a lid, was snuck out of Matthew's dad's toolshed. Corky didn't think that the box was big enough and debated it for a while. They all put their stuff in there and found that he was right. The box was just too damn small for what they had.

Travis took everything out of it—which was his, Corky, and Dusty's items— and tried to reposition it so it would fit. He failed. Dusty took a crack at it, telling them they were stupid and rearranged it. His attempt was worse than Travis's. Finally, growing tired of seeing the boys be boys, Danielle pushed Dusty to the side and knelt down. She meticulously placed the items in position. She was even able to put hers and Matthew's items into it. It was a snug fit, and the box perhaps could've been an inch wider on each side of the square, but it was fine. The lid was a little harder to close, but once pushed down and locked into place by the latches, the time capsule was serviceable.

"Yeah, sure, after we showed you how not to do it," Corky quipped. Danielle raised her eyes to her friend and shook her head.

With the business of the time capsule being locked in the metal box for however long, the five of them looked for possible places to bury it. Dusty suggested the spot over by the swing set that belonged to Travis's sister, Heather, but Travis said no. Corky walked over to where the basketball goal was. Travis said no. Matthew walked over to the rose garden and told everyone that would be a good place. Once again, Travis said no.

"Then where in the hell do you want it, Ms. Particular?!" Matthew shouted from across the yard.

Travis looked at the willow tree that was on the far end of the yard.

"Right over there will be perfect," he said.

The four of them and Dusty with the shovel, walked over to the willow tree. "Now look here, we're going to have to bury this thing away from the tree because of the roots. So I think twenty paces that way," Travis said, pointing east. He took the shovel from Dusty and walked over to the trunk of the tree. He took twenty paces east and stabbed the shovel into the ground. "Right here."

"You guys get started on that, me and Danielle will go get a bag of concrete and a hoe. You still got that water hose?" Matthew asked.

Travis nodded, "Yeah, it's right there on the side of the house. Should reach, hell, it's two hundred feet's worth."

Matthew reacted with a thumbs up, and he and Danielle walked across the yard side by side.

"You think they'll ever get together?" Dusty asked Cokry while Travis walked towards his house to get the water hose.

Corky shrugged, "Who knows with them two? But you can tell they like each other." Dusty nodded, watching them disappear in front of the house.

***

Dusty and Travis took turns digging the hole: two feet across, two feet in length, and eighteen inches deep. Corky put the metal box inside it, and it fit pretty good. "Fits pretty good, doesn't it?" Everyone nodded. Corky took the metal box out of the hole.

Matthew opened the bag of concrete he swiped from his dad's toolshed and poured half the bag down into the hole. Travis turned the water on and sprayed the concrete, getting it wet and ready to mix. Dusty took the hoe and began mixing it until it got thicker and thicker. Then, he took the hoe and smoothed out the roughness as best he could.

"We'll let that set for about thirty. Then we'll put the box in, pour concrete on it, and then cover it up," Matthew said.

In that thirty minutes of waiting, the five of them played a game of H-O-R-S-E where Danielle was the last one of them standing. It wasn't news to the guys. Danielle was one of the best shooters of the five of them. She had played point guard at Claxton Elementary School since sixth grade. When they got into high school, she was already on the starting five girl's basketball team and the first freshman, boy or girl, to make the starting five in over thirty seasons. She was that good.

"This is bullshit, you know?" Travis told her after he missed the easy layup she had made.

"Maybe, but you can't hit a layup, so what's that say about you?" Danielle said, laughing.

"Hell, I've been digging that damn hole over there. My arms are tired!" Travis exclaimed, shaking his arms out. The guys, even Danielle laughed.

"Excuses. Next time, we're playing for money," she said, taking the basketball and sinking a basket from twenty feet away, nothing but net.

"Is the concrete dry you think?" Dusty asked, getting put out of the game at H.

"I'd say so. Let me go check." Matthew walked over there, took the hoe handle, and jabbed it down into the hole. It seemed hard enough. "I think we're ready!" The four of them walked over to Matthew to finish off the process.

Matthew placed the metal box carefully down into the hole; Dusty and Corky poured the rest of the bag of concrete on top of it; and Travis hit it with water. No mixing it this time around. After another thirty minute game of H-O-R-S-E between Travis and Danielle where she won, putting him out at R, the concrete was finally settled. Corky covered up the hole with dirt, and the deed was done.

"Now," Matthew told them, standing there looking at the covered place where the time capsule lay in state, "we open this when the first person here dies. Are we still good on that?" They all said yes. "All right then. Let's go to Pappa Enzo's and get some pizza. Dusty's buying." They all laughed and walked away.

"I ain't got that much money," Dusty said, trailing behind his friends.

"Just get it from your mom. I gave her a twenty last night," Corky said from the front of the group, walking across Travis' backyard.

"Not funny!" Dusty replied, laughing himself. "Actually, that was pretty good."

***

Travis, Corky, and Dusty walked twenty paces from the trunk of the willow tree, which in the last twenty years had grown at an astounding rate. After walking the paces off, Travis stabbed the shovel into the ground. "Should be the spot, right?" Corky nodded as well as Dusty. Travis started digging and quickly five minutes turned into ten, then ten to fifteen. He found himself over a foot into the hole and still no concrete.

"I don't think this is it," Dusty said.

"Me either," an out-of-breath Travis agreed. "Maybe my pacing is off. Let's dig back a little ways and if that ain't it, maybe ahead a ways. Surely, it's close."

"I'll give you a rest, chief," Dusty took the shovel and dug into the ground two feet from where Travis had been digging. Ten minutes later and fourteen inches deep, according to Corky's tape measure, no concrete.

"Maybe it's ahead?" This time Corky took the shovel and started digging into the ground that was ahead of Travis' spot. After ten minutes, his shovel struck something solid, like a rock.

"I think we got it, boys!" Corky excitedly said.

Travis and Dusty walked over and again and again with each shovel strike, the metal against rock was heard. "Yeah, I believe this is it right here." Corky kept at the hole, digging around the sides, and making it wider so he could get the shovel on the edges of the concrete they had buried so long ago.

"Let me give you a rest here," Travis said, taking the shovel.

He picked up where Corky left off and kept digging out the hole on the sides, making it wider. In twenty minutes of work, Travis was able to expose the concrete.

"Yeah, this is it. Dusty, get that pry bar, and let's see if we can start prying this thing out of here."

Dusty took the yellow pry bar that was Corky's from his toolshed and jabbed it underneath the concrete the best he could. Several stabs later, the pry bar was under the concrete, just a little bit of a foothold, but it was the best they could do at the moment. Travis was on the other side with his shovel head under the concrete. Both of them worked and wiggled their instruments under the concrete, trying to get a better advantage to pop it loose from its grave.

Another twenty minutes had passed by, and the concrete was a little bit looser than it was when they started, but not by much. Then Travis had an idea.

"I'm going to see if they have a hammer we can borrow for a minute. Maybe we can beat that son of a bitch into pieces." Dusty and Corky agreed.

Watching Travis walk across the yard to his old house, Corky said to Dusty, "What if we do all this work, and there's nothing in that box except dry rot and dust?"

"That would suck, dude. But it should be good in there, right? I mean the box was latched and encased in concrete. I think it's going to be fine."

"This feels so weird doing this, doesn't it?"

"You mean without Matty?" Dusty replied, knowing exactly what he meant.

"Yeah. To be honest, I thought I'd be the first of us to go," Corky said, watching Travis disappear to the front of the house.

"Why is that?"

Corky shook his head, "I don't know. I ain't the healthiest person going, you know? Heart problems, blood pressure is consistently bad...I already had a mild heart attack last year."

"Bullshit? Really? Hell, I had no idea."

"How could you? Nobody talks anymore. The best we do is like a post on Facebook if we even get on there anymore."

"Nah, I hardly ever do. Mostly, it's ads nowadays. I stay off it. Leah is on there nightly being nosy, but I really go no use for it."

"I'm the same way," Corky was about to say something else when Travis appeared from the front of the house, carrying a hammer in his right hand. "I guess we got us a hammer now."

Travis brought the hammer and handed it to Dusty. He got on his knees, "Watch your eyes. Pieces will be flying." Dusty raised the hammer back and slammed it against the concrete, which flew chips as he figured it would. Corky and Travis held their hands up and shielded their eyes. They could feel the pieces of concrete hit them on the arms. Dusty closed his eyes and dropped the hammer several times, not knowing where the hammer was quite landing, but knowing the whole time that he was hitting it at least somewhere.

"Piece at a time boys...piece at a time," Dusty said.

After breaking as much as he could, Dusty got up to inspect the damage. Some visible damage, but hopefully it was enough to try to pry it out of the ground with the shovel and the pry bar. Corky took the pry bar and worked it underneath the concrete while Travis did the same with the shovel. It worked a little better than before, but there was still more work that needed to be done.

Thirty minutes later, after some more digging out the sides of the hole some more, they were able to finally pry the concrete mess out of the hole. After the three of them popped it up, grabbed it by its rocky edges, and hoisted it out, the three of them fell to the ground clapping and cheering. The time capsule was recused, and the only thing left to do was finish breaking the concrete off the metal box that was encased inside it and open the thing up.

"Well, let's get this hole filled back in, take this to the cabin, and bust it up. You guys bring the bags of topsoil?" Travis asked.

Corky and Dusty looked at each other while on their back on the ground, "No…we forgot." Corky replied.

"I called you guys not five minutes after we left the cemetery about running and getting several bags," Travis said in frustration which was more out of being tired. Travis looked at them and rose to his feet, "Well, I guess my ass is running to Lowe's then. Ya'll take that to the cabin, and I'll buy the bags and fill this in. Don't break that without me." Travis warned.

***

When Corky and Dusty pulled into the driveway of the cabin, which had been renovated twice since the last time they were all there the night of their high school graduation, they saw a silver SUV parked.

Corky pulled up beside the SUV and looked at Dusty, "Danielle decided to show I guess," he told Dusty.

Corky shut the engine off, and the two of them got out of his car and stretched their legs. "You know, I didn't know how much older I'd gotten until we were digging that hole. Man, I'm already sore." Dusty said, stretching his back out.

"Me, too, brother. Getting older is a bitch. So, I wonder where Danielle is. She ain't in her SUV."

Dusty stood and looked around a bit, considering the possibilities. "I bet she's out back down at the dock." The two of them walked away from the driveway and started along the side of the huge cabin.

"Man, this place looks different than the last time," Corky said.

"Yeah, Mom and Dad had some people up here working on it and changing stuff out. Twice, actually. But I think this is the last time they're doing anything to it. They're getting too old to come out here. Hell, this is the first time I've been out since last year."

"Why is that?" Corky asked, still walking in tandem side by side to the back of the house.

"I don't know. I guess there's no reason to, honestly. I've been trying to talk Dad into selling it, and I think I might have him convinced to do it. Property taxes are insane out here, and it's not worth spending money on something you ain't doing anything with. When I was married to my first wife and the kids were younger, we came out here a few times a year, but now the kids are grown and out living their lives. Me and the new wife don't feel like driving all the way out here. We just relax at home."

"How is marriage the second time around?"

"Better than the first, I can safely say that for sure," Dusty replied.

"Sometimes I wonder how long mine will last."

"Problems going on?" Dusty asked as they walked around the cabin to the back where the lake was.

"No, no issues, I mean, nothing out of the ordinary, I guess. Just regular problems that all couples have."

"Communication is the key, man. Don't let those regular problems become major ones. Take it from someone who knows."

The lake behind the cabin, majestic and wide and as long as the eyes could see, stunned Corky. Seeing it brought him all the way back to 1997, the night they graduated. He remembered what he had forgotten, or at least thought he had forgotten.

"What a great view. I forgot how awesome this place was," he remarked.

Dusty nodded. He was used to seeing it. But not Corky: the sight of the lake, as the towering trees off in the distance served as a backdrop, made it look as if they were walking in a Norman Rockwell painting. Down the hill a piece was the dock that stretched out a good twenty yards into the lake. At the end of that dock sat a woman, Danielle.

"There she is," Dusty said what Corky had already seen.

"I wonder why she came back?"

Dusty shook his head, "I don't know. Day like this, I don't think we know anything anymore."

Corky knew what Dusty was saying—cryptic as it was—he knew what his friend was driving at. They had buried their long-time friend, *best friend*, the one that this whole day was about. The sobering fact that they had lost one of their own was not lost on Corky nor Dusty while they walked down the hill to the dock where she sat at the end.

Danielle had her wireless earbuds in, legs hanging off the edge of the dock, listening to "Plainsong" from the Cure. It was their song, her and Matthew's when they dated that year as freshmen in high school. She had been crying, something she had not really done at the graveside in front of everyone. She had even kept it together in her SUV. Coming to the cabin, the last place they were all together, proved at moments to be overwhelming. She knew it would be, but had no idea how much of a gut punch it would be knowing this was the place where it all ended on graduation night. Danielle put her arms back behind her on the dock and leaned back, feeling the wind in her hair and listening to Robert Smith sing.

She had no idea that Corky and Dusty were walking on the dock calling to her. Of course, they had no idea she had earbuds. Danielle closed her eyes and soaked in every ounce of Smith's words to that song when all of a sudden she felt a hand touch her shoulder. She screamed, jumped up, and turned around to see who or what had touched her. In her surprise, she nearly fell off backward off the edge of the dock. Had it not been for Corky reaching out to her and grabbing her arm, she would have taken a swim.

"Damn it! You guys scared me!" she shouted, shaking inside and out.

"Sorry! Sorry! We thought you heard us and were just ignoring us or something. We didn't mean to scare you!" Dusty explained.

Danielle stood there for a minute and ran her fingers through her wavy blonde hair trying to calm down. She reached up and turned off her earbuds, "Did you guys get the time capsule?"

"Yeah, yeah we got it finally. It's in the trunk of my car."

"Good," Danielle said. "What kind of shape was it in?"

"It's still in the concrete. Travis wanted to be here when we bust it out," Dusty said.

"Where he's at?" Danielle asked.

"Probably filling in the hole we dug. We liked to never have gotten that thing out. For a minute, I didn't think we were, " Corky said.

"What brought you back?" Dusty asked.

"I was curious about the time capsule," she said. "Plus, I wanted to see you guys a little more before I left for home. Good for the soul."

"Come on, let's get up to the cabin," Dusty told them as the three walked back up the dock. "Why did you come back?"

Danielle, trailing behind them, took a few moments to answer that question. She wasn't sure that she wanted to truthfully answer it. But she did. "He was our guy...same reason I drove to the service."

Dusty believed it, had no reason not to. "Yeah...today has been a heavy toll, that's for sure."

"Still feels like a dream," Corky interjected as the three of them walked off the dock and up the incline of the backyard where the huge cabin stood atop the hill.

"Yeah, I know. I think it's going to hit a little harder when we pop that metal box," Danielle said.

The three of them made it to the top of the hill and around the cabin. They walked up the porch steps, and Dusty unlocked the front door with a key from the front pocket of his blue suit. The door creaked open, and the smell of the cabin being shut up for some time smacked them all in the face. It was a musty smell– not totally overpowering, but lingering nevertheless.

"Make yourselves at home," Dusty said, walking through the cabin's first floor.

The inside had not changed much. It still had that open concept on the first floor. The stairs that led to the second floor had been changed.

"Maybe I'm crazy, but didn't those stairs used to be on the other side of the room here?" Corky asked.

"Yeah, Mom decided years ago that she wanted them moved for whatever reason. No idea why. Dad just had it done," he replied, opening the cabinets for glasses.

"I can't believe I'm here again," Danielle said, looking around at the spacious cabin in awe.

"I wish it was under better circumstances," Corky said. "But then again, would we be here if it wasn't for Matt?"

Dusty heard him but didn't acknowledge it, and Danielle was the same way. No sense of replying to the obvious.

"What's your poison?" Dusty asked, leaning against the kitchen counter and watching them slowly mill about the place.

"For what?" Corky asked.

"Drinks? Water, tea, something stronger?"

Danielle knew that she was going to need something stronger. "Something strong."

Dusty nodded, "Wild Turkey it is. Corky?"

"Just water will be fine. Hey, is this the same deer head from graduation night?" He stood, looking up at the deer head hanging on the wall above the mantel. It was Dusty's dad's prize buck, a twelve-pointer, he shot and killed back in 1983 in the very woods that surrounded the lake they were at.

"Yup, same one."

"Crazy," Corky said to himself. "I think that's the only thing I remember in here."

"I'll be honest, I don't know how much of it was here when the last time we were all here. A lot of it has changed, but some has stayed, I guess. Years run together after a certain age."

Dusty poured himself and Danielle a shot of Wild Turkey and gave Corky his water from the tap straight from the well. He walked the glasses over to the kitchen table and sat them down. He took a seat in the chair. Danielle and Corky saw that, walked over to the table, and took their seats. None of them spoke, just sipped on their drinks, lost in personal thoughts.

Their high school graduation night, Corky's wedding, Matthew's graveside service, and now back at the cabin for the time capsule were the only times in three decades the best friends had been at the same place at the same time. It felt surreal, and also felt... foreign, like they were strangers to each other. Maybe they were. Three decades had gone by, and hardly anything was spoken between them all. They all promised to keep in touch, but promises are thin in the wee hours of the night.

Over time– and it didn't take long– the five of them were ghosts to each other. Social media came into play years later, and they connected with each other once again, but even those times were few and far between. A few likes on a post here and there, maybe a heart icon on a post. Sometimes a personal message to the other. That was about the sum of their relationship: friends on Facebook when thirty-plus years ago they were the Fab Five of Claxton.

"You remember that time that we all were riding our bikes down that country road? We all turned the curve really sharp; and Matthew's bike slid out from underneath him, and he slid into that dead possum?" Dusty recalled, laughing loudly. The others started laughing too.

"God, yes! He was covered in dead possum juice. I remember him smelling so bad for the rest of the day. I couldn't even stand being around him, he stunk so bad," Corky said through his laughter.

"Or remember that time that he got us lost in Hudson's Woods?" Danielle reminded. "I didn't think we were ever going to get out of there."

"Oh man," Dusty said, "I had forgotten all about that. Was that the night where Travis was running and went face first into that tree?" Everyone laughed. "I guess it was."

"You know," Dusty said after a few moments of silent reflection between the three of them at the table, "Matty really was the engine that made us go. We wouldn't have gotten into the shit we did had it not been for him. He just um...made being a kid awesome; always some adventure he was cooking up or wanting us to go on."

Danielle and Corky nodded their heads slowly, each thinking about the adventures they could recall as the images of their youths had faded over time.

"I feel bad because we didn't keep in touch," Corky said after that silence between them all had become too much at the table. "I mean, he was my best friend, and I didn't even call or text him to see how he was over the years."

Dusty sat there looking at his nearly empty glass of Wild Turkey, thinking of what Corky had said. *He's right,* he thought, *we all should've done better, hell, I should've done better.* Before Corky could say anything out loud to his friends about what he was thinking, the front door opened, startling the three of them inside.

It was Travis coming inside, disheveled in the gray suit he wore to the funeral, "Okay, holes are filled. Insert joke now, Dusty. Where's the time capsule? You came back?" he said, looking at Danielle.

"Yeah, the curious part of me wants to know what's in that time capsule. Plus, I wanted to see all of you again."

"Glad you came back," Travis replied.

"Time capsule is still in the trunk of my car," Corky said.

***

The four of them went outside and popped the trunk lid to Corky's car, and there it was: a hulking piece of concrete that held the metal box inside. Corky and Dusty lifted it out and walked it over to the front porch where the extracting process was to begin. Dusty hopped off the porch and walked to the small tool shed off to the side of the cabin. He came out of there with a hammer, a chisel, and a pair of safety glasses. "I'll take care of this. You guys make yourself at home. This might take a while." Dusty got down on his knees and started hammering away on the chisel, chipping away at the concrete.

Travis, Danielle, and Corky walked back into the cabin and milled about the place, soaking it all in.

"Does this place seem smaller to you guys since the last time we were here?" Travis asked.

"It kinda does, doesn't it?" Danielle replied.

Travis walked about the open floor plan of the first floor and looked at the décor of the place. He didn't remember everything from the last time and had no idea if the stuff inside the cabin was there from graduation night, but one thing remained the same: the deer head above the mantel.

"Hey, the deer is still here. That's awesome!"

Danielle took a seat at the table while Corky leaned up against the kitchen counter, looking around solemnly. "So," Travis asked, turning his eyes to Danielle, "what made you come back? I thought you were heading back home?"

She thought about why she turned around and came back. Thought about it a lot while coming back actually. She didn't want to tell them the truth, and lying was best. Besides, she didn't want to cast an unsavory image of Matthew to them. What had happened between the two of them needed to stay between the two of them, like it had for years. But if anyone would understand, it would be the boys. They always understood everything, no matter how crazy or personal. At least, that's how they all were back in the old days when they were kids. But they weren't kids anymore, and times had changed– decades had rolled by. Were they the same as before she left?

"He was our guy...same reason I drove to the service."

Travis stood next to the mantle, looking at her with what she thought was doubt on his face. Then it changed to trust as he nodded.

"Yeah, he certainly was. God, I hadn't seen him or talked to him in years, but I already miss the hell out of him," he said, dropping his eyes to the floor. He missed his best friend. They all did.

Outside on the front porch, the sound of metal on concrete could be heard. Travis walked over to the window and looked at Dusty who was methodically pounding away on that chunk of concrete.

"He ain't kidding...this could take a while."

"You guys want to turn on some music?" Corky asked.

Danielle turned to Corky, "Yeah, let's do that. Maybe it'll break the heaviness a bit."

Corky pulled his phone out, scrolled through his music app, and found one of his favorites. He selected the 80s/90s rock tab and hit play, turning up the volume a little on his phone and putting it down on the island across from him in the kitchen.

The first song, and maybe it was serendipitous, that played was Matthew's all-time favorite, according to him on one of their legendary campouts: "Losing My Religion" by R.E.M. Travis and Danielle turned to look in Corky's direction. They were well aware of the song playing.

"Did you select that song?" Travis asked.

"No, I just hit the 80s/90s rock tab and hit play," Corky replied, stunned that this was the very first song to come on.

Danielle smiled and tears nearly came out of her eyes. That was his song. "That's kinda spooky," she simply said. Travis and Corky looked at each other and nodded, thinking the same thing.

"Think I'll take a drink. He got anything strong in this place?" Travis asked, walking towards the kitchen.

Corky reached into the cabinet behind him and gave Travis a glass and the bottle of Wild Turkey.

***

Travis sat at the table slowly sipping on a glass of whiskey while Corky sat up on the counter in the kitchen. Danielle had moved to the loveseat and stretched out, looking towards her friends absently. "Losing My Religion" had gone off and next up was another one of Matthew's favorites, "Heroes" from David Bowie. That didn't get lost on any of them. They all knew that was one of his faves. Travis was going to say something like 'Maybe his ghost is playing the playlist today,' but he didn't say it; just thought it. Danielle and Corky thought the same thing

"Any of you ever met his family?" Travis asked.

Danielle shook her head, "No."

"Me either," Corky said. "I didn't even know he had kids until today."

Just then, the front door opened and in came Dusty, holding the metal box. His hand was bleeding as well. Danielle immediately got up after seeing this and walked over to him as Corky hopped off the counter, and Travis got up from his chair. It was the metal box from years ago Dusty was carrying into the cabin.

"I got it!" Dusty said in triumph.

Danielle looked over Dusty's hand and saw that he had taken a rather large chunk out of the side of his index finger.

"Do you have any bandages here?" she asked.

"Yeah, in the bathroom." Dusty put the dented metal box on the kitchen table.

"Let's get this cleaned out," Danielle walked her friend into the bathroom, remembering where it was from long ago.

Corky and Travis stood over the metal box marveling over it. It had several dents in it and had concrete dust on the sides and lid. The latches were still there but looked as if they were broken.

"Well, there it is," Corky said dryly.

"Yup. There it is. Are you nervous?" Travis asked.

Corky kept looking at the metal box, "A little bit. Is that weird?"

"Nah," Travis said. "Inside that box is our youth. What we all put in there many moons ago. It's like we're going back in time, Doc Brown."

Inside the bathroom, Danielle was treating Dusty's hand. First, she was running cold water over it in the sink, and then she looked in his medicine cabinet for alcohol.

"Now, this is going to sting a bit," she said. She opened the bottle and poured a little on the exposed cut, and Dusty howled with pain. "See, wasn't lying, was I?" She put the lid back on the bottle and returned it to the shelf. Then, she got some triple antibacterial ointment, squeezed a small amount from the tube, and put it on his open wound. She then put a bandage over it.

"There you go. Best I can do."

"What are you, like a nurse or something?"

"Close, I'm a doctor," Danielle said, patting Dusty on the shoulder. "You were such a good boy today. Now go see the young lady at the desk, and tell her to give you a sucker, okay?" Danielle giggled for the first time since she had been back in her hometown as she walked out of the bathroom.

"Wait a minute?! A doctor!?" Dusty asked. "Wow, that's awesome!"

***

The four of them were at the kitchen table looking down at the metal box, thinking silent thoughts about what was inside it, trying to remember what it was that was so precious to them back in the land of long ago. Then, another song played...the Cars, "Since You're Gone", another one of Matthew's favorites. The four of them looked at each other.

"Yeah, he's here doing the playlist," Corky said. They all smiled.

"So, who wants to do the honors here?" Dusty asked.

None of them spoke up. Tired of waiting, Dusty reached over and pried open the lid, which was stubborn. After several attempts, it wouldn't budge. "Let me get a butter knife."

He walked into the kitchen and Travis tried to open it to no avail. Then Corky. Danielle didn't try. Dusty came back over and worked the end of the butter knife into the crevice of the lid and the bottom part of the box and began to pry it open. It took until the end of the song, but he managed to open it enough where he could put his fingers inside it. With a mighty pull, Dusty pulled apart the lid, nearly sending all the items inside flying all over the place. He and the others looked down into the metal box at what was inside. And what was inside sparked their long-forgotten memories back.

"Oh my God," Danielle whispered.

The others stood there dumbfounded, in a trance at what was locked away from their youths. Looking at the items sent them back to a time and place where they were thirteen and fourteen years old, just as they were about to go into high school, where life as they knew it changed forever.

"Son of a bitch," Corky simply said. Nobody heard him utter those words. They were all too hypnotized by the items in the box.

The four of them sat down at the kitchen table and started taking stuff out. Travis got his boxing glove and slipped it on, looking it over. It was red and appeared to be intact, just like the day he put it inside the box. Wearing it on his right hand, he could remember hitting the heavy bag out in his garage. He wasn't paying any attention to what the others had taken out. He was too enamored by his forgotten item. How did he forget his boxing glove? It was the one thing that meant the world to him. It was his precious item of his youth.

"Man, I was going to be a boxer when I grew up, remember?" Travis said to the three of them.

But they weren't listening. They were too excited about their recovered treasures of the past.

"Man, I loved Mike Tyson back in the day. Wanted to be a boxer because of him. You remember when I knocked you out?" Travis said, looking at Corky.

Corky wasn't paying him any attention. He was looking at his Danzig 1 cassette tape. God, that tape brought back such vivid memories for him. He remembered buying that tape at Tape City and playing it over and over in his bedroom. Eventually, he brought the tape over to Dusty's house, and he and Dusty rocked to it. Then, they brought it over to Travis' house where the three of them head banged so much one night to the hard rock, that the next day they couldn't lift their heads.

"Man, remember this album? How many times did we listen to this? Millions, I bet," Corky said. "I totally forgot I put this in here. I still remember the lyrics to every song by heart."

"You should. You played that tape all the time," Danielle said, not really liking the music.

"Man, I know. Me and Matty used to play it while playing video games at his house. He always said he sounded like a hard rock Elvis," Corky remembered, reading the song titles on the A side and B side of the cassette as if he would have ever forgotten them. No chance.

Dusty was sitting back in his chair looking down at his lost treasure of youth. It was a picture– a group picture of the five of them down at the train depot. He flipped it over and it read: July 1990. God, they were so young in that photo. Matthew was wearing his Braves hat, which he always did, smiling back at him. God, he was so young in that picture. How old was he, twelve at the time? And what about Dusty? Dusty held the photo closer to his eyes, and he saw that he was smiling ten miles wide. And why wouldn't he? He was there with his four best friends in the world.

He sat there, and a thought crossed his mind. He never had friends like that when life came in and took them all in different directions, scattering them into the four winds. That photo represented hard proof that he had actually belonged for the first time in his life. He felt so happy looking at that picture that he held it up for them to see, "Want to see how we looked years ago? Here's a picture of all of us in July 1990."

Dusty handed it to Travis and he looked it over, smiling. "Damn, look at all of us. We're so young!"

Danielle took it from Travis to give it a look, "Oh my God! Look at my hair back then!" She looked at how the picture had held them all in their youths forever. She handed it to Corky as "Love Shack" by the B-52s came on the phone. But they were too enthralled with the contents of the metal box to notice. It was another one of Matthew's favorite songs. Had they been paying attention to the phone's playlist, they would've recalled how Matthew loved to dance to the song and how he could sing like Fred Schneider from that band.

"Man, this is crazy! This is the only picture of all of us that was taken, right?" They all thought that it was. "I want a copy of this, man. Don't forget me," he told Dusty.

Danielle, looked at her forgotten treasure and nearly cried. How could she have forgotten about it? It was a name tag for her golden retriever, Shaggy, that hung on his collar until the day he died. She loved Shaggy, and he had been a part of her family ever since she was four. When he died of old age, she took his name tag off his collar and kept it in her drawer. Sometimes she would get it out to look at it, smile, and then cry. "What did you put in there, Danielle?" Corky asked.

"Shaggy's name tag."

"Oh, I remember that dog. He was awesome," Travis said, flexing his hand inside the boxing glove.

"He certainly was. I had forgotten all about this tag and even putting it in here. Wow." She put his name tag in the palm of her hand and squeezed it tight. She could, if for a brief moment in time, feel her dog lick her face, the softness of his fur when she petted him.

The last thing in the metal box was the one thing that no one wanted to pull out. It was Matthew's contribution to the box. They had seen it in there when getting their stuff out, missing it on purpose. But they saw it in there and knew immediately what it was. What it was was an Atlanta Braves hat, stained with salt rings from sweat from all those summer games they played down at the park.

Dusty pulled it out, and the three of them sat back and looked at the old ball cap. On Corky's phone, another song, "Changes" by Black Sabbath came on cue and fit the mood of the group that sat at the kitchen table with all their forgotten items of youth. Matthew once remarked that this was the hardest song to listen to because there was so much pain behind it, and they all knew what he meant now.

The gravity of the situation was upon them in earnest. Dusty closed the lid to the metal box and placed Matthew's Braves hat on top of it. It was like he was there, with them at the cabin. Danielle started to cry. Travis just stared at it thinking about the kid that used to wear it. Dusty sat back and rubbed his fingers slowly over the bandage that Danielle had placed over his cut while Corky dropped his head and thought about their dead friend.

Finally, after several minutes of listening to a young Ozzy sing, Dusty spoke, "He never went anywhere without that damn thing, did he?" Nobody replied because they all knew it was the truth. It was rare that he was without it. He had two Braves hats, but the one that he put in the time capsule was his first hat and the one that he loved the most.

"What happened to us?" Corky asked them as another song played. This time it was, "Pictures Of You," from the Cure.

It took some time to respond, but Travis finally did. "Life, man. Wasn't nobody's fault. Just life."

"Yeah, but why? What kept us from keeping in touch? It's like we all left each other...like what we all had back then wasn't important," Dusty said, looking down at the table at the picture of all of them.

"It was important...we just grew apart," Travis replied.

"I had gotten a text from Matty a few years ago. He texted me 'Happy Birthday!' He remembered mine, and I never even knew his. How's that for a best friend?" Corky said with some guilt in his voice.

"He called me once and left a voicemail and asked about how I was doing and such. I was so busy that I never called back. I just forgot...didn't think about it until we were at the graveside service today," Travis said.

"I had that lunch with him fifteen years ago. I could've called him and checked in on him, but I never did. He called my cell phone and text but like you, I was always too busy to return it. I always meant to, you know? Time got away from me. He must've thought we were real pricks," Dusty said, saying what Corky and Travis were thinking.

"What about you, Danielle? When was the last time you talked to him?" Corky asked.

She sat with Shaggy's name tag tight in her hand and thought about it. She thought about telling them the truth, spilling everything that she had kept secret from everyone. She considered finally breaking her silence in front of those she loved so many years ago, those she trusted. Could she trust them now? And if she told them her secret, would they look at her differently, or Matthew? Before she could run deeper into those thoughts, she opened her mouth, and the words fell out. It was too late to go back now. The point of no return had been passed.

"The night before he died." The cat was out of the bag.

The boys were stunned. Her words knocked them out of their trance, and they lifted their eyes to her where hers met them all.

"What?" Corky asked.

Danielle knew there was no turning back now. She had already taken that first step to unburden herself.

"Yeah," she lowly said, squeezing Shaggy's name tag harder in her hand. "Um...we were seeing each other for the last couple of years, off and on."

"Seeing each other?" Travis asked. "Like...what?" he was shocked as they all were.

Danielle shifted in her seat, feeling uncomfortable now in front of them. "I had just gotten divorced and was in a really bad place. I got this friend request from him on Facebook, and it really surprised me that all the years that had gone by, he remembered me. So I accepted his request, and we started talking. Things felt like they did back when we left it all those years ago. I think we both knew we'd end up back together somehow. Eventually, I invited him out to my place in Alabama...which he came. And then..."

"Wow, this is crazy," Dusty interrupted. "He was cheating on his wife with you?"

Danielle replied, "Yeah, that's about the size of it, I guess. We neither were proud of it. It just kind of happened."

The three of them sat there, stunned, shocked, not knowing what to say. But what could they say? They didn't know Matthew as a man, but just as a kid. How much had he changed over the years? They had no idea.

"What was he like? I mean, I didn't really know him as an adult," Travis asked.

Danielle gave a half smile, "Pretty much the same Matty we all remember. Just grown-up. He got married at twenty-two to Carrie, his wife at the funeral. Raised two boys: Dylan and Raylan. Worked over at Truist bank as a branch manager."

"Damn," Corky said, "He was a banker? I would've never guessed that in a million years."

"Yeah, he had been with that banking company for fifteen years before they changed their name to Truist. I think before he said they were called BB&T. But he seemed to love his job. When we reconnected, we were both in bad spots. I had divorced Bill, and his marriage hadn't been good in a long time, he said."

"So, elephant in the room," Dusty started, "Why didn't you guys end up together back in the day? We all thought you would in the end. Was it heading that way?"

"After we called it quits back in high school, we always were best friends. When I decided to leave for school in Alabama the summer after we graduated, we tried it one more time. It worked really good, but the distance was too much for us. I was going into med school, and that was going to mean more time for us being apart because I had gotten accepted into a school in Arizona. We talked about him moving out there with me, and he just didn't want to leave home. So... that was the end. I eventually got married and he did, too. Then, I got divorced years later, and he popped in.”

“Did he know about that?” Corky asked.

“No, I never posted anything about that. It was just serendipity is all. He came into my life when I needed him the most.”

“What was his married life like?” Corky asked as Travis and Dusty awaited her answer.

“Not good. He told me that she had cheated on him twice. The first time they went to marriage counseling, and he thought that might’ve fixed it. She had done it about a year after their first son was born. So, he forgave that. Chalked it up to her self-esteem after the baby and them still being young and making mistakes. The second time was about three years ago. He told me that it nearly devastated him. She wanted to go to counseling again, and he just shut her down. He told me that he hadn’t ever gotten over the first time, not really, and when the second time came, it knocked him out. So he was in a bad spot mentally. He was already talking to an attorney about getting divorced. She had no idea. We had planned to be together, get married, and live happily ever after like we should’ve done years ago.”

That’s when Danielle broke down and started sobbing heavily. Travis, who sat to her right, reached out with his arm and put it on her shoulder to let her know they all cared.

***

For hours in that cabin, as the light of day turned to night, Dusty turned the lights and ordered pizzas. They listened to music and talked about their lives, where they were, how they had been doing. Matthew was the topic of most of the conversations, as they told stories about their fallen friend. Most of those stories made them smile and laugh, and a few were personal ones that each of them had with Matthew.

“I remember when mom died,” Dusty said, recalling that sad day back in 1992, “he was there for me up in my bedroom and just let me cry the whole night. He didn’t say anything, you know? He was just there listening to me talk it out. I never forgot that night. God, I miss him, and I’m sorry we didn’t keep in touch.”

"I don't think he harbored any ill will towards any of you. Matter of fact, when we were talking, we always spoke fondly of you guys. He missed you, but he understood," Danielle told them. That helped ease some of the pain, not all of it, but some.

"I remember when I was going to quit high school," Travis began, "and Matty heard about it and came over to my house after he got off work and talked to me all night long about how stupid I was. Of course, I didn't listen to him, thinking I knew what I was doing. But when I went in there to officially drop out, I couldn't do it. His words kept replaying over and over in my head. You know what got me the most? Him telling me that if I did it, he'd be disappointed with me. For some reason, that bothered me so much. That was the reason I didn't drop out...it was because I didn't want to disappoint him."

"I remember him taking care of me when I was sick with the flu when Mom and Dad were out in Colorado. Remember that? Yeah, he came over and took care of me. Eighteen years old, taking care of his friend who was sick. That was the kind of man he was...one that I like to remember, you know?"

"I never thought he'd be the first one to die though. Hell, I guess I never could imagine any of us," Dusty said.

"You never know. Death stalks us every day," Corky replied to the group. "I want to propose something right here, right now...I want us to do this again, here in this cabin. Bring our families so we all can be together just like the old days. I don't want this to be it, and we come back when one of us dies. If Matty's death has shown us anything, it's that we're still best friends, even if we ain't seen or talked to each other in decades." The others considered this and nodded, and agreed.

"Well," Travis said, stretching out his arms and back in the chair, "I best be heading home. The wife will think I've got a side piece."

The group all laughed as they each got up from the table.

It was one in the morning and Danielle could see the full moon shining through the bay window of the living room. She was too tired to drive back home and walked over to Dusty, "Would you mind if I stayed here for the night? I don't think I'll make it home because I'm just worn out."

"Of course, no problem. Just locked up when you leave," he told her.

"Does anyone have any objections to me keeping his hat?" Danielle asked out loud. Travis looked at Corky who looked at Dusty.

"Keep it," Travis said. "He'd have wanted you to have it."

***

Danielle followed the boys out of the cabin, and they all hugged her and told her that they were going to keep in touch. A promise that they intended to keep. She leaned up against one of the posts that held the front porch roof up wearing Matthew's Braves hat. She waved to her friends as they backed out of the driveway and down the road, disappearing into the warm night. She smiled to herself, touched the bill of the hat, and tears came.

She took it off and held it to her face. She took a deep breath in, and she was shocked that the hat still had his scent: Old Spice, trapped within the fibers. At first, she thought her mind was playing tricks on her, smelling what she thought she would. But she smelled it again, and she was right the first time, it was his scent.

She put his hat back on and walked off the front porch and around the cabin. Aided by the light of the full moon above, she slowly walked down the hill towards the lake and to the dock that stretched twenty yards into the water. Taking a seat on the edge of the dock, she took her shoes off and dipped her feet into the cool water. From her front jeans pocket, Danielle pulled out her earbud case and plugged them into her ears. She took her phone from the other pocket and turned her music app back on, picking up where it left off when Corky and Dusty scared her earlier. She resumed playing, "Plainsong" from The Cure. It was *their* song.

Looking out across the shimmering lake that bounced moonbeams off the mirror-like stillness of the water, she started to cry thinking about Matthew; thinking about what was and what could've been; thinking about life and how cruel it can be at times, but at the same time, how magical and great exhilarating it was.

Danielle closed her eyes, laid on her back on the dock, and let the music take her away back to Matthew, back to Claxton, back to 1991 when she finally told him that she loved him on that hot July night in his front yard. That was her favorite memory of him. She could still see him standing there, facing her, wearing a newer Braves hat, not the one that he had put into the time capsule a week ago.

When Danielle told him about how she felt—which she was nervous as all get out—he stood there shocked at first. Then, he smiled, calming her nerves about a possible rejection. There was a possibility that he didn't feel the same way, and she nearly backed out of telling him. But something drove her to do it, because "Love," her mother had once said, "ain't something a person should keep bottled up".

Matthew stood facing Danielle who was nervously biting her lower lip. It was a habit of hers. "I love you back," he replied.

The two teenagers hugged, and Matthew kissed her. It was their very first kiss– the same kiss that would be forever remembered. It was a kiss that would be used to measure all others. The truth of the matter was their first kiss out in Matthew's front yard that night was the best kiss either of them would ever have.

Danielle, lying on her back, listening to the music of the slow strumming guitar, opened her eyes and looked at the stars. Tears streamed to the sides of her face, hitting the planks of the dock. Her tears were not of pain, but of how sweet that moment was– how he made her feel that night. She could feel that moment in time in her very soul lying on her back, looking at the stars.

It was 1991 in her mind, and Danielle Cooper was kissing Matthew Morgan in his front yard.

REGULAR PEOPLE

Eddie Eastman sat in the driveway of his home and looked about on that sunny May afternoon. It was six o'clock. He would've been home on time had it not been for the car accident that choked the two-lane highway for the better part of forty-five minutes. But he had texted Molly's phone while sitting at a standstill in traffic to let her know why he was running late. She worried about him when he was late.

Eddie sat in his car and looked at his house: a modest two-story home on an acre of property that was bordered by a white picket fence. The white picket fence was not there when Molly and he bought the place in 2001. It was added in 2005. It was a sign of the American dream– a status symbol of where they were in life. And where he and Molly were in good shape.

"We still are," Eddie mumbled, sitting in his car and looking at their home.

He got out of his car, opened the picket fence gate, and closed it behind him. He walked up the walkway and up the front porch, and he swung open the front door to his abode.

"Hey, Molly! Your handsome guy is home!" Eddie said with cheer.

He did this every day without fail. He started doing it back when they had first gotten married, and Eddie kept the gag going. Molly didn't seem to mind.

"How was work?" she asked, coming through the kitchen and toward him.

"Oh you know, same old office stuff as usual. HR never really changes much. It's either by the book, or it ain't," Eddie said, putting his Auburn University hat on the hook next to the front door.

"So you say," Molly replied, pulling her husband close to her for a kiss on the lips. The two of them still had that passion they had when they got married in 1998.

"Oh, I say," Eddie said while kissing her. "So, how was home today?" he asked as the two of them pulled their lips away from each other.

"Not bad. I tried a new recipe from a website I found online."

"For?" Eddie asked as the two of them walked into the living room where Eddie plopped down in his recliner. *God, this feels good*, he thought, taking his shoes off and placing them beside the recliner.

"Your favorite," Molly said from the kitchen.

Eddie turned in his recliner to look into the kitchen, "Chicken dumplings?"

"You know it!"

Eddie smacked his hands together. "Hot damn! I love you– you know that?!"

"You only love me because I can cook," Molly replied from the kitchen, in front of the stove as she stirred the pot of thickening chicken dumplings.

"Well, you do have other talents, you know?"

"Yeah, yeah, yeah. You play your cards right, you might see some of those talents later tonight."

"That's why I love Tuesday nights," Eddie said, laughing with excitement. He nestled deeper in his recliner, a recliner he had since 2001 when they first bought the house. It was the first piece of furniture they bought together. He told Molly that she could pick out any living room suit she wanted and decorate the entire house the way she saw fit, but give him this one thing: a recliner like his dad used to have. And he got one. It was old and had lost some shape over the decades, but it was just right for Eddie. It fit him perfectly.

"How long until the chicken and dumplings are done?"

"Ummm... about another thirty minutes, I'd say. Let me guess... you're going to rest your eyes."

"You know me so well." Eddie leaned the recliner out, stretching his tired legs on the elevated ottoman, and closed his eyes. He was dozing in no time—off to dreamland.

***

At the dining room table, he and Molly ate supper and talked about their day. For a long-term married couple, Eddie and Molly really never ran out of things to talk about. Sure, there were silences between them here and there; but for the most part, they could find something to talk about. Lately, the talk at the dinner table was about Eddie's work day.

"This supper, by the way, is out of this world. You did such a great job. But you always do."

Molly smiled, "Awww, thank you, honey. I'm glad it turned out okay. Sometimes when you try something new with something you already know how to do, you never know how it'll turn out. So, any more issues with that Steve Stone guy?"

Eddie shook his head with a mouthful of food. He chewed and swallowed before he answered, "Nope. We fired him today, around noon. He had it coming though. He'd been clocking in late and altering his time, making it look like he was there on time. Plus we got him on the sexual harassment beef I told you about last week. That guy is just a mess. I don't think he'll ever straighten out. Maybe he will, but I doubt it."

"How did he get hired anyway?"

"The HR manager before me hired him on. They were buddies. Sometimes the good ole boy system is alive and well," Eddie said.

"So...I've been thinking today," Molly said.

"About?"

"I'm going to go back to teaching after the summer is over. I'm going to call Leach and let her know that I'll be back."

"You sure?" Eddie asked, chewing his food. "I mean I support you either way– you know that. But I thought you liked just chilling at home doing what you want."

Molly sat there for a moment and thought about her husband's statement. "Yeah, it's cool and all, but I don't want this to be my life forever. I can only scroll FB and the internet for recipes for so long. I hate shopping. And flowers don't need any more attention since the season is up and going. I'm running out of things to do. I need to go back to my job, or I'm going to run amuck in this house Jack Nicholson style from *The Shining*." The married couple laughed together.

"Well," Eddie started, "if that's what you want, it's what I want."

***

After supper, Eddie took a shower and after that, he was sitting deep in his recliner, reading his phone for the sports news. Molly was on her phone playing Candy Crush while the TV was on an Atlanta Braves baseball game. They were playing the Phillies, and the Braves were up 2-0 in the third.

"You know, I remember my mom and dad doing this very thing back when I was a kid. Except instead of a phone, Dad read the newspaper, and Mom worked on a book of Find-A-Word. Funny how times have changed but not at the same time— you know it?"

"Yeah, my mom and dad were the same way. Except Mom liked to do crosswords in ink. That woman never made a mistake on those. I could never do them."

"If it's crosswords, I'm out. Especially in ink." Eddie laughed.

"Oh no, I can't do that either. I wouldn't even dare try. I can't even do them in pencil."

"How's your game going?" Eddie asked as he looked up from his phone to see Matt Olson hit a solo jack over the right field wall into the Chop House.

"It's going. Slow. I can't get by this level though. I've been on it for a bit. Gets frustrating sometimes."

"I'm sure it does. Let me ask you something. You ever regret not being able to have kids?"

Molly took some time to think about the question her husband asked. They had spoken about it before. Sometimes the question came back up but the answer was always the same from Molly.

"Sometimes, yes. But I love these moments right here. I always have. You?"

Eddie was quicker in his response, "Not really. I love these moments too. Besides, we still have our nieces and nephews. They're enough."

"Sometimes more than enough," Molly said giggling. Eddie agreed.

***

Later that night in bed—after a sexual romp under and over the covers—Eddie and Molly laid there in each other's arms, eyes closed, in the afterglow of what just was. It was warm under those covers, cozy, while their naked bodies held each other close.

"Molly?"

"Yes, Eddie?" Molly said in a state of near unconsciousness.

"Tell me this will never end."

"What, Eddie?" Molly asked with a dreamlike whisper. Had Eddie not been closer to her, he would have not heard.

"Us. These little moments right here. Promise me you'll be here forever."

"And ever," Molly said slowly from that place where dreams begin. "And ever."

Eddie's heart was so full of joy and sadness at that moment tears came from his eyes. He batted his eyes to clear his vision, but it was no use. The tears came rolling off his cheeks and down onto the sheet under them.

"I love you, Molly. More than anything. More than words can say. I hope you know that." Of course, Molly did not reply. She was lying there– her eyes closed, breathing softly. Eddie lay there holding his wife, his breath in sync with hers.

***

The next day, Eddie sat out in his car in the driveway, looking at the house that he and Molly called home. There was a time when he thought about selling the place and moving. He knew Molly would never go for it. Besides, why start over somewhere else at his age? Wasn't he starting over enough already? Sometimes life throws you a curveball. Right when you swing, it dips down at the last second, and you miss it. That's how it happened to Eddie—a swing and a miss after hitting fastballs down the middle for the better part of twenty-five years.

Eddie got out of his car, shut the door, and opened the picket fence gate. He walked up the walkway and up the front porch. Before he opened the door, he wanted to go around the house and look at something. He walked off the front porch and around the house toward the side yard facing Oak Street that was on the side of their acre of land in that suburb.

As he turned the corner of their house, Molly's rose garden came into view. It was a once vibrant living organism in their well-maintained lawn, but now the color was fading. Beetles had even chewed their way through all the red, yellow, and purple blooms. Molly had taken a lot of pride in that rose garden—spent a lot of time, years in fact—to make it one of the most beautiful spots in their yard. But that was before the accident. Everything changed after the accident. Nothing was the same, no matter how much Eddie tried to convince himself otherwise. You can only fool yourself for so long before the hard truths float to the surface.

***

He swung the front door open, announcing his arrival from another long work day.

"Hey, Molly! Your handsome guy is home!" Eddie said with cheer.

Molly came from the kitchen, wiping her hands on a towel.

"So he is!" She walked over to him at the door as he put his Auburn University hat on the hook next to the front door. She grabbed a hold of him and drew him in close. The two kissed passionately.

"Glad you're home," she said.

"Me too," Eddie said.

The two of them let go of each other and walked into the living room where Eddie met his recliner and plopped down. He took his shoes off and placed them beside the recliner. *God, this feels good*, he thought.

"How was your day?" he asked.

Molly sat on her usual spot on the couch adjacent to Eddie's recliner. "Not bad. Watered the rose garden. Put that new fertilizer in for them. I think they're going to look good this year. It already looks the best I've ever seen it. What do you think?"

Eddie looked at his wife and wanted to tell her the truth about the rose garden but couldn't bring himself to tell her.

"Yeah, Molly, it looks great. The best year I've seen."

Of course, it wasn't. But if Eddie admitted that to her, then he would have to admit everything else. He just didn't want to do that. He knew this was the best he was going to have since her accident.

"I have to remember to clip some and put in a vase for Mrs. Horshack. She just loves it when I do that for her. I haven't started supper. Any special request?"

"No, I think I'll eat some leftover chicken and dumplings."

***

After his shower, Eddie went into the kitchen and made himself a bowl of chicken and dumplings and heated it up in the microwave. Now he was sitting in his recliner, watching the Braves game while Molly sat with her phone playing her game. Eddie would look over at her from time to time and feel a rush of love overtake him. God, how he loved that woman.

"Does it get any better than this?" Eddie asked.

"What do you mean?" Molly asked, not taking her eyes off the game on her phone.

"Us, I mean just us here, right now. This. Me and you."

Molly smiled, "No, Eddie, it doesn't. This is perfect."

Eddie smiled and nodded his head. "It is, ain't it?"

"Don't forget you have to see Dr. Hudson tomorrow after work."

As soon as Molly evoked the doctor's name, his heart fell into his stomach. He knew what that meant.

"Yeah, about that. I don't think I'll go tomorrow. I may reschedule it," Eddie said, taking his eyes away from his beautiful wife and to the TV screen where the Braves were playing.

"No, you've already canceled on him twice in the last few weeks. You got to go this time," Molly said in that sweet manner that she had about her.

"I already know what he's going to tell me. No sense of going to hear that."

"Well, it doesn't matter. You have to go for your own good. You can't keep doing what you're doing, you know?"

"Why not?" Eddie asked. "I've been doing okay so far."

"Have you though? Really?" Molly asked, still looking down at her phone playing Candy Crush.

Eddie knew the answer to that. She was right, usually was. The truth was that he hadn't been doing good, and he knew it. He was coping the best he could, given the circumstances of recent events. He did an admirable job of fooling himself into thinking things weren't as bad as they were with him, but deep inside, he knew better.

"What's going on with me ain't hurting anybody *but* me. Actually, it makes me feel good. So what's the harm in it?"

"The harm," Molly said, "is because you know it's not healthy for you. The only reason you're pulling back from Dr. Hudson is because he's telling you things you don't want to hear. Which is what doctors are supposed to do. If you won't do it for yourself, at least do it for me."

"Molly, you don't understand," Eddie said, nearly breathless.

"Maybe not. But you have got to stop fooling yourself, Eddie. This is more serious than you think."

Eddie sat there in his recliner with his bowl of chicken and dumplings and knew that she was right. She usually was.

***

The next day, Eddie sat in Dr. Hudson's office, which was in his spacious three-story home on the other end of Claxton. He sat in a comfortable oversized chair and wondered if the doctor liked the fact that he could work out of his home and not have to venture to an office in a hospital or a medical village with other professionals. He also wondered if the doctor got worried about people who had mental issues coming to where he lived.

Before he could dive too deeply into those thoughts, Dr. Hudson opened the big heavy wooden door behind him. The hinges made a small creaking sound as the doctor entered the room.

"Mr. Eastman, how are we today?" he walked past Eddie to his desk to sit down behind it.

Eddie shifted in the chair to seem more attentive. "I'm okay."

"You canceled our visit two times already. Everything okay?"

"Yeah, same as it ever is, I guess."

"I reviewed the notes of our last session, and we had gotten to how you are coping with the loss of your wife. Does that sound about right to you?" Dr. Hudson asked.

Eddie nodded, "Yeah, sounds about right."

"So, have you been acting as if she is still alive? Going on like the accident wasn't fatal?"

It took some time for Eddie to answer. Answering the doctor's question was an admission that things were bad in his head. He knew they were, but saying it out loud was confirmation in the audible sense that maybe he was losing his marbles.

"Yeah. I know it's not healthy, but it helps me cope some."

"Eddie, I feel that you need to navigate your trauma in a more positive way. Being stuck in your mind, thinking that Molly is alive and well is not a healthy way to go, and one that I cannot endorse. Usually, I'm all for whatever coping mechanisms work, as long as they are not detrimental to the patient, but I'm afraid what you're doing is going to have long-term effects on your mental well-being as you go forward."

"I know, Doc. I'm just having a hard time, is all."

"I understand."

"Do you though?" Eddie quickly replied.

Dr. Hudson leaned back in his chair behind his desk and looked at Eddie through his big glasses.

"Yeah, I do. I lost my wife of thirty-five years to cancer three years ago. It was brain cancer. In a place where the doctors couldn't reach it. There was nothing they could do. So... I had to watch in slow motion as my wife died, as did my children. So yeah, Eddie, I do understand your pain."

Eddie sat feeling like a prick for assuming that the man had no baggage himself. For a long time after Molly's death, he felt as though he was the only one who had experienced death. He forgot there were countless others in the world who had taken a loss too.

"I'm sorry. I didn't know."

"It's okay. It's not something I go around advertising. But I do understand your pain. And pain to people is as unique as our fingerprints. We all deal with pain differently—we all cope differently—

but the main thing is that we have to guide ourselves to some sort of resolution, or it will eat our minds alive with grief."

"And I feel that's happening to me. As long as I see and interact with Molly, I'm okay. But if I don't— and I've tried— I fall to pieces. It hurts so bad. Part of me never wants me to stop seeing her like I do, but the other part of me is dying because I know she's not really there."

"You're stuck in a cycle of pain and grief. It's like a um...a hamster wheel. You can run forever on that thing until you get tired and stop, but you never really get off the wheel." Dr. Hudson said.

Eddie nodded, "Exactly. What hurts worse is not seeing her and talking to her—because when I tell you that I see her and talk to her, even touch her, kiss her—it's real, and I can feel her. It's like she's really there. And I don't want to lose that. But I know that it's all in my head."

"I know when my wife died– I swear I could hear her voice inside this house. Sometimes I still do. As trained professionals, we're taught to help those navigate the grieving process because there's really no timeline for when it's done. No finish line. I don't know honestly if we as human beings ever stop mourning the loss of those we love. I certainly haven't. It's easier, but it's not ever over, despite what the books and papers on the subject of grief tell you. However, I can say without a doubt—as a person who has lost *and* as a doctor— that it's not mentally healthy for us to stay in that constant cycle of grief... staying on that hamster wheel."

"It just hurts so good to see her, Doc," Eddie said, feeling the tears begin to form in his eyes.

"I know it does." Dr. Hudson replied. "How did you think Molly would feel, knowing that you're doing this to yourself?"

"She would tell me that I needed to stop."

"I've always said that those we love never really leave us. We catch some of their spirit within us. That's how they live on even after they're gone. I can feel my wife inside me—her spirit. And I bet you could too if you would begin to train your mind to stop projecting her outward and focus inward. There are still days, plenty of them, that I talk to my wife in this house. I don't see her, but I know she's with me in here," Dr. Hudson taps his heart. "But the difference between me and you, Eddie, is that my dead wife doesn't answer back. I've accepted what happened to her. And at some point, you must accept what happened to Molly. It may take years, but there'll come a time in your life where you will need to accept things as they are, or you will risk damaging your mental stability."

Eddie nodded. He knew the doctor was right. He was no dummy.

"But small steps turn into big gains. Remember that. What's the first thing you do when you come home from work?"

"I open the front door and announce to Molly I'm home."

"Maybe you need to not do that. Start there. Change that habit. Just open the front door and walk in. Try it when you leave here today. And then every other day. And then go for every day. Take it small and slow, and build from there. Are you a very routine-oriented man, Eddie?"

Eddie nodded, "Most definitely."

"Then after you conquer the front door, I challenge you to change something else about when you come home. Change up where you sit. Make a list of everything you do when you come home, your routine, and alter it. What you're trying to accomplish with that is making yourself a new normal. In my professional opinion, if you don't pry yourself slowly out of the way things were, you're never going to get out of the old ways."

Again, Eddie nodded. "Makes sense. I will certainly give that a shot. I'll see if I can start with the front door first and work on a list of things I need to change up some."

"Our next appointment, in two weeks, I want you to bring me a list of things you normally do versus the things you have changed from that list. Doesn't have to be wholesale changes at first. Remember— just small things, one by one, no timeline. Forward progress is progress no matter how small."

***

Eddie sat in his car in the driveway and looked at the house he and Molly called theirs. He had given a lot of thought to what Dr. Hudson had told him in his office. And the doctor was right. He had to start making some changes, but those changes were going to be difficult to enact. If Eddie didn't make those small changes—or at least attempt— his mental state would go up for grabs, and who knew where he'd go from there.

"I think I can do this," Eddie told himself, sitting inside his car and looking at their home. "You bet I can."

Eddie got out of his car and shut the door. He knew once he entered through the picket fence gate, up the walkway, up the front porch, and to the front door, there was no going back. If he was going to begin to heal—at least some—from Molly's death, from that car accident, it had to start when he opened that front door. He had to not announce that he was home, see Molly come to him, and pull him close for a kiss. It had to start somewhere, and that front door was the first step.

Eddie looked around his neighborhood and saw that it was just another regular day of the week, with regular people doing regular things. Mr. James was outside, cutting his front lawn across the street. Albert Kinney was sitting on his front porch, whittling a piece of cedar, like he did every day around that time of day. Marge Plinkton was out with her water hose, watering the flowers in her flower beds. Everything outside in his neighborhood was regular. That gave Eddie some relief. *Maybe I can be regular too*, he thought as he opened the picket fence gate and came through it.

He walked up the walkway slowly with a knot in his stomach. This was going to be the first day in forever that he didn't swing that front door open and say, "Hey, Molly! Your handsome guy is home!" That had been a trademark of his for decades now, and to think of changing it was frightening, to say the least. But there he was, walking slowly up the walkway and preparing himself to alter things—to change small things—little by little. A new normal.

Eddie reached the end of the walkway where it spilled to the front porch steps. Eddie paused briefly and looked around the white picket fence of their acre of land and thought to himself that the American dream was dead—at least his was. *What good is having anything if Molly ain't around*, he wondered.

Eddie lifted his right leg and touched his shoe down on the first step of the front porch. It was do or die now for him, no turning back. If he was going to get better, it had to start when he opened that front door. He knew he had to start getting better; even Molly was concerned about him, and she knew him better than anyone. Up the four rungs of the front porch he went. He crossed the small front porch that wasn't big for anything but a few potted plants and a decorative chair that neither he nor Molly ever sat on.

Eddie trembled a bit as he placed his hand on the cool silver knob of the front door. Old habits are hard to break, and this one was going to be the hardest—at least to begin with. He took his hand off the knob and stood, thinking to himself if he really wanted to get on with the healing process of losing his wife. The fact of the matter was that he loved seeing her, even if she was a profoundly grief-stricken mind trick he was playing on himself, projecting her as if she was alive and well.

It's only hurting me, nobody else. So what if I see and talk to my dead wife? Does it matter to anyone but me?

"Eddie, you know that you'll get worse if you don't start breaking the cycle now. It's already been too long doing what you're doing," he told himself out loud on the front porch.

I know, I know. But I don't want to start to lose her all over again. I start changing this, then I'll have to change other things and eventually, I won't see her again.

"But you can't stay like this forever," he said out loud in front of the door, his hand now back on the knob, ready to turn it. "You have to make a choice right now. Change small things right now, right here, or continue to stay stuck where you're at."

Eddie closed his eyes, twisted the knob, and entered the house.

"Hey, Molly! Your handsome guy is home!"

SIGNS AND WONDERS

I had seen him around the place from time to time. A tall, lanky kid they called Lefty. Why they called him Lefty, I have no idea. Maybe he was left-handed– I don't know. Still don't. At my age, you don't really care for things like that. How someone got their name or nickname was not high up on my list of priorities; getting old forces you to set different priorities. Priorities like what's on TV, what's for dinner, what's the weather going to be like tomorrow—you know, things like that are high up on my list of concerns.

Other priorities were not pissing myself or babbling on and on about stupid shit. My mind had gotten a little mushy– I could tell. Maybe it was destined to happen to me. Maybe it was being cooped up in this retirement home for the last few years. I don't know. Maybe it's a little bit of both, to be honest. But then again, it could be in my DNA to get soft in the brain or just plain old age.

I ended up at the Blue Water Retirement Home because I could not handle the pressures of my house anymore. I could've opted to go live with my daughters and their families, but the last thing I wanted to be was a burden. Trust me, no man worth his salt wants to be a burden on anyone. I could've had someone come and sit with me night and day, but that would've cost too much. And besides, who can you really trust these days? I don't like strangers much; let alone them being in my house.

So, I ended up here at the retirement home. It's not bad really. There are some people my age and older. The staff keeps us going when some of us don't want to. Seen a lot of people come and go in this place— that's for damn sure. Sometimes, I think of this place as an animal shelter, except no one is coming to adopt us. We're dropped off, most of us, and left to die. Not me. I came here on my own terms, and I'll leave on my own terms– thank you very much. Plus, I can go see my family on the weekends. If I don't feel like it, then I don't. I have to say that it's a pretty nice place and should be for the amount of money I'm paying to stay here and live out my final years. I guess the pension from the CSX train company I worked for all those years finally paid off in the end, didn't it?

***

I was sitting out on the back pavilion that late October evening. It was around six, and darkness was already around. The lampposts were all lit up around the grounds. I was sitting in a pretty comfortable rocking chair, listening to the Atlanta Braves play. I usually like to sit out in the pavilion when the temps get colder. I used to do that at my house. I'd go outside and sit on the back porch at night and just gaze around the place I'd lived for over fifty years. Now, this is the best I have. Ah, it's not so bad. I think life is partly about having creature comforts, and boy, do I have them here. Thank God for that.

Lefty came walking up the walkway, hands in his pockets, head down, as he was apt to do most times. He always seemed to have something on his mind. *So young to be carrying all that weight,* I always told myself. I wondered what could be bothering him so much. I didn't ask before that night out at the pavilion. Honestly, I didn't care to. Wasn't any of my beeswax. That's the trouble with most people nowadays; they get into people's business. People post their stuff on Facebook all the time. Why? Attention, that's why.

As far as staff goes around the place, Lefty was always pretty good. Polite, always helping out. Never a smart ass. He wore his hair nice and short. A real All-American boy. He helped me learn my new Android phone a while back. Lefty was an okay guy in my book. Just quiet, is all. I knew a guy kinda like him on the railroad back when I worked it. His name was Gus Meechum. Gus and Lefty could've passed for father and son if I'm telling you the truth.

"How's Blue Water's favorite retiree doing tonight?" Lefty asked, walking up into the pavilion and taking a seat on the railing on the same side as me. The two of us looked out across the huge pond across the way. The lights from the lampposts glistened off the water, setting

60

a calm mood. Sitting out there at night and looking across the water always relaxed me.

"I'm okay, I guess. Just listening to the ball game," I said, taking the wired earbud from my left ear.

"You ain't gotta stop on my account, Buzz."

"It's a runaway right now. Braves ain't hitting the gas. They're already going to the playoffs. They're letting their bench guys play tonight."

"They look good this year?" Lefty asked, blowing cigarette smoke into the crisp fall air.

"Best hitting team I've ever seen in Atlanta. But can they get to the World Series and win it? Who knows? Vegas never does."

I could tell Lefty wanted to be silent while out there, which was the norm when I saw him from time to time. Blue Water is a sprawling place, and sometimes you don't see the same people all the time, just here and there. I can count on both hands the amount of times that I've seen this young man. I will say every interaction that I had with him was good.

"I never got into baseball. My dad took me to a Pirates game once when the Braves came to Pittsburgh when I was a kid back in 2003. If I had to pick a favorite baseball team, the Braves would've been it. My dad watched them all the time on TV."

"That was back during the TBS Superstation days. A player I loved to watch play was Greg Maddux. Boy, he was a great pitcher. Probably the best I'd ever seen in my life," I told him. "Him, Glavine, and Smoltz. Damn, that was a pitching staff right there in the 1990s. Throw in Avery for a few years, wow. Damn shame they only walked away with one championship though. Of course, they blew the '96 World Series. But this new batch of Braves...this group could win a few."

Lefty blew more smoke out into the night air and looked around at the dark landscape in silence.

"How long you worked here, Lefty?"

"About a year and a half now."

"You like it?" I asked.

He nodded, "Yeah, it ain't terrible. Some of the old people get on my nerves. I mean..." Lefty turned and looked at me and stammered, thinking he offended me.

I laughed him off, "Don't worry kid– some of the old people in here get on my nerves too."

"Nobody's ever had a problem with you, Buzz. All of the people on the staff really like you."

"Well, part of my winning personality, I reckon. I just try to treat people right, is all."

"Well, you do a good job at it. How come you ain't living at home?" Lefty asked.

"Well, my kids didn't think it was a good idea, and I started to think they were right. I can get around pretty good, but sometimes I forget stuff like leaving the stove on or leaving candles burning. Nearly caught my house on fire doing that. The candle I was burning was next to the curtains in my living room, and they caught somehow. That's when the kids and myself figured it was time for me to come here. I didn't want to go to their houses and live because the last thing I wanted to be was a burden."

"You like it here?" Lefty asked, puffing on his cigarette.

"Yeah, it ain't bad. I got certain freedoms. More than most around here. But I like it okay. I like being around people sometimes. When I don't, I come out here. Never met a man that didn't like his alone time."

"Ain't that the truth," Lefty said.

"You ain't got a Southern accent. Where you from?"

"Pennsylvania. A town called Ridgway."

"Ah, okay. How in the hell did you end up in Claxton, Tennessee?"

"Met a woman on Facebook, and like a dumbass, I moved down here to be with her. It worked out for about a year until it didn't. She ended up going back to her ex-husband. And I didn't want to go back home as a failure, so I hung around here. Plus, I like the climate. Back home can get too much snow."

"Women. Get you every time. Got me," I told him.

"Yeah, well, mine got me good. I moved down here and moved into this house with her. I got a job with Renzo Manufacturing. I was making really good money for around here anyway, and we were talking about getting married. Then one day I came home from work, and she was packing up and telling me that I could have the house and that she was going back home. End of story. So, I work at Renzo from seven to four and then come here and work until eleven."

"Sorry for your run of bad luck. You need the money that bad you have to work two jobs?"

Lefty shook his head, "No, I just don't want to stay at home because all I do is think. And thinking for me is bad. I tend to get depressed a lot. And I don't have friends down here, so it's just best that I keep myself busy. I just feel for the first time in my life that I don't have any goals or direction in my life. The girl that I loved is gone. My home back in Pennsylvania is bad, which I didn't mind leaving at all. I feel like a man on a deserted island most times."

"How old are you?"

Lefty took a draw off his cigarette, "Thirty."

"I got fifty years on you. But I'm here to tell you, things will get better."

"I wish that I could believe that," Lefty said.

"You a college-educated man?" I asked.

"A little bit. Went to Penn State for a couple of years, and it just didn't work for me."

"I went to Auburn University, class of 1963. Had a professor down there, Dr. Clapper. Smart man, sometimes too damn smart because all of us in his classes couldn't follow him sometimes. He taught psychology. And one of his favorites was Carl Jung. You heard of him?"

"No," Lefty replied, fishing for another cigarette from the pack that was in his jacket pocket.

"He developed this theory called synchronicity, which means that they are meaningful coincidences that can't be explained by cause and effect. Sometimes there's a deeper meaning behind what has happened to us."

"Like what?" Lefty asked.

"Well, have you ever been singing a song in your head that you haven't heard in a long time, and then out of nowhere you hear it? That's synchronization. I was grocery shopping a few years back; and when I checked out, my bill was $77.77, and I was at register 7. I go get into my car, and all the mileage on my odometer read 77,777 miles. So naturally, I got to the gas station and played the lotto. Lucky 7s. I buy seven of them and bring them home and scratch them all off. Won $777 bucks all together."

"That's a pretty neat story, Buzz."

"Yeah, it is. But my point is, sometimes the universe talks to us. If we're able to hear it, it can guide us some– maybe tell us if we're on the right path."

Lefty smiled at that, "Sounds like a bunch of cult stuff to me."

"I used to say the same thing back when I was younger, too. But I believe there's meaning behind everything we come across. What that meaning is, I have no idea. Sometimes, though, sometimes, we get a totem that lets us know things are going to be okay. You a religious man?"

"No."

"I mean I don't go to church or anything like that. But I am a very spiritual man, meaning that I believe in God. I talk to him every day. I make sure to carve out twenty minutes for a one-on-one with the Big Guy. It helps keep me centered."

"You know if he talks back and you answer, they'll put you away, right?" Lefty said with laughter.

"Yeah, well, he does talk to me through the universe. That's what I think Jung was maybe getting at. Maybe when we come across these meaningful coincidences, it's God sending out messages to us to pick up on."

"He doesn't talk to me, that's for damn sure."

"Maybe you ain't been listening."

I could see that kind of struck a chord with Lefty. He turned and looked at me with a look that wasn't disbelief but rather curiosity.

"What are you saying, that my life has turned out the way it has, all the losses I've taken– is because I'm not listening to God, or the universe, or this Jung dude?"

I shook my head, "You got time for a story?"

Lefty blew smoke out of his mouth and repositioned himself on the railing he was sitting on. "Sure. Only for you, Buzz."

"Good. This is a story about a deer. And God. Or the universe, if you want to say that. Whatever is your choosing. But this story is as real as me and you sitting here, you understand?"

Lefty nodded...

***

"It was 1982. I had just told my wife at the time that I wanted a divorce because she was cheating on me with this dude at the post office. I mean, it just tore me to shreds, you know? We had been married for about twenty years up to that point. We had two kids and a nice house. We were living that American dream. Just a normal married couple. She stayed home, and I worked on the railroad for CSX.

"Somewhere along the way, she and I became distant. Instead of being a team, we started becoming more and more isolated from each other. That's not what I wanted, and I don't think that's what she wanted. It just started happening over time. Before we knew it, we were fighting all the time about the craziest stuff. Sometimes those fights got out of hand. I never hit her, mind you, but there was a lot of yelling and cussing back and forth. Shit got broke sometimes. It was totally unlike us.

"Anyway, after our last big fight, I got into my truck and rode around all night, trying to clear my head. I didn't want to leave her, but I couldn't stay, either. It was becoming an impossible situation. Man, I put a lot of miles on that truck that night– I tell you what. And you know what I came to the conclusion of? That I was done. Yup, I was too tired to fight anymore. And keep in mind, this was before I found out about the guy at the post office.

"So when I got home, it must've been around twelve, I reckon. I sat out in the driveway for a spell to gather the courage to walk in there and tell her I was done. It was the hardest thing I ever had to do in my life. Nobody gets married to get divorced, okay? Nobody. I think everybody who gets married goes into it with the best intentions and the right mindset. Things happen along the way that can sometimes test a marriage. Sometimes those things break it. But nobody gets married to eventually get divorced."

"Did you go in there and tell her?" Lefty asked.

I nodded my head slowly, lost to a time that was years ago, but still fresh in my old mind. I can still to this day feel that night in my bones.

"Yeah, finally I got out of my truck and went inside. I told her how I felt. I did it calmly because there was no more fight left in me. She was fine with it. A little too fine with it. I'd eventually find out why."

"The guy from the post office, right?" Lefty asked.

"Yeah, the guy from the post office. Andy Stephens. She had been dealing with him for a bit."

"How'd you find out?"

"Doris Deeds, the old woman who was my neighbor, had been seeing him pull up in his mail truck and stay for long periods of time. Of course, I had no idea. I was away on the trains. And she didn't think anything of it until she saw Mary packing up her car. Then she heard through the grapevine that we were getting divorced.

"About two months later, I mean I'm just plum torn up about it. My whole family just evaporated in an instant. The kids didn't talk to me because they thought it was my fault the marriage didn't last. Mary had them convinced that I was the one cheating on her instead of the other way around."

"How old were the kids?" Lefty asked.

"Melaine was sixteen at the time and her older sister, Jamie, was twenty. Jamie was already in school that semester over at Hiwassee College when it all went down. It didn't affect her as much as it did Melaine."

"When my parents split, I didn't care much. All they did was fight. My old man walked out one night after a fight and never came back."

"You two ever reconcile?" I asked him.

"No. I heard he died several years back. We never talked after he left. I was, like, fifteen at the time and had my own shit to deal with. I figured if he loved me, he'd reach out or something. He never did. So, I finally gave up on him like he did me."

"That sucks, kiddo. Kid needs their father."

"Do they, though?" Lefty asked sarcastically.

"Well, yes, they do. Need both parents. It took years for Melaine to even talk to me. And I'm talking like fifteen. She was thirty when she came to my house to talk. I thought I'd never see her again. Jamie, she was always around. She wasn't on Team Mom. Wasn't on mine, either. I'll give it to her, she stayed impartial because she loved me and her mom, and she wasn't going to pick sides. Melaine did. She and I lost a lot of time on account of her mule headedness. But it ended better than it started."

"So what about the deer, Buzz?" Lefty asked, getting me back on track.

I tend to get lost sometimes in my head when I tell stories.

"Oh, right, the deer. Sorry. Anyway, when Mary left and went to go be with that guy at the post office, I was in a tailspin. I felt like a stranger in my own home. Food didn't taste right; couldn't sleep good. I mean, me and Mary slept together in the same bed for nearly twenty years, and then it went to nothing. That was one of the hardest adjustments to make I think.

"I had a pretty rough depression and attempted suicide a month after she packed her bags. Obviously, I didn't go through with it. But I was close. I was laying on the kitchen floor that night, held the knife to my wrist, and was going to just let her fly. I'll tell you the thing that scared me the most, Lefty. The silence. Man, there was silence in that house when I was getting ready to do it. I mean, I didn't hear nothing. That scared me right there because it was as if I was on the edge of something and if I jumped, I'd never come back. Very sobering moment in my life up to that point."

"What stopped you?"

"I don't know. I just remember I stopped crying all at once and got up from the floor. I put the knife on the counter and just was calm for some reason. To this day, I don't know what came over me. Must've been God calming me down. That's the only thing I think it could've been.

"The very next day, I drove down to the park. They have this oval walking track down there. I walked it a lot back in those early days of the divorce just to have something to do after work and on my off days besides sitting in the house, driving myself crazy. I can't tell you how many miles I walked down there on that track.

"Anyway, that day of the deer, I had lapped that track like ten times. Four times was a mile, keep that in mind. I was tired and thinking about my life and where it was going; where I was at; and how all to shit it had gone. I started crying, talking to God. I mean, having a full-on conversation out loud with Him.

"I was asking Him why things happened the way they did; why I couldn't keep things together; why Mary cheated on me. I was just getting everything out in the open, you know? I was an emotional wreck out there on the walking track. Of course, I was alone on it as usual because nobody used it. Never knew why, though. It was a nice park. I remember when they built it, and I used to go down after work and watch the guys use the bulldozers and backhoes…"

"The deer, Buzz, before I start collecting my social security," Lefty said, half joking.

"Right, sorry. Anyway, I'm just crying, talking to God. I remember this clear as day. I said, 'God, I need a sign that you're listening, and that things are going to be okay'. I came down the hill off the right turn, and I was walking on the straightaway that faced Hudson's Woods on the other side of the chain fence.

"Out of nowhere, right out of the woods, this deer, a doe, comes slowly walking out of the woods and over to the fence. That thing stood over there, waiting for me to come over to it. I see it, and man, I just stop walking. I'd been down there at that park when it was nothing but woods and fields as a kid and knew that place well. I ain't never seen a deer in there.

"But there she was, big as Billy Be Damned. My heart is just a-flying out of my chest, and I'm shaking a little bit by seeing this deer. I started walking faster towards it from the straightway. Tears came out of my eyes not because I was sad, but because I knew God had heard me. I started running toward the fence and the deer.

"I get there out of breath, walk off the pavement of the track, and across the grass to the fence. And do you know that deer didn't even flinch, not nary a bit. I walked up to him, and he and I just stood there looking at each other, neither one of us blinking. There was a peacefulness that just washed over me, and I knew that I was standing before the presence of God right then and there.

"I'm crying pretty hard at this point, right? I stuck my fingers through the chain fence, and the deer started licking them. I ain't never had that happen to me. Then the deer let me pet her muzzle, and that just put me at peace for whatever reason. Now, I've seen deer in my lifetime, but nothing like that to where I could approach one and touch it. You know deer are really skittish around humans. But not this one. No, sir. She and I stood there and just looked into each other's eyes. I remember saying 'Thank you' and the deer flicked its ear.

"It turned slowly away from me and walked back into the woods from where it came. Didn't run, wasn't in a hurry. Just turned and walked back inside. Never saw it again. I went down there and into

Hudson's Woods for days and months afterward to see if she was in there. No trace. But that day, that was God coming to me to give me a sense of peace. I always believed in God, but after that, I *really* believed in Him.

"Things were up and down since that day with me mentally. But I always talked to God, and it gave me peace. I knew that He was hearing me. I never doubted it. He blessed me more than I ever thought or deserved. Since that deer, every day, me and God have had conversations on the daily."

I sat there feeling emotional about the recount of that day at the park. It still gets to me when I think about it. I don't tell many people about it because it's an unbelievable story. If I'd heard it from someone, I don't know if I'd believe it. I tell it to those that I think need to hear it, like Lefty. I think he needed to hear it for whatever reason. Do I think Lefty believed me and my deer story? At that moment, I don't think he did. He just sat there letting an old man walk down the road, telling a story about a time he wasn't even alive for.

"That's a good story, Buzz," Lefty said as he got off the railing and stretched out. "But I'm going to head out of here. Break took a little longer than expected. You need me to walk you up?"

I waved him off, "No. I'm going to sit out here some more. Peaceful night."

"Buzz," Lefty said before he walked out from the pavilion. "What about synchronicity? Was there a connection to it and the deer?"

"Yeah. I was supposed to meet God that day. Meaningful coincidence, just like Jung said."

Lefty looked at me and smiled, "Goodnight, Buzz," he said, turning to walk back to the main buildings.

That was the last I saw of Lefty. Until two months ago. He returned to the retirement home over a year later to see me. And when he visited me, he had a story of his own to tell.

***

It was in March when Lefty came back to the retirement home; nearly seventeen months had gone by. His return was a few days after a huge spring storm came rolling through that caused some damage to the east wing of the retirement home. Luckily, my quarters are in the west, and I was fine. I think it was a tree that had fallen over there and busted up the roof pretty good.

The temps had cooled off that mid-March, back down to a high of sixty-five, which was fine with me. I had been playing checkers with Clyde the day Lefty came back to see me. I had been playing checkers with the old retired police officer ever since he came into the retirement home a year ago. Every other day at 3:00 pm sharp in the common room. His mental abilities had begun to erode some as I beat him every time. Sometimes though, I'd let him win to keep his confidence up and going. I think Clyde knew about his mental decline but us old geezers don't like to admit much, even if we do know about it. So, we played like we were both in our youth.

I finished up my game with Clyde and decided that I was going to take a stroll around the grounds. I walked into my room to fetch my Atlanta Braves hoodie that I had gotten for Christmas , threw on my Braves hat, and off I went. I walked down the hall and told Rachel Glasnow, the lady who works on the dayshift and is in charge of the part of the wing where I stay, that I was going for a walk.

"Be careful out there. You have your buzzer with you?" she asked.

I didn't answer. I raised my hand which had the little black plastic box, much like those things they give you at restaurants to buzz you when your table is ready. This gizmo, given to all the old folks like me who like to wander around outside, comes in handy. If I were to fall or feel sick, all I have to do is press a call button; the signal pings to the iPads of the staff; and through GPS, they can find me. Got to love technology.

***

I found myself sitting on a park bench down from the pavilion looking out across the man-made pond. It goes on for miles, it seems. A fella could get lost in his thoughts, looking out at that water for too long. Why do I say that? Because it's happened to me a time or two.

It was nearly sundown, and the wind was blowing just a touch— making it just a might cooler than I would have liked. But the Braves hoodie kept me warm for the most part. I was sitting there thinking about much of nothing really when suddenly a voice spoke to me from my right. That voice nearly made me jump out of my own skin. It was Lefty.

"Damn it, boy! You almost gave me a heart attack!"

"I'm sorry, Buzz," Lefty said, wanting to laugh. "I thought you heard me walking up on the gravel."

"Hell no, I didn't! Oh man…someone needs to tie a bell around your neck so we can hear you coming. Grab a seat, would you? You're already making me edgy standing there."

Lefty sat down on the park bench next to me as I scooted over. "What brings you down this way? Last I heard, you had quit your job here like the night after we talked up at the pavilion."

"Yeah, I had hit a bad stretch." That was all he said.

I waited for him to elaborate, but he sat there looking out at the water. "Well, are you going to define 'bad stretch,' or did you just come here to sit?"

A minute or two later he said, "I came here because I needed to talk to you."

"About what?" I asked him.

"Me and you had a conversation that night up at the pavilion. Do you remember?"

"Son, I've slept since then, and my mind ain't as sharp as it once was. You're going to have to be more specific."

"You talked about Carl Jung, synchronicity, and the deer."

"Yeah, seems like I remember talking to you about that. You came all the way out here to ask me that?"

Lefty kept his eyes on the water in front of us. I didn't think he was going to say anything, but he finally spoke.

"Something happened to me that I need to tell you. Everyone else thinks I'm crazy. But I need you to weigh in and see what you think."

"Okay," I said, while I shifted around on the park bench to get more comfortable. "Fire away."

"As you know, the night you and I talked, that was my last night here. I didn't tell you that I had already planned on quitting. I always liked you, thought you were a good guy. You reminded me of my grandpa back home. I just wanted to come out and sit with you and shoot the breeze before I left."

"Why didn't you tell me?"

"We got to talking about that deer story of yours, fate, and God, and all that. I didn't want to slow your roll. By the time you were finished, I figured that we'd just leave it at that."

"Fair enough, I reckon," I said.

"Do you still believe all the stuff you told me that night?"

I turned to him and looked at him. His eyes were still fixed on the water. But he knew I was looking at him. "Of course."

There was a few minutes of silence between us before he spoke. "I have my own story, but it's about a hawk."

"A hawk?"

"Yeah...I believe everything you talked about now. I gotta admit, that night I thought you were full of shit, but...you were right about Carl Jung saying that there's no such thing as coincidences– that they are meaningful ones."

"Yeah. Everything means something in our lives. Just like that night at the pavilion. You and I were meant to have that talk."

"Yeah, I believe it was supposed to happen that way. Like the day I was born, you were born, all the roads we took, or didn't take– led us to that pavilion that night talking about the deer and stuff. I get it now. I get what you were telling me."

"So my deer has become your hawk. What led up to that?"

"Well, that's the story I'm going to tell you."

***

"I had a drinking problem that was becoming more and more of an issue. I had quit here because it was either that or get fired since I had been coming in to work drunk. I mean, I could function most times, but the staff knew most of the time that I wasn't particularly good. So, Edgar James gives me the choice to quit or be fired. But he did give me the option to come back if I would go to rehab and get help."

"Did you?" I asked.

Lefty shook his head, "Hell no, I thought I was good enough to keep going at the time. The drinking was getting more and more, yes, but I thought in my mind I was doing okay. Turns out, that wasn't the case. I said, 'fuck you, I quit.' I walked out the door, and that was it."

"What happened after that with Edgar?" I asked.

"I went to the Neon Tiger and had a few drinks. But that wasn't enough. I was driving down the streets, and I saw Matt's Liquors was still open. So, I pull into the parking lot and go inside. I bought my favorite whiskey, Hawk's. God, that stuff was so smooth going down. Burned just a little bit after it went down, but nothing major. Just a burn, you know?

"But at the time, Hawk's was a sign: that Carl Jung thing... synchronicity. Universe, or God, or fate... whatever you want to call– it was tapping me on the shoulder. But I wasn't clear enough in my head to figure that out yet.

"I drove out of the parking lot and over to the park where I sat and drank that whole bottle of whiskey. Now here's the crazy part. I don't remember it, but somehow, some way, I ended up being woken up by the police in Auburn, Alabama, two hundred and forty miles from here."

Lefty paused, and he started to cry a little. He felt ashamed of driving all that way, drunk. I could feel his remorse for that coming off of him in waves on that park bench. I didn't say anything to him. I just sat there being an ear. That's why he came. Sometimes a man needs to stay quiet and just listen.

"I drove all that way drunk– didn't even remember driving there. I could've killed someone. Or myself, and I would've never known it. God, that hits hard with me. The police get me out of the car, and the next thing I remember, I'm waking up in jail with the most horrible headache I've ever had in my life. It was hurting so bad that I was seeing double for hours.

"To make a long story short, I bonded myself out of jail and called my buddy Cliff to drive all the way down there to pick me up. I still had court and all that I had to do, but that was later. I told Cliff on the way back to Tennessee that I was finished drinking, and that I was going to get into rehab. That night, Buzz, that night... scared me. I'd never gotten that bad before. Ever.

"Anyway, I went to court down there, got hit with a big fine, and I didn't have to serve any jail time. My lawyer had the intake paperwork for the rehab place I was going to and gave it to the judge. He was glad that I wanted to get help and since it was my first offense, he gave me a suspended sentence. Thank God for that, right?

"So I go from the courthouse back up here to Tennessee to this place called Blue Pines. It's got people like me in it: people who are on drugs trying to get clean. Some of those people were worse off than I was. I was an ace compared to some of them. But I was there, willing to do the work. I didn't realize how hard it was going to be because drinking was such a thing for me.

"I'm doing the twelve steps you know, and man, I wanted a drink so bad. Like I'm going into withdrawals, getting sick, the whole nine yards. There is this preacher there, Mitch Williams, who counseled me. He and I started talking about God, and he wanted to know what my relationship with Him was. I told him that I didn't have one. He asked why. I didn't know what else to say. I told him I just never thought about it.

"On step five, I'm supposed to admit to God, myself, and another human being the exact nature of my wrongs. I told Mitch about it, and then he told me that I needed to go admit it to God. Now, I've never spoken to God. Just never had the need. But I did as Mitch told me.

"I go outside on the grounds of the rehab place that's way out in the middle of nowhere, right? Trees all around. When it's night, it's so dark, but you can see millions of stars up in the sky. I'd never seen so many in my life. I found this tree that's kind of off to itself beside a pond, pretty much like this one is, and I knelt and closed my eyes. I talked to God for the very first time and told Him everything I've ever done. As if He doesn't know already.

"I finished up with my conversation. When I raised my head up and opened my eyes, I saw this huge hawk perched up on a limb, watching me. Like, it was as close to me as the two of us, sitting on this bench. Me and this hawk are having a moment. It's looking at me; I'm looking at it. I get up on my feet, and it flies away.

"I don't feel any different from that conversation with God. I thought I would magically feel something, you know? But nothing. I started to think how stupid I was for even going out there in the first place. But Mitch told me that God heard me, and that it wasn't a waste of time.

"A couple of weeks later, I went out there to that same tree again. I knelt down and talked to God again. I asked him to please forgive me for everything that I've done, the people I've hurt, and to give me the power to break my habit. All the fancy talk in that rehab place still didn't curb my thirst for alcohol. I felt like most days I was losing it. I was hanging on, but just barely most days. But I was there to fight it.

"I opened my eyes, raised up, and there's that hawk again. The same one, looking at me. Me and the bird had this moment, just like last time. It flew away as I turned to head back to the center.

"The next time I was out there– this was about two weeks later– I went to the same spot by the tree, knelt down, and talked to God. No sign of the hawk. I told Him that I didn't think he heard me at all. I told him that I was losing what little faith I'd been given since I'd been at the rehab. I started to cry because all I heard was that God was the way. But at that moment, I felt as if He wasn't even real, how stupid I was for thinking that He was, and that He couldn't help me.

"So I said, 'If you're real, and you're listening to me– give me a sign. I'll do anything you want. But I just need a sign, God. Just something in good faith to let me know you're there, and that I'm going to be okay'.

"At that moment, as my eyes were closed with tears coming from them, I heard something jump off that tree limb where the hawk perched when I came to it. Its wings touched the back of my neck, and when I opened my eyes, I saw it flying away."

"And that's when you knew God was real?" I asked, feeling what Lefty was feeling. I knew how he felt.

Lefty nodded, "Yeah. He had been there as the hawk, watching me the entire time I'd go out there. I know it sounds crazy."

"Any crazier than a deer coming to me when I asked God for a sign?"

Lefty smiled to himself, "Right. You see, I drank Hawk's Whiskey for years. It was my poison of choice. Carl Jung was right. There are meaningful coincidences out there, not just random ones. They all mean something."

"So what happened later? You get straightened out?"

Lefty nodded, "Oh yeah. Everything is fine now. I'm sober. I got a new job. I even bought a house a few months ago. Got a nice girlfriend. Things are really good. And I talk to God every single day as I go to work. Not a day has gone by since that day by the tree when God touched me where I don't talk to Him. I see signs all over now to point me in the direction I need to go.

"Take my job, for example. I had no idea that I'd ever work for Pepsi. But I kept seeing Pepsi trucks, people drinking Pepsi, commercials for Pepsi. All of that in, like, a span of two days. I never noticed Pepsi all that much, you know, because I don't drink sodas. So knowing what I know about God, Carl Jung, and synchronicity, I go online and apply for a job with Pepsi. In under a week, I got the job servicing eight stores around here. The route supervisor said I came in at the right time, and he had just posted the job not even an hour after I put in for it. It was perfect timing."

"Now you can see things that others can't."

"Everything really does mean something, doesn't it?" Lefty asked, after being silent for a few minutes.

"Yup. Everything means everything."

PICKING UP THE DEAD

Deputy Danny Jones of the Brook County Sheriff's Department was on patrol that Halloween night. His shift had started around six when the sunset had darkened the landscape. That Halloween night, young and old alike were coming out of their homes dressed in costumes that would frighten and amaze those who saw them. Halloween night was always a busy time for the police department in Claxton, where Deputy Jones helped patrol.

Jones didn't mind working Halloween night. He always took the night shift after his kids had gotten too old for him to escort door to door for candy. Nowadays, his two children were adults taking their kids, his grandkids, trick-or-treating. He saw Halloween as a night for the young and the young at heart. Jones considered himself still young at heart and could've stayed home to give out candy, but he'd rather be out riding around soaking in the night. There was something different about working on Halloween night—something different in the air—a certain magic that the other nights of the year never could have.

He expected the same amount of calls as the previous Halloween nights he worked. There would be normal things like traffic accidents and domestics he'd have to work. But Halloween added to all of that. He would get calls about exploding pumpkins from Mr. Hudnell over on Exodus Street. That was the first call of his shift at exactly 6:36 P.M. It never failed. Mr. Hudnell was always a target of malicious mischief in one form or another.

Jones stood out on the front lawn of the three-story home while Jake Hudnell– one of the grouchiest old men Jones ever had the displeasure of coming across– cussed and yelled, waving his arms like a madman. Jones had responded to calls from him in the past and hated going over there. Ninety-nine percent of the calls were for nothing outrageous—just minor things. This night was no different. This was Jones and Jake's tenth meeting this year—the third Halloween in a row.

"I want something done, and I want it done tonight, damn it!" Jake shouted so all the kids in costumes who were walking by could hear. Jake wanted them to hear it because Jake liked an audience.

"Listen," Jones started. "We'll be out all night long. And whoever blew up your pumpkins on the front porch will be doing it someplace else. We'll catch'em."

"Yeah, yeah, yeah, you cops are all the same! Always show up when a crime has already been committed! Just once I'd like to see one of you here before it happens! Don't forget, my taxes pay your salary!"

"Do you not have cameras on your house like everyone else in the twenty-first century?" Jones asked in a snarky way. He meant it in a snarky way because he was already tired of the old man.

"Why the hell should I?! If you were doing your job, then I wouldn't have to have them– now would I?!"

"Look, I'd like to stay out here and talk to you some more...but I'm not going to. So, I'll write the report up, file it away. Hopefully, we'll catch the people responsible." Jones turned and walked away from Jake standing there with his arms folded.

"Those pumpkins cost me about fifty damn dollars! I catch'em, I'm going to stick an M-80 up their ass is what I'm going to do! Lousy ass cops!"

Jones didn't even turn to say anything back. It was pointless. Jake would stand and argue all night long. He found out the hard way years ago when he first encountered Jake Hudnell. It was a call over his mailbox getting bashed in. A simple game of mailbox baseball. Jake had Jones out there going on and on about it for nearly an hour. That was all it took for Jones to make sure that he kept Jake at bay by not giving in to him. He just took the report and talked to him as little as possible.

***

7:13 P.M.

Jones was called out to County Road 500 for a traffic issue.

Jones hit the blue lights on that country road and saw a car pulled off the side of the road. Headlights and red tail lights were on. Jones pulled up behind the silver Lexus and got out as did the driver. Immediately, Jones put his right hand on the grip of his gun. You just never knew what a call was going to entail anymore. He had never fired his weapon in his twenty-year career, and in that split second hoped he didn't have to.

The driver saw Jones place his hand on the grip and quickly threw his hands in the air, "Don't shoot! I'm the one that called!"

Jones eased his hand off the grip of his weapon and walked slowly over to him. "What's going on tonight? Dispatcher said, mannequins being thrown in the road?"

"Yeah, me and my wife were driving down here, and something flew across our windshield. We both were scared to death because we thought it was a guy. But I stopped and got out thinking we'd hit someone, you know. I got out, and it's a mannequin."

"A mannequin? Where's it at?" Jones asked, taking his flashlight from his belt, switching it on and scanning the dark road.

"Over there in a ditch. I left it for you guys."

The driver walked Jones over to where it was, lying in the ditch on the other side of the road. Jones bent down and picked it up. It was a mannequin, all right.

"So what happens now?" the driver asked.

"I'll take this with me. Probably some damn kids pulling pranks. Halloween after all. Just be careful driving the rest of the way, okay? See anything else, just call." The driver thanked Jones, and both went back to their cars. Jones opened the trunk and tossed the naked mannequin inside, closing the lid.

***

7:45 P.M.

Jones was called out to The First Baptist Church's block party they put on down at the park. It was always good down there and was the last place that Jones thought he'd wind up. This call sounded like a simple disturbance—at least that's what he hoped it was.

Jones pulled into the parking lot of Claxton Town Park amongst all the kids and adults celebrating Halloween. There was a live band at the pavilion playing all the classic Halloween songs. Jones parked his cruiser and got out. He was quickly approached by Debbie Monrow. She was the organizer of the block party. She was a pretty woman, fifty, still had her looks. If Jones was honest, he still had a crush on her that stretched back to the eighth grade.

"Debbie...what's going on tonight?" Jones asked.

"Well, Jonesy, there were the teenagers out here, three of them, cussing and throwing rocks at the kids. One of them was that Watkins boy."

"Tracy?" Jones asked.

"Yes. You know who I'm talking about then."

"Yeah, he usually hangs around with the Wright brothers. Always into something."

"Well, we ran them off, but we're afraid they'll come back and do something worse. It's a wonder that none of the kids were hit."

"Yeah, I'll ride up the streets here and see if I can find them. Looks like y'all have a lot of people this year."

"Oh yeah, I think it's the biggest turnout yet. It's not even eight o'clock, and we're pretty much out of candy," Debbie remarked.

"Say, that is a busy night then. I'll go around and check the streets. If I see them, I'll take care of it. In the meantime, if they come back, here's my cell. You call me direct." Jones told her his cell number, and Debbie put it in her phone.

The two made small talk for about ten minutes off topic of the three boys who were throwing rocks at the children. Jones was about to ask and see if Debbie was still seeing Ernie Wills, but before he got it out of his mouth, his radio went off, calling him to another place.

***

8:20 P.M.

Jones pulled up to Randy and Lois Linkletter's house for what was a possible domestic. He got out of his car, blue lights flashing, and assessed the situation. The Linkletter house was in a nice part of

Claxton. They never got calls out there, at least he never heard of anyone catching one. Everything was quiet around the posh neighborhood as Jones took his flashlight from his belt and switched it on. Not that he needed to, but it was more for comfort than anything else. Plus, he never knew what he was going to get into. He might have to cold cock someone with the three-cell battery light.

He scanned around the home, and everything was just as it should be for homes around there. Just then, the front door came flying open and out stepped a man. But not just a man– a man dressed up like Leatherface. That sight alone nearly scared Jones to death. He froze in the moment and was thinking that he needed to draw his weapon, but his arms weren't working. He dropped his flashlight, and the only thing he could manage to say was, "Sheriff's Department!"

Leatherface stood on his front porch and looked at the officer, realizing who he was. The man took his mask off. "Oh, hi. Sorry! I am so sorry! I can explain."

After calming his nerves down, Jones, Randy, and Lois talked outside the house for a bit on why the cops were called. The Linkletters loved Halloween and loved to pull pranks. They had only lived in the neighborhood for a few months and said that most of the neighbors were too high in cotton to fool with them– a Southern term for being too good and too wealthy to associate with others below them. They just wanted to pull a prank, is all.

What happened, the thing that got Deputy Jones out that way on Halloween night, was that Randy and Lois had devised a plan a few weeks ago. That plan was to scare the living daylights out of any one of the neighbors who liked to walk around in the gated community. What would happen was: Lois would run out of the house, covered in fake blood; while Randy, dressed as Leatherface from the *Texas Chainsaw Massacre* films, would chase her out the front door with the chainsaw running. No chain on the saw, of course, safety first.

That's exactly what happened. The plan went off without a hitch. Mr. and Mrs. Murray were out walking their dog that cool night in the safe confines of their gated community. That's when all hell broke loose. As the Murrays turned the corner at the end of their small street, they saw and heard a woman screaming, running out of the house from the front door and into the road. She was screaming for help. Randy was right behind her, trailing a safe distance, with the chainsaw buzzing.

The Murrays, a mid-sixty couple, who probably never laughed or had a good time in their lives, took off running in fear. Mr. Murray called 9-1-1 from his phone as the couple ran the fastest they had in decades.

Lois stopped running, watched the old couple sprint back home, and laughed and laughed with her husband.

"How long you think it'll take the cops to get here?" Randy asked his wife.

Back at the scene of the crime, Deputy Jones warned the couple to not do that again and said that he could arrest them for several things, namely disturbing the peace.

"And if I get another call out here tonight, that's exactly what I'm going to do to you two. Understand?" Jones asked.

Both Randy and Lois lowered their heads and nodded like scolded children.

"I mean it. No more." And that was that. Jones turned to walk back to his cruiser when his radio squawked at him, calling him to another place that needed the police.

***

8:57 P.M.

The Haunted Trail down at Harper's Farm was the latest call. Every year for as long as Jones could remember, the Harpers always put on a haunted trail and hayride. It was like the block party down at the park the church put on. Nothing ever happened that required the police to come any other day of the year. But Halloween night was different. It always was.

Jones pulled into the field that was a makeshift parking lot, and a swarm of people were standing and talking, discussing what had just happened. Some of the ones involved were still cussing back and forth with one another. Jones took a deep breath and got out of the car. He could sense the situation was volatile and called for backup.

On the ground was a man, mid twenties, and standing over him was a man that the Brook County Sheriff's Department knew all too well. It was Rob Robinson, the local hothead Rob was in his mid-forties and still potent, just like he was back when he and Jones were kids in the same school. Jones and Rob never had any problems with each other— even though Jones had to cuff him on several occasions down at the Neon Tiger. Rob was an okay man but with a very short fuse. Piss him off, and it was lights out.

"All right everybody, clear out of here!" Jones ordered as he walked closer to the situation. "You heard me now! Go on! Git!"

Rob was hovering over the guy on the ground with his dukes still up, ready to go if the guy got to his feet. Jones knew that Rob was hoping for more fighting. He also knew that Rob wasn't the type that got down on the ground to fight—he liked to square up, toe to toe.

"Rob! Stand down! You mind telling me what's going on over here tonight?" Jones asked, standing off to the side. The crowd that he told to go on was still standing there— some with their phones recording.

"Jonesy?" Rob asked with a sound of surprise in his voice. "You doing all right?"

"Yeah, been a busy night, is all. What happened here?" Jones asked while a friend of the guy on the ground helped him up to his feet. They couldn't have been no more than twenty-two.

"Punk kid right there pushed me into the pumpkin display over there right before we all went into the haunted trail."

"You pushed me first!" the twenty-two-year-old shouted, along with some of his friends. "I was just defending myself!"

Rob, the twenty-two-year-old, and the twenty-two-year-old's friends began to shout over each other. Jones could tell that Rob was about to fly into them. He could see it in his eyes even in the darkness of the haunted trail.

"All right, Junior, come with me!" Jones walked over and grabbed the twenty-two-year-old by the inside of the arm and walked him over towards his cruiser. "You're under arrest. I've had it tonight!"

"For what?! I was just..."

"Way to go, Jonesy!" Rob shouted from behind.

"You're going to jail too!"

"For what?!" Rob shouted back.

"Assault! Both of you! I've had it tonight!"

"My mom is going to be so mad at me." the twenty-two-year-old said.

"Well, it'll be fine. Simple assault. You'll go to jail, be booked, bond out, and be home in no time. You'll just be paying a fine. But you've got a record now, young man. Choose wiser in the future."

Eventually, the backup came, and Rob was arrested too. It took nearly thirty-plus minutes for everything to get back to normal at Harper's Farm. Jones leaned on the hood of his car as Deputy Horner came over to him.

"Busy night over this way?" Deputy Horner asked.

"Yeah, I'll say. I ain't stopped since I started. How's everything your way?"

"Ah, you know, same old Halloween prank stuff, I reckon. Had a bunch of mailboxes and pumpkins explode tonight. A low-riding green Honda been seen leaving a few of the scenes. You seen that car?" Deputy Horner asked.

"Tell me a kid that ain't driving one of those low-riding Hondas. I had a call earlier back in town over some pumpkins exploding. Same guy, you reckon?"

"Probably so. At any rate, I ain't too worried about it. We either catch him, or we won't. Rob went peacefully tonight? You think he's getting tired of fighting?"

Jones shrugged, "I wouldn't take him on. He's still got it. Don't let tonight fool you. Maybe he was just tired."

"I'm going to run Rob here to the jailhouse, and then I'm heading over to grab something to eat before Deb closes for the night."

"Okay, I'll be right behind you in a little bit with Junior here. You see a green Honda pull it over, and check it out, would you?" Deputy Horner said.

"Of course. Goes without being said. Maybe we'll get lucky tonight and catch whoever it is."

"I hope not. Just more paperwork," Deputy Horner said laughing.

***

10:22 P.M.

Jones called ahead to Deb's and placed his usual order: a double hamburger with steak fries and a lemonade to wash it all down. He ate in the parking lot of the restaurant in his car and watched as the small town began to wind down for the evening. The block party down at the park was cleaning up, and the trick-or-treaters were all at home, going through their candy and posing for one more photo in their costumes. Some of the more festive adults were still going strong with Halloween parties at their homes, and some were still having a spooky time down at the Neon Tiger. Halloween 2024, as it was, was coming to a close. Jones was hoping the rest of the night would be as quiet as it was while he sat and ate his supper for the night.

***

11:55 P.M.

Not much had happened since Jones had eaten supper in his car. He had a few calls about noise from some houses, which was the usual on Halloween. He showed up, knocked on the doors, and was greeted warmly by the owners. He just told them, the few houses that had the music blaring, that there had been some complaints, and that they needed to dial it down a bit. No issues, and everyone complied. That made his job so much easier.

Rain began to come down pretty hard, and Jones hated the rain, especially at night. He had a problem seeing at night anyway while driving, and the rain made it much more difficult. He was on County Road 550 when he turned the sweeping curve, and his headlights hit on someone walking in the rain.

Jones slowed down and stopped, rolling his passenger side window down and getting rain all over in his car. "Hey! You okay?"

The person stopped and looked inside the car. It was someone that Jones knew—knew since birth.

"Martin Watters? What in the hell are you doing out in this mess?!" Jones shouted to be heard above the rain.

"Oh, hey, Jonesy. I don't know really," Martin replied.

Jones observed that the kid. Martin was like his own: a kid who was his best friend's eighteen-year-old son. "Here, get inside. You'll catch your death out there." Jones said.

Martin got in the passenger seat and closed the door.

Jones took off slowly down the dark country road, not being able to see much of anything. The rain was really coming down now.

"Martin...I'm going to ask you, son. Are you drunk or high right now? Because if you are, I need to know."

Martin looked straight ahead out the windshield as the wipers worked back and forth as fast as they could, trying to keep up with the rain. A few silent moments passed before the kid answered. "Nah, you know that I don't do that stuff, Jonesy. Dad would kill me."

"Well, I didn't think so either. But I had to ask. What are you doing all the way out here anyways?"

"I was coming home from Denton's party at his house. His parents were gone..."

"Oh God!" Jones interrupted. As they turned another curve, Jones' headlights hit on a vehicle off the side of the road. Through the rain, he could see the red tail lights.

"Stay put," Jones said as he turned on his blue strobe lights and exited the cruiser. Through the pouring rain, he jogged over towards the wrecked vehicle with a flashlight in hand.

Jones saw that the vehicle—a green low-riding Honda— had crashed head-on into a tree. He eased his way into the ditch and over to where the car was. With his flashlight, he saw the driver slumped over into the passenger seat as the motor of the car was nearly in his lap. It was at that moment that Jones knew the driver was dead on arrival. He had seen too many accidents like this and much worse for there to be a happy ending.

Jones got on his radio and called for an ambulance and rescue and gave the approximate site of the accident. Jones tried the door, but there was no use. It was too crushed in. The driver-side window was busted out from the impact, which meant that Jones could reach and try to pull the driver, just to see if he could check vitals.

Jones reached in as far as he could and was able to grab the deceased driver by the collar. He pulled as mightily as he could. When he raised him up, and what Jones saw frightened him more than anything he had ever encountered in his life. That driver, the dead kid, was Martin Watters. Jones let go of him immediately, and Martin's bloody and broken body fell back into the position that Jones found him in.

Jones backed up from the driver's side, slipped, and fell in the ditch. He scrambled to his feet, maintaining his grip on the flashlight the whole time. He got back to the wet road and ran over to his car. He looked inside it, and Martin was gone. Jones stood in the rain dumbfounded.

—For Victoria

I'M THE MAN WHO KILLS THE MONSTERS

1

Eddie crept with caution across the kitchen, keeping his eyes glued on the window above the sink. He could not see anything yet, but the window was beginning to take shape. He could see some reflections of the lights from the dining room and the living room, but still nothing in terms of what was tapping on the window from outside. Tap...tap...tap...tap...

The closer Eddie walked, the more in view the window was becoming; the reflection of the dining room lights was now blotted out by his own body. In what seemed to be no time, he was standing in front of the sink that faced the window. He saw what was making that tapping sound. It looked like a man but was not a man. It had two eyes that glowed red, staring at him as it tapped its crooked and decayed index finger against the thin glass of the window in a slow cadence...

Months earlier...

The day that Jake came across the house, it was by pure accident. Jake had an assignment to survey some property out on the other end of Brook County when his GPS had taken him down County Road 550 as a shortcut. It only took six minutes off his time, but hey, it was saving him some gas. On that drive to survey property going up for sale at an auction, Jake drove by a house that stunned him to the point where he slowed down a bit to give it a look.

It was a three-story home– looked like it needed some repairs from what he could tell from his car– a big front yard and side yards. In the back of the house were sprawling woods that towered over the home, making it look as if the trees were lording over the home...being watchful. There was a woman up at the house: well dressed, blonde, youngish the best Jake could tell, getting out of her silver Lexus. Jake wondered briefly who she was and if she lived in that house that for some reason or another spoke to him. Jake drove on down the road towards his job, trying to look at the house until he turned the curve and it was out of view.

At the land, all eighty acres of it, he surveyed the area and made his notes of what used to be the Kirby Farm. The farm used to be a fully operational outfit, but now was nothing but an empty husk of what used to be and times gone by. The entire time that Jake was there mapping out the land for the auction, the image of the house he drove by never left his mind. There was something about it. Maybe it was because he could see himself growing old there with Leigh. As an added bonus, it was the only house for six miles either way on that stretch of county road. That was a plus.

He hated where they lived back in the city. The house they had lived in for nearly fifteen years seemed cramped now, too close to neighbors that he only tolerated over the years. He did not like most of them. They never gave him any real personal trouble, but it was those little things that Jake hated: barking dogs late in the night, police/ambulance sirens, loud music from cars driving on the streets, kids yelling and playing in their yards, people shooting off firecrackers on the Fourth of July. It was all basic neighborhood stuff, but Jake was over it. At his age, he wanted some peace and quiet— somewhere he could just live and be.

Being in the city and in that close neighborhood, Jake was beginning to lose his sense of privacy. One of the last straws came a few months back when he was on his back deck grilling out. His neighbor, Mr. Blankenship, a retired cabinet maker, came over to the fence that separated their property.

"Smells good over there!" Mr. B yelled.

Jake was good with his older neighbor but hated when the old man would grace the fence. Jake would go over and talk to be neighborly, but deep down, he hated having to do that. He wanted to be left alone in his yard. Grilling, mowing, planting flowers, shooting basketball with Eddie, or even sitting out in the hot tub would provoke Mr. Blankenship to come outside to talk to Jake. Mr. Blankenship always meant well, but it irritated Jake to no end that he could not just go out into his backyard and be.

"Yeah, thought I'd throw some burgers on the grill today," Jake said, walking off the back deck and over to the waist-high fence where the old man wearing a blue tropical shirt was standing, smoking a cigar.

"Good day to do some grilling, I tell you that," he replied. Mr. Blankenship held Jake in conversation for fifteen minutes that day.

The burgers on the grill nearly burned. All he wanted to do was grill out, sit on his back deck, and just decompress a little. But every time he stepped out into his backyard, there was the old man. Without fail, Mr. Blankenship would always use the term, "I tell you that," at least a few times during a conversation.

His neighbors on the other side of him were Nancy and Wilma, the lesbian couple that everyone in the neighborhood talked about. They were nice, kept pretty much to themselves– took care of their yard and house and minded their own business. On Saturdays when it was warm, they would be out in their driveway washing their cars. For the most part, Jake did not mind them at all. What he did mind was their dog, a small Boston terrier, named Tux.

The name of the dog– Nancy once told Leigh– was because the dog was black and white, and it looked like it was wearing a tuxedo. She laughed. Jake did not think it was cute. He hated the dog that they would let run loose on the daily. When Tux would run wild and free, he always, without fail, would come over and shit in his front yard. Jake would go out to do his weekly yard mowing and step in a fresh pile made by the dog. He had complained to his next-door neighbors several times, but it never made any difference. They still allowed the dog to come out and do his business wherever he damn well felt, mostly in Jake's front yard.

Across the street from his house was the Keller family. They were nice except for the twin boys that Jake hated with a passion. They were a little younger than Eddie, and most of the time his son avoided them. The twins, Trevor and Travis, always liked to get into trouble around the neighborhood. Sometimes they would TP someone's house several houses away from theirs so their parents would not find out. One time, they went down the street and set off some firecrackers on Mrs. Woods' front porch in the middle of the night. Though there were never any witnesses nor doorbell cameras to catch the little bastards at the time, everyone in the neighborhood knew it was the Keller boys at it again.

The one time that they fooled with Jake was on Halloween, the year before Jake moved his family. Halloween fell on a Thursday that year, and Jake took a four-day weekend. He loved Halloween and decorated the house in thick gothic décor on the outside. In the front yard were some foam tombstones, making it look like a graveyard; ominous carved jack-o'-lanterns on the front porch on either side of the front porch stairs; cardboard skeletons adorned the front door; spooky cobwebs hung on the outside of the windows. Jake's house was the only house in the neighborhood that was like that on Halloween. When Christmas came, he was not as festive. That was the Knobbs a few houses down on the other side of the street. They had their house lit up like Clark Griswald from *Christmas Vacation*.

That Halloween night, after Jake had given candy to the forty or so trick-or-treaters, he turned off the TV that was playing a *Halloween* movie marathon. Leigh had gone to bed several hours before, and Eddie was up in his bedroom playing *Halo,* where he had been nearly all night after coming home from the Halloween block party. With the house nearly dark sans the bathroom light that he always left on, Jake went through the house, like he did every night and made sure the back door was locked as well as the front. They always were, but Jake was funny about stuff like that. One more thing he did before walking up the stairs to bed was that he looked outside the front window out at the street to make sure things were good. This night, they were not. He saw someone, two someones, about the same height as the Keller twins. They were out and about near midnight on that warm Halloween night.

Jake watched them for a while, moving around in the shadows. They were going from house to house, using the cover of darkness as their protection. Sometimes Jake lost track of them, and they would reappear under a streetlight. He watched them for a while until he started yawning and getting tired. Jake let go of the blind flap and decided the two kids were just goofing around. He climbed the stairs to his and Leigh's bedroom, and once in the bed, he did not move. As soon as his head hit the pillow, he was out.

The next morning Jake woke up, stirring about the house. Leigh was in the kitchen, cooking breakfast. She had taken the day off from school. Eddie was still asleep, taking an off day as well. Jake decided that he would go out to the mailbox and pick up the mail he had forgotten the day before. In nothing but his sleep pants, robe, and slippers, he walked out of his house and down the concrete driveway and to the edge of the street where his mailbox stood. He opened the door and attempted to stick his hand inside. His hand was stopped about an inch in.

Jake leaned over and looked to see what was in his mailbox. It was dirt. The entire mailbox was full of dirt, packed plum full. Jake gritted his teeth; and if he did any harder, he would have surely broken them. He wiped his fingers on his robe and turned toward the Keller's house. He knew who was responsible for this prank: it was the twins. Although he could not prove it, sometimes you just know. That was the final straw for Jake. He wanted to move. He was tired of the dogs barking at all hours of the night; the sirens; the dog shit in his yard; the guy that gets drunk on the weekends down the street who likes to play Hank Williams, Jr. music really loud; Mr. Blankenship who always likes to chat him up and just being generally nosey. Jake was over it. The Keller boys had finally pushed Jake too far.

2

On that day he found the house, Jake had finished his assignment with the Kirby Farm, packed up all of his gear, and left the acreage. He typed in his GPS for home, but the route the device planned had wanted him to drive in the opposite direction from where he came in. Jake wanted to go back the other way so he could see the house; for whatever reason, he needed to see that house again. There was a draw for him, that much he knew. Jake canceled the GPS route, pulled out of the driveway, and headed back down the road where the house was.

When Jake got close to the house, he slowed down. He was excited to see a FOR SALE sign from Cloud Realty standing at the edge of the driveway. The silver Lexus that the blonde woman got out of was still parked next to the house. Jake stopped in the middle of the road and considered pulling into the driveway to get out and take a look.

Are you really serious about this? You know Leigh ain't really going to think you're serious about moving, the voice inside his mind told him.

"Yeah, but I think I can swing her once she sees this place." Jake let off the brake, pulled up into the driveway, and parked behind the silver Lexus.

Jake honked his car horn and got out slowly, taking in the house and the scenery. He walked into the front yard and stared at the house. It was a big house, three stories, but what impressed him most was the silence and the forest behind the house that stood looming over. *God, how tall are those trees,* he wondered. Before he could estimate in his head best guesses, the blonde woman emerged from the front door of the house. She was gorgeous, but Jake did not care one bit.

"Can I help you?" she asked, a little nervous.

"Maybe," he replied. "I passed by a little bit ago to do some surveying down the road; and when I came back through, I couldn't help but to notice this house is for sale. How much?"

Still standing safely on the front porch the realtor said, "Listed for one eighty-five."

The first thing that went in Jake's head was that it was a steal for that price. He knew of homes that were much smaller that went for nearly double that. Yeah, there were some cosmetic things that he could tell needed fixing: like the hanging gutters off to the side of the house; some shingles that had blown off on the western part of the house's roof; the vinyl siding had some rather large chips in it; and the front porch looked as if it needed some TLC– still...not a bad price.

"I know that it's last minute, but any chance I can look around?"

"Yeah, you sure can. I was about to leave for the day. But help yourself to walk the land. It comes with what you see here and behind the house, there's forty acres of woods."

"Wait?" Jake said with surprise. "Did you say forty acres? And this house? For one eighty-five?"

"That's right," the blonde realtor replied, "but you better hurry because this house won't be on the market long at that price."

Jake stood there dumbfounded, "How can that be? I mean, you got to know that all of this is much more than what the price is, right?"

The blonde realtor nodded, pulled the front door to, and walked off the front porch and across the yard over to Jake. She no longer felt spooked by him.

"Makes no sense does it? Hi, I'm Amanda," she extended her hand, and Jake took it and gave it a slow pump, still in awe at the price of the house and the land it came with.

"I'm Jake. Jake Avery. So tell me something...what's wrong with this house on the inside? Is it tore all to hell and back? No running water? No electricity? Copper wiring been stripped? Triple homicide?"

Amanda shook her head, "Nope. The house on the inside is great; nothing bad that I know of. The owner, Mr. Rogers, moved to California in a hurry and told our company to sell it for as much as he bought it for twelve years ago."

"So he's not making any profit on this place?"

"I don't think so," Amanda replied. "I've been doing this for a few years, and I've never seen anything like it before. But seriously, if you're interested, you better start the ball rolling. If me and my husband didn't need to live in the city, we'd take a swing at this place."

"Me, my wife, and son are ready to move out of the city," Jake said, lying about Leigh and Eddie. He was not entirely sure if Leigh was ready to move or not. But when he told her about it and showed her the house, she would surely change her mind...maybe. At least, that was Jake's train of thought.

"Well, this would certainly fit the bill for being out of the city. One feature that will be on the description when I put it up online this evening: you can get great Wi-Fi and phone signal here...which is kinda surprising, being out in the knobs and all."

"Can I see the inside of the house? I mean I know that you said you were leaving, but I just want to maybe have the ten-cent tour. Just give me five minutes...all I'm asking here," Jake begged.

Amanda looked at her smartwatch and bit her lower lip and considered for several seconds, going over in her head what she needed to do. "Five minutes."

3

"A steal, huh?" Leigh replied when Jake came home to tell her about what he had found while out working.

"Yeah, hon," Jake said while pacing slowly around their living room, contemplating that house and how much land came with it, "it'd be perfect for us. We could finally get the hell out of here and away from all of them."

"We've nearly got this one paid off. I mean, we're what, ten years left on the mortgage? And you want us to get back into..."

"That's the good part," Jake interrupted, "we sell this, pay off the bank, and we've got enough to cut off at least fifteen years on a thirty-year note. I've done all the math. We're golden."

Leigh sat on her side of the couch, watching her husband pace about the living room. She knew that he had wanted out of the neighborhood for some time and maybe she did, too. If she was being honest with herself, she could stand to have some space and privacy when she walked out of her house and out into the yard.

"What does this house look like?"

Jake smacked his hands together with excitement, "Get your shoes on! We'll drive out that way before it gets too dark and walk around the property. Maybe tomorrow I can get them to open it up for us so you can see what I saw inside...you're going to fall in love with it, I swear!"

4

Jake Avery stood in the middle of Leigh and Eddie, looking at the front of the house from the front lawn. The FOR SALE sign that had been posted into the ground by Cloud Realty had the red lettering of SOLD across it. It had taken several months to buy the house, but finally, it was all theirs: a nice home way out in the country; peace and quiet, and most of all...no neighbors. No neighbors always nosing around or playing their music really loud, or letting their dogs shit in Jake's yard. Nope. Out there, it was just them on County Road 550. The closest house to them was a double wide up on a hill six miles down the curvy back roads that were surrounded by trees on both sides, blotting out the sun every day.

"You hear that?" Jake asked. Leigh and Eddie looked at each other and looked around, trying to hear what he heard.

"No, honey. I don't hear anything," Leigh replied.

A smile stretched across Jake's lips, "Me either. It's peaceful. No sirens. No barking dogs. No Hank Williams, Jr. Nothing. Hell, not even birds chirping."

"At least we got good Wi-Fi here," Eddie said, breaking away from his parents and heading to the house and up to his new bedroom to unpack.

Leigh put her arms around her husband and her head on his shoulder, "I hope we like it here."

"Me, too," Jake returned. "What's the worst that could happen, right?"

5

Two months had passed by rather quickly for the Avery family and their new home. They had unpacked nearly everything– the essential things at least. Stuff they did not feel much like dealing with: like the Christmas decorations along with the tree; the tens and tens of cookware that Leigh's mom always bought her for her birthday; and the clothes that none of them wore anymore but were too lazy to donate, all sat in the garage, taking up most of the room. Leigh's SUV was the only car that could be parked in that two-car garage. Jake did not mind. He continued to park his vehicle outside in the driveway, much like he had at the old house in the old neighborhood.

Two months had gone by like a rocket for the Averys. Life continued to spin much like it always did: Jake still did his job as a surveyor; Leigh still taught at the same high school; and Eddie still went to the same school where his mom taught. Nothing really changed at all for them except for having some peace and quiet and being in a new-to-them home. Life was good...and peaceful.

"This is the life, ain't it?" Jake asked his wife one dusky evening while sitting outside on the front porch.

They both looked out at the county road and the landscape of the countryside. Nothing was going on, which in the two months they had lived there, nothing much did.

"I'm loving these rocking chairs, by the way."

"I have to admit," Leigh began, "at first I wasn't so sure that I wanted to move. But I guess you don't realize how much noise goes on around there until you live way out here. It's so...still out here."

Jake nodded, "Yup. I'm glad I found this place. It was like it was meant to be or something. Had I not gotten that assignment to survey that property down the road, that prick Jensen would've seen the house, and he'd have bought it."

"You really think so?" Leigh asked.

Jake nodded his head slowly, "I do. A house like this and a price like that almost never happens unless there was a triple murder inside or something."

"And you're sure nothing like that happened?" Leigh asked with a hint of doubt. She, too, wondered why such a nice home was so cheap, especially one that only had minor problems that were not going to be a pain in the ass to repair.

"Scouts honor, babe," Jake said. "They were all pretty straight up with us. The people down at the realty company, and our bank couldn't believe it either. I had Denny check records at the police station and nothing. Not one call out here. Ever. Maybe the guy that sold it just wanted it gone."

"But why though?"

Jake sat there and mulled over her question. It was the same question he had asked himself many times before. He never came up with anything really good. "I don't know. Maybe we'll never know why he moved to California."

"You still got his phone number that Amanda gave you?"

"I think so...somewhere, hell I don't know. Pretty sure I have it."

"You should call him one night, and thank him for selling the house so cheap. And then ask him why he moved."

"Maybe."

"Either way, I think you were right about us moving out here. I can't believe how nice it is to just sit out here and not hear dogs barking or loud music. Just nice to be able to sit and not have Mr. Blankenship always poking his head over at the fence talking to us...I tell you that." They both laughed.

"Or those fucking Keller twins. I hate them bastards," Jake said.

Leigh laughed out loud at Jake's open honesty. She knew that he did not have an infinity for those boys nor really anyone from the old neighborhood. She looked around at her new home and smiled. She was happy here– happy that she went along with selling their old home and moving out here in the middle of nowhere.

Off to the side of the yard, in the woods to be precise, Jake and Leigh were being watched. They had no idea of it then nor of it the other times over the last two months. The woods that Jake thought were cool to own held a secret– a terrible one. The eyes that watched the new homeowners wondered if they were going to run away like the old man had when things got bad. Things would eventually get bad because they always did. The eyes from within the forest watched the man and woman on the front porch until total darkness gripped the countryside, sending them in for the night.

6

On the second night of their staycation during the month of July, just a shade after the Fourth, Jake woke up hungry. It was odd because Jake never woke up in the middle of the night, especially hungry. He tried to lay in bed next to his snoring wife, thinking that the hunger would abate, but it did not. It only grew. Finally giving up, Jake flung the covers off to the side, got out of bed, and headed downstairs to the kitchen to find something that would quell his stomach.

Jake opened the fridge and found the usual suspects: a half gallon of milk, leftovers from suppers gone by, half a dozen eggs, something that looked like bacon but for the life of him he could not remember eating bacon recently, and some homemade cookies. Jackpot! Jake reached inside the fridge and plucked the plate of cookies out. Walking them over to the island in the middle of the dark kitchen, he sat them down and took the Saran Wrap covering off the plate.

Three cookies in– damn, they were good– Jake decided that some milk would surely hit the spot. He walked back over to the fridge, opened it up, and brought out the half gallon of milk. Taking a cup from the cabinet next to the sink, he poured a half cup and turned it up to wash down the cookie residue in his mouth. That's when a sound came from outside that caused the hairs on his arms to stand on end. It was a shrill scream that broke the tranquil nighttime.

Jake put the empty cup down and looked out his French doors that led to the back of the house from the kitchen. It was pitch black outside, and it had taken some time for the family to get used to the total darkness save a shed light that overhung on the garage. It was different living out in the country, but the hardest adjustment was not having street lights every fifty yards down a street. Jake hated to admit it, but at his age, he hated this kind of darkness that the country provided. If he was being honest, the only thing that he missed about the city were the streetlights. He wished that he had one right now.

Jake knew that he heard a scream; a high-pitched scream coming from the backyard, more notably, in the woods behind the house. He slowly walked up to the French doors and was so close to the glass that his breath fogged it. His hand ran up along the wall for the switch to the backyard light that was affixed to the side of the house where the French doors were. Nothing. He flipped the switch on and off several times and remembered that the bulb inside the fixture had blown a few days before.

"Well, that's just awesome," Jake said to himself.

He squinted his eyes and tried to look through the darkness but saw nothing—as if he really could. Jake slowly shook the doorknob and made sure that the locks, the one on the door and the deadbolt, were safely settled. They were, but for good measure, he twisted them. You never really knew, especially out in the country, especially out in this kind of total darkness.

Jake stood there feeling scared, feeling the warm milk residue still inside his mouth. He stood there looking out into the darkness from the inside, only protected by a thin pane of glass. But for what? What was he waiting for? That scream again? Yup. *Or was it a scream*, he wondered. *Maybe it was something in the house, like it settling or something. What if it was a cat?* Standing there for a few minutes longer looking into the backyard in the cover of darkness, Jake began to feel stupid.

"It was probably a damn cat," he muttered under his breath.

He backed up from the French doors keeping his eyes on– what, exactly? He did not know, but he was starting to feel silly about being scared in the first place. Getting his breathing regulated from the scare,

Jake turned his back to the door and started to walk through the kitchen and over to the island where the cookies sat. A loud series of bangs rapped against the French doors and screams like nothing he had ever heard before caused Jake to jump a few inches off the floor and scream out loud. He rushed over to the other side of the island for protection and dared to look in the direction of the French doors. *That was no fucking cat!* Jake thought frantically. He was trembling now, and the breath that he had just regulated was back up.

Jake wondered what in the hell he was going to do now. He turned his head and saw the kitchen drawer. *Knife, I need a knife!* He quickly pulled open the drawer from behind his position there at the island and without looking, he ran his hand inside the drawer, going over wooden spoons, a pizza cutter, several forks, and finally the large kitchen knife he knew they had. His fingers found purchase on the handle, and he pulled the large knife from the drawer and brought it close to him. He was ready. Ready for what? Whatever hit against the back door, that's what!

Crouched behind the island for a minute—maybe five; could have been ten, who knew— he was not counting. What he knew was that whatever it was beyond those French doors wanted his attention; maybe even trying to get inside. What then?

"They'll get this knife, that's what," Jake said to no one.

Breathing heavily, he knew that he had to protect his family. His gun, a silver Colt .45, the gun that won the West, was upstairs in a safe ready to be used just in case. *Well, this is a just-in-case if there ever was one,* Jake thought.

Jake got up from his crouch slowly, keeping his eyes on the French doors and his right hand tight on the knife. He was going to rush upstairs and fetch his gun. That should even the odds up a bit with whatever it was that made that blood-curdling scream and loud banging against his doors...at least that was what Jake counted on. Standing there looking at the doors and into the darkness, Jake steadied himself, planted his bare feet on the cool floor, and with a rush, he ran out of the kitchen— knife to his side because momma did not raise no fool— and up the stairs. Jake was going to get his Colt.

He paid no mind to how much racket he made doing all of this. Eddie was in his bedroom playing Call of Duty, headset around his ears, and Leigh was one of the heaviest sleepers he had ever known. Nothing could wake that woman up. Jake rushed down the hallway, into their bedroom, and to the closet. His hands were shaking, and he dropped the knife and pulled out the small safe that held the gun. He pressed his thumb against the biometric lock, and the safe popped open like magic. Inside laid the fully loaded Colt .45 in all its silver glory. Jake took it, forgot to close the lid and gave a quick look at his sleeping wife. She had no idea what was going on downstairs. Did Jake?

Coming downstairs, creeping actually, as it were, the hammer on the colt was pulled back, ready to do its job if the situation called for it. He had only shot twenty bullets through the gun since he had it and was pretty good with his aim. That was at the shooting range under no pressure at all with a steady hand. What about now with rapid breathing, sweat populating on his forehead, and his hands shaky at best?

Jake entered the dark kitchen and kept his eyes locked on the French doors which, to be honest, he was ready to find open for some otherworldly reason. To his surprise, they were still closed, still bolted. Jake's finger was poised over the trigger of the Colt, ready to start shooting. He crept to the back of the island and crouched down on his bare feet, ready to open fire at whatever came through that door.

***

The darkness grew thin as the sun was breaking through that early morning. The rays were pouring through the windows, brightening everything up and making the kitchen less scary for Jake. He had been behind that kitchen island, gun-cocked and ready, for hours. The morning had found Jake sitting on his ass, back propped up against the cabinet behind him. He was tired, and the adrenaline that had coursed through his veins for hours was now gone. He felt more at ease with the sunlight because, after all, nothing bad happened in the daylight, right? Jake un-cocked the Colt's hammer, placed it on the floor, and tried to get up. His legs would not cooperate, so he turned and used the cabinets to hoist himself up. It was a struggle, but he got up on his legs as they started to tingle. His legs had fallen asleep.

After several minutes of trying to get the severe tingling out of his legs where his blood could flow once again through his veins, Jake tried to walk it off. He looked over at the French doors and wanted to scream, but the sheer horror and surprise at what he saw closed his mouth. Then it gaped open, and nothing came out. His eyes were wide in terror at what he was looking at. On the outside of the glass of the French doors, there were splashes of dried blood.

How do you know that it's blood? his mind asked.

"Because what else could it be?" he replied in the kitchen.

Jake forgot all about the gun because it was daylight; nothing bad ever happened in the daylight. Jake took small steps over to the French doors for a closer look. The blood was red as can be and looked as if it had been wiped across the glass of the double doors with a mop head. He approached the doors with some caution and looked out through the crimson swaths. From what he could tell, there was just as much blood on the concrete patio next to the French doors and in the green grass as there were on his doors. He stood there in the kitchen, his mind trying to process it all, the entire scene.

"What the hell?" he asked no one.

7

The rest of July came without incident as did August. All was silent around the Avery home. Even though Jake still had no idea what was outside that night or what produced that much blood in his backyard, on his patio, and on the glass of his French doors, he figured that maybe it was a one-off. He hated letting it go like that, but what other choice did he have? He never told Leigh or Eddie about what happened that night; didn't want to scare them. They would not have believed him anyway. Jake had the scene cleaned up with a water hose by eight o'clock before Leigh stirred from upstairs and into the kitchen for breakfast.

September came and along with it another incident; this time Eddie was with him...

8

It was dark that night out in the backyard where Jake and his son sat around a fire adjacent to the patio. It was a cool night that Friday as a cold front had brought with it rain from earlier in the day; nothing soaking, but a mist for several hours, enough to make everything wet. Fall was set to begin next week. It was Jake's favorite time of year, and he was anxious to see all the leaves change color from the trees of the woods that surrounded three-quarters of his yard in the form of a horseshoe. He bet that it would be a sight to behold.

He had not given much thought to the night in the kitchen in July. Eventually, the memory burned off, but it was still there sometimes, especially when Jake was mowing or working out in the backyard. He had never mentioned that night to Leigh although he nearly did one evening while the two sat out on the patio. He had opened his mouth and was about to tell her during a moment of silence between the two, but then Leigh broke in talking about going to see her mom later that week. Jake closed his mouth, thinking that it may have been for the best that she spoke. *Maybe one day*, he thought.

When he and Leigh would go outside in the evening and sit either on the patio or on the front porch, Jake brought along his Colt. Leigh asked the first time when her husband did this.

"What's with the piece?"

"You never know," Jake replied, looking around like he was expecting something.

"You never know what?" Leigh pressed.

"What?" Jake replied. "Oh, just a little extra protection. You know how crazy people are these days. Walk right up to you on your property and cause trouble without thinking twice about it."

Leigh looked at her husband and said, "You're jumpy lately."

"I'm not jumpy," Jake replied to his wife. "Just cautious is all."

"When we sat outside back in the city, you never carried your gun outside. And back there, anybody could have just waltzed up on us from the street. Out here? You'd see them coming a mile away."

Unless they come at you at night from the woods, Jake thought. "It's no big deal, okay? Relax about it. Just...peace of mind, is all."

After that, Leigh just got used to Jake always bringing out the Colt when they would sit outside in the evenings. She could tell her husband was becoming a little paranoid but decided to allow Jake his notion about bringing the gun. Leigh figured that eventually whatever was eating at him would go away.

***

That cool night in September, Jake and Eddie were sitting in chairs around a small fire pit. Jake's Colt sat on the ground to his side. Leigh had to work the high school football game that was at home that Friday night, and miraculously, Eddie had no plans. All his friends had gone to hang out at the football game, and he elected to stay home and hang out with his dad. It was the first time in a very long time that the two of them just hung out together. Jake sat there looking up at the night stars while Eddie was on his phone messaging back and forth to whoever it was on the other end.

"School going okay?" Jake asked absently.

"Oh yeah. Not too bad," Eddie replied, typing quickly.

"Good. That's good," Jake replied, trying to make out constellations in the dark sky. "Any girlfriends?"

"Um...there's a girl I like. She's okay, I guess. But we're like, not official or nothing."

Jake nodded his head slowly, approving, "Keep your options open. You still got a long ways to go."

Jake was going to add to what he had just said, but something from inside the woods caught his attention. That sound was walking or what sounded like walking. He looked over at his son, but he was too enamored with his phone to notice anything in the real world. Jake raised up in the chair, took his eyes away from searching for star constellations, and looked into the darkness of the woods.

He slowly reached down for his Colt, all the while keeping his eyes locked into the darkness of the woods. A few minutes ticked off the clock and nothing. The sound was gone. *Probably an animal walking around,* he thought. Jake settled back in his chair and went back to looking at the stars, holding his gun just in case.

Thirty minutes later, Eddie, who had been sitting in his chair messaging like crazy and keeping his eyes on his phone screen, straightened his back and stretched out. When he took his tired eyes off his screen, they caught something in the woods as he looked around. He stopped stretching and looked for a second or two, and it looked to him as if there were a series of red eyes looking back at him from the darkness of the woods. Eddie blinked, and they were gone. He rubbed his eyes and chalked it up to nothing more than eye fatigue. He was going to tell his dad about it, but he knew how his dad was; he did not believe in stuff like the supernatural. Eddie gave the woods one last scan before he went back to his phone.

Jake needed something to drink, got up from his chair, and asked if Eddie wanted anything.

"Mountain Dew, if there's any left." Jake gave him a thumbs up, and he disappeared into the house through the French doors.

While his dad was gone, Eddie began to hear walking and shuffling around in the woods, this time, more so than what his dad had heard earlier. It sounded like several people moving around in there. Eddie took his eyes off the phone screen, looked into the darkness, and waited for his eyes to get adjusted from the light and colorful images of his phone. When they did finally adjust, he saw nothing but maybe a few outlines of trees.

Jake came back from the house with a can of Mountain Dew in his right hand, and a bottled water in his left. He pitched the soda over to his son, who quickly looked at his dad as he came walking back over to the fire pit.

"What's wrong with you?" Jake asked, sensing that Eddie's fur was up.

"I don't know. I thought I heard something in the woods over there. Sounded like walking."

Jake stood there, looking into the darkness and saw the same thing that his son had seen: a few outlines of trees, and that was it.

"Might be a deer...getting time for them to be running around." Jake twisted the cap on his water bottle and sat down, looking over at the woods and hoping deep down he was right. The fear of that night in the kitchen a few months ago crept back into his mind as he sat there. *I hope it's a deer*, Jake thought.

"Maybe...but I swore earlier...," Eddie stopped himself right there because he did not want to sound stupid to his dad when he was about to say that red eyes were looking back at him from the woods.

"Swore what?" Jake asked.

Eddie looked at his dad and then the woods. In those few seconds, his mind was trying to resolve the situation on whether to tell his dad about what he saw, or thought he saw, in the woods.

"I thought that I saw a bunch of red eyes in the woods right before I heard the walking. Like, they were all over."

Jake's blood ran cold. Now, it appeared, Eddie was having an experience of the unknown that originated from the woods, *their woods*, now.

"Red eyes?" Jake asked, not realizing that it came out just above a whisper.

Eddie heard him, though, "Yeah," he replied. "My back was hurting, and I stretched it out; and when I looked over, I could've sworn that I saw these red eyes looking at me from over there...and over there. There were a bunch of them. Kinda made me think they were surrounding us."

Jake looked at his son and then into the darkness. He did not see anything, not like he thought he would. He believed his son; had no reason not to. Was what he said any more unbelievable than what had happened to him that night in July in the kitchen around midnight?

"I believe you."

Eddie sat there stunned, "Really?"

"Yeah," Jake simply returned. "I think there's something in those woods."

When Jake told his son that, Eddie then got scared for the first time in a long time. His dad, a man who did not believe in much of anything otherworldly, just confirmed to him that he believed him about seeing red eyes. Why? Why did his dad suddenly believe him about something so crazy, so bizarre?

"What are you not telling me? Because you don't believe in the supernatural," Eddie inquired as they both looked into the woods.

Jake sat there debating inside his head, much like his son had to, whether or not to tell him what had gone down that night in July while he was in the kitchen. Finally, he did. Jake turned his attention from the woods and looked at his son from across the fire. Jake put the water bottle between his legs and held the Colt in his right hand...just in case.

"I've got a story to tell you. Now, it may sound crazy, believe me, but it's true."

Just then more walking around in the woods– sticks snapping, dead leaves being stepped on. It sounded to Jake and Eddie that it was more than one something; maybe several somethings, walking around inside the woods and coming for them, spreading out, flanking the outer edges of where the woods and the backyard came together.

"I think we'd better go inside," Jake advised.

9

September closed out and October was the new month on the wall calendar in the kitchen. It was Saturday afternoon, rainy, cool enough to see your breath. Jake and Eddie stood in the backyard where the woods and their backyard came together.

The night where the somethings stirred inside woods while they were sitting by the fire, Jake and Eddie rushed into the house, bolted the doors, and made sure all the windows were fastened. They went through the house and shut off all the lights.

Jake and Eddie stood behind the kitchen island much like Jake did that night in July when the first incident came about. The two of them looked at the double French doors, through the glass where a faint flicker from the dying fire danced. Nothing stirred about: no red eyes, no screaming, and no banging up against the French doors. All was calm. Jake, feeling less scared than he was thirty minutes ago, uncocked the hammer to his gun and placed it on the kitchen island.

"What's this story? Is it about what's in the woods?" Eddie asked.

Jake nodded, still looking out the French doors from across the dark kitchen, "Yeah. I believe so. So it was in July around midnight. I got up because I was hungry..." Jake began his story...

By the time Jake was finished telling his son the account of that night, they saw car lights pierce the darkness from within the home. Leigh had returned from working the concession stand at the football game.

"Not a word to your mother. You understand?" Eddie nodded.

***

Jake and Eddie stood there where the yard and the woods came together; neither was ready to go in there and explore uncharted parts. Down in their guts, they both knew something was in there, but since they owned the property, those woods were theirs and it was their duty to figure out what was lurking behind those trees at night.

"You ready for this?" Eddie asked.

Jake did not take his eyes away from the trees that stood before them and shook his head, "Not really. But we gotta figure this out."

Jake placed his hand on the grip of his Colt that was snug in his holster attached to his hip. "Let's go."

Jake and Eddie walked into the woods and were quickly consumed by the trees, the branches, and the entanglement.

10

The afternoon was overcast and cool while drizzle fell about the area. Neither of the Avery men was too sure about walking through the woods. There was a sense of dread about it sitting in their stomachs. For Eddie, this excursion seemed like the real deal all because his dad was taking it seriously. The story that his dad had told him about that night in the kitchen stuck in his mind so much that Eddie slept with his bedroom light on for a few weeks. He had trouble sleeping after that story that he believed one hundred percent. After all, his dad would not lie about something like that. Just his dad being out in the woods, carrying his gun, made the situation that much more serious. What did Eddie think they were going to encounter out there in the woods that day? He had no clue, but something was in there that much father and son knew.

The woods had an instant aura about them– an energy that Jake and his son quickly felt. Both of them stopped and looked at each other. "You feel that, right?" Eddie asked his father.

Jake nodded, "Yeah, like um...an energy. Maybe like a low-grade electrical current." He and his son stood there, not far from where they entered from the backyard. "We could do this another day if you want?"

Eddie considered it for a few moments, looking around at the scores of trees and walls of thickets. Inside the woods was a different world from where they came from. Eddie looked back towards their backyard, and he could still see their house and patio through the skeletal branches. They were not far in, not by a long shot. Turning back would be the easiest thing to do, sure, but was that the best thing?

"We turn back, we'll never come in here again," Eddie said with some conviction in his voice.

Jake knew that he was right. Feeling the energy inside the woods vibrating, Jake knew that it would probably get more intense the deeper they got in. He stood there looking at his son and then around at the trees. Jake nodded and started to walk a little deeper into the woods. Eddie followed.

***

The skies above them grew darker the deeper they got in. After twenty minutes of walking in the woods, Eddie was trying to figure in his head how far they were from the house in case they had to run back. At least half a mile, maybe even three-quarters, he estimated the best he could. He watched his dad ahead of him stepping lightly, stopping sometimes to look around. Maybe he heard something or maybe he was considering that this expedition was not worth the time. Whatever it was, Eddie felt that his dad did not want to go any further. If Eddie was being honest with himself, he was ready to turn back. That energy, the electrical current that seemed to pulsate in the air, was now a little higher; he could feel it sometimes making his stomach flutter like he had butterflies.

Jake had no direction, no compass, no nothing. He was in the woods, blindly walking around and hoping that he did not get him and his son lost...or worse, killed. *You own these woods, Jakey, why in the hell are you afraid of them?! They're yours! You own them! They don't own you!* Jake scolded himself when fear would creep in. The voice inside his mind was right; they were his woods and he owned them. But still...

About middle ways in the woods, although unbeknownst to Eddie or Jake, Jake stopped and looked at a particular sight on several trees. Eddie walked up to his dad and stood beside him looking.

"What do you think those are?" Eddie asked, looking at what appeared to be skeletons tied to various trees.

Jake gulped hard and licked his lips which had gone dry.

109

"I don't know. Looks like animal skeletons...but I can't say for sure."

He walked over to one of the trees to get a closer inspection of the bones. While he stood there looking, Eddie walked to another tree with another skeleton tied to it. Jake considered himself pretty woodsy. He had hunted with his dad growing up and saw all kinds of animals alive and dead; had even seen several skeletal remains of animals. What had been tied to that tree in front of him with what looked to be twine was no animal he'd ever seen. The skeleton looked to be upside down, the head towards the ground. It seemed to Jake as if it was a large bird of some kind. The bird's huge wings—or what was left after the flesh and muscle were gone—were wrapped around the tree. This caused Jake to shudder with cold chills underneath his jacket. He had never seen anything like it before.

Over on the other side, Eddie was looking at something that looked to be about his height, maybe human, which caused Eddie to want to panic. He kept his panic at bay because he did not want to freak out and look stupid in front of his dad. The skeleton that was tied to the tree in that same twine looked to have what Eddie thought were medium-sized horns coming up from the skull. It looked human, but humans do not have horns.

"Dad," Eddie said, not sure that his call for his dad even escaped from his throat. "Dad," he tried again, "you need to really see this."

Jake stood there mesmerized, looking at the skeleton on the tree before him. He thought it looked like a huge bird, but looking at it a little bit more closely, maybe a bat? Jake knelt down and looked at the thing's head, which was pointing towards the ground. It most certainly looked like a giant bat. Jake started looking around at the other trees that were scattered about that had skeletons tied to them. His mind began to get overloaded at the graveyard they had unknowingly wandered into.

"Dad!" Eddie called out again, this time yelling.

That snapped Jake back into reality. He turned and looked at his son from his crouch. Eddie stood there and pointed to what Jake thought was a human skeleton tied to the tree. He walked over to where his son stood and gave the skeleton a once over. It was about Eddie's height and looked to be human. But there were those medium-sized horns that grew from the skull.

"This place…," Jake struggled to find the words to articulate what he and his son had found in the woods. "what are we looking at here?"

Eddie stayed silent and looked at scores of other skeletons tied to the numerous trees from where they stood as far as their eyes could see; some of those skeletons looked to be human, and there were shreds of rotted-away clothing hanging off the bones. Others looked like giants and over-sized bats, and other winged creatures too large to be any birds they'd ever seen. Jake spied several more human-looking skeletons, but they had horns which made them what…devils?

With closer inspection of some of the other skeletons tied to trees, Jake and Eddie concluded some of them were honest-to-God people at one point. Eddie gulped without knowing it before he spoke to his dad.

"Whatever these things are and whatever happened to those people over there," Eddie pointed to the human remains tied to the trees, "it ain't natural…could be something bad in here."

When Eddie said that, Jake turned his eyes away from the human with horns and looked at Eddie, "You might be right. As crazy as this all is…you may be right."

"Do we keep going?" Eddie asked, secretly hoping that his dad would call it a day. The skies above were getting darker and the drizzle was starting to become a little harder; their breath could be seen a little better in the air. That crazy energy that they had first felt when they entered the woods was buzzing pretty good, standing there amongst the skeletons. The energy from whatever was generating it was palpable.

"I think we have to," Jake said looking at all the trees around that had some sort of skeleton tied to it.

How many trees? Too many to count. One thing that Jake knew for sure was that they were standing in a graveyard of sorts where the dead were not buried, but resting above ground. How long had they all been tied to those trees? How long did it take for the decomposition to take part in stripping the flesh off, leaving nothing but bare bones behind? Jake had no idea.

11

Father and son walked away from the graveyard and headed north on a slow trek. The day had grown darker, and the temp had fallen some.

Thankfully, the wind did not stir about, but the rain had picked up some. The drizzle had turned into a steady cold rain, smacking angrily against the dead leaves on the ground and causing a popping sound throughout. Eddie kept his eyes sharp and looked around, staying close behind his dad as he led the way into parts unknown.

Earlier, before they happened upon the graveyard, Eddie had figured they were probably a half a mile– perhaps three-quarters in the woods. Now, he guessed over a mile in. That estimation scared him because if something did happen there in the woods, running back would take forever– no matter how much adrenaline pumped throughout their bodies. They could die out here, and no one would ever know. *Maybe they would find our skeletons tied to trees weeks later like all those things back yonder*, Eddie thought.

Jake led the way, looking around, keeping his head on a swivel. He wanted to make sure that nothing could take them by surprise. He was well aware that something was inside these woods; could feel it as that energy he and his son had felt earlier became more pronounced, vibrating more the deeper they got in.

"You feel that?" Jake asked his son without turning to look behind him, keeping his eyes on all the trees about them and walking aimlessly in no direction at all but still heading north at the same time.

"Yeah. Shaking my insides. A lot more than before," Eddie replied.

Jake nodded his head, "Yeah, me too."

12

After fifteen minutes of walking through the woods that were thick with bushes, trees (both large and small), and brambles, the trees began to thin out some. Up ahead of Jake, he could see a barrier of sorts, running from right to left as far as the eye could see. It looked to him like a bunch of trees that had been cut down and stacked helter-skelter in piles, seven to ten feet high in places. Jake stopped walking as his son got up to his side and stood with his dad.

Both of them stayed silent for several moments until Eddie finally asked, "What is this?"

"It's a deadfall."

"It goes all the way down that way and down that way. God," Eddie remarked and observed. "It looks like it goes on forever; like a border wall or something."

That's exactly what it looks like, Jake thought. "Yeah, you're right."

Eddie reached inside his pants pocket and pulled out his cell phone. He had forgotten all about it while walking into the enchanted forest. He pressed the button on the side of the phone and the screen lit up with his locked background of a yellow Ford Mustang GT. He looked at the top of the screen and realized the words NO SERVICE appeared. The time on the screen read 4:55 p.m. "Dad, what time did we come into the woods?"

Jake stood there looking at the deadfall barrier from left to right in amazement. He wondered how in the hell someone was able to build such an elaborate wall. Most importantly, he mulled around the question of why.

"Dad?" Eddie again spoke, this time a little louder.

"Yeah?"

"What time did we come in here?"

Jake, still looking at the wooded barrier, turned to his son, "I don't know, around noon. Maybe a little afterward."

"It's 4:55 right now. You're telling me we've been walking in here for nearly five hours?"

Jake's face grew contorted, "That can't be right."

Eddie held up his phone for his dad to look at, "Right here." Jake looked at it. It now read 4:56 p.m. with NO SERVICE. "There's no way we've been walking around in here that long."

"No, you're right. There's no way. It feels like maybe an hour max. Not no five hours." Jake turned his eyes towards the right side of the wooded barrier and caught a faint glimpse of something– a structure off in the distance that he somehow missed earlier.

"There's something down that way." He pointed in that direction.

Eddie's eyes followed his dad's finger and saw what he saw: a structure off in the distance amongst the protection of the trees. Hard to see at first, but if you looked long enough you could see it; the father and son duo saw it.

"Think we should go have a look-see?" Jake asked.

Eddie looked around, his insides still jittery from the strange energy that radiated throughout the woods, and then looked in the direction of the structure. He was not sure about going in that direction, not at all. He felt that his dad was not exactly keen on the idea either.

"I guess," Eddie replied. "We've come this far."

Jake nodded and absently put his hand on the grip of his Colt. The feel of it comforted him, but the question remained, would he have to draw it and use it on someone...or something?

He liked to think that the gun offered the ultimate protection for him and his son, but would it? Would a bullet stop the creatures that roamed the woods? Would a bullet stop whatever created that long deadfall barrier? What about what lies within that structure they were going to investigate? Could bullets stop something that came from the supernatural world? Jake had no idea. Before July, Jake never believed in the supernatural.

13

Jake and Eddie walked along the side of the deadfall barrier towards the structure that was coming into better view with each step. The skies were getting darker above, and the rain had gotten noticeably harder. Eddie pulled his phone out of his pocket and pressed the side button to turn on the home screen. 5:24 pm.

"Now it says 5:24," Eddie told his dad as they walked side by side through the trees.

"Yeah, that ain't right. Maybe something is wrong with your phone."

"Or maybe we've walked into something where time doesn't exist. Or maybe that energy we feel is messing with the phone. I mean, it's messing with us. I don't know about you, but I've got this ringing in my ears now," Eddie replied. Jake did not refute any theory from his son. It was very possible...in those woods, anything was possible.

14

Jake and Eddie made it to the structure that was really no bigger than a shack. It was old and rustic; it had windows but no glass in them as far as either of them could tell. The roof was made of tin and was rusty red.

The shack leaned to the side some and looked to Jake like it could fall any moment, especially if a big gust of wind came.

"You think someone lives in there?" Eddie asked.

Jake shook his head, "I don't know. I doubt it. The place looks ready to fall over...might have been here a hundred years. Could've been like a hunter's place to rest or something." Jake was right about that last part. He had no idea how right he was.

"Think we should go inside?" Eddie asked.

Jake looked around and noticed that the skies were darker, and the daylight was growing very thin. The last thing that Jake wanted was for him and his son to be caught out in the woods in the dark. That possibility was becoming a reality with every passing second.

"What time is it?" Jake asked, afraid of what the phone would show.

Eddie reached into his front pocket to retrieve his phone. He pressed the side button and the home screen came on– not with the yellow Ford Mustang GT, the NO SERVICE message, nor with the time. On the front of the now red screen were the words, "LEAVE NOW!" Both father and son looked at each other, at the shack, and then up at the skies as the rain fell. The wind began to get up and the trees began to sway, causing some leaves that were barely hanging on to drift down to the forest floor.

"We gotta go!" Jake said over the rain and wind. Panic ensued as they turned and trotted back where they came.

"Do you remember how to get out of here?!" Eddie asked over the rain and wind, jogging alongside his dad.

"I hope the hell so!" Jake said, trying to keep calm.

On the inside, he was scared to death. The air began to feel different, much like it did when a storm was coming. The rain fell harder; the wind blew with more force and off in the distance the two of them could hear trees fall, crashing down with brute force. The splintering sounds of those fallen trees scared Eddie as he felt that he and his dad were dead in those woods. He just knew they were not going to make it out alive.

They ran, weaving in and out through the trees, nearly falling sometimes, slipping on the wet ground, but they maintained their footing for the most part by the grace of God. But did God exist in those woods where it appeared that time held no court? Eddie did not think so. He thought that the woods were something out of a H.P. Lovecraft story and wanted no part of it.

If Eddie was being honest, he felt that the woods which formed a horseshoe around their house was a gateway into another dimension. *But would Dad believe that*, he wondered as they ran for their lives before the darkness caught them. When it got dark, then what? What creepy crawlies and beastly beasties lurked in the dark recesses of the woods? Eddie thought he already knew judging from the skeletons tied to the trees back at the graveyard.

15

Running for what seemed to be only minutes, which made no sense at all, the two of them ran through the skeleton graveyard and towards home. As the two ran by, the human-looking skeletons each lifted their heads all in unison and looked in the direction of the Averys. In no time flat after running past the skeletons, Jake and his son could see light at the edge of the woods. From within the woods, Jake and Eddie could see their house through the limbs of trees. They were almost out. The wind grew stronger, and the rain now came down in sheets, hard. It was as if the elemental forces inside the woods were trying to keep them inside for whatever nefarious reasons.

Jake and Eddie busted through a wall of limbs and within a blink of an eye, they were back in their yard, on the grass. The woods were safely behind them now as they stood in the overcast afternoon. They ran a safe distance from the woods, stopped, and turned to give the woods a look. No rain or wind. It was dead calm. Eddie, thinking quickly, reached into his front pocket and fetched his phone. He pressed the side button and the screen came on showing a yellow Ford Mustang GT. The words NO SERVICE were no longer there. In its place was 4G and some bars.

"Dad? Look," Eddie said, holding up the phone for him to see the time. It was 12:15 pm.

16

It was Halloween, and it fell on a Friday. Leigh had to work the concession stand again at the high school football game. That left Jake and Eddie to their own devices. It was cold that night. The woods that formed a horseshoe around their house and property had lost all the leaves after the last two weeks of unseasonably cold temperatures. The trees, which made up the forty-acre forest, had been stripped bare, showing now only skeleton limbs and branches, which created an eerie backdrop behind the Avery house. When the moon was just right, like it was the night before– not a full moon but damn near close enough– the moon shone through those woods, making them appear to be something out of a horror movie.

They never said anything to Leigh about what had gone down in the woods earlier in the month when the two of them went to explore. That was a secret they kept to themselves. Jake thought about telling his wife about everything but stopped because when he would practice telling her in the mirror in their bedroom, it sounded insane. Hearing the words coming out of his mouth, trying to explain that night in the kitchen, that night he and Eddie were out by the fire, and that day in the woods sounded ridiculous. Jake just kept his mouth shut, and he and Eddie discussed it at length between the two of them. It was their secret.

Eddie, who had believed in the world unseen long before his dad ever had, knew about such things they had encountered. He had fancied himself as a Fox Mulder type from that classic TV show, *The X-Files*. He believed in the unseen, researched it, and filed away everything he read inside his mind as it pertained to the supernatural. What was more supernatural than outside his bedroom window out in the woods? It was a hotbed of paranormal activity, but exactly what kind of paranormal activity was it? Eddie guessed that the woods were a portal to another dimension, where a door could swing both ways.

A few days after their hike in the woods, Eddie and his dad sat at the dining room table one evening while Leigh had to help her mother paint one of the bedrooms in her house. Jake and his son sat discussing what the woods were. Jake previously had not believed in the supernatural but loved a good scary ghost story. Those woods out in his backyard were more than just a ghost story; they were the real deal. They made him a believer.

Eddie began talking about what he thought the woods were. His working theory was that the woods were a portal of some sort and that the deadfall barrier was just that, a barrier.

"For what?" Jake asked, leaning back in his chair as Eddie laid it all out.

"To keep something back— to keep whatever it is on the other side *on* the other side. I mean, you saw it. That deadfall goes on forever. We didn't have a chance to climb it and look over, did we? I really wished we would've."

"So you think that the skeletons that were tied to those trees came from over the deadfall barrier?" Jake asked, already knowing what his son was going to say.

Eddie nodded, "Oh, for sure. I think that what was screaming and slammed up against the French doors that night you were down here was where one of them made it all the way through the woods."

"Question is," Jake began, "what's been stopping whatever they are from reaching the house except that one night? Someone or something had to have killed those things and tied them to the trees to rot away. I mean, something is taking care of those things. And what about that night last month when you saw those red eyes everywhere?"

Eddie had thought about this for a while and had arrived at a pretty good conclusion based on his research.

"I think someone has been protecting that deadfall barrier for years. Maybe they're the one that keeps whatever those things are at bay from getting loose. We don't know what's all in there or what has crossed over. And that night when I saw the red eyes, I don't know. Maybe some of them got loose."

Jake sat and looked at his son and marveled at how smart and, at the same time, crazy he sounded. The entire situation was unbelievable. Never in a million years did he think he would be having this conversation with his son, much less giving credence to such things, but here he was at the table talking about things that go bump in the night.

"You think that's what the shack is that we saw? Maybe whoever is guarding the deadfall barrier lives there?"

Eddie nodded, "I think so. But we never got to look inside there. We got chased out. But I don't think it's very smart to go back in there to see over the barrier or in that shack either."

Jake nodded in agreement, "You got that right, kiddo. So what do we do?"

Eddie leaned back in his chair. He had already thought about that.

"Halloween is coming up. It's on a Friday this month and on a full moon. That night the veil between the dead and living is at its thinnest. I'll bet my Xbox that we're going to see and hear some stuff that night. I think we stay around and wait for whatever it is that may come out of those woods."

"I'll be honest," Jake started, "I don't know if it's a good idea for us to be here. I mean, what if whoever takes care of the deadfall barrier takes the night off or is dead or whatever?"

Both of them sat for a while lost in their heads, treading on their hamster wheels going nowhere fast.

"Then I think we might not need to be here that night," Eddie said. His dad agreed.

17

The plan was simple and should have gone off without a hitch. Leigh was going to be gone working the concession stand at the high school football game again, and Jake and Eddie had planned to go into the city to the town park to walk around the block party that all the city's churches put on. It was usually fun there: live music at the pavilion, games, hay rides around the park and the service road beside what used to be Hudson's Woods. The woods stood tall for decades upon decades until someone burned them down years ago in an act of arson.

There were all kinds of games for the kids and a costume contest for both kids and adults. It was usually a grand time and a way to burn a couple of hours from giving out Halloween candy at their doorsteps. Most of the town usually showed up at least for an hour and it was most of the time packed.

***

Two days before Halloween, on the twenty-ninth, Jake came down with the flu. It was a nasty strain that literally put him down on his back in the bed. He put off going to the doctor because Jake did not do doctors.

"Maybe you need to go," Leigh told him as he lay there in bed the night of the twenty-ninth. She was leaning up against the door frame of their bedroom, knowing what her husband was going to say.

"I'm fine, hon. Just a cold. That happens when you work out in the rain sometimes. Plus, it's been so cold lately– bad mixture."

Jake was so stopped up that his wife could barely make out what he was saying. She looked at him and saw that he had something more than a common cold; she thought it was the flu because it had been going around her high school like a mad bastard.

Leigh walked from the bedroom door, over to her husband in the bed, and placed her hand on his forehead, "God, you're burning up."

"I'm fine," Jake said.

***

On the thirtieth, Jake knew that it was more than a cold. He thought maybe he had the flu. He woke up that morning and could barely move. Everything hurt; even opening his eyes hurt. He turned over in bed and noticed that Leigh had already gone to school. *What time is it,* he thought. He turned and looked at the clock that sat on the nightstand. It was 8:45 in red digital numbering.

"Oh God. I'm late for work," Jake groaned. He tried to raise himself from bed but failed miserably. Three more feeble attempts proved that he had no energy to even get out of bed.

Eventually, he mustered up enough strength and raised himself up, turning himself to the edge of the bed where his bare feet touched the floor. It was cold. Matter of fact, he was shivering. He slowly got up off the bed and felt lightheaded immediately, and his legs nearly gave out on him. He crashed back down on the bed and decided that maybe he needed to take a knee today. He looked outside through the window, and it was dreary. He could hear the wind and rain against the bedroom window. *Not a good day to be out surveying land, that's for sure,* he thought.

Deciding that his wife may have been right, he reached for his phone that sat on the nightstand next to the digital clock. He got his phone, turned the screen on, and called into work. Ian Morton, his younger boss fresh out of college, answered.

Before Jake could tell him that he was not going to be there and that he might go see his doctor, Ian said, "Your wife already called me and told me how bad you are. You sound like hell."

Jake agreed and Ian told him to take until Monday off and get well soon. Jake ended the call, went through his contacts, and called Dr. Anderson for an appointment.

***

On Halloween, Jake was in bed asleep. He had been in bed since being diagnosed with a very nasty strain of the flu. Picking up his prescription from Walgreens, he took the meds that may cause drowsiness and in no time, Jake was out like a light as his system and medicine began to work together to fight the infection. The only time that Jake did wake up was to go to the bathroom to pee. That was it. Leigh even checked on him from time to time to see if he was still alive. He was, just deep sleeping is all. It was the deepest sleep Jake Avery had ever encountered.

All day at school Eddie was nervous. He and his dad were not supposed to be at home later. The plan was to go to the Halloween block party and burn off a few hours and after that? Well, they did not really know where to go or how they were going to keep Leigh out of the loop. She would come home around ten-thirty after the football game that she had to work, and they could not just up and tell her what had been going on. Leigh would laugh them out of Brook County for that.

"There's no use in trying to even talk to her about it," Jake had told his son a few days before the flu set up shop inside his body. "She doesn't believe in stuff like that. But then again, neither did I."

As the days went on and after they settled on not being at home when Halloween came, the plan, as far as keeping Leigh away from home, was never settled. Jake told his son that he would come up with something. Eddie did not pursue it any further after that. He figured his dad would cook up something. When his dad came down with the flu, all bets were off the table now. It was Eddie trying to figure out how in the hell he was going to get them both out of the house for the night and keep his mother from coming home. He was sure that something was going to happen on Halloween night; could feel it in his young bones. Now that his dad was sick and deeply in a prescription medicine-induced dreamland, he had to figure out what to do *if* and *when* something came from the woods.

Eddie got home from school via the bus and walked up the driveway. The towering trees that made up the woods stood skeletal, ominous, stripped bare of their leaves. The day had started off cold, around fifty, and the weather forecast was for it to dip down into the upper thirties by nightfall. The weatherman on Action News Channel 5, Chip Chrisman, told all those trick-or-treaters "...to bundle up because it was going to be a cold one and couldn't rule out some passing showers before the night was over."

Eddie walked inside his house and up the stairs to his bedroom. He un-shouldered his backpack and took his Braves hat off, tossing it onto his never made-up bed. He walked out and down the hall to his parents' bedroom to check on his dad. He quietly and slowly opened the bedroom door and heard snoring. Jake was deep under covers, sweating out the infection inside his body.

Eddie closed the door silently and walked down the hall and downstairs. He had to prep for tonight...just in case. There was no way he could get his dad out of the house and stop his mother from coming home. Eddie was just going to have to make do with what he had...which was nothing really.

18

Leigh came home after school and did her normal daily thing. Eddie was up in his room trying to keep the nerves down. The best he could do was pace back and forth inside his room, but before his mom got home, he was all over the house going over in his head what he was going to do if a situation arose. *What if something happens like it did to Dad that night,* he wondered. *What am I going to do? What if a bunch of stuff comes from the woods and attacks the house? What then? Call the cops? Take dad's gun and start shooting? This ain't going to be good. But what if nothing happens? What if it's a normal night just like any other? Come on, Eddie, you were in those woods and know what happened. You saw what you saw that night by the fire.*

"Eddie, I'm heading back to school to do this stupid concession stand!" Leigh yelled from downstairs up to the second floor.

Eddie heard his mother and came out of his bedroom and down the stairs, "What time do you think you'll be home?" he asked, standing half way on the staircase looking at his mom.

"No later than ten-thirty…I hope. You keep an eye on your dad. I don't think he's been up and coherent since he took the medicine the doc prescribed for him. It really knocked him out up there."

Eddie nodded, "Yeah sure thing."

Before Leigh turned to walk away, she got a feeling from her son. Maybe it was mother's intuition, but there was something odd about how he was looking at her. She felt it coming off him, "You okay? You're not getting sick, too, are you?"

"Nah, I'm good. Just a little tired from school is all."

"Come down here and let me feel your head," Leigh told him.

Eddie came down the rest of the stairs and she placed her hand on his forehead and waited a few moments. "Well, you ain't got a fever. That's good. But keep a watch out for that at any rate. And watch your dad. You need me…call. I love you," Leigh said and that was that. She turned and walked away and out of the house leaving Eddie and his sick dad alone on Halloween night.

19

Eddie watched his mother drive away from the living room window and as soon as her car vanished from sight down the road, he felt a pang of fear deep inside his stomach. It was at that moment that Eddie felt alone. Yeah, his dad was inside the house with him, but what did that matter? Eddie knew that if anything ever came from the woods to the house, he was going to have to defend it…somehow. Exactly how he did not know. It was a good thing that he knew how to shoot his dad's Colt.

Speaking of the Colt, Eddie went back upstairs after seeing his mom off and crept inside his parents' bedroom. His dad was still in the same position he had seen him in earlier, still facing the closet, still deep under the covers. He could hear his dad faintly breathing a congested snore. Eddie tiptoed across the floor and went over to the closet. He looked over at his dad and could see his face peeking out from the three covers. His eyes were closed. Eddie turned his eyes to the closet, opened the door, and looked around. On the floor, next to the outer wall, was the safe. He reached in and saw that it had that biometric fingerprint pad on it. Eddie stood there dumbfounded. *Well ain't this a bitch,* he thought.

He reached inside and pulled the safe out. The gun was safely locked inside it, and the question was how to get it out. He looked back over to his knocked-out dad and came up with an idea. He carried the safe over to the bed and laid it beside his dad. He then, not carefully at all because he figured his dad was deep under, pulled back the covers just enough to find his dad's hand. He reached in and took his right hand, moved the fingers around, got the thumb, and placed it on the biometric lock. It popped open like magic. He tucked his dad's hand back close to his chest and pulled the covers back over him. Eddie took the fully loaded Colt out and laid the safe down on the floor. That was that; no fuss, no muss.

***

Eddie sat in the living room scrolling through his phone on various social media sites, seeing what his friends were up to that Halloween night. Most of them were down at the block party having what looked to be a great time according to the posted pictures. The loaded Colt sat waiting on the end table next to the couch where Eddie was sitting. He had gotten up several times to double, triple, and quadruple-check the back and front doors to make sure they were locked.

They were just as they were the first time. He also went to every room of the house to make sure the windows were locked as well. In the living room, he had the TV on. AMC was showing their annual Halloween movies in consecutive order in the franchise. He had seen those movies a million times with his dad and paid them no mind at all. The TV was just on to provide some comfort as background noise.

At six o'clock was when things got going...when the darkness settled over the land the things from the woods began to stir about.

20

Eddie sat there immersed in his phone when suddenly something broke the spell– a tapping, like someone was tapping their finger on the window in the kitchen. It was loud enough to travel through the kitchen, dining room, and into the living room over the loud sound from the TV. Eddie looked up from his phone as his heart came up in his throat.

"What was that?" he asked quietly in a panic state. He thought he already knew what it was, the tapping.

Again the tapping came, tapping a little louder this time. Eddie stood up from the couch, put his phone in his back pocket, and stole the gun from the end table. He held it firmly in his right hand. Was he ready to battle the unseen forces from the woods? No way, but did he have a choice? Not really.

Eddie followed that tapping sound that came from the kitchen. He crept through the dining room, holding the Colt to his side. The hammer wasn't cocked just yet; eyes straight ahead. His heartbeat was going a mile a second. The tapping sound on the glass was getting louder with each step the closer he got. All the lights were on inside the house at this point to make him feel safe. Did he feel safe? No, not with whatever it was that came across that deadfall border and roamed the woods stirring about. "Safety" was just a word to Eddie Avery that meant nothing more than an illusion.

He got into the kitchen right on the very edge where the dining room ended and the kitchen began. The tapping was coming from the kitchen window above the sink. He figured it would be the French doors like his dad had dealt with months before. Eddie stood there and heard the tapping, which was slow and consistent, and ran his hand along the side of the wall to turn off the lights. He could not see a thing through the window from where he was at.

His fingers found purchase on the wall, and he shut the light switch down to OFF. Although there was light emanating from the dining room and the living room, the kitchen was not in total darkness. He still could not see what was causing that tapping on the kitchen window. He knew that he was going to have to walk closer to the sink and come face-to-face with whatever it was. He cocked the hammer back on the Colt single-action gun.

Eddie crept with caution across the kitchen, keeping his eyes glued on the window above the sink. He could not see anything yet, but the window was beginning to take shape. He could see some reflections of the lights from the dining room and the living room, but still nothing in terms of what was tapping on the window. Tap...tap...tap...tap...

The closer Eddie walked, the more in view the window was becoming; the reflection of the dining room lights was now blotted out by his own body. In what seemed to be no time, he was standing in front of the sink looking out the window and saw what was making that tapping sound. It looked like a man but was not a man. It had two red glowing eyes staring at him as it tapped its crooked and decayed index finger against the thin glass of the window in a slow cadence.

Eddie's heart skipped a beat at the sight of what he thought looked like a zombie– a true figure that had returned from the grave somehow and was standing outside the kitchen window tapping. He figured that those two red eyes belonged to what he saw when he and his dad were sitting by the fire that night. Chicken skin covered his arms by that revelation.

Eddie did not know what to do at that moment. He had the gun, but then what? Shoot through the window, giving the zombie a headshot like in the movies? His mind was turning and burning on what to do when suddenly something shook the locked French doors on the other side of the kitchen. Something was trying to get in, and if that was not bad enough, there was a loud ear-piercing screech that came from whatever it was trying to pull open the double doors.

Eddie looked at the zombie through the window and its two red eyes, and over at the French doors that were being pushed and pulled making all kinds of racket. With the hammer cocked, Eddie raised his arm, aimed the gun in the general direction of the French doors, and squeezed the trigger. The shot rang out so loudly that it hurt his ears. The gunshot did nothing to stop what was going on over at the doors.

Cocking the hammer back again, he looked at the kitchen window and saw what he thought looked to be a zombie was still tapping on his window. He squeezed the trigger a second time. The bullet came out of the gun and through the window hitting the zombie dead square in the head. At least that was what Eddie thought because the tapping stopped.

Cocking the hammer back again, he walked over to the sink and looked through the busted glass into the night the best he could. Although he did not see the zombie tapping on his window anymore, to his horror he did see what looked to be fifty sets of red eyes coming from the woods as if they were surrounding the house. The left side of the

French doors had finally broken, and whatever it was trying to get inside was nearly in.

Eddie rushed over to the middle of the kitchen, a safe distance from the French doors, raised his arm and pulled the trigger again, shooting through the glass of the left door. He hit it and it gave a loud squeal mixed with a rumbling roar. Eddie could not see very much through the glass and darkness, but he could have sworn that whatever it was looked like a pterodactyl.

Eddie had to know what he hit. He rushed over to the French doors and flipped the wall switch to turn on the back lights that lit up the entire backyard. The floodlights his dad had installed last month came on in a flash showing everything. Thank God Dad installed these! Eddie looked through the busted glass and could see and hear what looked like a pterodactyl, writhing around on the ground in pain. It screamed into the night. It had a long, slender head and neck. The tail, the best he could tell from his view, was short. All of the red eyes from the woods were getting closer to the house, and the light from the floodlights showed Eddie that he was right; they were zombies shuffling from the woods groaning and moaning.

Eddie was frantic. He knew that his house was about to be overrun by the undead and was not too sure that the beast that he shot was dead or just injured. He did not stand there to allow himself to think about how dire the situation was; he was in full survival mode now. Eddie ran across the kitchen and placed the gun on the island and into the dining room he went.

He grabbed the dining room table, a huge oak one that was heavy as hell, and he dragged it across, scraping the hardwood floors as he did. He dragged it to the French doors that had already been breached. If the zombies knew what they were doing, they would make a beeline to the broken doors. He pushed the oak table against the doors, and then he rushed back into the dining room and grabbed the oak chairs, which were heavy too, and stacked them on top of the table. Eddie picked up the Colt from the island and cocked the hammer back and waited. He had forgotten he only had three bullets left in the silver barrel.

He could hear the groans from the zombies outside and the screaming and squealing from the pterodactyl-looking creature. Something else made a sound; something smashed against the side of the house, and it sounded as if it was climbing up to the second story growling as it did. Eddie wanted to scream, cry, and piss his pants at the same time, but for whatever reason, he was locked up. When he saw the first couple sets of red eyes through the French doors, Eddie began to aim and start shooting. He fired the remaining three shots towards the double doors, not knowing if he hit anything or not. He cocked the hammer back, pulled the trigger, and dry-fired. Nothing came out, and it was then that Eddie realized that he was out of bullets and out of options.

Jake was having that dream of riding a motorcycle. At this particular point in the dream, while Eddie was doing battle with the undead and strange creatures, Jake was sitting at a red light on a two-lane road in a town he had never been in before. Sitting there on his bike, looking around at the fields and woods around, he heard what sounded to be gunshots, three of them, off in the woods.

"What was that?" the woman who was not his wife asked from behind him on the seat.

"I don't know. Sounded like gunshots, didn't it?" The light turned green and off Jake went down the road, not giving the gunshots another thought.

The zombies were beginning to break the rest of the glass from the French doors and push their way inside the home. Eddie now screamed and tears came from his eyes. He knew that he was a goner. He quickly gave some thought about rushing up the stairs, but in every horror movie he had ever seen that was how the character died.

As the zombies began to force their way inside the home; the thing that was crawling up the side of the house growling; and *Jurassic Park* still screaming in pain in the backyard, Eddie closed his eyes and screamed at the top of his lungs for someone to come and help him.

From the woods came a man...

21

Just like in the movies, the hero came out of nowhere and took charge of the situation. The pterodactyl stopped screaming. Eddie had not noticed because he, himself, was screaming his head off in the kitchen hunkered down behind the island. The thing that was climbing up the side of the house had been shot down and stabbed in the heart with a stake...the zombies that had entered the house were one by one pulled back outside and decapitated with an ax until the kitchen was free of them.

Eddie sat there, hands to his head, eyes closed, and screaming. He did not see how close one of the zombies had gotten to him; within inches until it was decapitated by the hero from behind. Blood flew everywhere in the kitchen, and the man pulled the zombie out by the arm from the kitchen and tossed him outside with the rest of the dead, through the broken French doors and scattered dining room table and chairs. The undead, the pterodactyl, and the thing climbing up the side of the house were all taken care of within a matter of five deadly minutes and Eddie did not see any of it.

When he finally stopped screaming, he slowly opened his eyes and saw someone standing at the kitchen sink. He could hear running water as if someone was washing their hands. Eddie slowly rose to his feet and cleared his throat, "I've got a gun," Eddie weakly said.

Without turning to look at the boy he just saved, "Yeah, and I bet you're out of bullets, too."

Eddie stood, trembling, looking at the man who had his back turned to him, "W...who are you?" he asked after a few moments of trying to gain some sort of composure.

The burly, shadowy man finished washing his hands and shut off the water. He turned to look at the boy in the darkness, "I'm the man who kills the monsters."

A NIGHT IN THE MEADOW

"What is it?" Paul asked.

"It's called, *A Night in the Meadow.*"

"Well what the hell does it mean, I guess I meant to ask?" Paul asked his ex-girlfriend, Sandra.

"You got this dark landscape going on here...this cottage just sitting...," Paul said, waving his hand at the painting that hung on the wall at the Spritzer's Art Gallery.

"It's simple," Sandra started, "you have the small cottage here alone in the meadow at night. The house is a representation of a human's desire to be alone in tranquility. The full moon is a manifestation of the inner light that lies within all of us. The darkness of the landscape is my interpretation of how darkness can, over time, creep into your soul if you don't have the right amount of light to ward it off– hence, the full moon."

Paul turned and looked at her, then at the painting, and back to her again. "You painted this...thinking all of that?"

"I did. The old Native American guy that sold me the colors you see here, told me about them being transformative. I asked what that meant. He told me to just beware and warned me that if I painted a picture with the colors, the picture could change. So far...I haven't noticed any changes. He probably tells that to all the out-of-town customers. Either way, the colors were a lot different than I'm used to working with. They had a...uniqueness to them for lack of better words. Textures were different. What's funny, after I painted this piece, all the colors that I had used disappeared...almost as if they evaporated overnight after I was finished; never had that happen before." Sandra told Paul as a waiter carrying a tray of wine glasses approached her.

"How long did it take you to paint it?" Paul asked, never minding the curious story about the colors.

She took two wine glasses with a smile and handed Paul one. He was still looking deeply at the painting.

"Strangely...one night. I had this image in my head all day and tried to sleep that night but did nothing but toss and turn. So, I got up and went into the studio to paint this. I don't even remember painting it...like I was on automatic drive or something. You don't like it?"

"No, I like it. I guess I just see a painting. I don't get all your deeper meaning craziness...transformative color bullshit...but then again, I never did. Probably why we didn't work out, right?"

"No," Sandra said, taking a sip from her wine glass, "we didn't work out because you like to fool around with anything that gives you the least amount of attention. And you were drinking too much for me."

Paul grinned, knowing that she was right. She usually was. "Yeah, there's that, I guess. So... any takers?"

"Not yet. Most of the people are over there looking at what I call my 'Forgotten Years' display. It's all the stuff that I painted when I was still in high school."

"Well, I want this one," Paul said.

"Pauly, you don't have to buy anything. That's not why I invited you here tonight."

"I know. Listen, I like it. It speaks to me for some odd reason. I think it'll look good in my office. Maybe even in my living room. Somewhere, hell, I don't know. So...how much?" Paul took a sip from his wine glass and swished the fine wine around in his mouth.

"Six-fifty," Sandra replied.

Paul nearly spat out his wine, "Six-fifty? For this?!" Paul saw that his words cut her a little, and he regained his footing. "I meant, six-fifty...for this? Surely you want more?"

"Yeah, good save. You don't have to buy it."

"Listen, you're one of my best friends, and I want to support you."

"I get plenty of support."

"I'm buying it. Do I take it now and have the cashier ring it up, or..."

Sandra smiled and wanted to laugh at Paul's ignorance of being in a fine art gallery. "This isn't Wal-Mart. You just don't take pieces of art off the wall and go to a cashier. Here, I'll go tell Vigo that this painting has already been sold. He'll come over and place an index card next to it with your name and how much you paid for it."

"Vigo?" Paul asked, smiling. "You have a guy here named Vigo? Ohhh, is he like that guy in the painting in *Ghostbusters 2*? I mean, we're in an art gallery, and there's paintings all over the place...I'm just saying...it might be haunted. You never know."

Sandra wanted to laugh and tried not to because laughing would only encourage Paul.

Paul bought *A Night in the Meadow*, and hung it for display in his living room. He tried his home office at first, but it felt too bulky in there, too shoehorned in. He tried his den– not a good fit there, either. The living room had nearly bare walls, and the six feet by six feet work of art fit nicely on the left side of his flat TV that hung on the wall. After affixing the painting to several Command Strips on the wall, Paul stood back to give it a look. It was still crooked, a little bit lower on the left side than the right. Paul took the painting off, repositioned it, and hung it back.

He stepped back and smiled, "That's it."

The next evening, Paul was walking through the living room, holding a glass of chocolate milk when his eye caught the painting. Something was different about it, something small, but different all the same. Paul walked over to the painting, stood in front of it, and stared deeply at it. It was the moon. Sandra had painted the full moon just above the cottage, but now the full moon was...what? Just a shade past the house– almost like it had moved. How was that possible?

"What the hell?" Paul quietly asked no one but himself.

He thought for sure Sandra had positioned the moon above the cottage, but wasn't one hundred percent certain. Would he bet his life on it? Paul shook his head at that question and backed away from the wall.

"Maybe I'm wrong."

2

The next day at work went about the same as they always do: reports to file, spreadsheets to create, emails to send, and meetings that went nowhere fast. Something did gnaw at Paul, chewing on the gray matter of his brain: it was that damn moon. Had it moved? The thought of the moon randomly streaking across his mind that morning; while at his desk, he worked on the TPX reports for his boss, Howard. Once the thought of the moon over the cottage flashed in his mind, it hung around there for a while– impossible to block out.

He had gotten up earlier that morning and did his normal routine of going to the bathroom, walking down the hall and through the living room that spilled into the kitchen. From there, he would get his morning coffee– maybe some cereal if he was hungry– and sit at the small table reading the news on his phone. That morning, Paul took his piss, walked down the hall, and into the living room where he stood in front of the painting. The moon was in the same place it was the night before when it moved.

"I know it moved," Paul uttered to himself. He stood there staring at it, wanting to see if anything else moved within the painting. Paul snuck a peek at the wall clock and realized that he had been standing there for ten minutes, and by doing that, it put him behind on his morning routine. Now, he felt rushed all because of that damn painting.

Sitting at his desk, Paul stopped working on the TPX reports for Howard when the thought came to him about the moon moving to the right of the cottage. *It moved. I swear it did,* Paul thought to himself.

"But what if it didn't, Pauly?" Paul said loud enough that anyone passing his cubicle could hear him.

That means I'm seeing things...like I used to when I was on drugs.

"Maybe I'm making something out of nothing. I probably didn't notice it before, and for some reason, it's caught my attention," Paul replied.

Maybe...or maybe not. You're not one to make up crazy things. I mean, something had to have happened for you to notice it, right?

"Maybe," Paul said, trailing off at his desk. Paul sat there for a good two hours– thinking about the moon, the painting, the dark landscape of it all.

Howard came pecking on his cubicle wall stirring him out of his trance. "Are they finished?"

"Are what finished?" Paul replied, wiping the drool from his bottom lip from where his mouth had hung open while in a state of trance.

"The TPX reports. I needed them before lunch," Howard said, looking at his wristwatch. "And it's ten minutes before noon. So...I need them...now!"

"Yes...yes, sir. I've got them here somewhere. I'll email them to you. I just forgot, is all," Paul said, scattered-brained as he shuffled around at his desk, looking at his computer screen to pull up the file.

Howard gave Paul an angry look and hurriedly walked away back to his office. Paul pulled up the TPX reports, and they were not completely finished. But with some fancy wording and some numbers that he plugged in that sounded close to being right, Paul finished and emailed them to his boss in under a few minutes. It was not the best report he ever filed, but it would do. Besides, Paul figured, Howard wouldn't even know because he's dumb as hell.

3

Paul had arrived home later that evening from work, and the situation with the moon had still hung around in his mind. It evaporated some, but the remnants of his thoughts and his growing obsession over it caused his productivity at work to sharply decline for the day. Paul put all his work stuff down and walked into the living room, and the first thing he did was walk over to the painting. To his surprise and horror, something else had changed about the painting: a light was on.

A light was on inside the cottage, glowing a muted yellow from what Paul guessed was the kitchen, at the back part of the cottage. Paul stood there dumbfounded and horrified. He looked up at the moon, and it was still in place or at least he thought it was but who knew for sure. But that light turned on in what Paul figured was the kitchen...that was something new, and it happened while he was at work.

Paul wondered if he could watch this stuff inside the painting happen in real-time. So, he took a seat down on the ottoman that was placed in front of the couch and stared at the painting. He wanted to see something happen– something move or something like the light flick off. Or maybe even see another light come on inside the cottage. What about the moon? Maybe the moon could move a little more to the right, and he would catch it in real time.

At any rate, Paul sat on that ottoman and looked into that painting until his phone's alarm rang out. Paul took the phone out of his pocket and saw that it was 7:00 a.m...It was time to get up and start the day.

"I sat here all night?!" Paul shouted, rubbing his face and feeling the pains in his back from sitting so long without moving a muscle. When he stood up, it took forever for him to straighten his back which barked and groaned.

He looked at the painting, and nothing that he could tell had changed. It was still the same: the light was on in what he thought was the kitchen, and the moon was still hanging in its position. Paul was extremely tired and had been up for approximately twenty-four hours now. And for what? Trying to catch the things inside the painting moving as if there was life going on inside of it? Yes...precisely.

Paul got his coffee, skipped the news and skipped a shower. He went into the hall closet, got his security camera, and placed it on the ottoman, aiming it up at the painting. He then slid the ottoman closer to the painting, so the camera could catch anything that might move while he was gone for the day. He took out his phone and linked it up with the camera so he could watch the painting while at work, a live feed. If anything changed– the moon moving or the light going off– he would be able to see it.

"Foolproof," Paul said dryly.

4

The day at work was a busy one. He sat in meetings all day long listening to regional managers drone on and on about this, that, and the other. None of it mattered to his department. Those meetings never did. But Paul, being a department head, his presence was required. He was not as tired as he thought he would be. He guessed the five Red Bulls he drank along with his coffee turned that trick. While sitting at the table in the conference room, Paul would pull his phone out to check on the painting. He zoomed into the live feed, and it still looked the same as it did when he left the house. He did this every couple of minutes it seemed sitting there and each time the painting remained the same.

After work and the all-day meetings which ran four in a row over different things in different departments, Paul rushed out of the office building, holding his phone up to his face the whole time watching the live feed. He did this at the lunch break, sitting off to himself in the cafeteria, just watching for something, *anything*, to happen to that painting. He skipped eating because he did not want to avert his eyes for just a second for that hour he was on lunch. Still, there was nothing. Paul got into his car, put his phone in his phone holder that was affixed to his windshield, and pulled out of the parking lot headed for home. He was playing a dangerous game now...he was paying more attention to the live feed of the painting than he was on the road.

Two miles from his house is where the accident took place. Paul became so enamored with watching the painting that he less and less watched where he was going. Sometimes his eyes would look out the window and catch the road and see where he was at. And then his eyes slid back over to his phone. He figured driving was nothing but muscle memory, anyway. That was until he rear-ended the car in front of him at the stop sign. His airbag deployed, and his face smacked against it. He was not hurt, neither was the old woman he hit at thirty-five, but it was enough to scare the hell out of him and her.

Paul got out of the car, and for the first time that day, common sense overrode his obsession over the phone's live feed of the painting. He rushed over to the driver's side door of the car he hit and checked on the old woman. A police officer just happened to be at the four-way stop and saw the entire thing. Who says there's never a cop around when you need one? Paul apologized profusely a million times to her, hoping that she was okay. She appeared to be, just shaken up is all.

After talking to the officer as he wrote the report, Paul was free to go after insurance info was collected. Paul went over to inspect his car; his front grill and headlights were busted up pretty good. The hood was caved in, and it would take a mechanic to pry open the hood now because when Paul tried, it was too smashed in for him to open it. He wanted to see how much damage was done to the engine or radiator, if any.

He dropped to all fours there in the street and looked underneath for any leaking fluids. To his surprise, there was nary a drop on the pavement. The back end of the old woman's car was crushed in, and the left and right back fenders were crushed against her back tires, making it impossible for her to drive it home. A tow truck eventually had to come and retrieve it. When the officer asked Paul why he didn't stop, Paul lied and said that he had not been sleeping the day before. It really was not a complete lie; he had not slept in over twenty-four hours, and he was feeling it there at the scene of the accident.

Eventually, Paul got back into the car and looked at his phone. The light in the cottage had gone out. Paul looked at this turn of events for a few moments and then pounded his fists on the steering wheel screaming so loudly that the officer and the old woman gave him a look.

"Fuuuccckkk!"

Paul put the car in gear and drove it home. When he was clear of the police officer and the accident that he caused, he pressed the gas and hit seventy down the little street he lived on.

Paul rushed into his house and just as he saw on the phone, the light was off in the cottage. He had missed it. He ran his fingers through his hair in frustration and then pulled on it, screaming. He walked up to the painting so close that his nose was nearly touching it.

"Move! Fucking Move!" Paul commanded. "I know you can because you've been doing it! Move! Turn on a light! Something!"

Nothing happened. Paul stepped back and was so mad that he tore his button-down shirt off and flung it across the living room. Then he picked up his gaming chair and tossed it against the far wall in a fit of rage. He took the camera off the ottoman and crushed it with his bare hands before slamming it onto the living room floor and breaking the rest of it by stomping on it. Breathing heavily, he turned and looked at the painting once again. He wanted to pull it off the wall and tear it apart and nearly did...but he stopped himself. Why? Paul didn't really know.

5

That night Paul finally crashed and crashed hard. He was hungry and had not eaten since the morning before, but he was too tired. And a shower? Forget about it. He went to bed in his work clothes and did not take his shoes off. All he wanted to do was go to bed and sleep the sleep of the dead– which he did. Paul slept a good ten hard hours, and no dreams came, at least none that he could remember.

When he woke up, it was not by his alarm, but by music playing. It was some slow 1920s big band music– sounded like what a couple would dance to in a ballroom. It was loud, echoing around in his house, causing Paul to open his eyes and scan his dark bedroom. At first, he thought he was dreaming. He sat up on the edge of the bed and gathered his senses the best he could. His mind and body needed more sleep, but that slow big band music was loudly playing.

Paul slowly got out of his bed, crept across the bedroom and down the hall, which led him into the dark living room. The music was louder in there. Paul stepped into the living room and instantly saw another light on in the cottage, this time at the front part of the house. The big band music was coming from there– from the painting, inside the cottage. Paul walked across the living floor, his shoes crunching the plastic broken pieces of the camera, and he stood in front of the painting.

The music played and as Paul stared into the painting, he thought he saw someone dancing in the window of the cottage. It was! Paul inched closer to the painting and saw with his own tired eyes a blonde woman in a sundress, gliding in the living room of the cottage to the music. Chicken skin flashed all over his arms and legs. He was scared but at the same time mesmerized by the dancing woman inside the cottage.

6

"So...let me get this straight...the moon has moved...lights are coming on in the cottage...and you saw a blonde woman dancing to music that you heard coming from the painting?" Sandra asked while sitting at the table in her art studio.

She did not believe him one bit. Paul was on the other end of her phone, on speaker actually, as it sat on a stool. Sandra was turning the pages slowly of an art magazine where she was a featured piece, absently listening to him.

"Yeah...that's about the size of it, I guess," Paul said, sitting at his desk in his cubicle at work, fighting off sleep. He was so tired, and the bags under his eyes were proof of that.

"When you get home, I want you to snap a picture of the painting. I want to see this. I think you're full of it though, you know that right?"

"Yeah, whatever. I'm sure as I'm sitting here– all that shit happened. You sold me a haunted piece of art, you know that right?"

"Pauly...there's no such thing as haunted. I think you've been drinking again and with your past history with..."

"I ain't been drinking, goddammit!" Paul snapped at her. Sandra had never heard Paul be so mean before, so cross.

"Listen, all this shit in the painting is real. I tell you what...I'll send a picture of where that moon has moved to, okay? Then you tell me I'm crazy!" Paul ended the call and sat there in frustration. He sat at his desk, leaned back in his chair, and closed his eyes. In a minute flat, he was asleep, snoring.

7

Paul stood back from the painting later that night when he got home and snapped a picture of it with his phone. He pulled up Sandra's name, attached the photo to it, and hit the blue arrow. The message was sent, and he was just sitting there, waiting for it to show READ on his end. Paul stood there holding his phone in his hand and looked at the painting. He thought hard about the position of the full moon, where it was when first saw it inside the gallery. There was something about that full moon that bothered him in particular; something that made him obsess over it. His phone chirped, and he looked down at it. It was Sandra with a text back that said:

It's in the same place on the night that I painted it. You need to lay off the alcohol

Paul was not so sure, but he had no way of proving her wrong. After all, she was the artist who painted the piece. Paul closed the message, stuck the phone into his front pocket, and walked away from the painting. He was not satisfied with Sandra's answer, but what was he going to do about it? Nothing. Out of frustration, he punched a hole in the wall. His hand found a stud, and he nearly broke his hand. When he pulled it out, he could barely flex it when he tried to make a fist. He turned his watery eyes towards the painting, and nothing else had happened...yet.

8

A few more days had passed by, and nothing about the painting had changed: no music, no lights, no nothing. The moon was still in the same spot as when he spoke to Sandra about it a few days ago. Paul, during that time, gave the painting a once over, inspecting every inch of it: every dark blade of grass in the meadow, the cozy cottage, the creek, and the full moon. Everything was where it should be.

On that night of deeper inspection, he wondered why he was so intent on making sure the painting's images had not changed.

"I've got to stop this...I'm losing my grip here," Paul said to himself, standing there a couple of feet away from the painting on his wall.

That night he went to bed, satisfied that nothing else had moved or changed within the painting, if there was anything at all to begin with.

Paul began to wonder if he was just seeing things. Back in the day, Paul had done a lot of hard drugs, powerful ones that affected his mind. Sometimes, when he was younger while doing those drugs, Paul would see things that were not there. After he kicked his habit of psychotropic hallucinogens, doctors told him that he might still see things from time to time; that the damage he had done to his brain could not be one hundred percent healed. He had gone a long time not having those hallucinations, but the painting...was that even real, or was it his mind going back into those drug-infused states of seeing things that were not there? Paul was not sure of anything those days.

9

The next morning, Paul got up and got ready for work, determined to start back on a clean slate. He walked over to the painting and stared at it again with the same intensity as the last several nights. As the morning sun was coming through his house windows, he could see the painting in natural lighting. It looked the same. That full moon though...that moon was still just a shade off to the right away from the cottage. That's what bugged Paul the most: the moon. Everything else? Well, all appeared to be fine...for the time being. Paul turned, walked away from the painting, and went into the kitchen to fix himself a cup of coffee to get his morning going.

He sat in his small kitchen— freshly showered, coffee cup to his right on the table, his phone in front of him, scrolling through the latest news. He had no idea why he bothered with the news anymore: tales of woe at home and abroad; protesters in the street screaming about something they think is important; and the staple headline of the president's comments on whatever was going on in the country. Yet, Paul scrolled through the news to find something useful, maybe even uplifting. There was nothing.

Paul finished his coffee, turned his phone screen off to black, and stuck it in his pants front pocket. He walked from the kitchen and through the living room, not giving the painting a moment's notice. Had he stopped to look at the painting, Paul would have seen something from the right side of the painting– all the way over to the edge, to be exact. It was a black shadowy outline of an arm, holding an ax. It was barely visible, not in plain view; but it was there, creeping slowly, much like the moon had crept to the right, above the cottage.

10

Paul had returned home from another long day at work and tossed his keys down on the end table next to the front door. He had a personal victory that day: he had not thought about the painting at all the entire day. He felt free from, *A Night in the Meadow*, for the first time in a bit. He took his shoes off and flung his Braves baseball hat onto the hook on the wall. He went through the living room that evening, picked up the remote control to his TV, and hit the power button, absently leaving it on whatever channel it was on when he shut it off the last time. What was he watching last time? Paul had not a clue. When the TV was on, it was for the most part just background noise unless college basketball was on or the Atlanta Braves.

Paul walked through the living room and into the kitchen to grab a snack, just a little something to hold him over until he made supper. What was for supper? Paul opened the cabinets to get his bag of Doritos and looked around for something that would stand out.

"Ramen it is," Paul said, answering his own question.

He pulled an orange package of chicken-flavored noodles out and tossed it onto the kitchen counter for later. "Mystery solved." Carrying his bag of half-eaten Doritos into the living room, Paul went over and fell into his deep-seated couch and propped his socked feet on the oversized ottoman, pulling his phone out of his pocket.

As he scrolled through the various social media apps, checking in and being nosy on what his friends were doing or what stupid memes they were posting, Paul paid no mind to the painting. Had he looked up, he would have noticed that the arm that held the ax from the right edge of the painting had moved closer into view. Now, a half figure, a tall standing man covered in darkness with an ax, was coming into view. Not the whole man in view just yet, but that was coming...soon.

After watching College Basketball's Greatest Buzzer Beaters of All-Time on TV while eating his bowl of Ramen Noodles, Paul made a phone call to his mother, and they talked about his sister's Lucy's health and her choice in men well into the night. He did not talk to his mother much and tried to avoid it as much as he could. He regulated having to deal with her twice a month, once every two weeks. Paul and his mom had some issues, but those issues would never have a remedy. They just went along like everything was fine. Paul had decided a long time ago that things between the two of them were never going to be right. He took what he could get. To Paul, there was a victory in that.

Taking a shower, brushing his teeth, and getting all his clothes and such laid out for tomorrow morning, Paul went through the house shutting off the lights room by room. He hated sitting in his house with the lights off in the other rooms. He always felt that it made the house on the outside look lonely at night. So, he turned every light on in the house, making it look as if the house were alive when the night came while he was home. His dad would have been so mad.

As Paul walked out of the kitchen, he flipped the switch off and stepped into the living room. The TV was still on as well as the lights overhead in the living room. He picked up the remote and pressed the power button, and off went the TV for the night. Paul was about to walk over to switch off the wall lights when the painting caught his eye. There was something different about it...something that was not there the last time he looked at it.

Immediately, Paul noticed that the full moon had moved a little more towards the right, further away from the cottage. The landscape appeared to be a little brighter, too, thanks to the moonlight. Over to the right of the painting, Paul saw something shadowy. It was too dark to tell what it was; but to Paul, it looked like a half-man coming into view, and what was that he was holding in his hand?

"Is that an ax?" Paul asked himself.

He was puzzled over this new finding and wondered if that tall shadowy figure on the right edge of the painting had been there before. He could not remember. Then it hit him: his phone.

He rushed into his bedroom and took his phone to open the pictures app. He scrolled all the way to the bottom where the most recent pictures were, and there it was...nothing. The picture he had taken days ago was gone. He closed the app, went into his messages to where he sent the picture to Sandra. It was gone from the message thread as well. Paul stood there, stunned. He thumbed up the picture album, and then slowly went through each one of the nearly five hundred pictures. Nothing.

The picture that he had taken of the painting and sent to Sandra had vanished from his phone. Paul began to wonder if his drug-damaged mind was playing tricks on him again or if this was really happening. Tears formed in his eyes, and he started to cry. He slowly sat down on his bedroom floor, back against the wall, and sobbed heavily. Paul felt as if he was losing his mind.

After a much-needed crying spell, Paul walked back into the living room and over to the painting. He knew that the artwork was changing; there was no doubt in his mind about it. He dashed away any thoughts that his mind was going back to producing hallucinations again. He raised his phone, snapped another picture and made sure that it was in his picture album. He even sent a copy of it to his email just in case. He also sent it to Sandra with the message that said LOOK AT THIS. Paul stood there and looked at the painting that seemed to be alive...but how?

11

A few days later, nothing remarkable about the painting had changed; not one single thing. However, Paul did discover a strange thing on his phone: the picture that he snapped a few days ago, where the moon looked to have moved again and the shadowy figure coming into view with the ax, had been erased from his phone– even gone from his email and in the message thread with Sandra. He called Sandra and asked her if she had gotten the picture of the painting that he had sent.

"No, I just got something that said, LOOK AT THIS," she told him.

"What about the picture I sent you a while back of the painting? Tell me you still got that one?" Paul asked.

Sandra scrolled through the messages and found the messages from that night but no picture, "That's funny...it's gone. I know that I saw it because I looked at it when you sent it. I even replied back to you... I know that I didn't erase it because I've still got the message where I told you 'to lay off the alcohol...'" Sandra trailed off in thought, trying to figure out what was going on. "What's going on here?"

"I don't know," Paul replied, "but I need you to come here and look at this in person to make sure that I'm not going crazy. There's a dark figure that looks like it's coming from the right side of the painting now, holding an ax."

"I can't. I'm about to drive to the airport," Sandra told him.

"When will you be back?! Because you got to look at this! I mean, this is serious! Either this painting is haunted, or I'm losing my grip on things!" Paul returned in a panic.

"A day or two...depends on how I feel when I get there. I'm a guest speaker at an art gallery opening in New York City tomorrow evening."

Paul stood there, holding his phone and looking at the painting that was what? Moving? Transitioning into something else? Alive? *Is that where I'm at now in life?* Paul wondered.

"When you get back, get here when you can. I'm sure it'll still be here...maybe worse."

Paul ended the phone conversation and stood there trying to make sense of it all. Now he was worried as was Sandra. Paul had sounded desperate to her. She had never heard him act like that before. She wondered if he had found his way back to drugs.

12

The next night, Paul was awakened from his sleep by the sound of someone walking, maybe even jogging, through what sounded like grass. He opened his eyes and lay there for a few moments, and the sound stopped. Laying there thinking that it might have been a dream and nothing more than that, Paul looked around the dark bedroom where some streetlight barely made it in from the blinds, and slowly closed his eyes. Before his mind could whisk him away back to dreamland, that sound came again. Paul's eyes flew open, and he rose in the bed and looked around, hoping to catch that sound. It had stopped...again.

"What the hell is that?" Paul whispered to no one. He waited for the sound to come again– nothing.

In the silence, Paul decided that he was going to investigate what the sound was because he knew that he heard something, like someone running through tall standing grass, and it sounded like it was coming from the living room. He remembered back when he and his sister Lucy were kids, and they would go to their grandmother's house. She lived way out in the country, and every time he and Lucy would go out into the fields to run and play, Paul remembered the sound that the knee-high grass made against their pants as they ran. That was the sound that he was hearing: tall grass smacking against the legs of pants while someone ran.

Paul stood in his bedroom after getting out of bed and then tiptoed through the room, keeping his ears fine-tuned to any sounds the house was making. Before he made it halfway through the bedroom towards his door, the sound of running or jogging came– the sound of grass swiping against the legs of pants. Paul's insides started to turn to butterflies as he figured out what the sounds could be: the painting...it was moving again.

Paul rushed out of the bedroom and down the hall and into the living room. He flipped the overhead light on and looked at the painting. He did not have to get a closer view because he noticed something different right away. The half-shadowy figure that appeared to be holding an ax on the right edge of the painting was now full-blown, smack dab in the middle of the painting, standing in the middle of the field and heading towards the cottage. Paul could see the dark man in full with the ax and knew that he intended to get to that cottage. For what reason?

Paul stood and watched the painting for a few minutes. Nothing moved. He stepped closer to the painting, hoping that he could see it move. Paul, tired of standing and watching *A Night in the Meadow*, decided that he was going to take a seat on the ottoman and just stare at the painting.

"Maybe I can wait you out," said Paul.

He took a seat, and for the next few hours, he did nothing but watch the painting to see if the dark man carrying the ax would get closer to the cottage. For the rest of the night, nothing happened. What Paul did not realize or hear, was that the dark man was inching his way towards the cottage in silence, inching his way closer and very lightly stepping when Paul would blink. He knew that he was being watched and had even slowly turned his head to look at Paul through his point of view from within the painting. Paul had no idea the dark man was watching him. He never saw the subtle movements he was making. Just as Paul was waiting for the dark man to make a move, the dark man was waiting for Paul to leave. It was as if the two were playing Red Light, Green Light.

13

A loud crack of thunder stirred Paul awake. The thunder was so loud that it shook the entire house. He slowly opened his eyes and realized that he must have fallen asleep on the ottoman while on stakeout. He rose from the ottoman and right away felt how stiff his back was. He looked at the painting: the dark man carrying the ax had gotten closer to the cottage. He was two-thirds of the way there now. Another loud crack of thunder again shook the house as he sat on the edge of the ottoman and inspected the painting with tired eyes. There was no doubt that the dark man was closer to the cottage. Why was he heading to that house?

It was morning at six o'clock, and judging by the darkness outside his blinds, there was a storm coming as the dark clouds blotted out the sunlight. Paul got up from his ottoman and walked over to the widows. He flung open the curtains and opened up the blinds. The outside was dark and gloomy that Halloween Eve. Leaves were blowing all around as the winds were ushering in a cold front that was set to spark off an all-day rain– a cold rain at that. Paul stepped away from the windows and walked over to the painting. He stood and stared at it like it was going to do any good.

"This is like some episode of *The Twilight Zone* or something," Paul remarked, looking at the dark man.

What Paul did not know– how could he?– that the dark man was looking back at him from within the painting, waiting for Paul to go away so he could do what he needed to do. He was so close now.

Being off from work that day and the next, Paul was determined that he was going to solve the mystery of *A Night in the Meadow*. He knew something otherworldly was taking shape in that painting, but what could he do about it? He thought about taking the painting off the wall and burning it out in his fireplace in the backyard. That thought ran through his mind a lot that stormy Halloween Eve morning. As he drank a cup of coffee and watched the painting, he thought about taking some paint and painting over the dark man, or just painting the entire canvas blue. He thought that he still had half a gallon of paint left in the utility room from where he painted his bathroom a few weeks prior.

As the rain came down and the storm grew with intensity outside, Paul rested his Iron Man coffee cup on the ottoman and got up. He walked over to the painting, raised his hand, and placed it on the cottage. Then, something happened...

14

Paul found himself standing inside a strange room in the dark. Not total darkness as the full moon's rays came through the open windows of the cottage. Paul looked around and discovered that he was inside the cottage, inside the painting.

"What the hell?" he managed to ask.

The cottage itself was medium-sized inside. He was standing in the middle of what was the living room.

There was an old box-style TV on a stand with long rabbit ear antennas, two end tables next to a recliner, a coffee table with some magazines and books on it, and a couch. To Paul, this was just an ordinary-looking living room, just like in someone's house...nothing odd about it. Paul heard someone creeping down the stairs. It was a blonde woman dressed in her robe– the same one he watched dance in her living room while the big band music played. She screamed at the sight of the intruder as she ran back up the stairs in a hurry. Paul could hear the bedroom door slamming and locking behind her. That scared Paul. Hell, the whole scene scared Paul.

He looked around in the darkness of the strange house looking for the front door. It was across the living room over to the right. He walked hurriedly over to it, not before whacking his left shin against the coffee table. Limping to the front door, he opened it and before he could leave the living room and cottage forever, the dark man had made it to the front porch of the cottage carrying his ax. Wide-eyed, Paul pulled back inside the house, slammed the door, and locked it. He backed up, figuring out what was coming next because he had seen these kinds of scenarios before in horror films. Paul stood there and waited for the banging to start. And right on cue, it did.

The dark man from outside swung the ax against the wooden front door, trying to chop his way through. Upstairs, the woman in the robe could be heard screaming her head off. Paul stepped back and had no idea what to do next. He looked for the back door, and he thought he saw it on the other side of the kitchen. He raced through the living room, hitting the coffee table with his right shin this time, and went sprawling onto the floor. Paul got up, limping worse than before from the pain towards the kitchen.

The dark man kept chopping his way through the front door, trying to get inside. Paul made it to the back door and flung it open, running outside into the night. He ran a few yards away and turned to look back at the cottage. The sound of the dark man chopping his way through the front door while the woman in the robe upstairs screamed could still be heard in that quiet countryside, inside the painting. Paul was going to keep running, but the screams from the woman in the robe caused him to stop. He had to save her.

15

Paul, who never thought of himself as a brave man, became just that. He went back into the cottage through the open back door and stood inside the kitchen, looking across to the living room where the door was nearly gone. It would only take a few more swings from that ax to turn the trick, Paul figured. He looked around for some sort of weapon– something that he could use against the maniac who was trying to get inside. He rushed out of the kitchen and into the dining area.

Over by the fireplace, he saw something metal leaning up against the brick. It was a long fireplace poker. Paul ran over, grabbed it, and held it tightly in his hand. He marched back into the kitchen and through into the living room where he awaited the dark man to finally bust his way through. Paul steadied himself, ready to do battle. The final pieces of wood that held the front door together broke free, sending the fragments of wood flying into the living room.

The dark man had breached the front door and invited himself inside. Paul stood there against the burly dark man: he with his ax and Paul with his poker. Paul could not see any distinct features about the man standing before him in the doorway. All that he could see was just shadows swirling all around him. Paul's grip on the poker tightened even more.

"I could've had this done already if you hadn't been watching me," the dark man spoke in a gruff voice.

Paul did not respond. He was too scared. The dark man began to walk inside the home further as the woman in the robe screamed bloody murder from her upstairs locked bedroom. Paul raised the poker and swung in mid-air as a warning to the approaching man.

"Get back!" Paul demanded.

That act did not make the dark man pause. He kept walking slowly towards Paul, carrying his ax. Every step that the dark man took was a step that Paul backed away. He was scared beyond belief.

Paul took another hearty swing in mid-air. To this, the dark man laughed sinisterly. Paul, backing up, did not realize that the coffee table that he had nailed his shins against twice before would still be there and would be his undoing. Backing up and not taking his eyes off the dark man who was walking slowly towards him, Paul took one more step backward and tripped over the coffee table, landing on his back, the poker coming free from his hand. He tried to scramble the best he could to his feet, but before he could, the ax came down on him catching him in the chest flush.

Blood spewed upwards for just a moment and then poured out from his deep wound. His eyes were wide in terror as he lay on his back, struggling to catch his breath and struggling to stay alive. The dark man hovered over him and pulled the ax out from his chest. He raised it again while Paul tried in vain to crawl away on his back. Again, the ax fell on his chest, this time taking what little life Paul managed to cling to. He was dying and would be dead very soon.

The lady upstairs was still screaming as loudly as she could. The dark man pulled the ax out of Paul's chest, and he made his way up the stairs towards the screaming. It was what he came to the cottage, through the meadow to begin with: the woman. He slowly, rung by rung, walked up the stairs, her screams getting louder. It was as if she knew that he was coming, knew that her doom was near.

In the hallway, three doors were closed: two on the right and one on the left. The one on the left was where the woman was. He tried the doorknob to the one on the left, and just as he expected, it was locked. So, just as he did with the front door, he stood back, raised his ax, and began to chop his way through as the woman in the robe screamed for help.

Out in the country, especially as far out as she lived, no one could hear her screams. The dark man chopped, chopped, and chopped his way through the wooden door until he was inside. The woman was crouched down in a corner, screaming and begging for her life as the dark man slowly walked over to her from around the bed.

16

Sandra had finally made it back from her art gallery speaking engagement in NYC on Halloween. Instead of going straight home, she had her Uber take her to Paul's place. She paid the man that rainy Halloween late afternoon and walked up the walkway to Paul's house as the Uber pulled away. She had tried messaging and calling Paul, but no answer.

His car was still parked in the driveway and Sandra did not know if that was a good sign or not. She did not inspect the front of the car at the moment, just saw it from the back. Thoughts, crazy ones, danced throughout her mind as she walked up on his front porch to knock on his door: *What if he's dead in there? What if he had a heart attack and died in his sleep? What if he was killed in a home invasion?* All these thoughts flooded her mind as she rapped on his door several times. No answer. Then, she wondered if Paul stayed true to his routines.

Back when they were dating, Paul used to put a front door key deep in the dirt of his flower pot. He was always locking up his keys inside the house and numerous times, more than Sandra could count, she would have to come with her spare that he had given her and unlock the front door. She told him to hide a key somewhere he would know where to look. He decided inside the dirt of the flower pot next to the front door would be a good idea. Sandra looked at the flower pot, and the dirt had turned to mud from the rain. She made a gross face and stuck her hand down into it. It was wet, slimy, and oh, how she hated sticking her hand in there. But it had to be done. She moved her fingers around and went deeper into the mud. Finally, her fingers touched something that was metal. It was the key.

She pulled the muddy front door key from the flower pot and gave it a good wipe on her jacket sleeve, which she did not want to do, either. Sandra stuck the key into the doorknob and twisted it, unlocking the front door. She slowly pushed it open and peered inside. All was quiet.

"Paul?!" Sandra shouted, walking inside the living room.

Her shoes crunched some broken pieces of plastic from the camera he smashed a while back. The gaming chair he had thrown was still where it was against the wall. Over on the other side of the room, on the wall, was a hole, like someone had punched through it. Sandra began to wonder, *What if Paul was the victim of a break-in, OR did he just finally snap?*

"Paul?! It's me...Sandra!" She kept walking slowly through the living room and then into the kitchen.

She checked one of the bedrooms that he used as an office and then another bedroom where the rowing machine was. No sign of life in either room. Sandra walked into Paul's bedroom. The bed was unmade but that was typical of her ex-boyfriend.

Sandra checked the bathroom, and the utility room next, and even went out the back door and into the shed in the backyard...nothing. She also made sure that he was not in the car slumped over. All clear there, too, although she did see that the car had been in an accident at some point. *That's concerning*, she thought.

Sandra went back into the house and stood in the living room. It was then that she was scared that something awful had happened to Paul. She pulled her phone from her pocket and dialed 9-1-1. After she gave the address and what was going on to the dispatcher, who said the police would be there shortly, Sandra ended the call and looked around the living room. Then, something caught her eye...

There was a painting hanging on the wall next to Paul's TV. It looked like her painting, but there was something different about it...something not right. She walked closer to it, not taking her eyes away from it. It was her painting all right...but it was different. *A Night in the Meadow* had turned into *A Day in the Meadow*. Where the full moon was, was now a bright yellow sun. The landscape that was silvery and shadowy was now bright and vibrant. The creek off to the side seemed to glisten in the sunlight. The grass of the field was deep green and soft. Something else odd, something strange...

Sandra got closer to the painting and looked deeper into the canvas, specifically at the cottage. It looked to her that the front door of the cottage had been broken to pieces.

"What the hell is going on here?" Sandra asked no one as she stood back looking at the painting, puzzled.

LIKE A ROCKET

I first discovered Bob Darnell and his friends back in 1988. He was a man who lived in a single-wide trailer at the end of Jeralds Street back in my hometown when I was a kid. He and his wife, Faye, were two of the nicest people I had ever met. I had lived on that street ten years before our paths crossed on that hot day in late July. I had always seen him outside, sitting on his front porch and watching the late afternoon traffic go to and fro. When I would ride my bike past his house, he and his wife would tip a wave, and I would return. Every time I saw them, she would always be in a housedress, and Bob would always wear a white tank top with blue jeans. I don't think they ever changed clothes.

I never stopped over there to speak to them. I was only ten and stayed away from people that I didn't know. When I asked my dad about Bob, he told me he was a good guy.

"How long has he lived in that trailer at the end of the street?" I asked my dad.

Dad tipped his Braves cap up in a state of thinking while he and I were working on his brown Dodge. I say "we," but I was just handing Dad tools. He was the one working on it.

"Well, let's see here...I'd say about a good twenty-five, maybe thirty years." I nodded and thought that was a long time– ancient times for a kid like me to wonder about.

"Why you asking?" Dad asked.

"No reason," I replied. "I always see them out sitting on the front porch, and they wave and I wave back."

Dad ducked underneath his car hood and tightened whatever he was tightening.

"Yeah? You should go over there and sit a spell with him and Faye. Good people. I tell you what, he can tell some of the best stories. Him, J.M. Casteel, and Walt Bain hold court over there usually on Friday evenings."

"Hold court?"

Dad grinned as he rose up from the hood and snuck a look at me, "It's a term about a group of people gathered together talking. They tell stories over there. Some of the best ones I've ever heard."

"You've been?"

"Well, yeah, I've been a time or two. It's been a long time since the last time, I reckon. But man, can those old men tell the stories. Thousands of them, I bet," Dad told me as he slammed the car hood shut.

***

A few days after helping Dad with his car, me and J.J. took off on our bikes all over town and in the county scanning the ditches for soda cans. We wanted money to buy some comic books, and collecting cans in trash bags that we brought along with us always helped get us the newest copies of *Batman* or *Green Lantern*. Sometimes with that money we got from the cans—which wasn't much by no means—we paired it up with our weekly allowances that we had gotten from our parents. It was always enough to buy a us a comic book, a candy bar, and a Coke from Wilson's Drugstore.

That day we were out, me and J.J. had collected four big trash bags, full of tossed soda and beer cans. It was the most we'd ever gotten on a ride. We rode our bikes in the country, way beyond the city limits. It was hard for us to pedal up hills while carrying those bags of cans, which were heavy, to say the least. Sometimes, we'd have to get off our bikes and walk them up the steep hills, heading for home.

When we got back into town, we went to Jack Rutherford's house. He was the fella who always took old scrap metal and cans from anyone and everyone. We had been doing business with him since last year when me and J.J. started doing the can collection. Jack was a rough man, not talkative at all, and stood about six-five and burly. We would ride our bikes into his place, and usually he was outside at his truck, talking. Transactions were him taking our bags, holding them, and giving us his best guess on how much they weighed. We had no idea if he was accurate. For all we knew, he could've been ripping us off. But we usually managed on average six dollars. For a kid back then, six dollars was a financial boon.

Me and J.J. cruised into Jack's backyard where the action was always going on, and for the first time, we didn't see Jack outside. We called out for him and nothing. I laid my bags down, went to the back door, and knocked. I heard the footfalls of someone inside— too light on their feet to be Jack. A woman answered the door, and I could tell she had been crying; eyes were red as fire, and she looked as if she had not slept in days. I had only seen his wife a few times, and she always looked kept up, but not that day. That day she looked worn down.

"Is Jack here? We got some cans to bring him."

I could see tears forming in her eyes, and she managed to tell me that Jack had been in the hospital sick last couple of weeks.

"He had a heart attack and ain't doing too well," she told me as her voice was starting to crack.

I was stunned by the news. I was only ten, but I knew what a heart attack meant. My grandpa had one of those back when I was eight, and I saw how my dad dealt with it. I knew Jack's was probably serious business.

"You boys can take them cans to Bob Darnell's house. He's doing cans now." She tried to smile the best she could, and that was that. She closed the door, and I looked over at J.J.

"Who's this Bob guy? You know him?" J.J. asked, sitting on his bike with his bags of cans on the ground.

"He lives down the street from me. Dad says he's a good guy. Come on, let's go."

***

We drove to the end of Jeralds Street and to the single-wide trailer that was nestled in between two houses: a brick one and a two-story farmhouse that was owned by Bobby Milton, the town mayor. We parked our bikes on the front lawn of Bob's place. I got off to walk up the porch stairs to the front door. The front door was open, but the screen door was closed. I knocked on it, causing the wooden frame to vibrate. No one answered, but I could hear faint country music playing in the background. So I knocked again, louder this time. That knock did the trick as a woman who I would come to know as Faye, his wife, came walking out of a room to the left and called out.

"Who is it?" she asked.

"Hey!" I replied as friendly of a 'hey' as I could. "I'm Joey Powers from down the street. You might know my dad, Randy?"

Faye came into my view and to the screen door with a smile, "Why, yes I do, young man! I've seen you zooming by here on that bike of yours a million times, I bet! You better be careful on this street; sometimes cars come flying so fast down here– why, me and Bobby can't even tell what color they were when they went by! What can I do for you, son?"

"Me and my friend over there got some cans, and we were going to take them to Jake Rutherford's house, but his..."

Faye nodded telling me that she already knew, "We've been taking cans and other such things from people– been keeping Bobby busy lately. You boys go on to the backyard. He'll be out there."

I thanked Faye and walked off the porch. I told J.J. that we needed to go over to the backyard.

We left our bikes and carried our four bags of cans around the edge of the trailer and into the backyard. There were all kinds of metal back there, undoubtedly from what Jack wasn't able to take anymore. Looking at the sprawl in that smallish backyard, I wondered to myself how much more this yard could hold– not much by the looks of it.

Me and J.J. kept walking in silence until he heard a loud bang of metal. It sounded like a .22 going off. We both jumped, and J.J. screamed with fright.

"Who's over there?" a voice from the side of a shed hollered.

"Joey Powers...from down the street!" I yelled.

"Randy's boy?!"

"That's me!" I shouted from a distance.

"Well, all right then! Come on over!"

Me and J.J. both looked at each other in relief. What were we afraid of? I haven't the foggiest– didn't know then or now. We walked with our bags of cans rattling around and when we turned the corner of the white shed, there sat Bobby: white tank top, blue jeans, and a Braves hat on like me.

He sat on two brown milk crates from Mayfield's Dairy Farms and had an ax in his hands. The loud bang we heard was that blunt side of the ax coming down on top of a can that sat on a large tree stump; that's how Bob crushed his cans: a stump, an ax, and milk crates to sit on.

"We took these cans over to Jack's but…"

Just like Faye, he nodded that he already knew, "Yeah, just sit them over there."

Mine and J.J.'s eyes followed Bob's pointed finger and to our surprise, we saw a slew of bags filled plum full of cans, just like ours.

"That's a lot of cans," J.J. remarked.

"Yeah, it's a lot all right. Keeps me busy though. How much does Jack give you boys?"

"Usually about six dollars," I replied.

Bob sat there on his stack of milk crates and pondered for a few seconds, "I'll give you eight. Jack likes to lowball people too much. Eight sound good to you boys?"

We both nodded and smiled. Turns out that Jack *was* ripping us off.

"Usually Seaton's gives me about seven cents a can. And I figure I can pay about half that with people who bring me cans. Ain't no sense of trying to rip people off, you know? Plus, I'm retired, and I don't need the money, really. The money I'm making off the cans puts gas in my mower and trimmer." Bob laughed, and we laughed. I'm not sure what was even funny but hey, when in Rome.

I liked Bob already. He had a calming demeanor about him, a soothing way his words came from his mouth. He wasn't like Jack, that's for sure.

"Well thank you for the extra money," I told him.

Bob nodded, "Ain't no problem. How's your daddy doing?"

"He's all right. Been working a lot lately."

"What about you? What's your name?"

J.J. told him his first and last.

"Green? Any kin to Delbert Green? Any of the Greens on the west side of town?"

J.J. said that he didn't know, but maybe.

"Well if you are, let me tell you, Delbert Green is about my age and when we were little kids, we used to go down to this old house out on County Road 17. Now that house was so rundown, rats wouldn't even live in it. Three stories, used to be owned by David Peters. That family name used to mean something around here; don't anymore, but used to.

"Anyways, me and Delbert are hanging around that house feeling like grown-ups for whatever reason, and Delbert gets this idea about breaking in the house. I wasn't sure about it because it didn't feel right, you know? Anyways, Delbert talked me into it, and we walked up the porch and to the front door. That porch, you could feel it about to give way any moment, it was so rotten.

"Delbert tried the doorknob and of course, it was locked. So, what did we do? We both started kicking it in. Eventually, we busted the door open, and in walks Delbert first. As soon as he walks in that house, he falls through the floor and down into the basement." Delbert started laughing so hard, gave such a cackle, I've never heard anything like it before or since coming from a man. His laugh made me and J.J. laugh.

"I thought the damn fool broke his legs!" Bob said through his laughter.

"Did he?" I asked.

Wiping tears from his eyes, Bob shook his head, "Nah, just got the wind knocked out of him, is all. Got bruised pretty bad, but nothing in the way of broken bones. God, I can still see him falling through the floor that day like it just happened. Well, boys, I hate to talk and run; but Faye is supposed to be making me lunch, and I'm starving. You two get any more cans, you just swing them by here. Oh, and before I forget, here's that eight dollars."

Bob got up from the stack of milk crates with a groan and straightened his back out. He pulled out a five and three ones and handed it to me.

"Ya'll come back one day and sit a spell. And Joey, tell your daddy I said hey, would you?" I told him that I would. We told him goodbye and walked away as he disappeared into his trailer for lunch. In the few minutes I met Bob, I knew that he was a good, honest soul. He didn't talk to me and J.J. like kids, and that's what made me like him even more. He treated us like...old friends.

***

Sure enough, the Friday after we first met Bob, I was riding my bike down the streets of Claxton. I was heading home that hot July evening around nine from playing baseball with my friends down at the park. As I was riding, heading for home on Niota Road, I saw a group of men sitting on Bob's front porch holding court, as Dad said. As I got closer, the more in focus they all became. You could hear them a block away laughing. I pedaled a little faster towards Bob's house and made a decision to stop in for a spell; maybe listen to these stories being told.

At first, I was intimidated by just rolling up into his front yard and hopping up on the porch to sit on the edge of it. The closer I got, the more I was afraid, for some reason. I had decided last minute to make the turn to the right and go down Jeralds Street and go home. But the men's laughter made me want to be a part of what they were talking about. All I wanted to do was listen. So, I slowed down in front of Bob's house and cruised on into his driveway. The men kept talking, like they didn't mind me being there. I laid my bike down in the yard and sheepishly waved to Bob and the rest of the guys, who didn't miss a beat with their talking. They smiled and politely waved back at me.

Bob was sitting in his rocking chair and a large, blue cooler sat beside him. Beside him: was Walt Bain, his neighbor from across the street; J.M. Casteel on the other side of the street, sitting in a chair at the edge of the porch facing Bob and Walt; and Johnny Cook, who lived on the other side of Bobby Milton, sitting on the opposite side of J.M.

I smiled and sat down on the edge of the porch, taking my place.

"Hey, Joey! Want a Pepsi? They're cold!" Bob offered. I nodded my head, and he reached in, got one, and tossed me a can. It felt good on my sweaty hand.

"That'll be ten dollars, young man! Regan's in office! Everything is high right now!" Johnny said, laughing.

I just smiled as I popped the top. The old men asked who I was and before I could introduce myself, Bob told them for me. They nodded and told me what a good guy my dad was. I agreed with them. He was the best. I sat, drinking my cold Pepsi and relaxed some, listening to the old men get back to their storytelling. What they were talking about I hadn't a clue because I walked up on them mid-story.

"Well," J.M. said, getting back to his story, "I never played cards with him again. No, sir!" The men all laughed.

"I tell you, a son-of-a-bitch that would cheat you every which way but loose was Bert Meany."

The men all nodded and agreed with Johnny.

"I saw him one time down at the junkyard sell a man a car that didn't even have fifth or sixth gear in the transmission. He had no problems selling people junk and taking their money. The bitch of the bunch was that if you called him on it, he'd pull a gun on you..," Johnny said.

"Well, hell," Bob said, interjecting quickly because once Johnny got going it was hard to get him to stop talking. "He pulled a gun on Jessie Cantor when he had that tractor he bought off him towed to his junkyard. I remember Jessie telling me that Bert aimed to shoot him right there, and over what? A bum tractor that Bert rigged up good enough to start so he could sell it?"

"I bet ol' Jessie didn't get his money back neither," Walt said.

Bob shook his head, "You know he didn't. Eventually, people stopped dealing with Bert. He wasn't going to make any money doing people the way he was doing. Small towns talk."

I took another swig of cold Pepsi and pieced together that the subject they were discussing before I interrupted them was about cheaters; and more notorious than the man they were talking about before I got there named Bert Meany, one who I had never heard of before. I was pretty sure that I never heard Dad mention his name. He could've been dead for all I knew. Just then, a car whizzed by so fast, none of us even saw it as it went by. That sparked another story between the old men.

"People fly down this road," Walt said, stating something I was quite sure they had said at least once while holding court on Fridays.

"Ol' Punk Davis used to drive fast, didn't he?" Bob said rhetorically. They each agreed. I giggled at the name Punk. I had never heard anyone named that before. It was comical to me. I asked Bob years later what Punk Davis' real name was. He told me that it was Stephen. How they got Punk from that he didn't even know.

"He had that '58 Plymouth Fury, and that thing would fly."

"It wasn't a Plymouth Fury," Johnny said. "It was that '56 Thunderbird that had the V-8 in it. Remember? He crashed it that night of the high school prom down on 232. God, I remember responding to that wreck that night. Killed all three of them: Punk, Cindy Howser, and Bobby Blaine. Just kids about to graduate high school."

"I remember hearing some fellas telling Punk's dad down at the hardware store one Saturday that he bought his son too much of a car starting out," Walt recalled.

Bob threw up a passive hand and waved that off, "Ah, you know how Dennis was. He had money and liked to flaunt it around. But I know he regretted buying him that car. Hell, he was never the same. Neither was Nancy."

"These young people got to learn not to drive so damn fast," Johnny looked over at me, "You remember that story, son. You get old enough to drive, slow it down, or you'll end up like ol' Punk and his friends did." I nodded and told him that I would.

Those old men sat around and talked about cars for another good hour or so. My dad would've loved being there, listening to all the stories. They talked about racing down Highway 39, which they warned me not to ever do. They talked about who had the fastest cars between them all, and they told me never to buy a fast car because I'd want to drive it fast.

They got into a heated discussion right before I left, just as it was getting dark, about who had the best football season at Central High: the 1946 team or the 1947 team that won the only state championship. I figured out through all their stories that night they had grown up together, gone to the same school, and played on the same football team while in high school. They were lifelong friends and used those Friday nights to regale themselves with memories of a time that was nearly forgotten.

The only thing that kept it current and somewhat relevant was that they remembered it all, or at least to the best of their abilities. Which was fine with me, I had no idea if they were remembering it wrong or not. I wasn't there, and they were. And if one of them misremembered something, the other three would quickly correct it.

I told them that I needed to get home and thanked Bob for the Pepsi, handing him the empty can.

"Come back and see us next Friday, Joey. We'll be here," J.M. said to me.

I smiled and told them I'd be back next week. I jumped off the front porch and got on my bike and pedaled away. Before I got too far, I could hear them hollering and laughing down the street some. I wanted to turn around and stay until they all went home for the evening, but staying out too late would surely get me grounded. No kid wants that, especially during the summertime.

***

I sat on the porch, right there on the edge, listening to the same cast the following Friday night. I was drinking a Pepsi given to me by Bob while they were discussing health problems. One thing that I figured out way before hanging out at Bob's on Friday nights was that older people loved talking about their ailments. Why? I don't know. It's right up there with them talking about the weather.

"Ever since I got out of bed the other morning, my knee has been giving me fits," Walt told them, actually stretching out his leg and rubbing it for them to see that he was telling the truth. *How would they know*, I sat and wondered. That thought made me giggle a little bit, but not enough for Walt to hear me.

"Probably Arthur letting you know he's still around," Bob replied. I had heard them speak about Arthur briefly last Friday and wondered who he was, or for that matter, what it was. I didn't ask them. I tried to figure it out on my own. I eventually asked my dad, and he told me what it was: arthritis.

"It's all those years pouring concrete. Up and down on ladders. Bending down, raising up. Son," Walt looked over to me, "don't have a job like I did. Go get you a good job with minimum labor."

"But just enough to keep you in some kind of shape that's not round," J.M. said, leaning over and smacking Johnny's bloated stomach.

The men howled with laughter, and I did too. Those guys did that to each other. They would cut on each other and all have a good laugh about it. I guess as long as they had been friends, they earned the right to say whatever they wanted to about the other. I had friends like that with J.J., Alton Downs, and Raymond Price. We would go camping out in my backyard, and we would cut on each other and our moms. Nothing was funnier than a good mom joke. I could tell these guys had a secret language between the four of them. I guess they should've considered how many years they were friends. That Friday night I chimed in and asked that very question.

"How long have you guys known each other?"

"Too damn long," J.M. said, laughing.

"You ain't kidding about that. Seriously though...what? Fifty years? Met ol' Walt there back in '34 or '35, I reckon, when we were ten. J.M. and Johnny came a little bit afterward," Bob tried to recall to the best of his knowledge.

"Sounds about right," Johnny said. "Met right over there at Kirby's Farm. Damn, it was hot, remember?"

"Hell, Johnny, every summer is hot," J.M. said.

"We all worked in that field, throwing them hay bales for old man Kirby for basically nothing. I think we did it for bushels of corn to take home, if I ain't mistaken. Hell, everybody was hurting back then. People weren't out of the Depression yet. It was bad around here, growing up," Johnny said.

"Yup, you kids got it made compared to what he had it at your age. But you're supposed to have it better. Every generation needs to make sure that the next one ahead of them has it better than the last," Bob articulated thoughtfully. The others nodded in agreement.

"When did things get better for us, you think?" Walt asked, keeping his bum leg stretched out.

"I'd say around 1950 maybe? When did you come home from Korea?" Bob asked Walt.

"Well, I enlisted in the spring of 1950...got sent over there in the summer of '50. I think I came home around fall of '51, I want to say."

"By the time you got back home," J.M. began, "we had all gotten married and found work."

"Didn't you start at Eureka Textile out of high school?" Bob asked J.M.

"Yeah, hired me right on the spot. Seventy-five cents an hour. Was forty until the government raised it," he told us.

"You went there, and I went and worked at Miller's sawmill. Eventually, he brought me on the crew. You see, I built houses for a living," Johnny remembered and then looked over at me to tell me what he did.

"Bob, what did you do?" I asked.

"I was a bagboy and shelf stocker over at Ed's Grocery that used to be in town. You know where Tape City is now? Well, back then, it used to be Ed's Grocery. I worked there for a year or so when I graduated high school until I figured out what kind of trade I wanted to get into. Went to trade school and learned how to be an electrician. Wired up all the houses that Johnny helped build. Hell, did that until I retired. We all stayed at our jobs until he aged out, didn't we?"

The other old men nodded and grunted in response.

Sitting there listening to them talk some more about their jobs and listening to Walt talk about his stint in the war, I was just mystified by the four old men that I was listening to. They were an ocean of stories, and I was fortunate to be there, a willing audience member, probably something they had never had before. Let's be honest, how many kids my age wanted to spend their free time around a bunch of old geezers? My friends couldn't have cared less and made fun of me to some degree about spending my Friday evenings on Bob's front porch, but I didn't care. I loved the way they talked, cussed, carried on with each other. I loved hearing the stories, the antidotes, the way they would look at me and tell me to not do what they did. It was as if they were giving me a blueprint of sorts on how to be successful.

As the night closed in, I noticed on my watch that it was later than the Friday before when I left. I was leaving a lot later than last time, and that was a good thing. I told them goodbye and hopped off the front porch. I got my bike and pedaled home, thinking about what it was like to live back then and what the town I called home must've looked like in comparison to the current time. It was crazy to know that Tape City, a place where me and my friends would go in and buy tapes and used records, used to be a grocery store. I would've never thought it in a million years. I couldn't wait to go home and tell my parents about that nugget of information I received. I wondered as I turned into my front yard if they would be as shocked as I was.

I got off my bike and took a look down the street, towards the end of Jeralds Street where Bob lived, and couldn't see a damn thing. I wondered if the old men were still sitting there, talking in the night. I also wondered how long they sat out there and talked. Did they talk into the wee hours? Most importantly, did they ever run out of anything to talk about? I doubt it, really. Those guys loved to talk and had a million stories, I bet. I couldn't wait until next Friday so I could sit there and hear what kind of idle conversation they would get into.

***

The next Friday I showed up, one of the members of Bob's court was gone forever. When I got there, the three of them were sitting in their usual spots, but Walt's chair was empty. I could tell right away when I pulled into his front yard and lept on the front porch that something was wrong. The past two Fridays I had arrived they had been in mid-conversation, and Bob opened the cooler and tossed me a Pepsi. Not this time. The cooler was missing and so was Walt.

I sat down in my usual spot and could feel the energy– or I guess, lack thereof– had been zapped from the three old men. Bob said hello while J.M. and Johnny kinda tipped me a wave. I knew something was wrong but wondered to myself if I should ask. I decided that I was just going to sit there and not say a word; that I would piece together what was going on as I did for most of their conversations and stories, where I had no idea who the people were or from what time period they were talking about. Turns out, I didn't have to wait very long to figure out what happened.

"Joey, I don't know if your daddy knew, but Walt died yesterday morning," Bob said heavily.

That hit me like a ton of bricks falling from the sky. Walt– the old man from the war, the man who liked to laugh, who told stories like nobody's business– was dead. He was the first person in my life that I had ever known to die. I looked over at his empty chair and felt a hollowness all of a sudden. I could feel the others' pain. I didn't have years and history with Walt, but I could tell he was a good man, an honest man as the day was long. I also could pick up that the old men were shocked and grieving. I wondered sitting on the porch if I should pick up and go home, maybe see what J.J. was doing. Suddenly, I was feeling very out of place being there.

"I don't think he knew," I simply replied. "What happened?" I was hoping that wasn't a dumb question to ask and instantly regretted it as it tumbled from my mouth.

"We're thinking a heart attack," J.M. said. "Wife found him in the bathroom. She heard a loud bang and went to check on him...he was on the floor and..." J.M. didn't finish. He didn't have to. I got the picture.

For the first time, I saw Johhny Cook dig into his shirt pocket and pull a cigarette with a lighter. He lit the stick and puffed on it, blowing gray smoke into the air.

"Man had been through a war and a bad car wreck that killed everyone else in the car, but him to go out like he did? Damn shame."

"His doctor gave him a clean bill of health just two months ago, he told me," Bob said.

"Yeah, well that don't mean anything, does it? When it's your time, it's your time," J.M. said.

"You remember Kittybrew Dixon? Hell, he died while out mowing his yard just down the road here. I was driving down the street and saw him out mowing, and I stopped in to talk to him. He seemed fine. His wife told me at the funeral home a few days later that after I drove off– and I was only there five minutes, didn't even get out of my car– that he fell in the yard deader than a hammer right after I left. Boys, we just never know," Bob told us.

J.M. and Johnny nodded, and I nodded too, just trying to fit in. Not that they were paying any attention to me. I was the furthest thing from their minds at the moment. And rightly so.

"I hate it for Alma and the kids. Walt and them kids were close. So was him and Alma. How she doing?" J.M. asked.

Bob shook his head, "Good as can be, considering. Faye went over there to check in on her...said that she's still in shock. Hell, ain't we all?" Again, J.M. and Johnny nodded.

I did again because I was shocked about the news that the man who sat in that now empty chair was dead.

"You remember that time that he was over at the house, helping me put that roof on my barn? He was up there walking around to see how much of it needed replacing, and he stepped through a rotten piece and down he went right into the hay loft. Boy, he was cussing up a storm," Johnny said, making the others laugh.

"I do remember that," Bob said. "What about the time that he was cutting that piece of paneling? He decided that he was going to do it real quick like and didn't put it on the saw horses. He angled it up on the edge of the tailgate of his truck and was holding it underneath. Well, he got the circular saw and started cutting a straight line, not any more than a foot he had to trim off, he said, and he sawed right over his fingers that were holding it underneath. Blood was everywhere. His first three fingers were hanging on by strings. He's lucky that the doc was able to sew them back on. But he never had any feeling in them after that."

After five minutes or so of reflecting in silence, J.M. spoke: "He was one of the best men I ever knew. Give you the shirt off his back, the last dollar he had. He told me one time about finding this wallet lying in the parking lot of Wilson's Drugstore. He bent down to pick it up, and there was something like two hundred dollars in it. And you know that his family could've used it back then. What does he do? He takes it back inside to Wilson's and gives it to the pharmacist. Other men around here probably would have taken some for themselves or the whole damn thing. No...Walt was an American original."

"Boy, I tell you," Bob started, "him being gone makes you think, don't it? Like how fragile life is. Here one day, gone the next. Even in youth, we are in death."

Bob looked over at me and to be honest, that scared me. Was he saying that I could die? I was too young, right? That bothered me the rest of the night. I couldn't sleep, just tossed and turned and thought wildly if I was going to die. But as the days went on, that worry evaporated, much like things do when you're little.

***

I stayed away from Bob's for a few weeks after the news of Walt's death. I didn't even drive to the end of Jeralds Street. I steered clear when me and J.J. were out and about on our bikes. The summer was winding down, and school was approaching much too fast for me. I still shot glances down the street on those Friday nights and could see them all on the front porch. I wanted to go over there so badly but chose not to. I wanted the freshness of Walt's death to ease some. Knowing someone who had died gave me the willies, and me and Dad talked about that some. He put my mind at ease and told me the biggest lie ever:

"Son, you're too young to die. So don't worry about it."

I know now that was a complete lie, but back then, being young, I took him at his word. I never knew of my dad lying to me. Also, I had never heard of a kid my age or younger dying, so in my mind, it made sense to me. After hearing him tell me that, it did put me at ease. When

Freddy Downey, a kid in our town was run over and killed several years later, I knew that my dad had lied about little kids not dying. Of course, I was much older then and knew that my dad told me that to calm my mind down all those years ago.

August came, and so did school. I hated school mostly because I struggled with the classes so much. Learning seemed to come easier to most of the kids, but for me, it was like I was running uphill. My mom had enrolled me in after school tutoring in math, but like in my daily math class, it went over my head. I tried– I really did– and I still couldn't be the student I wanted to be. I remember being jealous of those other kids, the smart ones, who could raise their hands in class and answer correctly what the teacher was asking. I wanted to be one of those kids, not just in math class, but in all my classes. I wanted to be looked at by the other kids in a green shade of jealousy. As my school career went on until I graduated high school, I was at best a below-average student. "Sometimes, you have to work with what you got," I heard my dad say throughout my life. I wonder where he heard it?

***

I went to Bob's place that Friday earlier than normal. It was around six, and they were already gathered—the three of them—on the front porch. The first week of school was in the books, and I was happy about that. I dropped my bike in his front yard and hopped up on the front porch. Unlike last time, back when Walt's death was still new, Bob opened the cooler that was back and tossed me a Pepsi can. It was cold, wet from the ice.

"Set up in Walt's old chair. You ain't no dog," Bob invited.

I slowly got up and looked at J.M. and Johnny, and they didn't seem to mind. Taking my seat in that chair felt weird at first, I got to say. I was like I was one of them, a kid of ten, sitting there swapping stories with the old-timers. I leaned back and popped my Pepsi tab and took a deep swig. It felt good going down.

"How's school going, young man?" Johnny asked me.

I nodded, "About the same I guess. First week back."

"You know, I always hated school. Never liked it," J.M. replied.

"That's because you can't read or write," Bob said, laughing loudly.

"Oh, I can read, thank you very much. Joey, don't let that man tell you a lie about me. I can read just fine. Write, too. But nah, I never liked school. But...I had to go."

"I can't wait til I ain't got to go no more," I declared.

"You'll be graduated in no time, son. Believe that. Life goes by in a flash. Especially the older you get, the more time flies. Hell, it feels like I was in my thirties just a few weeks ago. Now, look at me." Johnny said.

"Yeah, you look like shit," Bob said, laughing again.

"Somebody's salty this evening. Faye not doing her wifely duties?" J.M. said.

"Not in front of the kid," Bob said, laughing again. That made me smile because they were smiling. I had no idea what in the hell they were talking about.

"Best Braves baseball player you ever saw?" J.M. asked the court.

Bob sat there and considered for a moment, "Eddie Mathews, hands down. Man could do it all: hit, throw, run– you name it."

"Mine is Henry Arraon. Better than Mays by far," J.M. said.

"I'd have to say Warren Spahn for me," Johnny said.

"Joey?" Bob asked. "What say you?"

I was a big baseball fan, still am, and the Braves were and still are my team. Back then, I was enamored with Dale Murphy. Every time he came up to bat, I would stand there and just be in awe at how he walked up to the plate and swung the bat. I would go outside and emulate his batting stance and swing. When I played Little League, I wore his number three and tried to be like my hero out there on the diamond.

"Murphy."

The old men all nodded, "Yeah, he's a good one. Won two MVP awards in '82 and '83. Got a great swing." J.M. said.

We all sat there on Bob's front porch and talked baseball, past and present, for hours. I joined in on the conversation quite a bit that day, a first for me. Walt's name came up a few times, and the men, I could tell, were still missing their friend. Hell, I missed him and only had met him a few times. Bob got up from his chair, cutting our time shorter than normal. Matter of fact, it was still daylight.

"Boys I hate to run ya'll off, but Faye and me got to go to a tent revival tonight over in Pikeville."

"Yeah," J.M. said, easing himself out of his chair with Johnny doing the same, "I got to be heading out, too. Claire is cooking a mess of chicken and dumplings this evening."

I got up and stretched, and all of us said our goodbyes. I hopped on my bike and not wanting to go home at that moment, I rode down the street to nowhere in particular. J.J. was out of town for the weekend, visiting his aunt and uncle in South Carolina, so that left me pretty much wide open all weekend. What was I going to do? I had no idea. But at that moment, I was feeling the wind of the August evening lick my sweaty skin.

***

A few weeks had passed by since the last time I was at Bob's hanging out with the old men, listening to them talk about nothing much at all. Usually, that was all it was, just talking about whatever came to mind. Sometimes it was about cars, sometimes about sports, women, the weather, and stories from days gone by. I liked sitting there listening to them for whatever reason. Mom had asked me why I liked going over there so much, and I told her I had no idea. But it was cool to sit there and listen and hear them laugh. Maybe it was because I felt like I was one of them. They didn't seem to mind at all that I was a kid, and that made it more special to me.

It was September, the middle part, when I came coasting into Bob's backyard with a bag full of empty soda cans. J.J., who had usually been my helper on such excursions, was no longer with me. He and his family had moved away to the nearby town of Etowah. We talked on the phone here and there, and I would come over and spend the night with him on Fridays. He'd do the same with me on Saturdays. Not having him to hang out with after school sucked for sure, but like any kid my age back then, I had to adapt to the new normal. I started playing with other kids from school. That was fine because they were good kids, and we all had the same interests.

I had ridden my bike to my usual places out in the county with the huge trash bag tied around my handlebar grip. I would ride slowly along the sides of those old country roads, looking for cans. Mostly what I found out there, even back when J.J. was with me, were beer cans. Once, on a dare, we found a beer can that had some left in it. You could still smell the alcohol. I dared J.J. to take a sip of it. With some hesitation, he did it, and I can still to this day recall the look on his twisted face as he spat it out and gagged. I laughed so hard.

He wanted me to do it, but I said, "Not after what happened to you I won't!"

Bob was sitting on his milk crate stack, smashing cans with the blunt side of his ax on that tree stump. I could hear the cans being smashed flat all the way to the side street next to his backyard.

"Hey, Bob!" I said.

Bob turned around, sweat pouring down his face. He saw me and smiled, "Joey! Come on in here! Where you been, son?!" He was happy to see me.

"All over the place," I replied. "I got you some cans here."

Bob took the trash bag I handed him and sat it next to his pile of bags next to his stump. "Thank you, sir. Boy, it's sure hot today, ain't it?"

"It is. I've already sweat through my shirt."

"Where's your friend been? That Green boy?"

"Oh, he moved to Etowah. We don't get to see each other much anymore. I'll go over there on Fridays some and spend the night, or he'll come over and stay the night with me on Saturdays."

"Right," Bob said, "work it out the best you can. How's your parents doing? Everybody okay?"

I nodded, "Yeah I think so."

"How's school treating you?"

"Not bad. Still hate it, but it could be worse, I guess."

Bob smiled and laughed, "Son, it could always be worse– trust me on that one."

"How's the boys doing lately? I haven't been over here in a few weeks." I said that, thinking he hadn't noticed or something.

"Good, good so far," Bob said. "J.M. has been helping his son work on a tractor, and Johnny has been helping his wife get around lately. She took a fall a couple of weeks ago and done something to her knee. So he's been helping her get around. He hasn't been here in a bit either. But, that's life, they say."

There was some, for the first time, awkward silence between us in that backyard. It was like we ran out of things to say, and I didn't think that was possible for Bob, who always talked. But I finally broke the silence.

"Still missing Walt?" I said that before I could realize I had spoken it. I was a kid back then, and sometimes my mind didn't govern what my mouth said.

Bob dropped his head and looked in another direction. He let out a long sigh, "Yeah, I do. He was such a good friend of mine. Friends are easy to come by, but good ones, now that's not so easy. I had the pleasure of calling him friend fifty years, give or take a few. Been an adjustment. It's like I lost a brother."

"That's a long time."

"But, when you get old like us, kiddo, you just never know. I always said once you get past sixty, you're living on borrowed time. Walt up and dying made me start to think— hell, all of us— to think a little bit more about our mortality."

"Do you think you know when you're going to die, Bob?"

Bob shook his head thoughtfully, "I don't reckon I do. I don't think there's any real warning on when it comes, except right at that very moment when it's happening. I think then you know. Like when that happened to Walt. I gotta imagine he knew he was dying right then and there."

Some more of that awkward silence between us, me straddling my bike, and Bob sitting on his milk crates at the tree stump, sweat sliding down our faces and backs. I didn't know what to say after that so I just came up with whatever hit my mind.

"You guys going to be out on your porch Friday night?" I asked, finally breaking the tension.

"Yeah, God willing. Probably will be me and J.M. though. If you want, we'll be here. If not J.M., it can be me and you." Bob smiled.

I smiled back and told him that I'd see him later. I turned my back around and pedaled out of his backyard. Before I could reach the beginning of Jeralds Street to head for home, I could hear cans being smashed.

***

That following Friday, I didn't go to Bob's. I had forgotten that Claxton Elementary had a football game that evening and me and my friends, Jake Abernathy and Clyde Freeman, decided to go. Of course, we had to practically beg our moms to let us go without adult supervision. Luckily, the school was only two blocks away from my house, and I could walk there in under five minutes. Reluctantly, Mom let me go after she and Dad spoke to each other about it. Of course, I got the sermon to go right there and back; and if she drove down there and didn't see me, I would be grounded.

"Mom," I remember telling her, "I just turned eleven. I think I'll be okay."

"I don't care, things still happen in this world, Joey. But I mean it," she said, "straight there and straight back...nothing in between. You understand?" I nodded and hugged her. She was worried about me walking two blocks to a night football game and had she known where me and J.J. had rode our bikes to, she would have had a stroke.

Jake, Clyde, and myself went to that football game. We crawled underneath the fence at the school and walked on in, without anyone noticing us. We didn't pay like those other suckers. And why should we? There was a perfectly nice fence that was loose on the north end of the school. Not many kids knew about it. Thankfully for us, Jake did. We crawled under the fence and made our way to where the football field was. It was all lit up, and we could hear the crowd cheering. It was the biggest game of the year so far for the school. The three of us walked down the hill from the playground and around the end zone to where the bleachers were. It was so loud there that night I could barely hear Jake talking, and he was walking right beside me.

We made it to the end of the bleachers and looked up to see if there was a place for the three of us to sit. Nope. It was packed plum full. So we decided to stand there, talk, and watch the game. But honestly, we didn't watch the game as much as we talked. Eventually, a few of our classmates saw us standing over there and came over to talk. After a while, there was a consensus with the eight of us that the game was boring, and Jake proposed that we go up to the basketball court that was up on the hill and play a game.

"We don't have a ball," I said.

"My dad has one in the backseat of his car. I can go get it," Paul Sizemore said.

Paul was a kid in our grade who got picked on kinda hard back in those days. I felt sorry for him because that kid was a good guy, but the bullies, always present, seemed to hone in on him. Maybe it was because Paul was thin and weak and wore thick glasses.

"Yeah, that'll be awesome," Jake said. "We'll meet you up at the basketball court."

Paul rushed in the parking lot direction while me and the other six boys walked around the end zone and up the hill to the school's playground where the basketball court was. It wasn't well lit up there, but good enough from the lights of the football field. I figured that our eyes would adjust once we got used to the dimness. I was right.

Paul came back with his basketball, and we all played four on four. I took Paul as my teammate and you know what, that kid was really good. He was dribbling between his legs, hitting long shots, layups– you name it. And rebounding, he was a beast. I started calling him Charles Barkley after that night in the school hallways. He seemed to like that and would sheepishly smile when I would yell out, "Hey, yo, Barkley!" in the school. I had taken a shine to Paul that night and saw him in a much different light, dim as it was, up there on the basketball court.

The school's football team had two Friday night home games in a row and me and my friends, which included Paul, went to but never watched. We elected to go to the basketball court and play basketball. Sometimes we had enough to choose teams, and sometimes we just shot around, talking about what kids our age talked about. I remember at one of those night games being up there on the basketball court, waiting for my turn to shoot the ball, thinking while looking at my friends and wondering if Bob and his friends did stuff like this when they were young. They had a lifetime of memories together; most of them good from what I've heard them tell on his front porch. I thought at eleven that I had some good memories and hopefully more to go, years to add to my story. I laughed to myself thinking that one day I would be like Bob, sitting on my own front porch with my friends, talking, shooting the breeze, remembering times long gone by. I could see myself doing that one day.

***

It was the first Friday in October, and I hadn't been to Bob's in some time. It wasn't that it was getting old to me. I loved going over there and sitting and listening to them talk. But being a kid took precedence over that. I had friends who liked to come over and play Nintendo, play baseball down at the park, or even walk around in newly mowed hayfields. When the guys weren't available, I knew on Friday nights Bob and his friends would always be there swapping stories. With my friends each doing something different with other kids that particular night, I told Mom and Dad that I was heading over to Bob's for a bit.

"Be home before eight!" Mom yelled from the kitchen.

Fall was here, and it got darker much earlier now. I hated it. It meant that my outdoor time was cut much shorter. I got on my bike and rode up Jeralds Street and saw Bob sitting alone on his front porch. He had his cooler sitting beside him. I pulled into his front yard, dropped my bike, and hopped up on the porch like always.

"Hey, Bob!" I said with excitement.

"Hey, kiddo, get you a seat!" Bob reached into the cooler and grabbed me a Pepsi. It was a little nippy in the air that evening just before sunset, and the can was cold in my hand.

"Where you been lately?"

"Oh, you know, here and there. Been going to the football home games and stuff like that."

Bob nodded, "How they looking this year?"

I had no idea actually, so I just made something up, "Pretty good. Not bad. Seems to be a good team this year."

"Good. Central High has lost three in a row. I don't know what's wrong with those boys over there. But they better get it together soon. Time is running out for them to get into the playoffs."

"Where's J.M. and Johnny?" I asked, not popping the top of my can.

"Johnny is still with his wife. She still ain't getting around too good. J.M. has got the flu. Change in temperatures, I guess."

"Is it bad?" The reason I asked that was because I heard that when old people got the flu, it can be dangerous. At least that's what I had heard my dad tell my grandpa one time over the phone.

Bob sat there and thought about my question for a few moments before he spoke, "You know, I don't know. When you get our age, something small like the flu can turn into something worse. I hope not.

But you never know. I talked to him the other night, and he seemed to be doing better. But this time of year, we sit out here less and less because of the cooler temps. I won't be out here much longer in the weeks to come."

"Think it'll be cold this year?" I asked, sounding like one of them.

"Almanac seems to think so. But you can see all the birds on the ground, looking for food and the squirrels already running around like crazy looking for nuts. I'd say we're in for some cold temps, maybe even some snow."

I smiled at the prospect of snow. I had only seen it snow there in my town a couple of times, once when I was barely four, but somehow I remembered playing in it with Mom and Dad. The other time was when I was nine, just two years ago. There was something magical about the snow: playing in it, feeling it in your hands, the brightness of it when the sun reflected off it. And let's not forget the school closures. That was a bonus.

"Dad hates the snow," I said, laughing.

Bob nodded, "Yeah me, too. I reckon why is because adults still have to go to work while kids can take the day off from school. In some way, we're jealous of kids."

"Why?"

"Because being a kid is the greatest thing you can be. Take me for example: I'm old, I can't do what I used to do back when I was young. I go to bed around nine o'clock most nights. I can't eat what I used to without it backing up on me. I get tired more easily than I did when I was a kid. Why, when I was your age, I could go all night long with hardly any sleep. Could do that back in my thirties."

"When did it change?" I asked.

Bob sat back in thought about that question for a few moments, "I'd say when I hit mid-forties. That's when knee pain started to creep in. My back hurt a lot more after I finished playing golf. I didn't have as much energy. Man, I haven't swung a golf club in years, come to think of it. I used to be pretty damn good, you know; even won a few local tournaments around here."

"I didn't know you played golf."

Bob nodded, "Yup. Me, Johnny, J.M., and Walt used to play all the time after work down at Shady Oaks. Walt was damn good, too. He had a natural swing. And, boy, could he putt. I saw him one time sink a thirty-foot put, like it was nothing. Hell, one time we were out, Johnny hit a hole-in-one. Ask him about that the next time you see him. He loves telling that story."

Me and Bob sat on his porch, talking about golf right up until it got cooler and time for him to go inside. I had no idea about the sport and honestly, no clue what he was talking about. I tried to understand what terms like eagles and bogeys were. He showed me what slicing and hooking were. Bob even went inside and brought out his bag of golf clubs for me to look at. They were nice, clean. I held them in my hand and he showed me on his front porch before the sun bowed out for the day how to hold one.

I was also taught what the numbers on the clubs meant and that each club served a purpose. He was excited to talk about golf, and I could tell it used to be a passion of his until his body couldn't do it anymore. And I think that made him sad. But I could see that twinkle in his eyes when he spoke about it. It was the last time I got to sit with Bob and talk. Had I known that, I would've asked him a bunch of questions about life and how to do it right. There was much more I wanted to hear from them, much more that I wanted to learn. But that night in October was it.

Throughout that October, I hadn't seen Bob out on his porch. He did tell me that when the cooler temps came and it got darker more that he wouldn't be outside unless it was warm and pretty. That October I remember it rained a lot and was cold. That Halloween, me, Clyde, Jake, and Paul went trick-or-treating, and it was just so wet and nasty that it wasn't any fun at all. We trick-or-treated at Bob's place. Johnny and J.M., who seemed to be feeling better by the looks of him, handed us candy from his front door.

***

November came, and it was about the same weather pattern: cold and rainy. I remember Bob saying that the almanac predicted that it was going to be cold, and he was right. It did spit snow for a few days, but nothing that would shut the schools down. That was a bummer for us kids, to say the least. When we saw it snowing mixed with rain while in school, we were all so hoping that the school would call the buses and send us on our way. No such luck.

In December, I heard the news that devastated me. Bob had died. It wasn't a heart attack or a stroke. He didn't fall nor was he killed in a car accident. What happened to Bob had been in his body the entire time. It was cancer. He had been battling cancer for the better part of a year. From what my dad had told me when he and Mom sat me down in the living room to break the news, it was stage four colon cancer. I had no idea what cancer was, not like I do now anyway, nor how deadly it was. But Bob was gone, and the news hit me in the chest like a hammer.

Bob had been dealing with the news that he was going to die the whole time I was visiting the old men on his front porch. I wondered if Johnny, J.M., and even Walt knew about it. I bet they had. It all started to make sense to me now, hearing Dad and Mom talk to me about my friend Bob passing away. I began to realize that they were all there, sitting on his front porch, talking about passive stuff like the weather and sports, and memories of people and places long gone– that they were there to comfort their friend in his time of dying. I had no clue that the man was dying, and even if I did, what would I say to him? Would I have acted differently around him? I don't know, to be honest. I knew how I felt when Walt died, and now, Bob was gone– gone from something that had eaten him from the inside.

I remember feeling sad and crying that night when the news was broken by my parents. I got on my bike after the talk and pedaled down to the end of Jeralds Street. I saw his trailer come into view, but there was no Bob on the front porch that cold, windy December evening. I stopped at the stop sign and looked at his place, where they all used to sit and laugh and talk. I sat there and looked at where I used to sit: right on the edge, drinking a Pepsi from his cooler, listening to everything. I cried looking at Bob's place.

***

Years later, when I turned nineteen, I had enrolled in college at Auburn University and was going to move down there to live on campus. I was excited about that. It was my first time being out on my own, away from my family and away from Claxton. I had packed up what I needed to make the move in my old Ford F-150 that my dad had gotten me as a graduation gift. It wasn't the best truck in the world, by no means, but it was mine outright. I loved that truck. Still have it today: just clicked over five hundred thousand miles if you can believe that. Dad and Mom were going to follow me down to the school to make sure that I got unpacked in my dorm and see me one last time before the Thanksgiving break when I came back home to visit.

I told them that I needed to see someone before I left, and I would be right back. I got in my truck, drove down the street, and made a left at Bob's place. The home was empty and had been since Faye died a few years back. The trailer sat empty as their kids tried to figure out what to do with it. The last time I saw Faye was back when I was a sophomore in high school.

She was out sweeping the front porch when I rolled up on my bike. I stopped in to talk with her for a few minutes. She seemed sad still because of Bob being gone. At that point, it had been about four years. To her, and even to me, it was still fresh. She and I spoke on her front porch about things. She asked how I had been: how school was going, how were my parents. You know, the usual banter. Then I asked about her and how she was feeling these days. She told me that her kids were staying with her some, helping out around the house and whatnot. That was the last time I talked to her. I know that I should've come over for a visit more often than that one time, but life got in my way. I always had intentions of going over there to sit with her for a spell, but something always managed to get in the way: sports, homework, girls– something always got in my way.

I passed by Bob's trailer, drove down the road to the next house, and pulled into J.M.'s house. Just as I hoped, he was sitting outside under an oak tree in the shade in the front yard. He started waving as soon as I pulled into the driveway. I got out, and I could feel the smile on my face.

He sat in his chair and waved me over, "Come on in here, young man! Get you a seat!" he said with excitement in his voice. J.M. had not forgotten about me.

I pulled a chair off his front porch, placed it beside him, and shook his hand. He had gotten older, and it was the first time that I had seen him up close in years. He was looking much older than the time I remembered him back when we first met, some nine years ago. He couldn't stop smiling and asked me how I had been doing over the years. I told him good, and that I was heading off to college but wanted to stop in and say hey before I left. It was long overdue.

We sat and talked longer than I anticipated, but it was good. We talked about Bob, Walt, and Faye. He told me that Johnny's wife eventually passed away, and that Johnny was living with his daughter over in Nashville. Happened about three years ago– J.M. told me.

"I'm the last of them, you know," he said.

When he said that, I could sense the fear in his voice. J.M.'s family was out of state, and it was just him in his house, alone. June, his wife, was also dead. I could tell that being all by himself weighed on him just by talking to him.

"Think you'll move in with your kids eventually?"

"Hell no!" he said, laughing. "I like living here. Hate being on my own, but I've lived here so many years now, there ain't any place I'd druther be. I just miss everybody, you know? Seems like yesterday, we all were sitting over there on Bob's front porch, talking. You were what, ten at the time? Man alive, where did the time go? Take some advice: appreciate your youth because it goes by like a rocket." I nodded and told him that I would keep that in mind.

We sat under that tree and talked for about ten minutes longer, about nothing much at all. It was like sitting at Bob's all over again. I didn't mind though. I knew deep down in my heart that this was going to be the last conversation that I ever had with the old man, and I wanted to savor it. Turns out, it was the final conversation. Not that it was by design, but rather that I was too busy to go for a visit. Life, for all intents and purposes, had gotten in the way.

"You do good down at that school now, you hear me?"

"Yeah, I will, J.M."

He tried to get up to see me off but struggled to get out of his chair. I told him to sit back, and I shook his hand and gave him a hug.

"You take care. Don't get yourself hurt around here, okay?" I told him.

He smiled and nodded, "Try my best. You come see me now. Good luck at that school!"

***

I drove down to the old neighborhood the other day while up for a visit to see Mom and Dad. Things had certainly changed around there. The once nice houses were torn all to pieces. Bad neighbors had moved in, devaluing the once best neighborhood in all of Claxton. It was a shame. Mom and Dad were selling their house and moving into a condo in a community called Meadow Heights on the outside of Claxton. They couldn't stand their neighbors and hated seeing what the place around them had become. They wanted out. The man who had bought up all the homes made them an offer, and they took it. They were sure that their home, which still looked great, would in time look like all the others once a certain element moved in– which it eventually did.

I parked my truck in Bob's driveway and got out to take a look around. I was sure that no one lived there and probably hadn't in a long time. At least, I've never seen anyone there all the times I came up to visit Mom and Dad. I walked across the yard and sat down on the edge of the front porch, just as I did back when I was a kid, and soaked it all in. I got a text message on my phone. I pulled the phone out of my front pocket and lit the screen up. The image on my phone, the background, was of me and my wife, a picture that was taken a few days ago. I smiled, as I always do when I see us.

I was older now. Gray hair was all over, signs of crow's feet already taking residence, and my eyes seemed to have lost some of their shine. Then I remembered what J.M. told me the last time I talked to him:

"Appreciate your youth because it goes by like a rocket."

"It sure did, J.M. It sure did."

HORIZON HOTEL

He had come back to the Horizon Hotel in 1965 just like the demon, Joseline, said he would a few years ago. It wasn't a visit to the five-star hotel for business or pleasure. Bill Barker stood in front of the Horizon Hotel as people walked to and fro on the sidewalk in downtown, and in and out through the hotel's glass doors. No one paid any attention to Bill standing there. No one saw the look of desperation in his sullen eyes, his slumped shoulders, or his shaking hands. Even though no one looked his way as they went about their business on that gloomy, drizzling Halloween evening just about sundown, everyone would remember what happened when the shot rang out.

Those that were in proximity of what Bill Barker did, would remember it for the rest of their lives. It was their, "Where were you when Kennedy was killed?" moment. Each of the bystanders recalled precisely where they were when the man in the gray suit and black topcoat pulled a gun from his pocket, stuck it under his chin, and pulled the trigger.

Some people like Robert Blinker, a man who had just walked out of the Horizon, didn't see what happened because his eyes were on the ground as he walked. He was thinking about hailing a cab to get to the airport to go home to Chicago. He didn't see Bill kill himself, just heard the shot. His body jumped at the sound of the gun, and he looked up, trying to locate where the shot was coming from. He knew it was close, and could smell the gunpowder. Then he saw the man on the ground.

Regina Roberts, a maid for the hotel who had just walked by the man in the gray suit and black topcoat, didn't see the suicide act but heard the gunshot as she passed by him. He pulled the trigger while she was only five feet away. Blood and some brain matter had gotten on her uniform. She screamed wildly as she turned around, only to see Bill fall limp to the concrete. Her eyes saw him fold to the concrete, but her brain took some time to register what had just happened.

Marie Plemons, a wife and mother, who was walking with shopping bags in each hand from Martindale's Boutiques, down the block from the Horizon, saw the whole thing. Bill had caught her eyes early on as he was standing there, looking at the entrance of the hotel and then at the glass entrance doors. She had a feeling that there was about to be trouble but had no clue as to what kind. Marie saw Bill reach into his topcoat pocket, the right side, and extract a silver gun. He slowly drew the weapon and put it under his chin. Before she would scream, maybe warn the people close to him or for him to stop, Bill pulled the trigger. She saw a red puff of blood exit the top of his head, and in a split second afterward, he fell to the ground. She remembered stopping dead in her tracks, trying to process what just happened and never minding that she dropped her shopping bags.

Others coming and going ducked for cover, screamed, and ran like scattering ants when their anthill had been demolished. Everyone looked around trying to locate where the gunshot came from. Was it a sniper? Was someone trying to commit a mass shooting? Was it a firecracker? Was it just one shot or two? Am I safe? Should I make a run for it? On that late Halloween afternoon, just around sundown, questions swirled about what was going on in front of the Horizon Hotel.

***

The scene had been secured, thanks to the police who arrived on the scene in a matter of minutes, with weapons drawn. Several were looking up in the windows of the buildings to see if they spotted a sniper. Officers spotted the man who was lying in a pool of blood on the concrete in front of the Horizon. A few of those officers rushed over to the man who was down and started checking him out to see if he was okay.

In about thirty minutes, the shops and eateries on the block were on lockdown while the police swarmed the area, getting statements from the people that may have seen what happened. Marie Plemons was talking to one officer off to the side while another officer was speaking with Regina Roberts about what had happened. Robert Blinker, on the other hand, didn't hang around to be interviewed by the police. He had a taxi to catch, which he caught several blocks away after running for his life when the shot came. He was already at the airport by the time the detectives came to the scene after the cops arrived.

Detective Rich Kruger, a newly minted detective as of two weeks ago, was on the scene, kneeling and inspecting the body of Bill Barker while crime scene photographers took the dead man's picture. He had investigated his share of murders and other horrible things in the city before, but this was a first for him. He had never investigated a suicide in front of a hotel before.

"What do you make of it?" an officer asked who had been one of the first on the scene.

Det. Kruger kept his eyes on the dead man as he answered, "I don't know. Obviously, it's a suicide. But why? This guy has money. Rich guys tend not to off themselves. They got it made."

"How you know this fella is rich?"

"You see this topcoat? It's a Thompson. These are high-end coats. He didn't buy this out of a Sears catalog, I can tell you that." Det. Kruger reached into Bill's back trouser pocket and felt for a wallet. He found it and pulled it out.

It was a nice wallet— black leather, felt good in his hands. Another high-end item on his person. The detective opened it up, thumbed through it, and found the dead man's identification.

"William Gregory Barker...1345 Western Pen Lane...Everett, Washington. Everett, Washington? That's a long ways away from here," Det. Kruger said, looking at the officer who was still hanging around him.

"Is it? I mean, we get all kinds of people from all over. It ain't that out of the ordinary," the officer pointed out.

Det. Kruger nodded, "Well, you got a point there. But still...why would you come all the way here just to kill yourself? Did he know the hotel? Had he stayed here before? I wonder..." Det. Kruger tailed off and checked the dead man's other back pocket. Nothing.

He rolled him over a bit and checked the right side pocket of the topcoat. Nothing there. Then the left. Bingo!

"What is this?" he asked absently.

What the detective pulled out was a very thick envelope. By the weight of it, there had to be several pages of something inside it. On the front of the white envelope, there was no stamp, no address to or from. Just blank.

"Got something there?" the officer asked.

"Maybe...might be a letter. I'll check this out. Might tell us why he came here and killed himself."

***

Back at the station, Det. Kruger sat alone in an interrogation room, door locked. He didn't want to be disturbed while exploring the contents of the letter. At least that's what he thought it was; a letter that maybe could explain the mysterious circumstances on why someone would travel so far to kill themselves in front of a ritzy hotel downtown. With a cigarette hanging loosely between his lips, the detective sat at the table and opened the envelope.

He pulled the papers out and unfolded the tri-fold. It was indeed a letter, typed out, dated on the upper right-hand, his name and address on the upper left-hand; Det. Kruger counted ten pages worth of the letter. He took a long drag from his smoke and tapped the ashes into a silver ashtray that sat on the table. He made himself comfortable as much as he could on that stiff wooden chair and began to read the last words of Bill Barker...

***

If you found this letter, then that means I'm dead. I did what I told myself I was going to do; what I needed to do, I guess. My name is William Barker, but friends call me Bill– sometimes, Billy. Either way is okay by me. And if you're reading this, that means you've seen my dead body, and I guess we need to be on a first-name basis.

I was a millionaire; made my money in the stock market fairly early by the age of twenty-nine. I didn't live lavishly, nor did I show people that I had money. Why should I? People who know that you have money want to be your friend for only that purpose. Family? I don't have any to speak of: parents are long dead; brother is in the Army abroad somewhere; and my sister...who knows where she is? Friends? None. Just a group of men that I consorted with. Those men were my eventual undoing, I guess you could say. Had I not ever met them, perhaps, I'd never walked into the Horizon Hotel. I would have never killed myself in front of the place for you to find. I guess you never know where you'll end up in life.

The men that I speak of were of the same status as me. All of them filthy rich– too much money, more than they needed. Unlike me, they flaunted what they had: big houses, nice cars, fancy clothes, whores on call, captains of industry.

Bert Billings was the oldest of the group. And he was the mastermind of what we got into. He was a former CEO of Windstar Oil. He made millions from that company over his tenure. The oil his company produced is probably the same oil that is in your car. He was a very interesting man. At least I thought so.

Next was Otis Ledbetter, his company got government contracts for the war effort in Korea and Vietnam. War is big business, and Otis cashed in. Odds are, if a place was bombed, his company probably made the bombs that were dropped. He made sure to convince the men in Washington to keep the wars going because if peace was found, he'd be out of a job. Not that he was hurting for money, mind you.

Our other man in the group was Dayton Moore, another multi-millionaire who had more money than sense. He owned several casinos in Las Vegas and had mob ties. He made a fortune on sports betting. Rumor was that he fixed any sporting event that he wanted. You should have seen the women he had and the places he lived. The man, much like the others, didn't want for anything and did whatever he wanted. He showed how much money and power he had. Dayton was a man that I was scared of. You crossed him, he'd fix you fast and put your body somewhere out in the Nevada desert.

How did I come to know these men? Good question. It started over a party that I was invited to. I usually don't do parties or get-togethers, but the girl that I was dating at the time was invited by her friend, Marcy DeBoard, who was friends with Burt's wife. We went to upstate New York in his mansion where there were all kinds of people that night. You could practically smell the money those people had.

There were mayors, governors past and present, war generals, mobsters, and even Harry S. Truman was there for a bit. He had left by the time me and Millie arrived. I was so out of place there that night.

Sure, I had just as much money as they did, but still, that house and those people were not my scene. Millie went off to see some of her friends, mingled about the house which was crawling with people, and left me alone leaning up against a wall, holding a glass of champagne.

I watched people talking, laughing, doing whatever they wanted to do there. Some were even in the big bedroom having sex. You could hear them over the live piano that was being played in the spacious living room. No one seemed to care one bit. It was like there were no rules inside that house. And why would there be? People like that don't abide by any rules; they make the rules you and I have to go by.

I was standing there people-watching when a man approached me in a tuxedo. He was older than me, balding, his glasses resting on the tip of his nose. He asked me my name and what I did. I told him. He introduced himself as Bert Billings, former CEO of Windstar Oil. We both shook hands, and he informed me this was his house but in no way was his party. It was his wife's idea for the party because she loved throwing them. "She loves being seen," he told me.

I could tell that he didn't like this type of atmosphere, and he told me as much. He wasn't a fan of large crowds. He liked to keep it intimate. I agreed wholeheartedly. We stood there and looked around at all the people for a little bit. He pointed out people within the crowd and told me who they were, how much money they had, and what their position in life was. It was interesting.

He then asked me if I wanted to get out of there and go down into his basement. He promised me that it was quiet down there, and we could get away from all the noise. He told me there was a card game that would be going on down there shortly. I liked cards, so I agreed to go down. He and I walked across the living room while people, mostly intoxicated, stopped Bert along the way shaking his hand, touching his shoulders, saying hi, and thanking him for the invite. Bert was smiling, nodding, and being a pleasant host. I could tell that he hated every second of being spoken to and pawed at.

We reached his office and closed the door. The noise was still loud even through the heavy wooden door. I closed it, watching Bert go over to a bookcase. He pulled a book halfway out, and just like in a Vincent Price horror flick, the bookcase turned and exposed a lit corridor that spiraled down into his basement. "Let's go," he said to me.

I followed him down the old stairwell and into the basement which was well lit and spacious. In the middle of the room sat a table where two men, Dayton Moore and Otis Ledbetter, were sitting and swapping stories. Bert introduced me to them, we shook hands, and I took the open chair next to Otis. Bert was right– it was quiet down there; couldn't hear a single voice from upstairs.

We played poker for hours. How long? I'm not sure. But it was long. We all talked about our successes, failures, women, the future, and all that stuff. What I didn't know was that I was being interviewed by these guys to be included in their tight group. We all meshed rather well, I got to say. I liked the three of them. They were rich, yes, but there was an honesty about them. I think they felt they could be themselves within the group. And for the first time, I had friends.

***

Things were going good for a long time between the four of us. We'd all visit each other from time to time at the Horizon Hotel. That seemed to be our meeting place. Dayton had purchased the hotel because he wanted a place to stay when he visited that part of the South. The hotel wasn't the nice place you see now. When he bought it, he brought me, Bert, and Otis to look at it to see what we thought.

It was rundown and probably should have been bulldozed if I'm being honest. When he told us how much he bought the place for, we all laughed at how stupid he seemed to be. But he told us to hide and watch because he was going to turn the old reputed whorehouse into a five-star hotel...he did just that in under two years of buying it. By the time he had the renovations put to it, it was magnificent and was in every magazine from California to New York. The Horizon Hotel was back and better than ever. It was a place where all the high class came to relax and be waited on. It was luxury at its finest.

What he didn't tell us, not at first, was that there were places inside that hotel that were haunted. I didn't believe in things like that. My grandmother did, but me...not so much. The other guys were the same except for Dayton. He said one night while I was in Vegas with him that the hotel had a bad history of death, and there were places within it that were haunted. He had even spoken to one of the ghosts– Mr. Withers, he called him– down in the laundry area.

I could tell that Dayton was not yanking my chain because he was as serious as a man that I ever met. But he told me that the hotel had a power over him– a draw, he called it. Eventually, he was spending more time at the Horizon than he was at his home in Las Vegas. We started seeing a change in our friend over time and not a good one. Things with him became strange.

Me, Bert, and Otis stayed at the Horizon a lot during the days when Dayton was falling apart. Our friend was on the brink of a complete mental collapse. The hotel management was having their own run-ins with the residence ghosts during this time as well. Most of the rooms on the fourth floor appeared to be the worst. Dayton's room was at the top, on the sixteenth floor, and had the best view of the downtown district. Matter of fact, all ten rooms on the sixteenth floor had a great view of downtown but Dayton's was the best because it faced the west side of the city. Man, I remember the lights being on in the buildings at night and looking at them from that room. It was breathtaking.

***

You see, that hotel is haunted. Still is and I haven't been back there since that night Dayton died. That hotel, I came to find out through exhausting research that I paid for, had a bloody and violent history. Some of it Dayton told me about. It was all that violence and blood that made the Horizon Hotel what it is today. I'm sure that the building is still haunted. That, I have no doubts of. The type of things that roamed the halls, stayed in the rooms, and dwelled in down in the laundry don't just vanish over time. I'm sure they are still there; still frightening as ever.

The owner and builder, Walter deStroman, a wealthy man, much like the four of us were, bought the tract of land and erected the original hotel. Eventually, the hotel became a hub of the downtown district and over time, a hub of problems. Murders, suicides, fights, you name it happened there. The hotel kept going and kept in operation even after Walter deStroman died.

New ownership took over after his death and still, the reports of the hauntings continued. New and old staff members were forced to sign an

NDA, a nondisclosure agreement, about not saying anything concerning the things that went on around there. The reason was that word had gotten out about the place being a hotbed for supernatural activity, and the reputation started spreading about how odd and spooky the place was. The staff, who had their own issues with the place, started quitting, understaffing the hotel until it finally went out of business.

People would stay in that hotel just to have an experience. Most people didn't, but those unfortunate who did left and never came back. They told stories about seeing ghosts, hearing people talking in their closets and under their beds, people running down hallways, gunshots, etc. When the hotel experienced fourteen deaths—ten of them suicides within a five-year span—the owners of the hotel went out of business. The Horizon Hotel had a bad reputation attached to it. People started calling it the Hotel Death.

The hotel eventually became a vacant relic of the supernatural in the downtown district, and its reputation invited all sorts of psychics, mediums, and paranormal investigators around the world. Books and magazine articles were written about the place and how badly haunted it was. During October, people would sneak in there, roam the corridors, and stay in the rooms to see if they could have an experience. I'm sure several did, but I think most, not all, of the stories that were told and printed were lies. I think the stuff that happened to some people they never spoke about, at least not to a lot of people. The things I saw— I never did. Who would believe me? You, the reader of this letter, may not. I don't care. What happened, happened there.

Years went by, and the hotel became an eyesore to the downtown district. City mayor Woody Wilson vowed to tear down the old hotel and pave over it, adding more parking to the nearby city shops. Would've been a great idea, too, but here came Dayton Moore. With his money and influence, he convinced the mayor and the city council to stop their plans, and he would buy it. He told them that he could turn the old Horizon Hotel into a five-star hotel. It didn't hurt that Dayton gave Mayor Wilson an extra $125,000 in his election coffer to win reelection. That's when Dayton told us what he had bought.

Dayton, over time, started to change. I noted that earlier in this letter, but I never explained things fully. I don't know if I even can. Dayton got taken over by something in that hotel: a demon named Joseline. That was the night everything changed. The night Dayton died or was killed. However you want to say it, Dayton was no more. We went our separate ways as a group after that. None of us could see each other after what happened in that hotel that night.

I remember us having Dayton strapped to a chair with our belts in his room that night. Joseline had possessed him. That was the reason behind his appearance becoming profoundly haggard and sallow over time. Dayton was slowly dying.

"He's mine now!" the demon growled using Dayton's voice. "Your friend is long gone! Get out while you still can!"

For a few weeks prior to Dayton's death, each of us had stayed at the Horizon with Dayton because we knew our friend was in trouble. But we didn't know how much, certainly not about Joseline. We all knew something wasn't right with him, and he looked to us to be falling apart. His appearance, which was always a suit and tie, neatly pressed, shoes shined, hair slicked back, had been substituted to an unkempt version. He wore the same suit for weeks, never taking a shower. He smelled to high Heaven. I never saw him eat or drink anything while I was with him. He had become incredibly thin over that time.

He was incapable of holding conversations for any amount of time, and making hotel business decisions on the day-to-day was a no-go. Otis ended up calling the shots most of the time to the hotel's management. Dayton would mostly sleep up in his room, but we knew things were going to get worse.

I was in my hotel room, Otis was down on the first floor, counting the deposits from that day's receipts with the hotel's chief senior manager, Tom Forbes, while Bert stayed with Dayton in his room up on the top floor. It was common practice for one of us to stay with Dayton during those days. I didn't dare walk out of my room at night because I had an experience with a little girl down the hall where I walked to the ice machine to get some ice. I was standing there with my bucket, waiting on the ice to dispense when a hand touched my back. I turned, and this little girl, a ghost, stood there and screamed out to me. I jumped a foot off the ground, bucket flying, and screamed as the ice dispensed all over the floor.

That wasn't the only time that I had had an experience in that hotel. Once, down in the laundry area, I was chased by something, to this day

I have no idea what it was. It growled, and I could hear it running. So I ran back up the stairs into the safe confines of the hotel's hallways. Randi Taylor, the lead maid of the place, asked what was wrong, and I acted like I saw a rat.

"You heard it running at you, didn't you?" she asked.

She told me it was common down there that "Ted"-- that's what everyone on the staff called whatever it was down there– scared people, running at them. I was floored that she took it so easily. To me, this was absolutely mind-blowing. To her and the staff, it was just another day at the Horizon.

On the night Bert saw what he saw, I remember I woke up in my room, turned on the radio that was on my nightstand, and laid there in the bed, listening to music. For me, sleep was thin, and had been since I stayed in that hotel. I was tired back in those days when we had to watch Dayton, so fighting bouts of exhaustion was the norm for me.

Otis was down in the office counting money, and Bert was staying with Dayton on the top floor. According to Bert, after a few hours, he wanted something to eat. He tried to call down to room service, but the phone wouldn't work. Which was weird because we had never had an issue with the phones in that hotel before. Making sure that our friend was fast asleep, Bert figured that it wouldn't hurt to take the elevator and go down into the kitchen to make himself something to eat.

Coming back from the kitchen to the sixteenth floor, Bert saw something when the elevator doors opened that caused him to drop his plate with the turkey sandwich, chips, and glass of tea. What he saw was Dayton crawling on the ceiling of the corridor like a spider– his head was turned around backward, with red glowing eyes.

***

I was lying in my bed, nearly dozing off listening to some music when a frantic knock came on my door. I got up, opened it, and in rushed Bert. He was a sight: shaking, stumbling over his words, looking around in a panicked state. I'd never seen my friend like this before. I calmed him down, got him over to my desk chair, and coached him to take deep breaths. After about five minutes, he was calm enough to tell me what he had seen.

By the time his story was over, I remember standing there in disbelief. Sure, I had experiences in that hotel: I heard things, saw things, and even was told stories from the staff about their experiences. I experienced and heard enough from everyone to fill a book of horror stories. But what Bert had told me legitimately scared me– so much so that I wanted to leave the hotel and never come back. That's when Bert told me what he thought was going on.

"I think he's possessed," he said to me. Now, I admit, I didn't and still don't know a lot about that subject. To my surprise, Bert did. I discovered that he was well-versed in the supernatural. Me? The only experiences I had were in the hotel. That was enough.

Bert was an occultist. So were Otis and Dayton. I had no idea at all. They never discussed anything like that around me. I didn't believe in that kind of nonsense.

"We were going to make you the fourth member of our chapter," Bert told me in my hotel room.

"A member of what?" I asked him.

"The Black Night Society."

***

What Bert told me was crazy. In a nutshell, The Black Night Society was nothing more than a bunch of ultra-wealthy men who gathered in small places around the world and tried to touch the other side: the unseen world. He said that the secret society had been going on in America ever since the days of George Washington; he even said good old George was one of these members. I had heard of the Illuminati, but Bert assured me that this was much more than that.

The whole purpose of the secret society was to break through the other side and make contact with things that weren't on our plane of existence.

"Ghosts, monsters, BigFoot, Loch Ness...how do you think all that stuff got here? Our forefathers brought them over...even demons," he told me. "Me and Otis had thought for some time that the reason that Dayton had bought this place was because it called to him."

When Bert said that, I distinctly remember Dayton telling me that same thing in his room at his casino back in Vegas– about how the Horizon Hotel seemed to call out for him.

"We think whatever it is in this hotel reached out and brought him here...along with us. For so long the three of us have been reaching out with sacrifices and séances...I think something is reaching out *to us* now. We brought a lot of stuff into this hotel from the other side. Things were already here, make no mistake. But...but we added bad things to it."

"What have you guys gotten into?" I asked.

Bert had this look of fear in his eyes like I'd never seen before.

"Honestly...I don't know. One night several months ago, me, Otis, and Dayton held a séance in Room 221...the most haunted room in the hotel. I think we might have made contact with something pretty strong. We might've opened a door that night to the other side...maybe we didn't close it all the way."

I still wasn't sold on what my friend was telling me. I mean, how could I be? What is it they say? Seeing is believing? Well, that was coming later. Ghosts are one thing. But what Bert was getting to was possibly something demonic and certainly not of this world had entered through a door that they didn't shut.

"We got to call Otis and let him know," Bert told me.

***

Instead of calling down to the office, I suggested that we go down to the office and get Otis ourselves. And that's what we did. We walked out of my room and made our way to the first floor and into the office where Otis had finished counting the money and was making time with Deanna, one of the girls from the front desk. She was a blonde bombshell if I'd ever seen one.

We opened the door to the office and there was Deanna sitting on the desk, facing Otis with her shirt unbuttoned. Had we gotten there a few minutes later we would've gotten a show, for sure! Deanna hurriedly buttoned her white shirt and adjusted her black skirt, profoundly embarrassed. She hopped off the desk and ran out, not making any eye contact with me or Bert.

Otis leaned back in his chair, flustered. We both walked inside the office and closed the door. That's when Bert told Otis what was going on. I remember Otis having that look that Bert did; that fear in his eyes was undeniable. I was certainly scared, but not like they were; they knew what they had done. They had been playing with fire; something they didn't completely grasp or fully understand. Now, it appeared that something more powerful and sinister than ghosts had been let loose in this haunted hotel, coming through a door that the men had created and forgot to shut.

Bert and Otis decided that it would be best to discuss this outside the hotel. The three of us walked outside of the hotel and stood in the cold January night. Bert and Otis stood and bantered back and forth while I stood people-watching from time to time as the city's downtown district seemed to never rest, even at this time of night. I tried to keep up with their conversation, to understand what was going on, but I was out of my depth. I knew nothing about this topic. I was along for the ride. I could've left them to figure it out on their own, but I was their friend; that meant something to me back then. Still does, I guess. I never had friends as a kid or as an adult. These guys were the best ones that I had, for better or worse. Well, this was worse.

The conversation on what to do turned into a blame game: Bert blamed Otis for sacrificing that homeless man in Room 221. I stood there stunned that they had actually done that.

I interrupted them, "Wait?! What?!" but they just kept on going, paying me no mind at all.

"Oh yeah," Otis barked back, "who was the one that thought using our own blood to draw the designs on all the doors of the hotel was a good idea? That sure as hell wasn't me. That was you, buddy-boy! And, if I'm not mistaken, who was the one who brought that book and made us start using summoning spells? Wasn't me or Dayton! That was you! All of this was your idea because you met that guy in London who told you about this secret society. And now…look at us!"

Otis was shaking, but I don't know if it was from the cold or the fear.

I finally broke in because the two of them were inching closer together, looking like they were going to duke it out right there on the sidewalk while cars and people passed by. "Boys! Boys!" I shouted as loudly as I could to get their attention. "We gotta figure this out. Dayton needs us."

They looked at each other eye to eye ready to have a go, but then backed down and inched away from each other, their bodies less tense.

We stood outside and the three of us talked as the cold wind swirled around us. Actually, it was more of them talking and me listening. I had no idea what to do. I had no idea what these men of wealth had been up to in their little secret boys' club. Had I known a long time ago, I would have never been their friend. I would have never kept coming around after that card game down in Bert's basement. Dayton had become a good, close friend of mine as was Otis and Bert. Like it or not, I was in it with them. Maybe I could help get everything back to good again. We still had a lot of work to do.

"I can't remember if we properly closed the door that night," Bert said.

Otis stood there, running his hands through his hair trying to think. He was thinking hard, I guess trying to remember that night. "Me either. We did that ritual so much and nothing happened that maybe we got sloppy and just forgot. I don't know. But if what you're telling me you saw up on sixteen with Dayton, then whatever it is has got him. It would explain his condition."

"So what do we do?" I remember asking.

***

We walked back into the quiet hotel and God, it was so warm. It was getting late and all the guests, all seventy-five of them, were tucked away inside their rooms asleep or having sex, or whatever it was they all did behind those closed doors. The three of us got on an elevator. We didn't talk at all, I remember, on our way up to see about Dayton. We stood there thinking thoughts alone. I remember thinking how crazy all this sounded...Dayton being possessed. I knew Dayton was not the same man he was before. He had changed over time; and if Bert was right in what he saw earlier, things had gotten from bad to worse.

We got out of the elevator on the sixteenth floor where Bert's room was. Otis had told the front desk a while back not to allow any of the rooms up there to be stayed in by guests.

"Everything on that floor is off limits until I give the all clear," I remember him telling the staff.

He had been staying in Dayton's room. It was his turn. But what we needed was in Bert's room locked in a safe. We walked down the long corridor, Bert unlocked his door, and went inside while Otis and I stood outside and waited. After a few minutes, Bert walked out of the room, carrying a black book that looked ancient. It was pretty big, not a normal-sized book, and had some signs of wear and tear on the edges. I guessed that it was the same book that they used to practice their secret club stuff. I can't say for sure, and I certainly didn't ask. I knew too much already and didn't want to know any more than I already did.

The three of us walked down the hallway: Bert leading the way with the book in the crook of his arm, Otis behind him, and me lagging behind. We turned the corner in the hallway that lead to Dayton's room. And as soon as we did, something unbelievable happened. The hallway had snow on the floor. Ice sickles had formed, hanging from the reprinted works of art and candle goblets that hung on the walls. The temperature down that hallway was so cold that we could see our breaths.

We all stopped and looked at each other in amazement. I could tell this was not normal, not even for the men who practiced in the dark arts. How good were they really? I don't know. To be honest, I don't think they knew what they were doing back then *or* when we were marching to Dayton's room.

"So what are we going to do?" Otis asked Bert.

"We're going to drive whatever it is out of Dayton. And then try to banish it," he replied.

"Maybe just figure something out in this book afterward to get rid of all the things in this hotel while we're at it."

"You mean the stuff you guys brought inside?" I quipped.

"This place had a lot of supernatural activity before we got here...but we definitely made it worse. This hotel has to be the most haunted place in the world by now," Otis remarked.

Before anyone else could say a word, Dayton's door to his room slowly opened, inviting us in. We all three looked at each other. I nearly turned and ran down the snowy hallway and out of that hotel for good. Why I didn't, I don't know.

A thick fog rolled slowly out of the room. We all stood there looking, wondering if we should go in. Bert held onto the book against his chest, and Otis had backed up closer to me. I think he was ready to run out of the hotel too. A laugh came from inside that room. It wasn't Dayton's voice, but something much deeper, scarier. I would find out in a few moments that it was a demon that had taken over our friend's body and mind; the thing that had been at the controls for a while at that point.

Bert turned and looked at us. I could tell that he was scared. I saw him shaking. Maybe it was from the bitter coldness on the sixteenth floor, or maybe it was because of what was inside that room. Maybe it was both factors. I was shaking and can attest that it was from both. I didn't want to proceed forward into that room. But we had to try to rescue Dayton...if we could.

We stood there, each of us thinking a mile a minute when that laughter started again, this time very loud, as if it was taunting us.

"Either come in or stay away...whichever it is...I've got him, and I'm not letting this tasty treat go for a while," the demon said, using Dayton's mouth in a guttural voice.

Bert opened the book quickly and thumbed through the pages. He was looking for something in particular, it seemed. I determined that he knew that book very well and knew where all the spells and whatnot were located. He must have found it because he looked up from the book and began to recite a passage. The demon howled like it had been shot, and the door slammed shut. Otis and I stood there as Bert looked at the door and then at us.

"I think I know how to get this out of him...but we may lose Dayton in the process," I remember Bert saying to us.

Me and Otis stood, considering the weight of what our friend said.

"Any other way?" Otis asked.

I remember Bert looking at him with soulful eyes and slowly shaking his head, "I wish there was...but this is the only thing that I think will work. It's the extracting spell."

***

When he told us what it was, Otis ran his fingers through his hair. I could tell that this spell was serious...maybe even deadly.

After a few moments of pause between us, Otis asked, "And there's nothing else? What about the Encantor's passage?"

"Not on a demon," Bert replied.

Otis leaned back on the icy wall of the corridor, never minding the coldness of where we were. He knew the gravity of the situation whereas I knew it was bad, but had no idea about what the spell was going to do, especially the toll it would take on Dayton.

The entire situation we were in was bad. Had someone told me this story, I would have told them they were crazy. I didn't believe in stuff like this...that was until I stayed at the hotel and had experiences on my own. And now we were staring down a demon that had possessed our friend. How's that for unbelievable?

Otis paced about the snowy, icy hallway, running his fingers through his hair. I stood there shivering from the cold and could see my breath while Bert clutched the book and looked at us both.

"We messed around with forces we had no business with. Why did I ever let you talk me into this?" I remember Otis lamenting.

"Oh, like I twisted your arm to join in," Bert replied. "We all benefited from it. Look at where we all got in life."

Otis stopped pacing and looked at Bert. "And look at the costs, Bert! Our friend is in there possessed...he ain't coming back!"

"He bought this hotel because whatever force it is in here led him here," Bert reminded.

"Yeah, and we helped amplify it! We brought something from the other side over. We ain't pros at this! We've done our share, but we are far, far from good at this."

"Well, what do you want me to do about it now, Otis?! Tell me! What is it that you'd like me to do about it now?! Because I'll do it! You got a better option?!" Otis stood and looked at our friend.

I honestly thought he was going to rush him and beat the hell out of him. It wouldn't have done any good.

"The only thing that I know to do is to use the extracting spell in this book. That's it. Unless you got any bright ideas, guy?" Otis wanted to say something, but in the end, he had nothing.

"Now...let's get this horrible business over with." Bert turned to the closed door, reopened the book, went to some page, and started what I guess was the extracting spell.

Suddenly, the door flew open and fog rolled out. A loud, blood-curdling screech filled our ears. Bert walked in cautiously, and I followed. Otis brought up the rear. I was scared to death walking in that room, I got to tell you. I wanted to run out of that hotel as fast as I could and never come back. But I went along with it. They were my friends.

***

Inside his room, which just like all the others on the sixteenth floor was spacious and upscale, Dayton was up on the ceiling, screeching and looking at the three of us with his head turned backward. I remember he had this crazy look on his face. That face was Dayton's, but it didn't look like him at the same time. His eyes were black, hair was a mess, and his mouth was all contorted. He was on the ceiling, on all fours, screeching and growling, cussing us with every bad word he could think of. I keep referring to the demon as Dayton, but in my mind, that's where I go. I didn't see the demon, I saw Dayton. It was a shell of his former self.

Bert stood in the middle of the room looking up at Dayton and kept on reciting the spell in a language that was completely foreign to me. Whatever it was he was speaking seemed to hurt the thing inside that had control of Dayton. A few minutes after we got into the room and with Bert's incantation, Dayton fell from the ceiling and crashed violently to the floor in a daze. Bert told us to hurry up, and get Dayton in a chair. We did just that. Me and Otis rushed over and picked our friend up. We dragged him to a nearby wooden straight-back chair and sat him down on it.

"Tie him up with something!" Bert shouted at us. I could tell in his voice that time was of the essence.

Me and Otis frantically looked around for something, but nothing jumped out at us. Then inspiration hit me: I took my belt off my pants, and Otis did the same. We tied a dazed and confused Dayton to the chair, with me wrapping my belt around his chest, and buckling the belt behind him. He seemed to be pretty well in place.

Otis, with his belt, tied his feet to the front legs of the chair. He was good and secure...at least I hoped he was. In no time, Dayton's eyes sprang open, and a sinister grin began to spread across his face. I remember backing away and looking at my friend in horror. The sight of his black eyes and that demonic smile scared me silly. Thinking back on that scares me now just recalling it.

"Ohhhhhhhhhh a good spell, my friend. Better count yourself lucky you spoke it correctly," the demon said.

Otis, me, and Bert stood before Dayton. It was three of us against him. But I guess we were still outmatched. What we were dealing with was not of this world that was inside of him.

"You've come here to die?" the demon inside Dayton spoke in a low guttural voice.

The hairs on my arms stood on end and even writing this, they still do. That voice of the demon still haunts my thoughts. I can still hear it ringing in my head.

"What's your name, demon?" Bert asked, sounding confident. I guess you'd have to be confident in a situation like we were in. Thank God we had Bert. He seemed like he knew what to do...or at least projected that. There was a steel confidence in him.

Dayton smiled, "Joseline," the voice came out as a whisper. Oh, that whisper, so soft and sinister.

"Where did you come from?" Bert asked.

"I came from the other side of that door you opened in Room 221," Joseline replied, now using Dayton's real voice. "You boys forgot to close it properly."

Bert looked over to Otis, and they both knew the weight of what they had done. Otis was right: They messed around with forces they had no idea how to control.

"Well...you're done here," Bert told Joesline. I could hear the slight tremble in my friend's voice.

Joseline laughed loudly and shook around in the chair. I thought for a minute he was going to break free. "Silly boys...with your silly book! You think you can just destroy me? I'm older than that magic book...I have roamed time and space for eons, and you think that a few middle-aged men are going to take care of me?"

Joseline laughed a long guttural laugh. "Give it your best shot! But just remember...what you do to me hurts good old Dayton here. Food for thought. So let's get it on! Let's do it! Let's see what you got!"

Bert opened the book and began talking in the weird language again. Joseline laughed, then shook as if he was hurt by the words a few times.

Then the demon spoke again, "Does your wife know about the whore in New York City, Bert? I bet she doesn't. Doris, isn't it? She knows how to hit all those right spots, right? That's why you go back to her, and then you go back home and kiss your wife on the lips– the same lips where you've been..."

Bert spoke some more of that weird language, and Dayton's body shot backwards in the chair, nearly flipping over. Bert told me to go over and hold the back of the chair because we couldn't risk Dayton coming untied. I did as I was told.

"Hey, buddy, you got to untie me and let me walk around. Bert's going to kill me...you know that right?" The voice was Dayton's normal voice– the voice I knew.

For a split second, I nearly unbuckled him; but then Bert's words rang out, and the voice of Dayton who was somewhere inside, changed to Joseline, "Damn you then! We'll fight this til the end!" the demon's guttural voice promised us.

Bert spoke some more of those words from the book. With each spoken word, Dayton's body rocked back and forth, writhed this way and that. His head snapped back several times, and I could hear the bones in his neck crackle. I'm pretty sure that his neck was broken by the violent snapping. Bert stood looking on as he stopped reading from the book. Dayton hung his broken neck, the flat of his chin touching his chest. I thought he was dead. Then, he slowly raised his head and looked about.

"Are you happy now? Huh? You've broken his neck. He's gone now. Even if you expel me from his body, he's gone...Like a Mickey Mantle home run." Joseline laughed wildly, and the thought that my friend— *our friend*—was dead inside hit us all hard.

We didn't have long to mourn him. At that moment Bert was trying to extract the demon from Dayton's body and maybe put it back through the door he, Otis, and Dayton had opened a while back.

"How many of the weapons that you've made killed your fellow man, Otis? Ever wondered? I know the number. Hmmmmm? Try tens of thousands of deaths on your hands. I don't know how you sleep at night. Oh...that's right, you don't. You've got a guilty conscience. You hate being a weapons maker, but you can't stop now, can you? Took over the family business from dear old Dad. He'd be disappointed in you if you were to quit. But then again, you've done nothing but disappoint him, isn't that right?"

Bert spoke again using that ancient language, and Dayton's body shot back– this time nearly pushing me over. It was the most violent of the shots from the book. I regained my stance and placed my hands on the back of the chair to keep it from tumbling over.

Dayton's head fell back, and he looked at me from behind, upside down.

"Then there's you," the demon said to me. "I know your secret. Oh yes. San Francisco, five years ago. A blonde named Trixie. Things got a little rough in the bedroom. You didn't mean to break her neck. It was an accident. But what wasn't an accident was when you dumped the body in the water."

"Grab that mirror over there! Don't listen to it!" Bert shouted.

I stood there stunned. Since this letter is my last statement as a living human being, I will confirm what Joseline said. I met a woman at a bar downtown called Clyde's. We had a few drinks. She asked what I was doing in town when she found out I was there on business. I told her. She and I went back to my hotel to have sex. It got rough because she said she liked it that way. I was behind her in bed. I reached and pulled her hair back. I guess I did it a little too hard. I heard her neck snap. That sound, among other things, I haven't ever been able to get out of my head. I dumped her body off into the Golden Gate Strait later that night. As far as I know, she was never found. I left town that morning.

Otis ran over to the far wall next to the bathroom door and pried at the full-length mirror. He nearly broke it by taking it off. I often wonder, had it broken, what would've happened that night? He rushed over beside Bert who was still speaking the words, open book in his hands, with some force and conviction.

I was still behind Dayton holding the back of the chair. His body was going crazy from the words, and a time or two he nearly pushed me over. I thought for sure that if that happened, the demon would get loose, and there's no telling what would happen to us; perhaps possess one of us. So, I gripped the back of the chair as tightly as I could and prayed to God that He would grant me the strength to keep him from falling over in that chair.

As Bert kept speaking the spell, Dayton's head twisted all the way around to face me from behind. Seeing that, I nearly let go and backed away. I wanted to. But I held on, no matter what. I remember hearing the bones, what ones that weren't broken already, crack and snap. No way Dayton was going to live now. I didn't figure he had any chance before that.

His eyes were as dark as night, and his breath, right next to my face, smelled like rotten eggs, "You'll come back...all three of you will come here to die!" Joseline told me in a voice that literally made my skin crawl with fear. "You will all be back! I've already seen your futures! It'll end here! No matter what! No matter what! No matter what! No matter what! No matter what! No matter what!"

Dayton's body rocked back and forth, and side to side more violently than it did before. I don't know if Otis and Bert heard the demon over Bert's shouting of the spell, but I sure did. Without any warning, Dayton's body stopped rocking, untensed, and sat there loose in the chair, head hanging against his chest from the broken neck.

Bert stopped and closed the book. Otis stood beside Bert while the two of them stared at our dead friend. I slowly took my hands off the back of the chair and walked around Dayton, keeping my eyes on him. All of a sudden, Dayton's head pulled up and a black cloud of smoke started pouring from his mouth.

"The mirror!" Bert yelled, dropping the book. Otis and Bert took the mirror and put it in front of Dayton.

Dayton's black eyes flew open as his mouth was wide with that black smoke coming out of it. Then a deep scream came from Dayton's mouth. Something happened, and as I write this, I can't be sure of what I saw, but I saw in that mirror an image of the demon trapped that possessed our friend. It wasn't our friend.

In what seemed to be seconds, Bert and Otis were knocked backward onto the floor, still holding the mirror. It still is a wonder that the mirror didn't break. Dayton's body went limp again in the chair. I looked at the mirror and saw the demon trapped inside it banging on the glass, trying desperately to break free of its new prison.

Bert and Otis got up from the floor and looked at the mirror. The demon was pounding on the glass so much that it was starting to crack.

"We got to get to Room 221...fast!" Bert yelled. We all ran out of the room with Bert carrying the mirror, all of us hoping and praying that the demon didn't break free. That would be catastrophic.

We got into the elevator and went down to Room 221. That was the room where Bert, Dayton, and Otis did God knows what. I didn't want to know what, to be honest. I had heard enough already that night. We got into the room, the most haunted room in the hotel, and man, you could feel it in there. There was a heaviness inside there. I can't explain it, honestly. It's one of those places, much like the hotel, you had to be there to understand the full scope of it. Words cannot do it justice. I wish you could fully understand the amount of fear I had. My mind still can't wrap around it.

We got into the room and in the middle of the floor was a big round area rug. Bert rushed over to it and moved it. Underneath it was a pentagram. Red, no doubt drawn in blood long ago. They placed the mirror inside the pentagram, and Bert and Otis recited some words but not in the language Bert had used up in Dayton's room. These words and their pronunciations were totally different.

The demon—still trapped in the mirror—was banging the hell out of it. The mirror's glass was cracking. I noticed it and wondered if it was going to finally break free and maybe possess one of us, one of the guests, or staff of the hotel. Bert rushed over to the far side of the room and picked up an end table. He carried it over to where the mirror was in the pentagram and slammed it down on the mirror. It shattered into a million different pieces. Bert didn't stop. He kept slamming that table into the glass until there was nothing but the smallest of fragments left. It was over just like that.

We swept up the broken glass, dumped the multiple dustpans out of the window, and let the winds carry it away. The deed was done. The demon was no more. We were exhausted walking out of Room 221. We went back up to the sixteenth floor and back to Dayton's room. The corridor that was snowy when we left with the mirror was back to normal. We walked into Dayton's room, and he was still there, tied to the chair and slumped over. He, of course, was dead.

Otis and Bert discussed what to do about the body, who to call, and all that jazz. I didn't get much into what to do about our friend. I listened to them debate while I looked at Dayton in the chair. It was decided that we would unbuckle him from the chair and toss him out of his window to make it look like a suicide. I didn't like that option at all, but who was I to argue? If we told the police the truth, they would have laughed at us and arrested us for his murder. So, we tossed poor Dayton out of the window of the sixteenth floor. None of us watched him fall. We dumped him over, and that was that. Otis closed the window, and we left the room.

***

I ended up leaving the Horizon Hotel the following day. That was after we were questioned about our friend jumping to his death. We all said that he had been thinking about killing himself; that he had some mob bosses out in Vegas who had been harassing him, and that's why he was living at the hotel. The cops took it and didn't poke around much at all. They figured it was a suicide.

I went back home hoping to wash the memory of my stay at the hotel and what happened that night at the Horizon off me. It didn't work. I was stained. I knew that had I lived to be a hundred, I would never get that hotel and the things that happened there out of my head. What I saw, and what I had to do has stayed with me and will forever if I choose to live.

I never talked to Bert or Otis ever again after I left the hotel that morning in 1962. I cut all ties. I can't say if the two of them stayed friends or not after what happened with Dayton. If I had to make a bet, I'd say they stayed friends. They had been through too much over the years. Me? I was just the newer guy who came in. It was okay. I was never good at having friends anyway. I was always a loner.

In 1963—a year later—I read a news wire in the paper where a man had jumped to his death from the sixteenth floor of the Horizon Hotel. It was Bert Billings. No motive was known at the time, and the event wouldn't have been so remarkable had he not been who he was. Also, the news article pointed out that Bert was the second man to have jumped from the building since last year. The last, was us tossing Dayton over. I wonder if he did it from Dayton's room?

Otis, in the following year in 1964, was found dead in his room at the Horizon Hotel. I read this in another paper while in Washington. He was found hanging in his closet by the maid crew. There was no note, nothing to give a clue about why he killed himself and why there. I have to wonder if his suicide was in Room 221. Something tells me that it was.

What the demon said was true that night: we would all come back to die. Are we cursed? I'd say so. Why? I'm not sure. Maybe it was because my former friends messed around with forces they had very little understanding of. I certainly didn't have any. I was just along for the ride. That was enough to seal my fate. Maybe I sealed my fate when I accidentally killed that woman that night in San Francisco.

There was a draw, a lure, that brought me back to that hotel years later; probably the same draw that lured Otis and Bert back. Whatever that magnetic force was/is, Joseline knew about it. It was in place when Dayton first purchased the building. Whatever forces are within that hotel, they're still there, waiting on people. The demon, Joseline, is long gone. At least I hope it is. But a big part of me wants to know what else those men of wealth brought from the other side while playing their dark ritual games. I don't think it's foolish to consider that the demon was the only thing they brought out. I think there are still things– nasty and malevolent things– lurking in the rooms and hallways of that place.

It's haunted, I have no doubt. I have experiences there that I cannot resolve. Maybe one day someone will figure it all out. I don't know. My advice: don't go into the Hotel Horizon. It's a poisonous place. It looks glamorous and like it's one of the best places going. Hell, a lot of magazines have said it to be true. But what those magazines don't tell you is how infested with the supernatural it is.

So, I'm heading back to the Horizon in a few days. I don't want to go. There's something that whispers to me to come back...like it's drawing me there, much like a magnet does a paperclip. It seems like I have no control over it. I fight it, but in my dreams, I talk to a man, a tall man, from Room 221 who tells me my presence is required back at the hotel. For what reason, he doesn't tell me. I don't ask.

"You may leave," he tells me, "but you can never *really* leave."

I have that dream of the tall man once a night and have since I fled the Horizon. I also dream of what was chasing me in the laundry room. I dream of a little girl that was all cut up in Room 213. I dream of the man who roams the hallways of the eighth floor that floats above the floor talking about losing it all in the stock market. I dream of the beautiful blonde woman that Otis was fooling around with that night in the office. Except she wasn't on the staff. She was one of the ghosts that's in the hotel. How do I know this? She told me.

***

Det. Kruger finished the last page of the letter and sat back in his chair. He did not quite know what to say about what he had read. It was fantastic, to say the least. He did not believe in that sort of thing, but why in the hell would someone write this if it wasn't true? He rubbed his eyes and got up to stretch his legs. He went over to the window and looked out into the darkness of the city on that cool Halloween night. Off in the distance, he could see the lights of the Horizon Hotel several blocks, looming over some of the other buildings.

A knock on the door jolted Det. Kruger back into the land of reality. "Det.Kruger?"

He turned and saw that it was his boss, Captain Raines. "Cap?"

"Heard you caught a suicide this evening. Wanted to know what happened?"

Det. Kruger put his hands in his front pants pockets, "Gee," he considered telling him what he had read, but he'd never believe him, "just a garden variety bullet to the head. A wealthy guy with problems that money couldn't fix, I bet."

"Local?" he asked, standing in the doorway.

Det. Kruger shook his head, "Nah. Not from around here. I'm going to look for next of kin tomorrow. But I think this case is closed. Let his friends or family, if he's got any, figure out the 'why?'"

"Good enough for me. Say, that happened over at the Horizon, didn't it?" Captain Raines asked.

"Yeah."

"That's a spooky-ass hotel. Place is haunted, you know," he said as he walked away from the doorway and down the hall.

Det. Kruger stood bewildered and then shot a look at the table where the last words from Bill Barker were. "So I've read."

MESSAGES

"It's been two months...but it feels like it happened just yesterday," Dee said, tearing up as the wave of emotions came flooding back.

Talking about him hurt—hurt just as much as thinking about him—which was pretty much all the time. Two months had passed by, that was true, but time couldn't remove Dee Rodgers from that moment when everything in her life changed forever.

"That's perfectly normal to feel that way," her therapist, Dr. Rose, replied.

"I know that it sounds selfish, but I wish that I could get over him and move on. Just make some sort of headway into the future. I just...I feel like I'm trapped in the past. And I know that sounds awful to say."

Dee was crying now, trying to talk through the tears. Sitting in the chair across from Dr. Rose's desk, a brief thought streaked across Dee's mind: *How do I have any tears left? Haven't I cried them all?*

"You have had a traumatic event in your life, Dee. Everyone processes things differently and at different speeds. I know that you want to hurry up and gain some distance from what happened, but you really have to process the event."

Dee raised her hand to her face and wiped her tears away. "Can you just say Alex's death instead of 'the event?' You've been calling it an *event* for the last two sessions now. It wasn't an *event*. It was...was his death."

"My apologies," she replied to her patient. "You have got to process the eve...Alex's death, and stop trying to run from it. Sooner or later, you have to embrace it and work within that world of hurt. You won't ever get over his death, but you will be able to manage it."

"I can't get him out of my head. I wish that I could go to sleep and wake up next year. Maybe then I wouldn't have his memory fresh in my mind. Two months and he's still in here, still around the house. I just want some peace for a bit...just a moment where I can breathe a little. I keep going through all five stages of grief in, like, five-minute intervals. I'm beyond exhausted. I can't sleep. I've lost fifteen pounds since he died. I had to take a leave from work because I couldn't hold it together."

"You're better than you were when you first came to see me three weeks ago. That's progress, Dee. No matter how small. And you've been using the tools that I gave you to deal with grief. But you must stay vigilant. Things creep, especially trauma. It has a way of creeping if not held in check. And what's the only way to hold trauma in check? Do you remember?" Dr. Rose asked.

Dee sat there and knew exactly what her therapist wanted her to say. It was what Dr. Rose told her in session two. "PAP."

"Exactly. Pause it...Acknowledge it...Process it in real time. Alex's death may creep into your mind while you're brushing your teeth. Pause it, acknowledge it, and process it. It may creep while you're sitting at a red light. Pause it, acknowledge it, and process it. When his death creeps, use the PAP method. Are you doing that, or are you being lax?"

Dee, biting her lower lip, looked around the room. Her eyes had dried up from the tears, and she felt okay for now. She looked at her therapist who was awaiting her answer.

"Lax. I let the thoughts of my husband creep, and it just consumes me. Sometimes for hours. It's like I don't have any control. I can be sitting there having an okay minute or two, and it hits me. I try to PAP, but it's usually too late. I get on that hamster wheel, and I just run forever, thinking about him. I tell myself that I won't let it happen again, but it always does. I hate myself for not being strong enough to push it back, to use your PAP method."

"It's okay, Dee. Death hits everyone differently. You know what that makes you?"

"What?"

"Human," Dr. Rose replied. It was the last session she had with the doctor.

***

Coming out of those once-a-week sessions, Dee always felt empowered. But that empowerment evaporated as soon as she hit the front door where she and Alex lived for twenty-five years. The silence of the home was deafening, to say the least. On the outside of the home, those times when she went to the park for a walk or a drive down some aimless country roads, she was good; not great, by no means, but she was good enough to manage her emotions.

It was only when she got back home, into her house, and shut the door behind her, that things became harder. That's when Dee tried her best to not break down, not fall apart like she had all those other days in the wake of Alex's death.

Alex was all that she had in the world. Both her parents were dead. She had no siblings or cousins, aunts, or uncles. She was it. And kids between her and Alex? None. The two of them didn't want kids at first. However, that notion changed later when Dee was in her early thirties. Her biological clock started ticking, and she and Alex discussed the possibility of bringing kids into the world.

He wasn't for it because of the freedom the two of them had both financially and as a married couple.

"The last thing that I want to be is to be tied down by kids, Dee. Right now, if we want to do something we can just go do it. We don't have to worry about a kid or who's going to look after them while we're gone. It's just us, you know. Plus, financially, we're in a good spot, but that could be blown up quickly because kids cost a lot. God forbid if the kid has special needs. I personally don't want to take that roll of the dice."

Dee knew everything her husband said was right. She felt that way too. But there was something inside her, something maternal, that wanted/needed a child. She should've let it go, but the notion and drive of wanting a child gnawed at her every passing day. A couple of months later, Dee brought up the subject again, hoping that Alex's stance may have changed some.

"I know how you feel about it. But I think we can make it work. I've thought about this for a long time now. And there's something inside me that wants to have a baby. It's like I have this need for one. I can't explain it, and I don't expect you to understand it. But it's like my life is unfulfilled," Dee explained.

"And you think bringing a child into this world is going to fulfill whatever it is inside you?" Alex asked.

Dee nodded, "I feel that way, yes." The two of them stood in the kitchen and looked around the room, trying to not catch each other's eyes. Moments passed by before Alex finally spoke.

"Okay," he said. "If it means that much to you, let's do it."

Dee couldn't believe her ears. "Are you sure?"

"No," Alex said with a nervous grin. "But I'm not going to be the reason for you not being able to have a kid. We'll just take things as they come. Me and you, together. Till the end of the line." Dee smiled and at that moment loved her husband more than she ever had before.

***

Months went by and try as they did, neither Alex nor Dee could conceive a child. Alex blamed himself, citing that it was probably him who couldn't come up with the goods– while Dee felt like it was her who couldn't hold anything. The fertility doctor, Dr. Hammerstein, told them that they were both to blame. Neither of them could produce a child.

"We call it, 'Reciprocal Infertility.' It affects both spouces, such as is the case with you two. The stats currently sit at anywhere from 10% to 15% of couples that are affected by this," the doctor told them in his office.

That was that. No kids. Sure, there were workarounds but all that seemed to be pseudo-science to Alex and Dee. In the end, they gave up and saw it as a sign. Months went by as the news settled into their minds.

Alex, although not one hundred percent on board with being a father at first, had been imagining a future as a dad. Weeks went by when he and Dee decided they were going to try and in his mind's eye, he saw a kid, hell, maybe even two before it was over with. With each passing day, Alex was getting warmer to the idea of being a dad. So when the news came that he was partly to blame for not being able to have a kid, he took the loss and told Dee that he was sorry.

"It's not your fault. I'm partly to blame here, too," Dee replied.

"Maybe it's for the best, you know? Maybe we're being spared something horrible down the road. Maybe in some weird way, we're not meant to have kids for whatever reason." Dee did not say anything to that. She felt defeated.

Where Alex said it was for the best, Dee felt more than defeated. She felt mortally wounded. That clock that was ticking inside her, that insatiable need to have a kid, was going to have to just burn itself out. There was nothing she really could do about it.

She did briefly look into adopting a child but later decided against that, too. What she wanted was one of her own, made from a mixture of her and Alex– *their* child. It was the toughest pill to swallow, and at the time, Dee felt that was going to be the toughest loss she would ever take. Little did she know that Alex's death would be the toughest loss.

That crushing blow came on August 3rd, 2022 at 1:16 P.M. That was the exact time and date when things in Dee's life changed forever. She would never forget that nor forget where she was when the news came.

She was at her desk in her office. Dee was the head of the HR department in the company she worked for, Simon and Randall, a steel manufacturer that worked for the federal government through governmental contracts. It was a job she liked and was good at. She was hired twenty years ago as a fresh-faced college graduate who quickly won over those who came to see her.

Betty Barrow, the lady that was head of the HR department when Dee was hired on, was a battle ax of a woman who was beyond burned out by her job and by life. Four ex-husbands, a horrible smoking problem (two packs a day), and twenty years at the job had done that to her. Dee figured Betty's problem was herself.

Just as sweet and thoughtful as Dee was with everyone, Betty was the opposite. Workers would come into Betty's office with an issue about their paycheck or a question about their healthcare, she would snap at them in that smoker's voice and tell them she didn't have time for their questions and to speak to their direct supervisor. That's when Dee would jump in and help those in need. It wasn't too long after word had gotten around the factory about how nice and approachable Dee was in the HR department that people came to her instead of Betty.

After five years of learning the job and putting up with Betty's bullshit; after all the vacations Dee and Alex wanted to take off together being canceled; after all the six-day weeks where Betty refused to work a Saturday, causing Dee to have to, Betty finally hung it up and retired early. Why she was not fired years ago was beyond Dee. She guessed that people were afraid of her and what she might do or say. Betty had that way about her. Dee usually gave people the benefit of the doubt, but not Betty Barrow. She knew the moment she met her that she did not cotton to her very well.

Dee was promoted to the head of the department, which meant nothing more than a pay raise and a number two person, like she was to Betty for those years. Dee had been running the department for the last two years anyway, and management knew it. They didn't care if she was doing all of Betty's work as long as the paperwork was getting filled out and filed away for safe record keeping.

Dee cared when management did not because there was a point where she had gotten tired of doing Betty's work and not getting paid for it. She and Alex had discussed her maybe leaving the company and getting an HR position someplace else. She was more than qualified, had a degree, and more importantly, had job experience in her toolbox. She went around and put applications into places she thought she'd like to work, but nothing ever came open. Even the positions in want ads she took a swing at to no avail.

Alex had told her to quit and find something else in another field. Dee didn't want to do that, didn't want Betty to essentially run her off from a job that on the face of it she liked, but had grown tired of Betty and all the work she was doing for entry-level pay years later. The day she walked in to hand over her two weeks' notice was when Delbert Winfield, the factory manager, told her to keep it— that Betty had notified them that she was retiring, effective immediately.

"The job is yours, kiddo," he said.

Standing in his office, a place she had been to many times to have him sign time sheets, purchase orders, and other such things of record, she was dumbfounded. She had come into his office to hand over her resignation only to have the HR director's job.

"Wow," she said in amazement at the turn of events.

"Yeah. I'm not going to open the position up. You're doing the damn thing anyways and have been for years. Everyone here likes you. I'll change your position status right away, and you'll be level five pay from now on. Any questions?" Delbert asked in that southern accent that reminded Dee of Foghorn Leghorn from *Looney Toons*.

"No sir," she replied.

"Good. Now get back to your office, Mrs. Moody. You've got purchase orders from millwork that were sent to you from overnights and a staff meeting you've got to plan for this Friday. Need me, call." Just then Delbert's phone rang, and he picked up greeting whomever it was on the other line. With a grin, Dee spun around on her heels and marched out of his office, feeling like a weight had been lifted off her shoulders.

***

On the day of Alex's death, Dee was sitting at her desk, working at her brand-new computer. She had been after Delbert for years about buying a new one but being the penny-pincher he was, he always said maybe next year. Finally, the computer she had been using for the better part of twelve years gave up the ghost. She emailed Delbert from Rae's computer and told him that it was time not only for her a new one, but for Rae, the new girl who she hired straight out of college, to be her number two just as she was many years ago. Delbert told her to take the company credit card and buy something state-of-the-art, no matter the price. Dee wondered where the real Delbert was because the one she came to know over the years would have never said that.

"Maybe he's getting too old to care," Dee said out loud, reading the email again and making sure that she read correctly..

Dee had bought her and Rae two new desktops, HPs, and had the IT guys from the factory came in and set everything up. Setting everything up was not as easy as she thought it would be. Nevertheless, the IT guys got her taken care of without any interruptions in workflow. Her and Rae had to relearn how to use the newer computers, which were different than what they had been using. After a few days, they were pros.

Rae had made a drive to pick up lunch at Sonic during their lunch and had brought back Dee a Route 66 blue slushy and some tots. Dee was sitting at her desk, keying in that week's overtime allotments when her cell phone rang.

"Hello?"

"Mrs. Moody...my name is Thomas Track. I'm an officer with the..."

That's all Dee would remember, those twelve words. The rest she heard and stored somewhere in her mind, but those words would haunt her for the rest of her days.

After the officer finished telling her the bad news, Dee dropped her phone on the desk and jumped up from her chair, dashing out of the office, leaving Rae behind to wonder what was going on. By the time Rae got up to see what was going on with Dee, she was already down the hall, running full sprint. She called for her, but Dee was already out of the building.

Dee ran out of the wing of the factory where the offices were, across the parking lot o her car, doing all of this on autopilot. The biggest part of her mind was in complete shock by what the police officer had told her. Thankfully the rest of her mind, the part that kept her functioning, was on autopilot, assisting her while she was in panic mode.

She got in her car, sped out of the parking lot, and down the street toward the hospital where Alex was waiting for her. Tears flowed from her eyes, and she was shaking all over, clearly in no condition to be driving. It was only by the grace of God that she made it there to the hospital in one piece; not killing herself or someone while driving like a maniac on the streets and blowing through red lights.

Dee found the closest available parking space and parked the car, leaving it running, never minding to shut it off or close the door. She frantically got out and ran to the huge red sign that read ER.

She nearly ran through the automatic glass doors before they opened just in the nick of time, sending her into the cool lobby of the emergency room. She stopped and looked around to where she needed to go. Then she spotted it: a small cubby on the other side of the room where a fat woman sat on one side of the glass at a desk, taking down information on a computer while a kid that looked to be twenty-two sat on the other side, fumbling through his phone and finding whatever it was the fat woman was asking for.

Dee rushed over to the cubby and wedged herself between the sitting kid and the glass.

"I'm Dee Moody!" Her voice was raised in panic. "I got a call that my husband is here! I need to know where he's at!"

"Ma'am, if you'll have a seat right over there, I can get with you in just a second..."

"I don't have time! I need to know where my husband is at! You don't understand— I got a call from the police that he's here!"

Just at that moment, the officer that called, Thomas Track, came back into the ER through the automatic doors. He heard Dee shouting over at the cubby and knew that was the woman he had the misfortune of calling ten minutes ago.

"Mrs. Moody? Mrs. Moody? I'm going to need you to calm down for me just a second, okay? Okay, Mrs. Moody? Just give me a calm few seconds, okay?" Officer Track said, walking over to her.

Dee spun around and looked at the cop who looked to be no older than the kid that was sitting in the chair scared out of his wits by her.

"My husband is here. I got a call from the police that…"

Officer Track nodded his head and touched her on the shoulder, "I know, Mrs. Moody. I know. I'm the one that called, okay? I'm the one who called. Now, I'm going to need you to go over here for just a second, so I can get you to your husband, okay? Can you do that for me?"

"Is he okay? I need to see him!" Dee said looking at the police officer and then back at the fat woman behind the glass who was typing away on her keyboard.

"Rosa, we need to get her to her husband. Can we get a nurse out there quick?" Office Track asked politely through the glass, trying to keep Dee at bay.

Rosa was already working on it. "Yeah, I'll buzz ya'll in. See Nurse Brooks at the nurse's station. I'll tell her y'all are coming."

The huge double doors opened automatically, and Officer Track took Dee's hand and gently walked her across the ER lobby and through the doors. The hallway was long, emotionless, and a neverending color of white that made Dee's head swim a bit. One thing about that day she would always remember was how long that damn hallway was. It seemed to never end.

When the hallway ended, the police officer and Dee walked up to the nurse's station. Officer Track knew several of the nurses who were on duty that afternoon. He went to school with one of them back at Central High several years ago. Another he had dated briefly.

"Samantha, I have here Mrs. Moody. Her husband Alex was brought in a little bit ago," Officer Track said, speaking softly as if trying to not cause any more panic in Dee's mind than there already was.

Nurse Brooks looked at the police officer and knew exactly who he was talking about. It had been a slow day around there, and Alex was only the second patient to have been brought in. He also was the second one to have died that day behind the automatic doors of the ER.

"Sure," Nurse Brooks said as she walked around her station to meet Dee. "Mrs. Moody. You're husband, Alex...it seemed that he had a massive cardiac event earlier this morning at work. He was brought in by the EMTs, but he was...we just couldn't get him back." Nurse Brooks out of the corner of her eye saw Dr. Louis coming down the hallway with a cup of coffee. "Dr. Louis. I've got Mrs. Moody here. She's the wife of the man that was brought in with the cardiac event."

Dr. Louis nodded and approached Dee with his free hand extended, "Mrs. Moody, I'd like to talk to you over here in private if I can." He guided her away from Officer Track, and Nurse Brooks and escorted her down the hall a bit where the two of them could be alone.

"What happened to Alex? She told me he..."

Dr. Louis nodded, "Yeah, I'm afraid so. He collapsed while at work. The EMTs got there and worked on him...they worked on him the entire ambulance ride here. Me and the staff worked on him, too. I'm sorry."

Dee stood there on legs that felt like jelly, a mind that was racing a million miles a second. "You say sorry...he's going to be okay, right? Tell me Alex is going to be okay."

Dr. Louis dropped his head. He had been here before, many times, to break the sad news. It was never easy, no matter how many hundreds of times he's had to do it. The looks of desperation and total sadness never evaporated from his thoughts after the workday was finished. He took those people home with him, those looks of devastation when he told them their loved ones were gone.

"No, Mrs. Moody. Alex is dead. We did everything we could do."

Dee raised her shaky hand to her mouth and screamed as she leaned against the wall and slid down, slowly crying. Dr. Louis reached for her, but it was too late. Dee was sitting on the floor, back against the wall, head in her hands crying and screaming, calling for Alex.

***

A couple of days after the ER, seeing Alex lying on the table dead for the first time, and feeling nothing but the coldness of his skin when she held him and cried for God to bring him back, Dee found herself standing in a room with several caskets. It was a showroom at the Zegler Funeral Home in Claxton. The owner of the place was talking to Dee about her options. His words were empty to her.

Dee was still reeling from the news—still a complete shock to her system— from when she laid eyes on Alex in that room in the ER. Dr. Louis had walked her from the hallway and into the room. Laying on a table was her husband, the man she had loved to the moon and back a trillion times. Her eyes grew wide in terror, and tears poured out as she ran to him. The doctor gave her as much time as she needed and closed the door behind him, giving her privacy.

Somehow, much like she did getting to the ER when the phone call came, Dee later that day found herself sitting in their driveway. She was stunned, her brain was scrambled– a million memories of them, her and Alex, played on a maddening loop. That day in the driveway turned to night, and Dee never made it into the house. She cried herself to sleep in her car.

She was standing there in the Zegler Funeral Home, looking at caskets, and hearing a man talk softly about each of them and the prices. Dee was trying her best to maintain her composure, her best to just stand up and get this business of the funeral and burial over with. The thing that Dee wanted most of all was for the man to just pick one for her, get to the Burton Cemetery, and bury him so she could just focus on Alex and not the business of funeral planning.

There was no funeral for Alex Moody. No receiving of friends. He had a few, and they called and dropped by the house to see Dee and offer their condolences. There was no family. Alex was an only child, and his parents were both dead, as Dee's were. The two of them were orphans in this cruel world. All they had was each other til the end of the line. Who knew that the end of the line would come so quickly? She had no clue that death was right around the corner for her husband.

The burial went as planned four days later after his death at the Burton Cemetery. It was only her, Rae, a few of Alex's friends from work and childhood, and the preacher that Zegler Funeral Home had recommended to perform the graveside service. That was it.

Once that was over, Dee said her goodbyes to everyone and walked with Rae down the hill and to her car. The two of them drove off through the rain that early August afternoon.

"Do you need me to stay with you tonight?" Rae asked, driving through the rain.

Dee looked out the passenger side window as the landscape flew by like pictures in a flipbook.

"No. But thanks though. You've done enough, and I appreciate it more than you know."

"You know I can stay with you again tonight if you'd like. It's really nothing at all."

Dee kept her eyes on the passing landscape, aimlessly watching houses and trees fly by at fifty miles an hour. "It's okay, Rae. I'll be okay."

Rae doubted it, but she was not going to push her, not today. She kept quiet and drove Dee back home.

***

In the days and weeks after Alex's death, Dee spiraled out of control mentally. She swirled in all five stages of grief all at once– forwards, then backwards, and side to side. Some nights stretched for weeks where sleep was thin and the dreams, when they came, were of Alex; always of Alex of days past. In those dreams, Dee would wake up from her couch, screaming and crying, calling out for her husband. Those dreams of him had a way of feeling real, as if her husband was still alive and kicking.

Slowly, Dee became a victim of her own mind and house. She took a leave from work, and Rae managed things admirably. She should, after all, Dee was the one who trained her. With the work situation put on ice for a while, at least until November, Dee began to exist– not live, but merely exist within the home.

She didn't eat and had lost ten pounds in the two weeks since Alex's death. It's not that she didn't try, but food did not taste the same. Even some of her favorites had no taste at all. In a weird way, Dee felt guilty for eating while Alex was dead. It didn't seem right to her. She would get hungry but kept her mind on that hamster wheel of Alex and the memories of him. God, how she loved and missed him. He was her soul mate, her touchstone, her best friend. He was all she had in this world.

A month after Alex's death, Dee contemplated suicide. She had gone as far as going into the closet in their bedroom and taking the gun out of the shoebox that sat on a shelf. It was never fired, the gun, but had given Alex a sense of security in the home in case of home invaders.

Dee, having never held that gun, nor any gun in her life, picked up the Colt .45 revolver. The first thing she noticed was how heavy the gun was. She carried the gun over to the bed and laid it down. She walked back over to the shelf in the closet and took the small box of bullets.

She fumbled around on how to open the chamber, and after close examination and a YouTube tutorial, she found out how to open it. She felt stupid after seeing how it was done. Nevertheless, she took the bullets from the box and inserted six, one by one, into the chamber. With the gun fully loaded, she pushed the chamber back into place. She felt as if she should be shaking or terrified out of her wits. But the truth of the matter was that she was exhausted and wanted to die. She didn't want to live without Alex.

Dee walked over to the full-length mirror in their bedroom and stood in front of it. She looked at herself and didn't recognize the woman she had become: the weight loss, the black under her soulful eyes, her hair—which was always kept nice and well-maintained—was all over the place and was in need of a good washing and maybe a trim. Dee had lost herself, lost her way, lost her will to continue on after Alex's death. Nothing was the same.

Dee took a deep breath and slowly raised that heavy gun up to the side of her right temple. She closed her eyes and pulled the trigger. She expected a loud bang...but there was nothing. The trigger didn't move. Dee opened her eyes and looked at the gun when she brought it down from the side of her head. Then she remembered from the YouTube tutorial that the style of gun she had: the person had to pull the handle back to engage the gun. Dee dropped the gun and fell to the floor in a sobbing heap where she eventually fell asleep.

***

"I think you may need to see someone, Dee," Rae told her over the phone. "I've been seeing a therapist since me and Billy split, and it's helped me."

Dee wanted to hang up on Rae the moment she suggested she needed to see a professional. She knew what was wrong: she missed her husband. The void in her life was much too great to bear most times, and

Dee was not the same person. She doubted she ever would be the same old Dee Moody. That version was gone– see ya, wouldn't want to be ya.

"I don't need to see a therapist, Rae," Dee replied dryly. "I know exactly what is wrong with me. I'm still trying to come to terms with what happened."

"I know. But talking to someone that is trained might be able to help you sort some things out."

"What is there to sort out? Alex is dead. I'm left with trying to get through the rest of my life without him. It's pretty basic, black and white, from where I'm at," Dee said with some spite in her voice.

"It is. But you know what I'm talking about. You can't hole yourself up in your house forever, you know? Eventually, you're going to have to come out and get back into life. I know it's hard..."

Dee cut her off right there sternly.

"Don't, Rae. You have no idea how hard this is, okay? No idea. I lost the only man that I have ever loved, the only family I had left. I don't think he heard me tell him that I loved him that morning." Dee started to cry again, which was the norm in those days.

Then, Dee's mind started to trail off as it often did in the wake of Alex's death...

***

The morning of Alex's death was just a routine morning indeed. Dee had gotten out of bed and started getting her morning ready for work while Alex did the same. Usually in the mornings, the two of them would greet each other with a kiss, just as they had every morning for as long as Dee could remember. It was such a simple thing to do, that kiss hello in the morning, but it was woven into the fabric of their marriage for the duration.

Dee was in the shower in the bathroom upstairs while Alex was in the bathroom downstairs finishing up his morning routine. When he was finished, he walked up the stairs to the second floor and yelled from the second floor landing towards the bathroom door that was cracked open.

"Hon, I'm outta here! I'm running a bit behind! You want me to pick up supper tonight since I'll be home before you?!" Alex asked.

Dee couldn't hear her husband very well over the loud running water from the shower head. It didn't help that Alex spoke softly. But she managed to put together a few of the words and figured he was talking about supper.

"Yeah, that's good! Anything you get will be fine!" she shouted back over the running water of the shower.

"Okay, I love you! Be careful going to work!" Alex shouted back as he ran down the stairs. That was the last time he spoke to his wife as a living, breathing person.

"I love you too!" Dee shouted while she washed her hair. Alex was already downstairs and never heard her.

***

"Dee? Dee? Are you there?" Rae asked.

Snapping back into reality from the past replaying in her head, Dee replied. "Yeah, I'm still here. But listen, thanks but no thanks. I'll get better eventually. I have to, right? I mean, I can't do this forever."

"No, you can't. Do you need some company tonight? Might do you some good," Rae asked.

"I'm not exactly ready to be seen right now. I look horrible. I saw myself in the mirror the other night, and I just didn't even recognize myself. But I'm trying..."

"I know you are, Dee. I know. Have you been sleeping any?"

"No, not much. A little here and there is about the best I can do. I think most times I'm just too exhausted to even sleep."

Just then, the smoke detectors in the house, all eight of them started going off. Not in regular beep...beep...beep...beep fashion, but intermittently like in Morse code. It was loud.

"What's going on over there?" Rae asked.

Dee, puzzled by the smoke detectors going off, slowly rose from the couch and stood in her living room looking around. The intermittent beeping was all through the house. It was the strangest thing.

"I don't know exactly. But all my smoke detectors are going off. Like in every room."

Dee walked from the living room to the dining room and then from there into the kitchen. She walked back through the dining room and back into the living room where she stopped at the landing of the stairwell. The smoke detectors up on the second floor were going off in that intermittent way as well.

"Sounds like some sort of Morse code," Rae said, pulling the phone away from her ear.

Dee stood with wonderment at all the alarms. "Yeah, it kinda does, doesn't it? I remember Alex a long time ago back when we were first married messed around with that."

At that precise moment, although Dee Moody had no idea of it, her life was about to be changed yet again. The smoke detectors stopped all at once.

"They stop?" Rae asked, putting the phone back to her ear.

"Yeah. I'm glad you heard it because had you not been on the phone, I would have thought I'd imagined it," Dee said as she still looked around the house in puzzlement and wonder.

"Has that ever happened before?"

Dee shook her head no as she walked over to the living room where the room's only smoke detector hung.

"Never. The only time that I've ever heard them go off was when Alex would change out the batteries. He would push the button down to make sure they were working. But this is a new one for me. Weird."

"Yeah, I'd say that's up there." Rae had to bite her tongue because she almost suggested that maybe it was Alex trying to communicate with her. She believed in that kind of stuff.

Dee was not a believer in the unseen world like Rae was. Just as Dee wondered what could've caused the smoke detectors to all go off intermittently, as if they were sending out a code of some sort, Rae on the other end wondered if it was indeed Alex trying to communicate with his wife.

Had Dee known about Morse code, like Alex had, she would have understood that the smoke detectors going off weren't just some random malfunctioning of the devices themselves. It was indeed a code: Morse code being sent to Dee from the beyond. That sequence of .. / .-.. --- ...- . / -.-- --- ..- through the beeping of the smoke detectors throughout the house was the message. That message was, "I love you."

***

The days after Alex's death had turned to weeks. During those weeks, Dee never felt so lost. She was lost without her husband and best friend. Death had come to take him away and how cruel it was that she never got to say goodbye. That was another added layer of her grief. She never got a chance to tell him how much he meant to her. But he had to know, right? She told him from time to time like long-term married couples do about how much the other feels for the other. Dee and Alex were no different. Both were still in love, and both would walk to the ends of the earth for the other. There was a bond there between the two of them that even death itself could not break.

Weeks were spent in the same clothes with no shower, no food, and no self-care whatsoever. Dee was aware even in her profound depression that she was spiraling towards nothing. And that seemed fine for her because not having Alex was a life not worth living.

Dee would sit around crying a lot during those early weeks that stretched on for eternity. She would walk around the house, downstairs and up on the second floor, looking out the windows into the world outside. Things out there seemed normal, the same as they ever were. Inside the Moody home, however, things had changed forever. *How could that be,* she wondered. *How could things outside still look the same since he was gone? Shouldn't everything outside change too?*

In that captivity inside her home, Dee would look at pictures, both physical in picture frames and loose ones from drawers, and those hundreds on her phone that had accumulated over the years. She would sit for hours lost in those pictures, lost in times past. Through those pictures, Dee saw vacations to Hilton Head Island in South Carolina.

It was by far their favorite place to visit twice a year. One in March and the other in late September. In fact, she had already booked the vacation two months prior at the same place they always stayed in, The Beachside, which was on the beach that overlooked the Atlantic. It was the most peaceful place in the entire world for the two of them.

Almost on cue, she scrolled to a set of snapshots of their last stay in Hilton Head. It was back in March, a lifetime ago now, it seemed. There were pictures of Alex sitting on the beach in a lounger, smiling and waving. Another of Alex sitting on the front porch of the place they rented for the week watching the sunset into the ocean. Then there was a picture of the two of them at their favorite place to eat down there, Steve's Lobster Catch. In the picture, the two of them were sitting close together, smiling for the waiter who snapped the pic of them. It was the last picture the two of them were in. The revelation of that picture being the final one made Dee cry out in pain as tears poured.

She closed the photo app on her phone and submitted to the wave of emotion she was riding high on at the moment. She revisited those pictures often during the weeks after Alex's death. It was all she had left of him. It hurt like hell seeing the pictures, remembering what he looked like, seeing his smile (as if she would ever forget him), seeing the two of them happy— frozen in a moment in time. Dee would go to that app often and make herself hurt all over again. She knew it would hurt scrolling through times past, but it also felt so good to see him again in a place other than her mind. Seeing him with her own eyes helped, but oh God, did it break her heart all over.

The pictures were hard to look at, for sure. But the hardest thing was the text messages between the two. Just like the pictures, Dee's heart busted into a million pieces as she would lay there in bed reading months' worth of messages. That made her break down countless times much like the pictures had. Those messages were just random in nature. Subjects like *hey, what do you want for supper* or *how's your day been so far?* And even the, *hey, just wanted you to know that I love you.* Reading those messages hurt, but that was okay. She was there for the hurt. That's why she opened the message app like the photo app. It felt so good to hurt so bad.

Dee would read through thousands of messages until she ended up to the final ones from the day he died. There weren't many that day. Just a few that were sent back and forth— nothing unusual, nothing that would indicate that those messages were going to be the last ones ever sent between the two of them.

Dee

Hey, I'm at work. I hope you have a good day

Alex

Me too. Sorry I didn't text when I got here. This damn meeting has got me all sorts of messed up. I'll do better, don't ground me lol

Dee

I would take your game system away but I don't think that would fix anything lol

Alex

Thanks Mom! Text you hopefully around lunch

And that was that. Those were the last messages that were sent between them. Nothing but the usual banter. If Dee would've somehow known that this was the last time they would talk, she would have told him how much she loved him, how much he meant to her. Reading all those messages nearly nightly stabbed her in the chest and when she got to the end, the last words, she fell to pieces. It was like she lost him all over again.

***

It had been two months since Alex's passing. Time didn't ease anything at all. His absence still was fresh, still raw on her emotions. Dee did manage to dip her toes back into some aspect of being normal. She started eating a little more here and there. She started showering more, started doing more self-care as August came to a close and September started.

When October had rolled around, she had lost another fifteen pounds, and the clothes she wore were hanging loosely off her. However, Dee was back to doing regular maintenance on herself. Although she hated the idea of doing things that were normal again since Alex was dead, it did feel good. Simple things like brushing her teeth and putting lotion on her skin after a hot shower brought her back to some of the old routine of days past. She wondered if that was wrong. She asked Rae one night on the phone what she thought, and Rae was happy that she was back to doing some things that were normal.

"Doesn't mean that you've forgotten him, Dee. It means that you have to take care of yourself, too. Do you think that Alex would want you not showering or not eating? What about not going outside the house?"

Dee figured that Rae was right. She also figured that she might be right on seeing the therapist.

The night that Dee finally laid in the bed, *their bed.* It was a huge milestone in her grieving process. She had not been in their bed for over two months and wondered how it would feel. That night, she did her pre-sleep ritual: brushing her teeth, rinsing her mouth, washing her face, and taking a hot shower. The hot showers always relaxed her right before bed.

Coming out of the bathroom from down the hall, Dee in nothing but a long tee shirt—one of Alex's Chicago Bears shirts—walked into their bedroom and looked at the bed. It was still unmade from that morning she and Alex had gotten up. She got in on her side of the bed and didn't think about it, just did it. That's when she took her phone off the nightstand, opened the messaging app, and began reading the messages, *their messages*, once again. That was when the tears came, causing her to forget all about being in their bed.

After closing the messaging app, she lay there on her back and cried even more while staring up at the ceiling. Eventually, she rolled over to face where Alex would be lying had he been alive. She could still smell his body lotion he loved wearing that he had gotten from Bath and Body Works: Noir, it was called. Dee was wild about it. That scent was intertwined into the bed sheets and comforter they shared in that king-sized bed. His scent caused even more tears, and she took his pillow and drew it close to her. She held it as if it was Alex, and eventually Dee cried herself to sleep, holding that pillow his head used to rest on.

***

That next morning, Dee was awakened by the sunlight from the October morning pouring through their bedroom window. This was odd because Dee had not opened the curtains and blinds since coming home from the ER that day of Alex's death. Squinting from the sunbathed bedroom, Dee got up from the bed and walked over to the window. She studied the window curiously. *I didn't open these,* she thought. She looked across the bedroom and saw that the hallway was drenched in sunlight. The curtains and blinds had been opened in there as well.

Dee walked out of the bedroom and down the hallway looking at the window. She then went into the bathroom and opened the door and just like the bedroom and hallway windows, the curtains and blinds were open in that window too. *What's going on here*, she wondered. She checked the spare bedroom by opening the door and saw the curtains and blinds were opened in there as well. Even more bizarre because she never went into that bedroom. That room had become a catch-all since there was not going to be a child.

Dee walked down the stairs into the living room where all the curtains and blinds were open, even the ones in the dining room and kitchen. The utility room, when Dee checked it, had the picture window blind opened. Dee walked out of the utility room and into the kitchen where she stood thinking about the recent turn of events. And in her waking mind, she figured it out, how the curtains and blinds were opened. It had to be Alex.

Every morning without fail as long as she could remember, Alex would wake up in the mornings and go throughout the house, pulling the curtains back and twisting open the wand to the blinds to let the daylight in. He hated a dark house and loved the natural light coming in. And at night, when darkness fell, Alex would go throughout the house and close all the blinds and curtains. That was one of his jobs around the house.

Dee stood in the middle of the kitchen and wondered with wild thoughts if it was indeed Alex who had done that this morning with the windows. It was crazy to think, but was it possible? There was no other explanation, no other options. What Dee did know was that it wasn't her that had done that. Those curtains and blinds had been left alone for over two months.

"Alex?" Dee spoke out loud in the kitchen. Just then, as if right on cue, the smoke detectors in the house started going off in that Morse code arrangement.

.. / .-.. --- ...- . / -.-- --- ..- "I love you" it coded out. But at the time, just like the first time it happened, Dee had no idea what the intermittent beeping was, or that it was a message.

***

Dee took Rae's advice and made an appointment to see the therapist Rae had recommended. It was the first time she had ever done anything like that, seeing a shrink, but thought maybe it could help some. Certainly wouldn't hurt. It also marked the first time since the burial that Dee had emerged from the house. She was actually wearing outside clothes instead of weeks-worn PJs.

It was odd coming out of her house. The wind felt different on her skin, and the air smelled crisp. Fall was in the air, and her neighborhood was in full swing celebrating the changing of seasons. Trees along her street, as well as all over town, were changing their leaves from green to brilliant reds, yellows, and oranges. Fall was her favorite time of year as was Alex's. They would drive up to the Smoky Mountains close to Halloween to look at all the trees in their beautiful rich landscape as the fall colors popped as far as the eye could see. Every year they did this, Alex was always dumbfounded by this change in nature.

"I think the colors get prettier and prettier every year," he would say each time.

Dee got into her car, a car that she had not been in since the burial, and started it up. It felt foreign to her at first. More than two months had passed by since she had done a lot of things, and driving was one of them. She had a random thought, sitting in the driver's seat: *What if I forgot how?* She pressed into the brake, pulled the gear into R and she backed out using the backup camera as a guide. On the street, she moved the gear to D, and off she went.

"Like riding a bicycle," she said to herself.

Inside Dr. Rose's office, she sat looking around the room while the doctor looked over her intake form. It was a form Dee had to fill out a few days ago online when she made the appointment. All it was was a form that wanted her name and address, medications she might be on, medical insurance, and the reason for the visit. On the reason for the visit, Dee just wrote, "struggling since my husband died."

"Sorry for your loss, Mrs. Moody."

"Thank you."

"Can you tell me about the event? How have you been coping since?" Dr. Rose asked.

"Well," Dee shifted in her chair to get more comfortable. "Not good. This is the first time I've been out of the house and out of my pajamas since his burial. I walk aimlessly around the inside of my home, hoping to find his presence, I guess. I look at pictures of us and of him all the time. I go through our text messages before I go to sleep."

"Do you feel closer to him looking at the pictures and reading the messages?" Dr. Rose asked but already knew what the response was going to be.

Dee nodded, "I do. I mean, it hurts to look at him. But I can't help it. I have to. And reading those messages, I can't NOT open that app to read them. I know it's probably not the healthiest thing to do, but it's all I have of him."

"If it helps you cope, within reason, then it's normal. The only time that coping mechanisms don't work is when people use drinking or drugs as a way to get along. Not doing any of that, are you?"

"Lord no. I haven't even had a sip of alcohol in my entire life."

"Have you accepted that your husband is gone?" Dr. Rose asked.

Dee wasn't sure how to answer that question. She knew that he was gone, dead. But did she accept the loss?

"Yeah, I guess I have. I mean, I know that he's not coming back. I get that part, you know? It's the everything else I'm struggling with."

"Tell me about 'the everything else' you're struggling with."

Dee took in a deep breath and let it out. "Well, I just recently was able to finally get into our bed and sleep. I struggled with that for the better part of two months. I just couldn't do it."

"How did you feel once you did it?"

"I mean, it felt good. But it was empty, you know? I had never slept alone before because Alex was always right there beside me for years. And now he's not. So it's been hard just doing that."

"What other struggles have you encountered?"

"Just everyday stuff. Like getting up without him. Not being able to talk to him. Not being able to see him. Not watching TV or a movie with him. I guess I didn't realize how much time we were together."

"And now it's a void," Dr. Rose interjected.

"Right. A void. Literally half of me is gone, it feels. I feel like I'm tail spinning out of control some days."

"Have you gotten the tail spinning under control any?"

"Somewhat. I don't have the days where I want to kill myself anymore, if that's what you mean. I still have breakdowns, still have those moments where something in the house reminds me of him. It's just been a hard road so far."

"When you think about killing yourself, how far has that gone? Suicidal ideation or actual planning?" Dr. Rose asked seriously.

"I mean, I loaded his gun and pulled the trigger next to my head. The only reason I'm here right now is because I didn't realize that I had to pull the hammer back to engage the gun. After that, I just put the gun away and took that as a sign, you know? Sometimes I don't want to live, and I wish I could just die in my sleep or something because it's hard living without him."

"Mrs. Moody, I'm going to tell you something. Just you being here, alive, is a testament to the courage you have to face the days alone after the event in your life. A lot of people succumb to suicide, or they just wither away into nothing at all– a shell of their former self.

"I want you to try something for me. When these waves of emotions come, and they will often throughout. One thing I know about loss is that you just don't get over it. You manage it. It's all you can do. We have to manage life, successes, and especially failures. But there's something that I call PAP.

"Its, Pause it...Acknowledge it...Process it in real time. When these emotions inside you come out from thinking about Alex or seeing something that reminds you of him, use the PAP system. Don't ever try to evade your feelings. Management of those is the key. Doesn't mean you're weak; it means that you are trying your best to deal with the event."

***

Dee was in the shower when another odd thing happened to her. It was around bedtime, and she was doing her nightly ritual– a ritual she started right before bed which began when she was a little girl. Dee was under the hot water falling from the head when all of a sudden, the door to the bathroom opened. Not slowly like in those old horror movies, but with a *whoosh.* The door slammed against the side of the wall, causing Dee to scream out in fright. She pulled the shower cutain and looked around, just knowing she was going to see a home invader standing there ready to kill her. Instead, there was nothing. Just an open door.

Dee turned the water off. She stepped out of the tub and looked around outside of the door and into the hallway. Nothing. It was still. She held her breath, trying to make her ears hone in on any strange sounds around the second floor. Again, nothing. She took the bathroom door, closed it from the inside, and pulled on the door knob. It wouldn't budge. Then she twisted the knob and gave it a jerk, and it opened like always. Dee wondered if she'd even shut the door to begin with. Even if she had left it somewhat ajar, what would have caused the door to violently open? These were the thoughts that Dee wondered as she began to towel off.

Another instance of something odd in the house occurred a few days later. It was by far the scariest of the strange things that had happened to Dee in the house. About twelve years ago, while on vacation in South Carolina, Alex and Dee visited an antique shop.

Dee wasn't about collecting junk and neither was Alex for that matter, but Alex had seen something in the window while they were walking by in the downtown district of Charleston that caught his eye. It was a jukebox, all lit up and playing. It was enough of a sigh to cause Alex to stop walking and stare into the window as Dee stood wondering what her husband was looking at.

"What is it?" Dee asked.

"It's a Rock-Ola jukebox. My granddaddy used to have one in his den when I was a kid. God, I haven't seen one of these in years. He used to play all the classics from this thing."

"Yeah?" Dee said, walking over to her husband who was pressed against the glass. "Yeah, it's nice, I guess."

"I remember playing records all the time there. His held sixty records I think. Man, I played the hell out of that thing."

"What happened to it?" Dee asked.

"I don't really know. When grandma died, I guess Mom and Dad sold it or something. I never saw it again. But this one right here looks exactly like the one he had. I'm going to go inside and have a closer look."

"You go right ahead. I'm going over to this ice cream shop for a sundae. You want one?"

He didn't answer because he was already through the entrance door to the antique shop.

When Dee came out with her sundae, Alex was walking out with a huge grin on his face. She just knew that he had bought the juke, could see it on that grin of his.

"Listen, Dee, honey, I…"

"You bought that jukebox, didn't you?"

"Yeah, you mad?" Alex asked.

"I ought to be. But you can work off the price."

"Something tells me that won't really be work," Alex said, reaching over to give his wife a kiss-peck on her cheek. "I paid the man, and he's going to have it delivered to the house in about two weeks. You should come inside and see it. She's a beaut!"

Being an engineer and able to fix and retro adapt just about anything mechanical or electrical, Alex redid the jukebox so that it could play nothing but CDs. He said it was simple actually and even tried to explain the process to Dee. She never understood anything her husband talked about but saw the fire catch in his eyes when he went into one of his explanations. Retrofitting the jukebox to play CDs was over her head for sure, but she loved that he was passionate about it. It was one of the things that she missed dearly about him.

Dee was sitting in the living room scrolling through pictures on her phone of the two of them, yet again. She was riding that wave of emotion and was doing the PAP system that Dr. Rose had told her about. She was surfing on that big wave all right.

She was going through pictures while sitting on the couch, looking at ones she had looked at hundreds of times over the last couple of months. Tears were forming, and the dam was about to break. All of a sudden out of the corner of her eye, she saw the juke light up in that green and blue neon. She heard the mechanical and electrical parts moving and buzzing inside it.

Then a song came on from the CD playlist. It was Alex's favorite: "Everlong" from the Foo Fighters. It was an acoustic version that he loved the most. Dee placed the phone down slowly and rose from the couch. She looked into the den from the living room. Chills ran up and down her spine. Gooseflesh prickled on her arms. She could even feel the inside of her mouth dry up.

She walked closer to the den, closer to the jukebox. The smoke detectors, the curtains and blinds, the bathroom door opening, and now this, was freaking Dee out when thinking about all of the incidents together at once.

Without any thought about it at all, Dee called out to her dead husband. "Alex? Are you here?" No reply. Dave Grohl just kept singing with his acoustic guitar.

***

"So. based on what you're telling me, you have a haunting," Rae said as she sat across from Dee in a chair in her living room.

"Maybe. I don't know. It's just so weird," Dee replied.

"All the things that's happened are tied to Alex in some way though, right?" Rae asked.

"Do you think it's possible that Alex is here?" Dee just came out and asked.

She knew how Rae was when it came to the supernatural. Dee, not so much. She didn't much believe in things like that. Maybe it was because if she believed in stuff of that nature she would spook herself. Hell, this woman couldn't even watch a horror movie. She watched *A Nightmare on Elm Street* for the first time a few years back, and it scared her so badly that she told Alex she was never watching a horror movie as long as she lived.

"I think so. He's tied to the house and to you. Could be trying to get your attention. Have you talked to him?"

"What do you mean?" Dee asked.

"Like, have full-on conversations with him in the house," Rae said.

"No, that sounds crazy. I did call out to him when the jukebox came on."

"Why did you do that?"

"Because I thought it might've been him that turned it on with his favorite song."

Rae sat back in the chair with a look of triumph, "Then you already believe he's here in some capacity. You should try to reach out."

"Like how?"

"We could do, like, a seance or something. I could try to channel him. But I'd have to be very careful..."

Dee cut her off, "No, I'm not bringing any kind of that stuff into the house."

"Well, how are you ever going to know?" Rae asked.

The answer to that question would come soon enough. Later that night to be exact.

***

Dee slid into bed after her nightly routine. The house was locked up for the night, and Dee lay there on her back with the conversation between her and Rae jarring around in her mind. *What if Alex was in the house,* she wondered. *Wouldn't I be able to sense him? It makes sense with all the stuff that's been going on lately. But could that even be?*

Dee rolled over towards her phone that was sitting on the nightstand to Google about ghosts when her phone chirped a text notification. She looked at the preview screen at the top and to her shock and horror– the name said Alex.

Dee's stomach fell to her knees and her hands began to shake. Seeing a preview of an incoming message caused her such fright, ten times worse than the jukebox ever thought about doing, that Dee sprang from the bed and stood and looked at her phone on wobbly legs. Could it be?

Dee ran her shaking hand through her thick gray hair while her other hand held the phone. She wondered what she should do next. Open the text? Or was she just seeing things? The jukebox was real, and so was the bathroom door, the curtains, and the smoke detectors. Dee stood in the dimly lit bedroom room and looked at her phone that was awaiting her decision. It was do or die now. She tapped the screen and it came on. On the bottom left, on the message icon, there was a number 1.

Dee opened the app, and there on her text message screen was Alex's name with a new message highlighted. She tapped the name and opened it up, doing all of this without any thought. Honestly, if she had thought about doing it, she would have run out of the bedroom and slept outside on the front porch for the night.

Dee's mouth hung open while she held the phone in her hand slowly sitting down on the edge of the bed.

Alex: hey

Dee began to cry. Tears fell on the phone screen. Her emotions weren't just a wave like she had been surfing on in the two months since he'd been gone; this was surfing a tsunami. She tried to type a reply, but her fingers wouldn't steady themselves long enough for her to do so. It took her several attempts, and the phone falling to the floor multiple times before she could type out a simple reply.

Dee: hey

A few minutes passed by before he replied.

Alex: you okay?

Tears fell even more from her eyes, causing her vision to become blurry.

Dee: is this really you?

Alex: yeah, it's really me

Dee: then tell me something only we'd know

Alex: let's see...um... remember that night on the beach at Hilton Head? We danced under the moonlight with no music. Just us that night. You were wearing that green sundress that I love. Your hair smelled like honeysuckle, my favorite.

Dee: Yeah, I remember that. How could I forget

Alex: One of my favorite memories of us

Dee: I can't believe it's you!

Alex: I've been trying to get your attention Dee. This was my last resort. Glad you answered.

Dee: The curtains and blinds, the bathroom door, the smoke detectors, and the jukebox were all you??

Alex: Yup. Sure was.

Dee: You scared me half to death, you know

Alex: I'm sorry. I wasn't trying to

Dee had stopped crying and was sitting in the middle of her bed now with the phone in her hands. They were shaking still, but she was in control of them. Her stomach was swarming with butterflies, that was for sure, but she was too focused on talking to her dead husband to really notice.

Dee: I can't believe this is happening

Alex: Me either

Dee: How??

Alex: No idea. I just know that I'm here in the house, but I don't ever see you. I feel you, but I don't see you

Dee: This is just so crazy! I don't know what to say. I'm just beyond freaked out at the moment

Alex: Do you need a second?

Dee: No! I've not talked to you in such a long time! I don't want to stop now

Alex: Good. Me either. Because I don't know how much longer I've got. I died and came here.

Dee: Do you remember dying?

Alex: A little bit. But the memory fades more and more. I know that I felt a horrible pain in my chest and I remember falling to the floor and my vision getting further and further away. That's all I can remember

Dee: I got a call from a police officer about you being at the ER. I got there but you were already dead

Alex: Dee, honey, I'm so sorry. I never meant to leave you like that. We still had a long ways to go, you know?

Dee started crying and hurting all over again as if he had just died, and she just heard the news.

Dee: I know. I just miss you so much. I wish I could see you and kiss you and hold you

Alex: Same here. I miss you. Man, we haven't been apart from each other since we've been married and this is so strange. I feel like I let you down

Dee: You can't prevent your own death. It's not like you gave yourself a heart attack

Alex: This is true. But I feel like I've hurt you

Dee: You didn't hurt me. I just miss you is all

Alex: I miss you too. How long have I been gone?

Dee: Over two months now

Alex: Wow! Is it close to Halloween yet?

Dee: Getting closer

Alex: I'm guessing you've not been in the mood for decorating the outside of the house for Halloween? Ah, well, that was my job anyways right lol

Dee: Yeah, you were the Halloween person of the marriage. I just supported you lol

Alex: You remember that time I was hanging those big spiders off the side of the front porch roof and I nearly fell off the ladder. Man, that was scary!

Dee: Yes!! If I hadn't been there you might have broken your neck!

Alex: Dee saves the day! LOL

Dee: Yeah, that was scary for sure

Alex: You know, I want you to know that it sucks not being able to see you and I miss you so bad!

Dee: I know! Does for me too! All I do is scroll through pictures all day looking at you and us. I cry most days

Alex: You're not falling apart too bad I hope because you still got to live. You've got a long ways to go honey

Dee: I have been yes. Started seeing a therapist. It's been way too hard dealing without you. I never thought I'd have to do it in my late 40s

Alex: Me neither. I wish that we didn't. I honestly figured I'd go first, but not at this age. I always thought we'd have more time and that maybe I would go when I was way old. Didn't work out that way did it?

Dee: No it did not. I nearly killed myself a while back with your gun. The only reason I didn't go through with it was because I didn't know that you were supposed to cock the hammer back. After that, I never picked it up again

Alex: Dee! What were you thinking?! Why would you do a stupid thing like that???

Dee: Because I'm so lost without you! Nothing is right anymore. Nothing is normal. Food doesn't taste the same. I can't sleep. I go outside and it's just different. It's going to be this way for the rest of my life. What I used to know is gone. I lost you and it has hurt every day

Alex: Well killing yourself is not the solution! God, I don't want you to think that way ever again. You still got to live!

Dee: Why? Without you there's not really any point. All I'm doing right now is just existing because this is not a life, certainly not the life I wanted or expected

Alex: Yeah, it might not be but that doesn't give you the right to throw it all away. I didn't have a choice, but you do. Promise me that you won't do anything crazy Dee.

Dee: I promise. Besides, I've not thought about it too hard in a long time now. That was just a one off. But I'd be a liar if I said it never crossed my mind. I knew one day that I'd lose you and I knew it would hurt, but I never thought in a million years that it would hurt as much as it does. If that makes sense.

Alex: It does. I don't know why I got pulled away from you. I miss us that's for sure

Dee: Are you in any pain?

Alex: No. I just feel sad. That's the only thing that I feel

Dee: I don't know how I'm going to make it without you. I'm barely making it now

Alex: I know. But you got to keep on keeping on. Not going to be easy.

Dee: No it's not going to be easy. I can't imagine going another 30 years like this

Alex: You won't have to. Eventually, there will come a time when you can manage the loss and the pain. Might not be for a while but you'll eventually get there.

Dee: I don't want to manage it! I want you back here with me!

Alex: Honey, I know. And if I could make that happen you know I would in a second. But that's not the reality right now. Let's be thankful that we have this moment in time. Because I don't know how long I can do this

Dee: What am I going to do???

Alex: You're going to live is what you're going to do. Live the best way you can. Don't stop. Things are different. It's a new normal. But you'll adjust. You have to.

Dee: Remember on our wedding day you said you'd be with me until the end of the line? I didn't think the end of the line would be this quick. It feels like there's a lot left undone

Alex: There is. And I remember saying that too. I never thought the end of the line would be me dying at work in my late 40s. Favorite memory? What is it? Come on, let's think of happy times here

Dee: That night we sat out under the stars on Big Hill right before we got married.

Alex: Yeah? There must've been a billion stars out that night. It was so peaceful I remember

Dee: Yeah. I think about that night sometimes still

Alex: You remember that big fight we had over that guy that I thought you were cheating on me with?

Dee: I sure do. That almost got us didn't it?

Alex: Yeah, it did. And it was my fault. I should've known you weren't like that. I was young and was afraid of losing the best thing I ever had. Because at that time I knew that I'd never find another like you.

Dee: Yeah, that was a rough run. A bad patch. But we got through it

Alex: We always got through it. Everything. Our parents' deaths, not being able to have kids. Man, we faced it all down though. Me and you

Dee: You and me. But this is not something we can do together though

Alex: No, unfortunately not.

Dee: Funniest moment we ever had?

Alex: Without a doubt that time we went to that couple's house you worked with and they got into that huge fight. Man! I was laughing so hard at how much they were going at it

Dee: LOL, Yes!!!! We didn't even stay to eat!

Alex: We had such a good time together and I know that it doesn't seem like it was long enough and trust me, it wasn't, but it was the time of my life. You were the best wife and my best friend through it all. I'm proud that I was with you for as long as I was. And I loved you to the moon and back times a million

Dee: I feel the same. I never loved anyone as much as I loved you. Even in the fights we had, which weren't many, I still loved you. I never wanted to be away from you, not for a second. I know you were meant for me. You are my other half and now you're gone and I don't know how to make it through. It's like half of me is gone. It just feels so bad and all I do is hurt.

Alex: One day, Dee, one day we'll be together again. I promise. And always remember how much I love you. This is not the end of us…it's just a pause. I love you forever and always.

There were several moments of silence between the two. Dee was trying to regain her composure from sobbing heavily on her bed. The pain of losing him was keen at the moment as what was left of her heart was breaking into smaller pieces. Finally, Dee wiped her eyes and looked down at her screen.

Dee: I love you too, forever and always, to the moon and back times a million

Dee sat there for minutes awaiting her husband to reply. He never did again. Whatever ghostly magic that had enabled him to reach out though smoke detectors, jukeboxes, and cell phones had vanished. Alex Moody, as it was, was dead again.

***

Before the year ended, Dee was able to scrape some of her life back together and report back to work. It was hard at first, but the work helped her get out of the house and helped her not think of Alex as much. At first, she felt guilty about that, but then knew that was what Alex would've wanted.

The days and nights, although rather difficult, were becoming easier. She still hurt most days, but she was managing better. When she needed her spirits lifted, she pulled out her phone and read the messages from that night. They made her smile, and yes, they made her cry. But in the end that was all she had of Alex: those messages and those pictures. Sometimes, when she was feeling low, she would send Alex a new message. An "I love you" or a "I miss you." Sometimes she would just text about how her day was as if he was still alive.

That was how she got by for the rest of her life. She never had another man in her life because Alex was it. The beginning and the end.

Dee ended up dying on her eighth birthday alone in her home. She had a heart attack like Alex did, decades prior. She was at home in the kitchen when it hit. Her body was found several hours later when Rae came to check on her with her daughter.

Rae, who was Dee's power of attorney, took care of all the matters that needed to be taken care of. Dee was buried alongside Alex in Burton Cemetery. And that was that.

Inside the Moody house on the night Dee died, it was quiet. It was October, and Halloween hung in the air. It was five days away. All the lights were out inside, and it was dark as a tomb. Then, the jukebox lit up in a fantastic green and blue neon, and a song came on. It was "Plainsong" from The Cure. It happened to be Alex and Dee's wedding song they danced to after they were married. It would always be their song.

In the living room on that night of Dee's death, the two appeared as ghosts, looking as young as they were on their wedding night. The two were reunited for the first time in over three decades.

They floated inches above the hardwood floor, slowly dancing to their wedding song just as they had that night. Dee rested her head on Alex's shoulder, and the two floated, together again, just as Alex promised.

HALLOWEEN MOVIE NIGHT

Bob loved Halloween and had ever since he was a little kid. He decorated his house and yard in a gothic and creepy way, affixing some lighthearted stuff like smiling skeletons and witches flying on their brooms to the front door and windows. He hung ghosts—made from old white bed sheets from years gone by—from limbs in the two oak trees in Bob's front yard. When the wind blew, it looked as if they were flying around.

Faux tombstones were planted to the side of the house, complete with a small rusty iron fence, to give his suburban graveyard an ominous aesthetic. Thick spiderwebs hung from the front porch with care, and menacing and goofy-faced jack-o'-lanterns lit up the front porch steps. He was the only one on the entire block who loved Halloween.

Halloween was upon them, and that meant another thing for Bob: his girlfriend. Sherry was coming over as she had done the past four years they had been seeing each other. She, too, had an affinity for Halloween. It was one of the first things they found they had in common when they met at a friend's costume party back then. Bob was a classic ghost, with a white sheet over him and cutouts for eyes, and Sherry was there as Morticia Addams. The two met at the punch bowl while the song, "Monster Mash" played. From there, the two were inseparable.

Every Halloween since that costume party, the two of them would hand out candy to the trick-or-treaters. Bob usually received more than a hundred on average. His reputation as a house to hit was on every kid and parent's list. Kids, as well as adults, from as far as the edge of town in any direction, made the trek to Bob's house to see all the decorations. He was "Mr. Halloween" to them. The local newspaper had written an article several years ago about Bob and his passion for the spookiest time of the year.

Sure, the cost of candy to hand out had gotten expensive over the years; companies charging more, and more kids hitting his house were the causes of that. But Bob didn't mind too much. He fixed it into his budget so that he could keep his status as the house to hit. He did, however, tell Sherry one evening over dinner last year that if he kept gaining kids, the Halloween candy budget was going to swell another twenty percent.

"Maybe limit the amount of candy per kid," Sherry suggested.

"You know, I never thought of that. I always just reached in and grabbed whatever. You're pretty smart," Bob replied, smiling at the love of his life.

"Well, you know. I try."

***

Halloween was also a time when Bob and Sherry would watch a slew of horror movies in between answering the front door for the trick-or-treaters. It had become a time-honored tradition with the couple. They had composed a list of some really cool spooky season films. This Halloween, the couple had decided that *The Addams Family/Addams Family Values, Beetlejuice, and Ghostbusters* were on the playlist. A stark departure from years past when their first Halloween was a *Friday the Thirteenth* themed movie list. The next year was the *Halloween* movie series, and the last Halloween was *A Nightmare on Elm Street* film festival. Next Halloween– it was determined by the two– that it was going to be a Universal Monster movie run.

Bob and Sherry would start their day around five-thirty that evening, just as darkness was beginning to spread. The earliest of the trick-or-treaters would show up on Bob's front porch, holding out their bags. Bob loved it and grinned from ear to ear when his doorbell rang.

There was something magical for him on this night. Some people loved Christmas, but Bob loved Halloween. Maybe the reason Bob loved the 31st so much was because it harkened back to when he was a kid, trick-or-treating all over town with his friends. Keeping the connection with Halloween allowed the adult to be a kid, even for just one day out of the year.

Bob went ahead and popped a movie into the Blu-ray player: *The Addams Family*, the classic from back when Bob was a teen. It was around five-fifteen that evening when Sherry texted him and said she was on her way there from work.

***

Bob looked at his watch and saw that it was fifteen minutes till six. It only took Sherry roughly ten minutes to get to his house from where she worked. Was he worried? Some. *Maybe she had to stop and get gas or pick something up*, Bob thought to himself. Maybe. Eventually, he tried calling her, but there was no answer. She always answered. It was getting closer to six now, nearly forty-five minutes after her text. Bob wasn't fully in worry mode just yet. However, his anxiety did increase.

At six-fifteen, an hour after Sherry first texted him, darkness finally took the daylight away. Streetlights flipped on throughout the neighborhood, and porch lights illuminated the homes along his street. Bob called her again in between kids at his front door. Still no answer.

After dealing with the last trick-or-treater, a mummy, Bob walked through the house with his now empty bowl of candy to the kitchen to replenish it. He set the bowl on the counter and grabbed a bag of Snickers and poured them in. Then, he heard the front door close.

"I'm here! Sorry I'm late!" It was Sherry's voice. Bob was now relieved and felt an incredible pressure lifted off him.

"I was beginning to worry about you. I called, but there was no answer," Bob said, leaving the bowl of candy to meet his girlfriend in the middle of the living room.

The two of them hugged and kissed, "I'm sorry. I don't know what happened. So...how many kids so far?" Sherry said.

Probably about thirty so far. But the night is young." Just then, the doorbell rang, announcing another kid. "Speak of the devil."

"Wouldn't it be cool if it was a kid dressed as the Devil?" Sherry asked. They both chuckled. "Let me get this one since I left you in the lurch."

Sherry walked into the kitchen to fetch the bowl of candy and went to the door. It wasn't a kid dressed as the Devil, but a zombie. She smiled, dropped a handful of fun-sized treats into his bag, and off he went.

***

Two hours had ticked off the clock since Sherry had gotten to Bob's house, and another movie was playing in the Blu-ray player. This time it was *The Addams Family Values*. It was winding up to the climax of the story. Sherry kept getting up to give treats to the costumed kids, telling Bob to take it easy and put on some music because they weren't really watching the movies anyway. They had seen those movies a million times, and they had become background noise.

Bob queued up his Halloween music playlist, and the first song that played was, "Midnight Monster Hop". Sherry closed the front door and placed the bowl on the end table next to the front door. She joined Bob as he danced in the living room.

***

Sherry answered every doorbell that night as trick-or-treaters came with their bags out, wanting candy. Bob didn't mind. He was having a great time being the DJ, dancing and changing out the movies that they weren't watching. Around ten that night, the trick-or-treaters were beginning to thin out considerably. The music was eventually turned off because the end of the playlist had been reached and was about to cycle back to the top with "Midnight Monster Hop." The last film of the night, *Ghostbusters*, was on TV as Bob and Sherry sat on the couch, eating what was left of the candy and cuddled up beside each other.

The doorbell rang again. Sherry was about to get up to get it but Bob stopped her, "I got this one. You've answered nearly every one of them since you've been here."

Bob got up from the couch, walked over to his front door, and opened it. Instead of there being kids in costume, standing there with their bags open, it was two police officers, standing there with serious looks.

"Mr. Myers?" the younger officer asked.

"Yes...can I help you officers?" Bob asked with nervousness.

The older officer cleared his throat and said, "Do you know Sherry Rammussen? You're in her phone as her emergency contact."

Bob stood there shocked and confused. "Yeah, she's my..." Bob turned to look behind him, and Sherry was gone from the couch. He turned back to the officers, even more confused.

"Sir, we're sorry to inform you that she was in an accident earlier this evening. Her vehicle ran off the road out on Country Road 435 and into a tree. I hate to inform you that she was DOA."

Bob stood there thinking that this was the craziest Halloween prank he had ever gotten in his life. More confusion sat in.

"She couldn't have...she's been here with me since... Wait a minute. Her car..." Bob stepped out onto the front porch between the two officers and looked out into the driveway. Only his car was sitting there. How was that possible?

"Sir, if you would like, we can take you to the hospital where her body is so you can I.D. her and fill out the paperwork. Do you know if she had any kinfolk around?" the younger officer asked in a low voice that was full of compassion.

Bob stood on his front porch and looked out at the driveway. Then, thinking that she was inside the house laughing at her prank, he rushed inside his house and yelled for Sherry to come out and clear this up.

He went through the entire house looking for her: under beds, in closets, everywhere inside the house he thought she might be hiding. Nothing. Sherry was not there.

Had she ever been?

DOOR TO DOOR

All four of them sat in Mrs. Clapper's eighth-grade science class waiting for the three o'clock bell to ring. The week had been a long one, and it usually was when kids and adults who loved Halloween had to wait for the best day of the year, aside from Christmas. Billy, Danny, Winn, and Eddie, best friends since way back in the second grade, talked amongst themselves about the night's festivities.

"Block party?" Billy asked.

"Don't we always?" Winn replied.

"We staying for the whole thing?" Eddie inquired, looking at Shawna from across the classroom, talking to her friends.

"No, I've got an idea for this year since it's basically our last time to go trick-or-treating," Danny said.

The three boys sat and looked at Danny for a few moments. "So, are you going to tell us, or are we going to have to read your mind?" Winn asked.

"We're going trick-or-treating at every house in town...even the creepy one out on Pine Street."

The three boys sat stunned. What Danny was thinking was crazy. "Man," Winn started, "there's no way we can hit every house."

"Yes, we can," Danny replied.

"You remember in the sixth grade when Charlie Morton tried the same thing you're wanting to do? He only got a hundred and fifty houses. Or so he claims. Do you know how many houses are in Claxton? Hundreds and hundreds. There's no way," Winn stated.

Billy said, "It's an awesome thought...but there's no way it can be done. Winn's right, Charlie got the closest, and remember last year when Laurie and Nick tried? They didn't even get close to Charlie's number. If his number was even real. I think it's impossible."

Danny, not one to give up, especially on this idea that would surely send them into the annals of eighth-grade lore, said, "I've mapped it out on Dad's map of the town. I've already got what we need to do and where we need to go first. We keep it inside the city limits, which won't be hard at all to do. Those others tried to hit the county houses along with the houses here in town. We can set the record for houses hit within city limits tonight."

The other three sat at their desks and considered what Danny had proposed.

"Okay, I'm in...I still say we won't be able to pull this off," Eddie said after some consideration.

"I guess I'm in, too," Winn said. "Billy?"

Billy looked at his three best friends and shrugged, "I guess. I had nothing else planned but hanging out with you losers anyways."

As soon as they all agreed, the three o'clock bell rang, and every kid in the classroom jumped from their desks and headed out. Halloween was underway.

"We'll meet at the block party," Danny told his friends as they walked through the jam-packed hallways of their school.

***

Danny walked out of his house and found his grandfather sitting in a chair on the front porch at just about five that evening. He sat whittling an old piece of cedar, the shavings laid at his old shoes that had seen their better days, for sure. Every time his grandfather whittled cedar, the smell, for whatever reason, made Danny smile.

"Love the outfit, kiddo," his grandfather said as Danny walked across the front porch.

"Oh, thanks, Grandpa. Handing out candy for the night?" Danny asked, looking at the huge dish that had all his top five favorites in it.

"Yeah, your parents are leaving for a bonfire tonight and asked me to keep the tradition alive. Ain't like I got anything better to do. Vampire this year, huh?"

Danny grabbed his black cape and spread it out behind him as if he was about to take flight off the front porch, "Yeah, last year was the wolfman. Wanted to hit another Universal Monster."

"Well, you look very pale with the makeup. Got your fangs, right?" his grandfather asked.

"Of course. A vampire can't leave home without them," Danny said, patting his black vest's side pocket. "Got time for a cool, scary story before I head out?"

His grandfather loved to tell stories. He stopped whittling and leaned back in his chair. "Well," he began looking up at the overcast evening, "let me see here...I think I do."

"Okay, cool. Go."

"Have I ever told you the one about the ghost boy that walks the streets every Halloween night here in Claxton?"

"No, I never heard that one before."

"Okay, good, making sure. Anyways, when I was a kid, back in the 1940s, there was this kid that had gotten run over by a car while out trick-or-treating out on what now is Maple Lane. He was a little bit younger than me and my friends, maybe a grade below us, I think. Anyways, we're out hitting all the houses and whatnot that Halloween. We get towards Maple Lane, and there's this commotion with a cop car and people standing all around.

"We ran over to where all the people were standing, you know, to see what was going on, right? We get there, and this person is lying under a sheet on the road. From what we could hear from the adults, the person under the sheet was a kid and was dead. He was running down the sidewalk and crossed the street without looking, and the fella driving the car smacked right into him. Now, sometimes, especially on Halloween, that kid's ghost can be seen roaming the streets in a white sheet...still trying to trick-or-treat. At least, that's the legend I heard."

Danny nodded and smiled, "Cool story, Grandpa. I'll have to tell that one to the guys. But tell me though, did that really happen?"

"Of course it did!" his grandfather leaned back in his chair and tipped his Braves hat up a little on his head, "I was there...me and Gabe Sitwell and all those others. Don't believe me? Go to the library. Check it out."

"Did you ever see the boy's ghost?"

"Nah, I never did. Don't reckon any of my friends did, either. But I heard tales around town that there were a few that spotted him over the years. Just an old legend, I guess– a spooky story for this time of year.

But...you never know. You might see him tonight while you're out and about. You better be safe out there, Dracula."

Danny nodded and walked down the stairs of the front porch, his cape flying in the wind behind him.

***

Danny, Billy, Winn, and Eddie all met up at the block party which was held at the town's park for as long as anyone could remember. The overcast daylight was still hanging around, but barely. The park itself was teeming with people, both kids and adults. A live band was in the center of the park playing all the cool Halloween-inspired songs. The one that was playing at the moment when the four of them met at the entrance gate was "Monster Mash."

Games, mostly for kids, were being played all over and the hayrides were beginning on the other side of the park. Winn, dressed as the Creature from the Black Lagoon, handed out the deep and thick plastic trick-or-treat bags.

"Think these will be enough?" Billy asked.

"I think so. They're pretty deep," Danny replied.

"So, you guys want to go mill around over there, or just start on the houses?" Eddie asked, adjusting the long sleeves on his red wizard robe.

"Let's just go hit the houses. We don't have time...unless you guys want to," Danny said.

"I honestly don't even see the point of going over there, especially if we've got all these houses to hit. It's going to take us a long time as it is," Winn told the other three.

"Well," Danny began, "I've got the map memorized."

"Where do we go first?" Billy asked, pulling his Michael Myers mask off, so he could breathe a little better.

"We head out to Eighth Street and work our way east to west. Then we'll hit Blue Jay Street north, and head south from there ending the night. But we're..."

Before Danny could say anything else, a few more kids: one dressed as a baseball player; another as a prisoner in black and white stripes; and Shawna, Eddie's crush, in a black catsuit with whiskers, a tail, and ears, walked up and joined them.

"We heard about what you guys are planning to do, and we want to go with you," Steve Miller, the baseball player, said.

"I kinda told him what we were planning at Wilson's Drugstore earlier," Billy said to Danny.

Danny was not planning on outsiders, but he was not going to turn them away.

"Sure, I'll give you guys the rundown on how we're going to pull this off. And I've got a really cool Halloween story to tell you as we walk."

The kids all walked out of the park as Danny started telling his crew how they were going to pull this feat off.

***

The seven kids walked from the block party that was going on at the town's park. They hit the houses along the way on Sunset Avenue where the park was located. That was ten houses right there in no time.

"How many houses did the map show?" David, the kid dressed as a prisoner asked.

"Approximately twelve hundred," Danny replied. All the kids stopped walking after he said that.

"Hold up," Billy said. "Twelve hundred?! And you think we can hit all those houses?"

All the kids stood there and looked to Danny for a response. "Yeah, because not all of them are within city limits. That number is just in Claxton as a whole...not within our city limits. Charlie, Nick, and Laurie tried to get every house...we ain't."

"Well, how many are in the city limits?" Shawna inquired.

"Eight hundred fifty-two."

"And you think we're going to be able to hit all of them...tonight?" Winn asked.

"Not if we're standing here, we won't. We've already gotten ten, in what? Ten minutes? Come on, we got to shake a leg here. Let's go!"

***

Drizzle began to fall as day turned into night. The kids, who had already taken care of Sunset Avenue going north, also hit the homes of Wicker

Street, Juniper Road, Cass Street, Thorney Bush Lane, Moss Street, and Harden Lane. On all those streets, there were a hundred houses that were hit. The kids' bags were not even a quarter of the way full, and by Danny's estimation, they were on track to get them filled all the way up to the brim towards the end of the night.

"But go ahead and eat some candy if you want to lighten the load," Danny said.

He looked at his watch under the light of a streetlight and saw that it was six-fifteen. They were in good shape.

They made it to Eighth Street and hit the houses there. Thirty there on that long street. Along the way, a few more kids joined the group, growing the traveling kids group from seven to ten. The newcomers were filled in by Shawna or Winn on what they were trying to do.

"How many houses have you guys hit already?" the girl dressed as a fairy princess asked as they followed tightly within the core group.

"One-forty," Danny replied.

"Cool...how many left?" the young kid that was dressed as Kermit the Frog asked.

"Seven hundred and twelve."

On Spangler Street, the kids racked up another forty-five houses. There were five of those houses that didn't have any lights on. That was a clear signal that the owners were either gone, had no candy left, or didn't believe in Halloween. In those cases, which would be several that night, Danny ran up the porches and counted the houses anyway. Tabby End Road yielded another twenty-five houses and along with it, a few more kids, swelling the number of the roaming group of trick-or-treaters from ten to fourteen.

The next rows of houses on the west end of town were on Dot Street, Cummings Lane, Vandal Street, Knofler Road, and Sage Wind Lane. Those streets had many trick-or-treaters coming and going already, and by the time Danny and his crew were finished there, sixty homes were hit and had candy.

"How many left, you think?" a kid dressed as a Ghostbuster asked.

"Five hundred eighty-two left to go...and it's..." Danny said, stopping under the streetlight to see his watch, "seven-twenty. Plenty of time."

The group of fourteen trick-or-treaters walked east to Lansing, Milford, Jacobs Streets, and Maple Lane. Seventy-eight homes were hit out of the hundred that were lined up on either side of the streets. Several more trick-or-treaters joined in the quest: a kid covered in a sheet, a kid dressed as a dog, a Santa Claus, and a football player, making the group now eighteen.

Clearing the east and west ends of town, the group headed north. It was eight-thirty. The group was still together, adding a few more kids along the way, making the group now at twenty-two. Heading north, the streets of Brock, Cardinal, Blue Jay, Carmine, and Stoker produced a whopping one hundred ten homes that gave out candy. McNamera Lane, Walnut Grove Lane, Connor Edition, Booker Drive, and King Road paid out with ninety-three houses that gave out candy.

"How many left?" Winn asked Danny.

Winn was getting tired as were some of the other kids in the group. Plus, the bags were getting heavier, and some didn't take any candy from the houses because their bags were already too full. Those kids were walking to be a part of something they could tell at school and one day maybe to their kids.

"Three hundred one...and it's eight-fifteen. We still got this, but we got to hurry." Danny said.

Clearing the northern part of Claxton, as well as the east and west, they headed south. The streets of Reading, Marble, Oak, Otis, Thurston, and Johnson produced a hundred fifty houses that gave out candy. The south end of town was more densely populated than any part of Claxton. A lot of that had to do with it being the part of the town to be settled. From the south end, the town grew over the years to the east, west, and north. Danny explained all this as he marched his group through the streets of Claxton that Halloween night.

As the night grew darker and the drizzle a little harder—not a hard rain, by any means—the group of kids began to taper off. By the time they made it to the last section of streets in the south end of town, it was down to the original four along with Shawna, Steve Miller, and the kid who was covered in a sheet.

"If all goes right, after this next batch of streets, we can call it a night and have hit every house within city limits!" Danny proclaimed. The kids were excited– tired, but excited.

***

Further down in the south end of town, on Cherry Lane, Brubaker Road, Lemon Avenue, Strider Place, Spring Garden Road, Burning Trail Street, and Elaine Drive, the kids finished up their night with the one hundred fifty-one houses that they needed. With the last house complete, the kids all rejoiced, screamed, and yelled in triumph, high-fiving each other. Poor Mrs. Walker had no idea what the kids were so happy about on her front porch at nearly nine-thirty that night as she was the last house on their Halloween march.

The group of seven walked back to where it all started: the park. The block party was winding down. Music was still playing and the older kids, the teens and the ones in their early twenties, were still hanging out laughing and having a good time. Shawna and Eddie had been walking behind the rest of the group ever since the north part of town, and Danny figured that they were getting to know one another. *Good for him*, Danny thought.

"Hey guys, this was awesome! We did it!" Eddie said, standing close to Shawna as they all stopped at the entrance gate to the park.

"We certainly did! I knew we could though," Danny replied.

"So...I'm going to walk Shawna home. I'll catch you guys later," Eddie said as Shawna waved goodbye. The two of them walked up the street disappearing into the night.

"Yeah, I'm going to go in here, and wait for my brother," Steve Miller said. "He's my ride. Later, dudes. It's been real." Steve walked into the thinning crowd of the block party.

"Let's call it a night. This bag is killing my back," Billy said. The four of them began to walk up the street and go to their houses.

***

Billy was the first to break off and go home. Then Winn. Danny and the kid covered with the white sheet were the only ones left walking toward Danny's house. Danny had done all of the talking while the two of them walked in the darkness and drizzle. Danny was talking about the night: how he had been studying the town for a while, and how to execute his plan to hit all the homes within city limits. He was pretty much patting himself on his back. He had even retold the story that his grandpa had told him before this night got underway just for the sake of talking because the kid under the sheet had not offered anything verbally.

As they reached the driveway to Danny's house, they stopped. "Where do you live? I can walk you home if you need me to. I can drop this bag of candy here at the house." Danny said.

Nothing from the kid under the sheet. Danny waited for an answer for a few awkward moments. Still, nothing. Danny stood there, looked at the kid, and asked, "What's your name? I didn't catch it earlier."

Again, nothing from the kid under the sheet.

"You know, it's been a long time since I've seen a kid dressed as a ghost. Let's see who's under that sheet."

Danny reached over to the kid and pulled off the sheet. To his shock and horror, when he pulled the sheet off, there was no one under there. Danny looked around the dimly lit street as if he was searching for the kid. Nothing. Holding the sheet in his right hand, the heavy bag of candy in the other, his grandpa's story flashed in his mind about the dead kid under the sheet those years ago.

Happy Halloween, 2022!

104

The meds he was prescribed weren't working, but it was all the doctor could do. Once you got the fever, you either lived or died. Those were the odds, fifty-fifty, across the globe during the pandemic as the fever spread far and wide across the world. Nathan had been sick for five days, and his condition worsened. Hospitals were packed full, and he was turned away, like so many were. Nathan still felt as if he could maybe beat it, but his wife, Marla, was doubtful in private. She had already lost several close friends to the fever and feared her husband would be next. And then what? Her? She hated seeing him in the state he was in, but there was nothing she could do but make him as comfortable as possible and watch after him. That was it. Barring a miracle, she had to sit and watch him slowly die.

The fever inside Nathan's body caused him to shiver with extreme cold. It was hot that August– the dog days outside. Inside the Brewster's house, the thermostat was set at a comfortable seventy-two. Nathan, suffering from Bumblebee Fever, was inside their bedroom under five, thick blankets and was still cold—still shivering.

Additionally, with the blankets, Nathan was dressed in his Atlanta Braves hoodie and a pair of sweatpants from decades past which still fit somehow; and on his feet, Nathan had two pairs of socks on. Yet with all of that, he was still struggling to stay warm. He couldn't remember a time when he was this sick and cold, and neither could Marla.

His fever, the last time Marla had checked, was still at a stubborn 103.4. She worried about her husband because he was the type that never got sick. When Bumblebee Fever became a thing, everyone was getting sick and dying off. It was a catastrophic virus and who knew how it was going to play out in the end, but she was worried about her husband. In the back of her mind, she worried about when her time was coming to catch it.

Marla's immunity to things like seasonal allergies and colds was not good. Even getting vaccinated for the flu during the cold months never prevented her from getting sick. She was scared, especially seeing on the news how many people had contracted the fever and then died from its complications.

She knew her time was coming and seeing Nathan—a healthy man in his mid-forties—struggle like he was, she figured when she caught it, there was not going to be much of a fight from her immune system. Bumblebee Fever had not grown with ferocious intensity… not yet. The worst was coming later; and when it did, humanity struggled to survive. Eventually, the world would shut completely down: people would drop off by the scores on the daily. Governments would crumble; financial institutions would cease to exist; and businesses would become dead relics of what used to be. The world would be thrown into a lawless abyss where the lines of bad and good were blurred by those trying to seize control.

For now, in the Brewster home, Marla was watching Nathan struggle, waiting her turn.

Nathan had been dealing with his fevers that would not break. The lowest they ever got was 103.1 and still, that was high. He took the prescriptions his doc had given him without any success in getting rid of the infection. Eating? Forget about it. Nathan had not eaten, nor wanted to, in two days. He tried some chicken soup at the kitchen table that Marla had made for him.

He was assisted from his bedroom by her and down the hallway as his body was wrapped in two blankets. He was freezing to death on his way to the kitchen. He took two spoonfuls of the soup, which was bland due to his taste buds being stripped away, and swallowed it down. He could feel the warm flow down his throat. It felt good, but after the second spoonful, Nathan could not manage to sit up in a chair. Marla picked him up, walking him back to their bedroom and back into bed where she covered him back up.

Nathan had dreams, crazy fever dreams, that were as wild as anything he had ever dreamed before. Not only were those dreams wild and crazy, but they were also very lucid, too. In one dream that seemed all too real, Nathan was a kid back in high school. But it was not the high school he had attended as a teen. This particular high school was foreign to him. Nathan saw himself—a kid of maybe fourteen—standing outside under a canopy while kids went to and from their classes. He was holding a piece of paper with his class schedule. He recognized none of the teachers' names, and the classes, ones like Business Topics, did not seem real to him. Looking at the piece of paper in his hand, he noticed a math class called, Adding and Subtracting.

"Where the hell am I?" Nathan asked in this dream.

He walked all over the school, outside and inside, down endless halls and into empty classrooms. It was like a maze for him to figure out. Walking into the cafeteria, a woman asked, "What are you doing in here?"

"I'm looking for Ms. Schazer's room," Nathan asked.

"Who?" the lady replied.

Nathan looked down at his class schedule and could not find the teacher's name on it anymore. "It was just here a second ago."

"Honey, are you okay?" This voice was Marla. Nathan woke up from his fever dream to find himself standing in the kitchen in a hoodie, sweatpants, and double-layered socks.

"How...how did I get here? Where's Ms. Schazer's classroom?"

"Honey, let's get you back to bed, okay?" Marla said, taking him gently by the shoulders and guiding him back to their bedroom.

"I never heard of her before...have you?" Nathan asked, still slipping back into his fever dream somewhat.

Marla played the role of whoever it was that he thought he was talking to, "Yeah, I have. But I think she's out right now. Why don't we get you over to this bed, and you lie down. When she gets back, I'll come for you, okay?"

Nathan was fully back into his dream now being guided by a woman down a school hallway, "Yeah...okay. This is my first day here. I guess I'm lost."

Marla got Nathan back into their bed and covered him up as he adjusted himself and closed his eyes, still dreaming of the school. Marla took the thermometer and scanned his forehead. In a few short seconds, 104.4 flashed on the display. She bent down to kiss his forehead, and it was burning hot on her lips.

***

A little while longer, Nathan had another one of those lucid fever dreams. This one featured his dad, who was long dead. Nathan showed up in the dream, standing in the same garage back home where he had grown up. He saw his dad leaning over the open hood of the 1981 Chevy Malibu Classic ratcheting something tight.

"Hand me that ½-inch socket would you, Nathan?" his dad asked, not even looking at him.

Nathan smiled, walked over to the bench, and found the socket to give his dad.

After a few turns with the socket, his dad raised up and stood there looking down at the engine, "Well, that ought to do it, I reckon."

Nathan stood there looking at his dad, mesmerized. The last time he saw him was in an open casket twenty years ago. Now, standing in the same garage back home, his dad looked to be mid-thirties. He looked so young and full of life, standing there looking down at the engine and thinking something over in silence.

"Dad?"

"Yeah, son?" his dad absently replied, still looking down at the engine.

Nathan looked outside the open garage door and saw his street in full view. "Nothing."

Nathan left his dad and walked out of the garage and into the bright sunny afternoon. It was his street: 1220 Maple Lane. Nathan stood there and looked around at the neighborhood in awe. "I'm back home," he said to no one.

Nathan turned to look back at his dad, who leaned back underneath the car's hood paying no mind to his son. Nathan walked out into the street and into the middle of it. It was like a ghost town. But that's how it was on Sundays. Was it Sunday?

"Hey, Dad!?" Nathan yelled.

"What?" his dad asked from underneath the engine, tightening up another bolt.

"What day is it?"

"Sunday."

Nathan nodded, "That's what I thought."

Standing there looking at the house he grew up in and around at all the other houses on the block, Nathan heard a car horn blaring. It made him jump, but when he turned his eyes to look in front of him, there was no car. Then the car horn blared again.

"Get the hell out of the road!" a voice roared. Nathan still could not see anything: no car and no person who belonged to the angry voice.

Marla had come in from the kitchen and just by chance looked out the living room window to see her husband standing smack dab in the middle of their street. A car was stopped in front of him with a guy standing at his open driver's side door, yelling at him. Marla rushed out the front door and across the lawn to rescue Nathan. It was another one of those fever dreams.

"Honey...honey...It's me, Marla. You got to get out of the street, okay?"

"What the blue hell is wrong with that son of a bitch?! He off his meds?!" the angry man shouted while he got back into his car and sped away once Marla gently guided Nathan out of the street and across their lawn.

Nathan, still in the dream, thought that Marla was his mother, "Mom? What's for supper tonight? Are you cooking your world-famous pizza casserole?"

"You bet, sweetie," Marla replied.

She managed him into the house and back into bed where she covered him back up while his teeth chattered and his body shook from cold. She once again took his temperature, and it read 104.2. It went down, but only by two-tenths. Nathan closed his eyes, mumbling something incoherent. In no time, he was snoring. Marla wondered if he was still having the same dream.

He was not.

***

His dream had now switched to when he, his parents, and his sister went to watch the Fourth of July fireworks back in 1997. That was such a grand time, and it was the last time that they all did anything as a family together. After that, Allison went off to college and only came home on holidays and breaks. Summers, she was working at Camp Lackawanna in Georgia.

That night watching the colorful and loud fireworks, Nathan knew that it perhaps would be the best moment he ever shared with them all. He was right; it never happened again, which made the memory that much more cherished.

Back in reality, Marla had to go to the store and get some milk. She hated the idea of leaving Nathan alone at home, especially with him having fever dreams and walking all over the place. But she needed other things, too: bread, coffee, cat litter for Sox, and some Hamburger Helper. She considered putting it off until she was more comfortable that her husband's fever would abate. It never did, not by much anyway.

All morning, she checked in on him. The fever was still holding at 104 or a few ticks above. But so far, Nathan had not gotten back up to wander around and act out his fever dreams. So, Marla decided that she would wait a little while before going to the grocery store, which was only a mile down the road.

Around five that afternoon, Marla, who had been checking in on Nathan off and on, decided that if she was going to go, then she needed to go already. She checked his temp one last time: still 104 but this time, 104 flat. She tightened up his covers around his neck and could feel him shivering underneath them. She kissed his forehead and walked out of the bedroom for the final time in her life. Unbeknownst to her at the time or even when death came for her, she was unaware of what was going to happen once she left their home. Even in the midst of life, death stalks us all.

Marla sat at the kitchen counter, made her small grocery list, and checked it twice. Everything was there, nothing was missing. She got up from the stool, gave the cabinets and fridge a cursory glance, and did not notice anything absent from the list. No additions at this time. She walked out of the kitchen and into the living room where her purse sat next to her rocking chair. She picked it up, slinging it over her shoulder as she walked out of the house.

Around ten minutes after Marla left the house for the final time and before she was struck and killed by the teen texting and driving in the Food Town parking lot, Nathan was having by far one of the craziest dreams he had ever had in his life. In reality, he was standing in the kitchen looking out his back door, staring out into their expansive backyard. Inside his fever-stricken mind, Nathan was awestruck. Out there was one of the biggest circuses he'd ever seen in his entire life.

There were huge tents: colorful ones with yellow, green, orange, and red stripes in the fabric. The biggest tent was in the middle, and the smaller and medium ones flanking it. Nathan betted a million dollars that the big tent had some really cool stuff inside it going on. The yard was abuzz with clowns juggling, trying to impress the children that were walking by. Over to the right on the far side of the yard, Nathan saw a booth where a small elfish man in a three-piece suit was talking to a crowd, telling those who gathered that he could guess their weight within a pound of what they actually weighed.

A bearded lady walked across the yard and looked at Nathan dead in the eyes. She smiled and waved to the sick man. Nathan smiled back and waved. Then she mouthed the words, "Come out here, and join the crowd." Nathan nodded, twisted the door knob, and stepped out into the circus atmosphere. He was swallowed up by the patrons, who milled about laughing, eating cotton candy, and drinking Cokes.

***

Marla pulled into Food Town and parked in the space right next to the handicapped reserved spot; she was very close to the store and had she taken the spot she had seen first a few spaces down, her life would have been spared. But the fates had it to where that spot was just available a mere ten seconds before she pulled in, as an Explorer backed out and drove away, emptying the stall.

Marla shut her car off, grabbed her purse, and got out of the car. Thinking nothing really at all, Marla was walking across the parking lot towards the store. The teen, who had just gotten his license a few weeks ago and was taking a shortcut crossing through Food Town, came in hot where the pedestrian crossing was between the parking lot and the grocery store. He was reading a text that his best friend, Hayden, had sent him about picking him up, so they could go shoot some ball.

Marla paid no mind to the car that was coming quickly down the pedestrian crosswalk. Another thing the fates had planned: her keys, which she for some reason or another did not put in her purse, had slipped from her grasp and clanged onto the pavement. She stopped walking and bent down to pick them up. That was her very last act as a living human being. Heath, the teen behind the wheel of his dad's car, did not see her and ran her over going twenty-five. He thought when the car jumped a bit that it was a speed bump. The only reason he stopped was because others in the parking lot that had seen to their horror what had happened, waved their arms and were screaming at him.

He then stopped and looked around at what all the commotion was. Then he happened to glance into his rearview mirror and saw a woman lying on the pavement sprawled, right leg and left arm in a position that was not natural. Blood began to pool where her head lay. Others had run over to Marla's aid, kneeling down, and some stood by watching with their hands covering their mouths. A few called 9-1-1 and told them to hurry. It would not matter if they would have gotten there faster, Marla was dead on impact. Her head smacked violently against the pavement, and it was lights out. The wheels that ran over her face and body crushed her bones and finished off any life that could have survived.

***

Nathan was walking in his yard where the festive circus was going on, but only inside that fever dream he was having. His fever had spiked again, and if Marla had been there to check it, she would have been very worried because it was now at a critical 105.3. His body in real life was shaking, and his teeth were chattering together. In his fever dream, he was walking around with a big dumb goofy smile on his face as he watched kids and adults mill about his backyard at the circus. Nathan stopped about a few yards from his backdoor and watched an animal band composed of monkeys playing drums, a bass, and a guitar.

"What is that tune? I know that song," Nathan asked himself, trying to place the tune in his head.

"It's 'I Melt With You'...our song," a familiar voice next to him said.

Nathan turned and saw who the voice belonged to: his ex-wife, Erin. He was stunned, completely taken off guard by her presence. She was his true love back in another life. They had been married for ten years, mostly good until the end came. Then the last year of their union was not so much good, but mostly bad. They ended things on a sour note, but that did not mean that Nathan just turned off how he felt about her.

"Erin?"

"How are you these days?" she asked, walking up to him, giving him the biggest hug he ever had.

He hugged her back and could smell the honeysuckle in her hair. God, she always smelled like that, and how that smell of her hair brought him back to where he loved this woman with the brightness of a million suns.

Nathan and Erin pulled themselves apart from each other and stood there looking deeply into one another's eyes, "I don't think I'm doing so good really."

"You don't look good if I'm being honest. You look very sick."

Nathan nodded in agreement, "I am. Probably dying."

"Let's me and you go take a walk," Erin told him as he took his hand and guided him to where she wanted to go, navigating them through the sea of people.

***

Nathan and Erin walked slowly side by side. Both were eating cotton candy, watching all the people enjoy themselves at the circus.

"So...let's get to it. You want to know why I left, right? Why things got bad for us towards the end?" Erin asked.

Nathan said, "Yeah. I never got any kind of closure at all when you left. It was like you changed on me when you hit forty...like you had a mid-life crisis or something."

"I did. I won't lie. I hit forty, started thinking that I needed to change things up for some reason. Started having that affair with that guy who was twenty...should have never done that. It was wrong. I know that now. And for what it's worth, I'm very sorry about how I treated you there towards the end. You were never the issue...it was me. You deserved better than I was giving at the time and I just...thought I could do better. Turns out I didn't. You were the best deal I would ever get."

Nathan walked alongside of her, munching on his blue cotton candy, soaking in everything that she was telling him. For the first time in his life, he was getting some sort of closure from the woman that he loved, still did, if he was being honest.

"You remember that night we met?" Nathan asked as the two of them stopped at a Test Your Might booth.

"Remind me," Erin simply replied as he handed her his cotton candy for her to hold.

Picking up an oversized wooden sledgehammer, Nathan looked at her and winked at the carnie who was working the attraction. He raised the hammer over his head and brought it down onto a metal red disc. When he hit it, the pressure from the blow caused a metal ball to fly up the pole, and it rang the bell.

"Winner! Winner folks! The winner gets the teddy bear!" the carnie announced loudly, handing Nathan a small pink teddy bear.

He took it and gave it to Erin in exchange for his cotton candy back. "You were coming down the aisle where the rugs were in Target, and I was walking in your direction on the other side. We locked eyes, and you smiled at me."

Erin grinned really big, "You stopped and told me that I had the prettiest smile you'd ever seen. I thought for sure that you were feeding me a line."

Nathan and Erin began to slowly walk again towards nowhere in particular, "No line. It was true. I've never forgotten that night. It really was love at first sight. At least, it was for me."

"It was for me, too," Erin replied.

"God, how I wished you would've stayed with me. Crazy what we could have had."

"I know. Trust me, I know. There were several times that I wanted to just pick up the phone and call you, just to hear your voice."

Nathan stopped walking, watched a clown riding an oversized tricycle, and then put his eyes back to her, "Then why didn't you? I would've taken you back, you know? We could've gotten through it...together. Your problem was that you never let me in." Nathan said, patting his heart. "All I wanted more than anything was you. All I ever wanted...was you."

Just then a muscular bald man in a green spandex suit came rushing over to them and blew fire from his mouth. She stood there and smiled as he ran away laughing.

"I was never good at talking...never good at feelings, you know that. But remember, I told you that when we first got together, didn't I? I told you that I wasn't a talker, and that might hurt us later on."

"You did," Nathan said as they somehow found their way to the big tent, where a man in a red suit and a black top hat was taking tickets for admission. "I thought that after a while, I'd wear you down and break through those walls."

Erin and Nathan stopped in front of the tent, standing there before the man with the suit and top hat, "Tickets?"

"Here you go," Erin said, handing the man the tickets she dug from her front jeans pocket.

"Enjoy the show," he told them as he reached over and pulled back the tent flap. They walked in and heard cheering and clapping.

****

Inside the tent, which was much bigger than it looked to Nathan on the outside, he found themselves sitting among the crowd watching a man with a whip and a chair taming a furious lion into submission.

"You know I could never be worn down, Nathan. The more you pushed me to talk, the more backward I went. Eventually, I just wanted out. I guess I wanted to be with someone who didn't like to explore feelings and talk about things."

"Which is why you colored your hair purple, started drinking, and got with that twenty-year-old. Makes sense, I guess. I mean, what guy that is twenty wants to talk about feelings?" Nathan said, eating popcorn from a bag. The cotton candy had mysteriously vanished and been replaced with some stale and extra buttery popcorn.

"You're right. I can't argue that point," Erin said. "But you did better after me, right? Marla seems really good for you."

"She is," Nathan replied as the lion tamer was finished, and a clown car rumbled about letting out fifteen clowns, who tripped and fell all over each other making all the kids in the audience laugh.

"I feel a 'but' coming on," Erin said, digging her hand into his bag of stale popcorn.

Nathan paused for a moment and was about to admit something that he never spoke to anyone. "She's not you."

Erin sat there in silence, chewing on the popcorn for a bit. "I'm sorry that I hurt you. It was never my intention, and if I could take back all your pain, I would. If I could go back and change all these years, I'd do it in a heartbeat. But I can't change the past. I can change the future...for both of us. Do you still love me? Like, really love me?"

Nathan didn't have to think about it. "Of course. With all my heart and soul. I never stopped. Even when you left me behind, I still did."

"I still love you, too," Erin said. "Let's get out of here. We're going to fix this. I'm going to put this right between us."

She got up, and so did Nathan. The two of them walked through the audience and back out the way they came in as the acrobats began to astound the crowd on the trapezes.

They walked out of the big tent where the man in the suit and the top hat stood, "Enjoy the show, I hope?"

"It was wonderful!" Erin said as she pulled Nathan's hand, leading him through the people that were enjoying the circus.

"Where are we going?" Nathan asked.

"You see. Just close your eyes."

"I'll fall," Nathan said laughing.

"Not if you trust me you won't. Just keep them closed, will ya?"

Nathan followed and did as she said; he kept his eyes closed, being led by his hand from the love of his life...his ex-wife. Where was she taking him? What did she have in store? Only she knew. He was excited about it, excited about being back with her. He hoped that it was true. It felt true down in his heart. Eventually, the two of them stopped walking.

"Can I open my eyes now?" Nathan asked.

"Yeah, go ahead."

When Nathan opened his eyes, they were no longer at the circus in his backyard. They were at Big Hill on the other side of town.

"You remember this place I hope?" she asked.

Nathan smiled, looked around, and giggled like a schoolgirl, "Of course I do! This is where we came and watched the meteor shower that night when I asked you to marry me."

Erin smiled and clapped her hands in excitement, "Right! Come on, sit down here in the grass beside me. It's about to start."

Nathan looked at Erin and then noticed that the daylight had turned to full darkness in a flash. Stars were everywhere in the night sky. It was so beautiful, just like it was that night the two of them came to watch the meteor shower, and he proposed to her. Nathan sat down with her, and for the first time in a long time, he was beginning to feel at peace.

In reality, Nathan had managed to walk down the street, across the town of Claxton, and over to Big Hill with no troubles at all on that very hot and smothering evening. He climbed the hill and sat exactly where he was in the fever dream. Had he been in bed and Marla been alive, she would have checked his temperature, and it would have been off the charts at 108. His body was dying, going into convulsions worse than it was when he was walking to Big Hill. Along the way, Nathan had fallen numerous times only to get back on his feet, but barely. In his fever dream, Erin, his true love, was pulling him by the hand out of the tent. In reality, that was what was pulling him to Big Hill for the final time: his love for her.

The two of them sat on Big Hill and watched the stars and the meteors streak across. They held hands and for the first time in decades, Nathan was happy...he was back with the woman who he loved with all his heart.

"I love you, Nathan...now close your eyes and lay down, okay? It's going to be okay now."

Nathan nodded and laid his head down in Erin's lap. He closed his eyes, and she started humming the tune of "I Melt With You." Nathan closed his eyes and drifted off to sleep.

In reality, Nathan had made it to Big Hill and collapsed there in the green grass and convulsed from the extremely high fever. Nathan Brewster died in the same spot where he and Erin were sitting in his fever dream—him laying with his head in her lap, her stroking his hair humming their song, putting him at peace.

THE WOLF AT THE DOOR

June 27th, 1986—Full Moon

It was already getting hot the morning when Lester Lowe's body was discovered out by his barn. He probably would have been out there all day in the rain had it not been for his wife, Mildred, who came out to check on him. Mildred had spent the night with her ailing sister in Vicksburg and had gotten back a little before noon.

She got out of her car and held her purse over her hair—which had been fixed by Missy Malcot at her downtown salon a few days prior—and jogged up the walkway as fast as her fat little legs would carry her. She went up the front porch steps, across it, and through the house. They never locked the front door—or back—for that matter. The Lowes still lived in that world where they felt safe sleeping with their doors unlocked and their windows open.

Inside the house, Mildred put her purse on the end table next to the front door and took her wet jacket off, hanging it on the hook on the other side of the wall. It was warm inside the house. She was walking through their home thinking that she would have seen or at least *heard* Lester by now.

Usually, he was up already. He was an early riser—an hour or two— before Mildred woke up. Lester, being a retired railroad worker for the better part of thirty years, was used to getting up way before sunrise. He thought that he would be able to sleep in more once he didn't have to be up at a job. He was wrong. His body had gotten conditioned over the years so when he retired a year ago at sixty-three, his eyes would open around three-thirty, at the latest four in the morning. He guessed old habits were hard to break.

Mildred went into the kitchen to see if there was any coffee made. Nothing. It was eight-fifteen and she would have bet money that Lester would have a freshly made pot halfway gone through by now. Standing at the counter, she could tell that there was not any coffee made that morning. Odd. The whole thing was odd. Lester should be up by now. He was home because his truck was still in the driveway. She parked right beside it. Then her thoughts became frantic. Something didn't feel right.

She walked out of the kitchen calling his name, thinking the worst— thinking that Lester was upstairs still in bed, dead of a heart attack. Hadn't they talked about something like that just the other day? Of course, they did. Midred climbed the stairs in a hurry wondering if they had spoken that very thing into existence. She climbed those stairs as quickly as she could thinking she was going to give herself a heart attack herself.

Mildred made it upstairs and from the long hallway, she noticed that the bedroom door to Lester's room was wide open. He never slept with it open nor was it open when he was out of it. The old door was closed much all the time. Another oddity. Mildred walked down the hallway to go to the door and half expected him to be lying in the bed dead. But when she got there, she saw his bed was unmade with no Lester.

Just by chance, she called out to him to check the upstairs bathroom. Nothing. Mildred then went to her bedroom. Nothing there either. Her bed was just as she had made it before she left. Mildred always made her bed as soon as she got out of it. It was a practice that her mother had browbeaten into her as a child—old habits.

In full panic now, she descended the stairs and nearly fell on the landing sprawling herself on the floor. She missed the last step and caught herself from doing just that, but barely. Her knee did get jammed and she would feel it later. Now, there was too much adrenaline coursing throughout her body to hurt.

"Lester!" Mildred called out walking from the living room to the dining room and kitchen again. She checked the den, the spare bedroom, and the bathroom. Nothing. The house was empty save her.

Her mind told her to go to the phone and dial 9-1-1 and have the police come and check this out because her husband was missing. But could he be outside? Mildred stood by the phone on the wall in the kitchen and looked out the window into the backyard. Surely not, she thought. Not out in this weather. But something told her to check it out anyway. Perhaps he was in the barn. That was a place where Lester liked to hang out some. Besides, there was a kerosine heater out there that he sat beside to whittle thick sticks of cedar when he was bored while listening to Paul Harvey on his radio.

Stepping back out into the rain, Milred raced across the yard as fast as her fat little legs would take her. The cold rain came down. She made it to the barn and opened the heavy wooden door fully expecting to see her husband sitting on a chair next to his heater wearing his flannel, whittling wood while Paul's voice filled the air. There was nothing.

She walked out of the barn and around it. Why she did that, she no absolutely no idea. Mildred would later tell the police that she had no recollection of walking out of the barn to begin with, let alone outside to the side facing the old cow pasture. And that's where she found Lester. Lying on his back torn all to shreds. She screamed the loudest scream she ever did and put her hands to her face in a harrowed look, just like the ones the women did in those old scary movies from the 1950s.

***

There were already investigators from the county sheriff's department at the Lowe home when Sheriff Dana McMurphy arrived at the residence. She sat in her cruiser for a moment, gathering strength to get out of the car. She had another one of those seizures last night that had just taken the wind completely out of her sails. Her head was still pounding and nothing she took seemed to knock the pain out.

Combined with the animal attack a month ago while on a hunt with her father in South Carolina, the young sheriff was not in good shape. But she had a job to do. Although sitting in her car—looking around at the Lowe residence and over at the barn—she had this weird sensation like she had been there before. But that wasn't right, not right at all. She had never been to the Lowe house. She didn't even know the old retired couple. Yet still, that now overwhelming feeling as if she had been there, right by the barn as a matter of fact, was constant and grabby.

She opened her door—man, that even hurt—and slowly got out of the car. Her body was still healing from the attack—still don't know what it was that jumped her—as deep wounds were on her back and chest and down the side of her neck on the left side. Her right leg was still a little gimpy and it felt as if it was broken but the X-rays were negative.

Dr. Cumbersome told her to rest and stay off it while he treated the rest of her wounds. A month had gone by and she was still sore. She hurt all over. The pain meds she took worked until they wore off. Her days were spent popping pills, usually more than she should've.

"You're a very lucky young lady, you know that?" he told her examining her wounds in his office a few days ago. They were healing but were going to leave scars.

"That's what Dad told me."

"And still no idea what got at you?"

Sheriff McMurphy shook her head, "No clue. One minute I'm crouched down behind a tree ready to shoot this raccoon when all of a sudden I hear something come running up behind me and it jumps on me. The only reason I'm alive now is because Dad was about twenty yards away and came running. He shot at it and claimed he hit it. But Dad's a terrible shot and he also said it was a small bear. I think he's mistaken on both accounts to be honest."

Dr. Cumbersome reapplied some new heavy bandages and gauze on her wounds, which were still bad. There were several of them across her body—deep ones that concerned the good doctor.

***

Sheriff McMurphy walked slowly from the driveway over to where all the commotion was over at the barn. The rain had not let up and was steady and cold for that time of year. Not the type of day to be out that was for sure. The sheriff was met by several deputies at the barn's edge.

"Pretty bad around there," a young deputy remarked. She only nodded and turned the corner.

The body of Lester Lowe was under a sheet while the county detective, a new one from the big city of Tallahassee, Florida stood over it writing stuff down on a clipboard the best he could in the rain. The crime scene photographer had walked by and shook his head, not acknowledging the top cop of the county. He was ready to escape that scene that made his guts turn.

"What happened to this guy?" Sheriff McMurphy asked, walking closer to have herself a better look. She hunkered down, man it was painful to do it, and pulled the sheet back some.

"Looks like an animal attack to me," Det. Stallings replied with a wet cigarette in between his lips.

Lester was torn to pieces. His right eye was missing, his stomach ripped open, and he was missing his left arm. It was a gruesome scene and she knew why now the crime scene photographer left. It was difficult to look at much less take pictures of.

"I'd say before the rain got here he was pretty much covered in blood. That's been washed away. I'd say he'd been out here maybe ten hours. A best-educated guess, given from when his wife last talked to him to when she found him."

"Good lord, this man is mangled," Sheriff McMurphy said absently, looking down at the old man.

"Yeah, large animals tend to do that, don't they? I mean, this could've been you last month, right?" Det. Stallings said matter-of-factly.

"Yeah, maybe. So, you going official with an animal attack?"

Det. Stallings nodded, "Yeah unless you got something different? Ain't no man doing all this."

Sheriff McMurphy raised and stood looking at the dead man as rain fell on him, washing his mangled body. She shook her head slowly, "Nah, probably an animal. Nothing else would make sense, would it?"

"Nope," Det. Stallings said as he pulled his cigarette from his mouth, flicking it out towards the field. "That's how it's going down in the books. Poor son of a bitch. Man, alive!"

July 28th, 1986—Full Moon

Ray Rawls was the second victim.

His body—what was left of it—was discovered not in a rural part of the county like Lester Lowe, but within the city limits. Right outside to be exact, right before Cogdill Street turned into Highway 39. There weren't many houses out that way from town. A few houses dotted here and there along the highway.

The houses weren't close like they were in town. Nearly outside the city limits, the houses had several acres between them, making it feel like they were living in the county but with city amenities.

Ray, an ambulance driver for the hospital, had just come home that evening around nine. His shift was over for the week and boy was he exhausted. His wife, Clara, had a nice chicken dinner ready but had to reheat it. Ray was about three hours too late to get home because he had to stay and help fill in for Steve Stone, who had something going on with his crazy ex-girlfriend. It seemed it was always something with Steve.

At any rate, Ray got home, sat at the table in the small kitchen, and ate his dinner. It was probably better when it was first made, but, hey, at least it wasn't cereal or Campbell's soup again. Since Harry was born, Clara had stopped cooking as much. The baby had consumed much of her attention and what time—little as it was—she did have she napped. Life of a stay-at-home mother.

Sometimes, this bothered Ray. But tonight, it was fine. At least dinner had some substance, not junk food or takeout that zapped their wallet. Ray was the sole provider and told Clara that she had to be careful about how they spent until she returned to work. Lately, she had been talking about not going back. Ray figured if that were the case, he'd have to work more hours to compensate.

Around ten that night, after Ray cleaned up the kitchen table and raked all the leftovers together in one plate. He told Clara that he was taking the scraps outside to feed the strays. Clara, barely awake snoozing in the recliner—Ray's recliner—just smiled and nodded and mumbled something incoherent to her husband. Harry was snoozing too in a bassinet beside her.

Ray walked outside in the hot, stale night air carrying the plate of a few leftovers. He had been tossing the scarps of food whenever Clara would cook over by the treeline to the east side of their home. The wind was picking up, and the talk of a bad storm was heading their way. Ray didn't mind storms. He usually slept soundly at the sound of the thunder and rain.

He walked over to the treeline like he had plenty of times before. He had no idea that it was going to be his last. While he raked the remains of the chicken dinner into the grass, the werewolf was standing directly in front of him camouflaged by a bunch of chest-high trees and shrubs. As the last bones of the chicken and a few mashed potatoes fell from the plate to the ground, Ray, who was still in his EMT clothes, turned and was about to head back inside to grab a shower.

The werewolf exploded from the treeline and tackled Ray from behind, sending him crashing to the ground face-first. The hit happened so fast that he didn't have time to know what hit him. The force from the werewolf knocked the breath clear from Ray's lungs.

The werewolf, in the cover of night, began to snarl and growl as it clawed Ray's face and down his chest, making deep gullies with its black razor-sharp claws. Ray tried to crawl away from the werewolf attacking him, trying desperately to scream for help. There was no more breath left in his lungs as Ray's life was about to flicker out.

The werewolf took a big bite from Ray's throat, silencing him forever. In three minutes flat, the werewolf had gutted and dismembered Ray Rawls who had just come home from work after covering for a fellow EMT. The werewolf howled loudly and viciously and fled the scene while Ray lay on the ground dead.

***

Sheriff McMurphy pulled into the driveway of the Rawls residence. The city cops, along with a few of her deputies from the sheriff's department, were already there. And of course Det. Stallings was there standing on the front porch looking off in the distance of the early morning just before dawn.

Sheriff McMurphy had a whopper of a headache again; another seizure last night, and it was a dozy. The sheriff woke up naked in her bed just like she had last month when the first one came. She never had a history of seizures before and now two in consecutive months. It was concerning her. Plus the memory issue. When those seizures came, she didn't remember anything, not even going to lie down. When she woke in her bed she was naked and she never slept naked. Even more odd, when she went into the bathroom, the tub was still wet from a shower. She didn't recall a shower either.

Getting out of her car, which was getting easier for her, Sheriff McMurphy walked slowly but better than she had been. The damage from the animal attack while she was raccoon hunting with her father was getting better every day too. She was happy about that and so was her doctor. The stitches in her deep wounds were getting itchy though.

"Hey, how's it going, McMurphy?" Dan Davis, the chief of police in town asked, meeting her halfway from her car to the Rawls house.

"Good. Better than them, I'm sure. What happened?"

"Well, just a little bit ago, the wife woke up because her baby was crying. She takes care of him and then notices that her husband ain't in the house and that the back door is still open. After a while, she gets spooked she says, looks for him in the house and nothing. Goes through the back door and sees him out there in the back yard."

"How did he die?" she asked.

"Looks like a damn animal attack to me. Seems to be what Stallings over there said too. Told me that ya'll seen something like this last month out at the Lowe place," Chief Davis said.

"Yeah, we did. How bad was he?"

"Pretty fucking bad. I ain't never seen anything like that around here. But it had to be an animal attack. Probably came through that treeline over there and got him. It's the best we can figure."

At that moment, Det. Stallings came walking up with a cigarette between his lips. His suit always looked too big for him and Sheriff McMurphy wondered why this city detective from Florida wore a suit around here. This was just a small rural county in Tennessee, not anything flashy like Nashville. A nice button-down shirt and some jeans would do.

"Looks like the same shit from the Lowe's last month."

"That's what he just told me," Sheriff McMurphy replied.

"Messed up pretty bad. He's already been photographed, bagged, and sent to the morgue. But I don't..." Sheriff McMurphy zoned out while the detective was talking and her eyes caught the treeline over across the way where Ray was raking the food out.

There was something about that treeline, something familiar. She sensed it just like she had last month while at the Lowe's place. Was it deja vu? No, that wasn't it. It was like she had been there before. That's how she felt at the Lowe's residence—like she had been there before.

"What?" she asked, looking at Det. Stallings.

"I said, but I don't think this is a man. I think we've got a wild animal on the loose attacking people."

"I'd agree with that since there's already been two dead men," Chief Davis said.

"We might want to tell the paper to run a story on the front page that tells the readers to watch out at night that a dangerous animal is on the loose," Det. Stallings said.

"You thinking a bear gone rogue or a big ass wild dog?" Chief Davis asked the detective.

Det. Stallings shook his head, "I don't know exactly. Whatever it is, is big enough to overpower two grown men and rip them to shreds. Maybe we need to get somebody down here to look at Ray who specializes in this kind of thing, like animal attacks. Maybe they can tell us what kind of animal is capable of it. I'm betting bear or wolf."

"That's a good idea. I'll reach out to the University of Tennessee and see if they can help us out," Sheriff McMurphy said.

***

A week later, Sheriff McMurphy and Detective Stallings sat in her office with Dr. Hanson from the University of Tennessee. He was a zoologist who was going over his findings from a few days ago when he examined the body of Ray Rawls and the crime scene photos of Lester Lowe. His findings and conclusions sparked some interest and at the same time several questions.

"There's no mistake. It's a wolf attack in my professional opinion," the doctor told them.

"Is that a common thing with wolves?" Sheriff McMurphy asked sitting behind her desk fidgeting with her ink pen.

"No. It's actually quite rare for wolves to attack humans, especially in the setting you have here. Wolves particularly avoid humans and there are only a handful of cases that I've read, now this is globally mind you, where this has happened in the last hundred years or so. The deaths here in your county have been at the victim's homes. So that means that your predator is actively seeking out its prey. In the manner of the attacks, this was not a feeding exercise. It's not a part of the behavior to act like this."

"So you think this might be a rogue animal doing this?" Det. Stallings asked, sitting on the edge of the sheriff's desk.

"I think so, yes. But what the trigger is, I haven't a clue."

"Could the wolf be rabid?" Sheriff McMurphy asked.

"Very possible. Even if the wolf was infected, and even though the behavior would change to be more aggressive, it's wired in their DNA to not approach humans unless they feel threatened in their territory."

"What would be our next step in protecting our community, Dr. Hanson?" Det. Stallings asked.

The doctor took his glasses off and rubbed his eyes before placing them back on his head. "Well, if it were me, I would hunt the animal and kill it. You do that, call me and I'll examine it. Maybe even write a paper about this maneater. But what you're looking for is a rather large wolf. The biggest wolf ever recorded was a male gray wolf. That animal weighed around one hundred and seventy pounds. Super rare. Keep in mind here, your average wolf weighs anywhere from seventy to one hundred and ten pounds. I think your wolf, I'm just estimating here, ranges from one ten to one thirty."

"Well," Sheriff McMurphy said, "I guess we'll assemble some hunters and try to hunt this thing. You think this wolf will strike again, doctor?"

The doctor shook his head, "I have no idea. Behaviorally speaking, the animal shouldn't have already killed two people, but here we are. Another thing that strikes me as curious...wolves aren't around here, especially in this area. You find it, then you have indeed found a rarity. It would be the equivalent of finding a Great White shark swimming in the Arctic."

August 29th, 1986—Full Moon

In the weeks before the next victim—Emily Anderson and her ten-year-old son, Noah—Sheriff McMurphy had assembled a team composed of ten men who were considered the best hunters in the county. She had met with them all down at the Elk's Lodge a day after Dr. Hanson drove back to the University of Tennessee. She and Det. Stallings explained to them the nature of what was happening and how if this wasn't handled and handled quickly, the wolf might go after someone else—maybe someone they loved.

"There is no money reward here," she told the men. "The reward comes from protecting your home, our community. This animal might be long gone, but it might not be. One thing I can say as your sheriff, we cannot sit back and allow this thing to kill any more of our people."

"There ain't any wolves around here. I've been hunting this county for decades and never seen not nary a one," Clet Clemens said.

"Yeah, I've got to go along with Clet. There ain't no wolf around these parts," Chester Chapman, another skilled older hunter said.

"Well, our zoologist up from UT says it's a wolf that killed those two men. We might not have wolves in this area, but that doesn't mean one didn't just come here," Det. Stallings said.

"What the hell is a zoologist?" Dale Drunkenberry asked, making all the other men laugh with his Southern drawl.

"Never mind that, Dale. We need to find this wolf and fast," Sheriff McMurphy told them.

***

The newspaper ran the story, warned the county that a man-eating wolf was on the prowl, and advised people not to be out at night, especially those in the country. Sheriff McMurphy was interviewed by phone and told Dirk Davenport—the lead reporter—that she was confident that the wolf would be killed but still warned residents to be aware of their surroundings, especially at night.

For nearly three weeks the animal was hunted all over the woods in the county. Hundreds and Hundreds of acres were covered and nothing. No sign of a wolf. There were a few wild boars that were killed during the hunts. Sheriff McMuprhy and Det. Stallings had just about given up hope; that was until George Gregory shot and killed something that was perhaps their wolf.

The wolf was shot and killed in an area known as Harker's Woods, just outside of the town, not even three miles from where Ray Rawls lived. George was sitting in a tree stand, not high off the ground, on the night of August 20th. He heard something rusting around ahead of him.

Probably was a deer, which it always seemed to be. He hit his ultra-bright flashlight and there it was…a wolf. A big sucker too.

The wolf didn't seem to mind the light. George gently placed his flashlight on the floor of the stand, keeping the light somewhat trained on the wolf. Being fast with his rifle, George unshouldered it, aimed, and fired into the direction of the light. He was always a good shot. That night was no different.

He shot the animal right in the back putting it down with a yelp. George picked up the light and shinned it on the animal. It wasn't moving. He climbed down the tree stand, managing the entire time to keep the light on the fallen wolf. He didn't want any surprises here. If this thing was responsible for killing two men, he didn't want to be the third.

He walked over to the animal, slowly, with the light on it. The animal was dead all right. Wasn't breathing, wasn't moving. George thought he had shot the wolf in the back. It was at the base of the neck. The gunshot nearly severed the wolf's neck. George stood in awe at not only his good shot but at how big the wolf was. George smiled and then laughed in the woods that night. He saved the county. He was a hero.

The following day, the paper ran a picture of the dead wolf on the front page. The headline read: MAN EATING WOLF DEAD.

Dr. Hanson had come down from the university to inspect this man-eating specimen. He was excited as well because he wanted to be the first in his field to be involved in writing a paper about a man-eating wolf. His entire two-hour drive all he thought about was the accolades and speaking engagements he would be invited to over this matter.

Back in her office, Sheriff McMurphy took phone calls most of the morning after her photo op, receiving congratulations from everyone, from local concerned citizens to county mayor Daniel Fielding. Deputies were swinging by her office, expressing their happiness that the wolf was dead. McMurphy was glad—elated—that the issue of the man-eating wolf was over.

"Well, I think you might have sealed your next election," Det. Stallings said in a joking way as he came into her office.

She smiled, "Hey, when you need reelection, just have a crisis, right? But really, I'm just thankful that this thing was killed. Could you imagine if it got ahold of a kid?"

"I don't want to think about that. But, we got our man. Well, wolf, rather."

"Dr. Hanson is coming down to examine the wolf," Sheriff McMurphy said from her desk while her phone rang.

"Where's it at?"

"Down at Summers Pet Clinic," she replied.

"Well, it's been an eventful morning already. I'm going to Hardee's to grab some breakfast. Margie didn't get up this morning to make anything. You want something?"

She shook her head, "Nah, I'm fine. I've got some cookies stashed around here someplace."

"Ah, the breakfast of champions. Well, I'm heading out for a bit. I've got to go down to Eddie's Pawn and see about a break-in."

"What happened down there?" Sheriff McMurphy asked, ignoring the ringing phone.

"Some lawnmowers and bikes were stolen. The front door was busted out."

"Well, you have fun with that. I'm going to sit here and take some more calls," she smiled as she picked up the telephone to answer it. Det. Stallings walked out of the room feeling hungrier than he did forty minutes ago.

***

At Summers Pet Clinic, Dr. Hanson was in the examination room where the dead wolf was lying on a table. It was too large for the table. Its back legs were dangling off the end while his nearly severed head rested up on the other end. It was a big wolf, and certainly not native to the area.

The doctor looked at the animal's paws and was curious. He took the paws and pushed out the claws. They were long, but not long enough to cause the amount of damage he saw with Ray's body and the pictures of Lester. He then examined the snout and teeth of the wolf. There were curiosities there as well. Things didn't match up with what he estimated vs. what he was looking at. Plus the weight seemed to be off.

This wolf looked to have weighed maybe eighty, maybe ninety pounds. Still fairly large, but not what Dr. Hanson had been thinking. He picked the dead animal up in his arms—heavier than it looked, but dead weight was heavy anyway—and laid the animal on the scale in the room. Approximately eighty-three pounds.

The only thing left to do would be would run a DFA—Direct Fluorescent Antibody test—a rabies test for the layperson. However, getting the results from the brain tissue would take some time. He could open the animal up there and run the tissue back to his lab at UT and examine it to see if this animal was indeed rabid. However, Dr. Hanson had grave doubts about this wolf being the one that had killed two men.

***

Back at the sheriff's office, Sheriff McMurphy was at her desk talking to the county mayor when a knock came on her closed door. It was the doctor.

"Sheriff McMurphy? Got a minute?" Dr. Hanson asked, opening up, disrupting their closed-door meeting.

"Yeah, come on in," she said.

Dr. Hanson walked in and sat down beside the county mayor. The two introduced themselves to the other.

"Sheriff, I just did a cursory examination of the wolf."

"Big one, ain't he?" Sheriff McMurphy asked.

"Yeah, he is. But I have some reservations about it."

"Such as?" the county mayor asked.

"Well, I...I mean...I don't think this is the animal you're looking for."

Both the sheriff and the county mayor were silent. Then the mayor spoke.

"We have a man-eating wolf that was shot and killed in woods not too far from here. Now, wolves ain't around this area, are they?"

"Well, no, not typically," Dr. Hanson replied.

"Sheriff McMurphy told me that you said that we should be looking for a large wolf and that it was a large wolf that did this to those poor bastards. What's in the vet's office right now? A large wolf. Right?"

"Well, yes, it's a large wolf, but it's not big enough to have caused the damage to those men. In my professional opinion."

"How many wolf attacks have you studied?" the county mayor asked smugly.

"None. This is my first. But I know about wolves and their..."

"So all you know is what you've read? No first-hand accounts? Son, I don't want to scare people around here thinking they can't go out in the woods or, hell, even their yards because of a wolf roaming around. I've grown up around here all my life and never saw a wolf. Never even heard anybody talking about a wolf. And the one time we get one that happens to come this way, it kills two men. We got the right one. You know why? Because it's the only one," the county mayor said.

The sheriff and the doctor sat back and didn't say a word for a few minutes. They were both letting the county mayor's diatribe marinate. Sheriff McMurphy felt that the county mayor was right. She had grown up there and gone on many trips with her dad in the woods, but she had never seen a wolf.

She had asked her dad about the possibility of a wolf around there a few days ago when the doctor came for a visit and her dad laughed and said "No way are there any wolves around."

He, like the other hunters and even the county mayor who had spent their entire lives in the county, all felt the same.

"What makes you think this ain't the wolf, Dr. Hanson?" Sheriff McMurphy asked.

"Well, the weight is not right. This wolf weighs eighty-three pounds. Fairly large wolf, but my estimation on what killed those two men put the wolf around one-ten, one-thirty."

"So about my size?" the sheriff said.

"Correct. Then there's the issue with the claws. When I examined the claws, they were profoundly shorter than what I would expect to see on the killer wolf. Typically a wolf's claws are an inch, but those can vary because of age, habitat, etc. The wolf that killed those two men I estimate those claws were a good two, perhaps two and a half inches long, maybe even three."

"That's what I hate about people like you. You always estimate but can never be approximate. Estimation just gives you wiggle room to make yourself seem right when the facts come out saying otherwise," the county mayor said.

"What else, Dr. Hanson?" Sheriff McMurphy asked, shooting a look over at the county mayor.

"The teeth. The canines, or fangs," he looked over at the county mayor, "are typically an inch and a half or two inches, again depending on the age of the wolf and different variables. For the wolf that I feel you are looking for the canines have to be a good three inches, maybe three and a half. To match the bite marks and the tearing that were present on the bodies."

"Rabies?" she asked.

"I've collected some brain tissue and I'm going to take it back to my lab at UT for examination. I can find out quicker than having it sent off. I've got all the tools I need there for an *approximate* determination," he said, looking over at the county mayor.

"Well," the county mayor got up from his chair and walked toward the door, "I'm not going to say anything else on this matter. The case is closed as far as I'm concerned. That redneck killed that wolf, people are safe, and that's all I care about it." He walked out and closed the door.

"I don't think it's the right wolf," Dr. Hanson said.

Sheriff McMurphy slumped in her chair and looked at the doctor. "What do we do now?"

Dr. Hanson shook his head slowly, "I'm not really sure."

***

It was around ten o'clock that fateful night when Emily and her son, Noah were savagely killed by the werewolf. They had just finished grocery shopping. It was late—way late—by their standards but by the time Emily had gotten off from work, picked Noah up from her mother's, and then got to the grocery store—they were practically out of everything at home—it was close to ten when they pulled into their driveway on Raven Way Drive.

The neighborhood was in the middle of the town, with nice, well-maintained homes all along both sides of the streets. It was safe there. Or at least it was before the brutal attack of the two out there on the front lawn. After that incident, everyone in the county, especially in the neighborhood, was worried. Doors were double and tripled locked as were windows. When the sun went down for the day, people stayed inside. Even the businesses around the towns in the county shuttered right before darkness came.

City and county police stepped up their presence as well. This was a full-blown crisis that the sheriff had on her hands. The newspaper had to retract their headline and now they were saying it was a serial killer, not a wolf. This angered Dr. Hanson because he knew it wasn't a man who was committing the acts of brutality. It was an animal, a beast.

Noah had gone into the house carrying a few plastic shopping bags in each hand. Emily was outside, hunkered down in the backseat gathering the rest in her hands. It was the last of it. Four bags was all that was left after spending nearly eighty dollars. Hopefully it would last the two weeks until she got paid again. But Noah, who was growing rather quickly it seemed, was starting to eat more and more. Emily told her mom that he was trying to eat them out of the house.

Emily shut the driver's side back door with her hip and turned to walk up the walkway when she came face to face with the werewolf. Before she could scream, she dropped her shopping bags and the werewolf raised its arm and swung, slashing the single mom across the throat. Blood gushed out violently in heavy streams of crimson as she fell. The werewolf fell on top of her and began to claw and chew its way through her body in no orderly fashion at all.

Noah came through the open door to see what was taking his mom so long when he stopped in his tracks and saw what his eyes could not believe. There was a werewolf tearing apart his mother on the ground. The kid screamed and the werewolf quickly yanked its head in the direction of the house, the front door. Noah saw the werewolf, blood, and a piece of his mother's blue nurse's uniform in its teeth and fur, and closed the front door. The werewolf got off the dead woman and ran across the lawn and up the concrete steps to the porch and busted through the wooden door with a mighty growl.

Noah ran up the stairs and screamed, terrified as the werewolf chased behind the kid growling and snarling the entire way. Noah had reached the top of the stairs and down the hallway to where his bedroom was, still screaming and crying, begging the monster to leave him alone. But the monster—the werewolf—was not going to stop. The curse wouldn't allow for that. The werewolf ran down the hallway and busted through another, weaker door, and found the kid wide-eyed and frightened. The werewolf wasted no time in killing the child.

***

Neighbors close by had called the police and in about ten minutes the house was under siege. By then the werewolf was long gone, running through the night aimlessly. The first body they came across was Emily's mangled corpse. It was bad. But inside, up in Noah's bedroom, it was much worse. The walls were splattered with the kid's blood and the kid himself looked as if he had been half-eaten and torn apart.

Police found Noah's right leg, what was left of it, over by his bed. His head had been torn off while his torso had been clawed through to his spine. There was so much blood that it squished when officers came into the bedroom from their shoes on the carpet.

While neighbors stood out on the sidewalks colored in blue lights from the police cars, Det. Stallings showed up. He went directly to the white sheet that was covering the body of Emily. He crouched down and uncovered her. He turned his head quickly and covered her up. The officers standing beside him didn't even look down when he uncovered Emily. They had already seen too much.

The chief of police, Lonnie Lankford, came walking out of the house looking as if he was going to puke. Det. Stallings walked over to him to have a chat, but the chief waved him off and walked over to the side of the front porch and threw up violently. The officer who was trailing behind his boss, looked at the detective and shook his head. It was all he could do.

"It's worse upstairs," the officer simply said to the county detective.

***

Later that morning, around six, Sheriff McMurphy woke up lying naked in her backyard. She rose and looked around, confused. She reckoned another seizure and had no memory of how she got out in her backyard.

She looked down at her body and saw broad swatches of blood on her arms, her chest, and her legs. "What the hell..." she whispered.

September 30th, 1986—Full Moon

The town was buzzing with the recent murders of the Anderson family—mother and son. The sheriff's department had been fielding calls the morning after. Concerned people were calling to ask what the police were doing to stop this spree. Sheriff McMurphy came walking in around noon—hair all put up, sunglasses on—and made her way to her office, not stopping to speak with her deputies when they approached her to ask a question. She kept walking.

She got to her office, closed the door, made it to her chair behind the desk, and fell into it. Just getting from her house to the station was a monumental task, to say the least. The seizure was the worst one she had. Her body was telling her that. Feeling like the room was spinning, she put her head down on her desk and that's about the time when Det. Stallings came in.

"Been trying to call you all morning. Where you been?" he asked, closing the door behind him.

Sheriff Mc Murphy slowly raised her head, sunglasses still on. "I had one of my seizures again last night. This one...this one really knocked it out of me."

"Well, we had another murder last night. Two of them. Mom and a kid. Happened over in Charleston. Same M.O. as Lowe and Rawls. This was in a nice neighborhood. Not out in the city limits or the country. Paper is telling everyone that it's a serial killer on the loose. But what has killed those people ain't a man. It's a wolf. I one hundred percent believe Dr. Hanson on that. I know a wolf was shot and killed by that Gregory fella...but maybe not *the* wolf, you know?"

Det. Stallings stood for several moments looking at his boss, wondering if she even heard him.

"Did you hear any of what I just said?" he finally asked her.

"Yes, Stallings, I did. But you're a little loud right now and my head is thumping. I'm going to lie down on the couch over there and get some sleep. Hit the lights on your way out and lock my door, would you? Tell everyone out there nobody knocks on that door." Sheriff McMurphy unplugged her phone from the wall and slowly got up, staggering over to the couch, and fell into it. Det. Stallings did just as she asked.

***

Back in Dr. Hanson's office on the University of Tennessee campus weeks after the recent murders, he was sitting in his office going over test papers from his students when a light knock came wrapping on the door, breaking him from his lull. Grading papers was not something the doctor liked to do. He loathed it. So when he saw who it was knocking on his door, willing to break him out of test grading prison, he smiled and waved his colleague, Dr. Dan Phillips in.

"How's everything on your side of the world, Doc?" Dr. Phllips asked as he grabbed a chair to sit on.

"Man, just sitting here grading these tests. First exam of the year and you'd think these kids would be ready for it. They never are. But at least this gives me a baseline to know what I'm working with."

Dr. Phillips nodded, "Yup, know that all too well. I've already lost faith in my classes' first text in." They both chuckled at that statement. "So, how's your wolf attack going? Anymore down there?"

"Yes, a matter of fact there was. A week ago. A mom and a kid. Right in the middle of a well-populated neighborhood in the town. I talked to the detective that's working the case and he gave me some of the particulars. This time the wolf busted through the front door of the home to get the kid. How that happened, I don't know. I knew that when they killed the wolf they claimed was responsible it wasn't the right one."

"But that was rare, right? A wolf being around that area." Dr. Phillips asked.

Dr. Hanson nodded, "For sure. That was an anomaly. Best way to explain it. Had rabies, too. So it was a good thing it was caught and put down. But what they are looking for is much..."

"Larger and stronger..."

"Right, exactly," Dr. Hanson said.

Dr. Phillips sat there looking up at the ceiling of the office. Dr. Hanson could tell his wheels were turning, thinking about something.

After a few moments of silence, Dr. Phillips said, "Maybe it's not a wolf, per se, they are looking for in the traditional sense."

"Look, it's not a man, I can tell you that for certain. It's a wolf..."

Dr. Phillips cut him off right there, "A werewolf."

Dr. Hanson sat there and looked at his colleague—a colleague everyone liked at the school but was sometimes viewed as a crackpot. He taught a folklore class at the university and although it was popular, especially around the first semester with Halloween coming up, other professors weren't impressed by the doctor. That was okay, he wasn't much impressed by them either.

Dr. Hanson started laughing, "You're putting me on, right?"

"I'm not. Given everything that you described to me from those first two victims, and now you say there are two more, this time with some property damage, I'd say the likelihood of it being a werewolf is very high. It's not a wolf in the traditional sense, but a cursed man inflicted with lycanthropy."

"I don't know how to respond to this," Dr. Hanson laughed, but he knew his friend was serious.

"It's fine, you don't have to. But you told me the details, and you told me everything that you know about wolves. You went into detail about how uncharacteristic it is for a wolf to attack a human and how rare it is for a wolf to be there in that area. You know animal behaviors. Is this wolf behaving like a wolf?"

"Well," Dr. Hanson began, "no, it's not. Not anything I've ever read. But that doesn't mean that it's a werewolf. Besides, those aren't real."

"There are things out in this wide world that cannot be explained by conventional methods. That's how folklore and legends start. It's a way to put some sort of explanation to something that can't be organized, categorized, and filed away. Folklore is an oral and written history of what someone has seen or heard that goes against conventional knowledge. Werewolves have an origin, just like everything else in this world. And how do you know that werewolves aren't real as you or I? Have you ever seen one?"

"No."

"So by your standards, if you haven't seen it, then it can't possibly be real, right? What about all the sea creatures that have yet to be discovered? Just because someone hasn't discovered them doesn't mean they don't exist, correct? You as a zoologist should know that."

Dr. Hanson knew that his friend had him there. It was Dr. Phillips using logic against him. Feeling as if his king was hemmed in with nowhere to go, Dr. Hanson decided to play along and go down this road with him.

"Okay, hypothetically, if this was a werewolf, how did it start and how do we stop it?"

"Whoever the werewolf is, has been bitten or scratched by a cursed werewolf, and then they, too, turn when the moon is full. It probably happened fairly recently. That nugget of lore seems to be transferable through time. I'd say the infected person was attacked in June or May. Then the full moon in June was their first transformation.

"Or then there's the possibility that it's a person who's recently moved into the area or maybe even visiting. The attacks are not localized or confined to one particular area. Which means when the transformation takes place it roams about. The next question is, how to stop it? Silver. It's the only way, right to the heart of the beast. Can't cure them, death is the only way."

Dr. Phillips got up from his chair and walked over to the far wall of the office. He took Dr. Hanson's calendar off the wall. "When was the first murder?"

"June 27th."

Dr. Phllips flipped to June and found the square for the 27th and there was the notation by the calendar company that read FULL MOON. "Full Moon. Next victim?"

"July 28th."

Dr. Phillips turned the page, and on the 28th square, there was a FULL MOON at the bottom of the square. "Full Moon. Next was the mother and child?"

"August 29th."

Dr. Phillips turned the page to August, found the 29th square, and saw where it read FULL MOON. "Full Moon. I will wager my paycheck that there will be a murder on the 30th on the full moon."

"That's a few days away."

"I know," Dr. Phillips said. "As fantastical as this is, and I know you don't believe or adhere to extreme possibilities, but once you have ruled out the laws of science to explain this, what else is there?"

"But I can't go down there and tell them to be looking for a werewolf. They'd think I'm crazy. They're fully convinced now that it's a serial killer stalking their county. I don't even believe that's a werewolf, Dan."

"But you do know it's not a man. You know it's wolf-like. Through your science you know this thing possesses wolf-like attributes through the clawing and bites. Listen, that town has a full-on werewolf on its hands. And it will not stop. Every full moon the curse will transform the poor soul into a bipedal beast. How many people will it go through until someone wakes up to what's actually going on? It's already claimed four lives."

Dr. Hanson laughed to himself for even entertaining the notion that his friends might be right. But when he thought about it, a werewolf—although an outrageous notion—did fit the M.O. "So what do I do?"

"Nothing. Let the 30th come and go. You'll call down there to your detective friend and ask if there was another death. There's always the possibility that the werewolf kills someone who lives alone and can't be accounted for for some time, giving everyone a false sense of security. There's always that variable. But make no mistake here: On the 30th, the werewolf will roam that county and attack in the night."

***

Sheriff McMurphy sat in the exam room with Dr. Cumbersome, who reviewed her chart. She had been feeling good since her last seizure and had finally gotten an appointment with her doctor. The old country doctor sat on his stool while Dana sat on the exam table. She hated being in there.

"So, let's talk about these seizures you think you're having," he said.

"I don't think anything. I know I'm having them."

"What's your symptoms?"

"Well, right before they happen, like a couple of days before, I've been getting these really bad headaches. I mean, they've been putting me down. Then after I get the seizure, I wake up not remembering anything and I'm confused and just tired. Like the kind of tired where I could sleep for days." She omitted waking up naked in her backyard and her bed.

"How long do these things last, the seizures?"

"I don't know. I don't have any memory of them. I just remember going to lay down with the headache and nausea and then I wake up the next day. But it's like I'm not asleep. It's like I can feel myself moving, running around. I know that sounds crazy but that's how I feel when I'm asleep."

"That is interesting. Do you see any stars or dizziness in your vision? Anything like that before or after?"

"Yeah, I have for sure. Usually happens right before the headache puts me down."

"Well, I can rule out blood pressure issues. Vitals there are good, where they need to be. Might be severe migraines or it could be a seizure."

Dr. Cumbersome pulled his pen from his white coat's front pocket and scribbled something on his notepad, and then on her chart. He tore the square of paper from the pad and handed it to her.

"Take this. It's a seizure medication called Phenytoin. What it does is, it controls and prevents seizures by stabilizing the nerve cells in your brain as it lowers the electrical activity there. Get this filled, take it as prescribed and I'll see you in a month. I want to see you before Halloween and we'll go from there."

****

Dr. Phillips was right about the possibility of a werewolf attacking and killing someone who lived alone. That happened on September 30th, around two in the morning out on Country Road 123.

Max Miller, an old man who was a widower and lived alone on his two hundred and fifty acres covered in darkness save a shed light, was the fifth victim of the werewolf attack. His body wouldn't be discovered two days after his death when Harlan Hannicker, the middle-aged friend, came to check on Max.

As soon as he saw all the blood on the front porch and the busted front window he knew it was bad. He would later find Max nearly ripped in half on the west side of his house. His face had nearly been chewed away, he was missing an arm, and his guts had spilled from his stomach and onto the ground. Harlan screamed. He ran away, got into his truck, and tore out of the long driveway nearly wrecking. By the time Harlan made it to the sheriff's department, he was having a heart attack and had to be admitted to the ER. Before the ER, Harlan was able to get his story—some of it, mostly broken pieces—to the deputy who helped him when he came inside the sheriff's department.

The night of the attack, Max was sitting in his recliner watching the eleven o'clock news like he did every night before bed. In his lap was his staple bedtime snack: a can of easy spray cheese and some Ritz crackers with a bottle of 7Up.

Max hated the news because it seemed to be the same old thing night after night. Why he watched it was beyond him. He didn't even really like the news that much. He didn't get out in town very often and the going ons around the local places didn't interest him much at all. The fact was that since Lucy had passed away—back in April this was—Max wasn't much for anything anymore, especially getting out of the house unless it was completely necessary.

The news went off and Johnny Carson was coming on. Max liked Carson and always caught the first thirty minutes of his show before turning in. He had eaten his crackers and cheese and was nearly finished with his 7UP when he heard something outside. A loud bang sounded like something had hit his old pickup truck outside.

A little shaken by this bang in the night, Max eased up from his recliner—which was getting harder to do—and shuffled his way to his living room window. He turned the porch light on and pulled the curtains back to see if there was anyone outside messing around. Sometimes being out as far as he was scared the old man. But what was he going to do? Leave? Nah, he built his house with his bare hands for him and Lucy. Leaving the house—a place he had lived for fifty years— would be blasphemy to Lucy's spirit.

His eyesight wasn't what it used to be and seeing in the dark, even though there was a porch light on the front, didn't help much. Max squinted out in the night and scanned the best he could. Nothing. Could have been a bird flying and hitting his truck, the old man guessed. Maybe. On the TV Johnny Carson was making a joke during his monologue about Bob Hope that made the crowd howl with laughter. Max closed the curtains, flipped the light switch off, and shuffled back to his recliner.

Before he could do some deep sitting—which he would regret later when he struggled to get out of it—there was that bang again. It was louder this time around and more aggressive. Max, out of fear, sprang from his recliner and hurried back over to his window as fast as his old body could go. He flipped the porch light on.

When he pulled the curtains back to see what was out there, his eyes grew wide and his mouth made a screaming sound but nothing came. The werewolf was on the other side of that window pane and reached through the glass, grabbing the old man. The werewolf pulled him through the window and outside into the night. That was all for Max as Johnny Carson mocked his marriages much to the crowd's pleasure.

***

The night of the attack was bad for Sheriff McMurphy. Not as bad as Max's night, but still bad. Her headache had come back and this time she was feeling worse than last month. She had gotten the prescription filled that Dr. Cumbersome had written for her. When she felt the headaches coming on, which meant a seizure wasn't far behind, she took the pills.

She had Deputy Logan take her home because she was in no shape to drive. He walked her inside her house and left her, asking three times if she needed help getting to bed. She shook him off and thanked him. She closed the front door and slid down, her back against it, to the floor. The room was spinning. She felt as if she was going to throw up. The headache was now thumping. Then came the stars flying through her eyes as her vision was grew far away as if she was looking down a tunnel.

***

Ten hours later, at three in the morning, a county police car was coming down County Road 234. Had his headlights not been on bright, he might have hit what was sitting on the road. It was a naked woman. But not just any woman. It was the sheriff of the county. He hit the brakes skidding for several feet before coming to a complete stop. He hit the blue lights and quickly got out of his car. At first, he didn't know who she was from the distance. It wasn't until he got closer that he saw that it was Sheriff Dana McMurphy, the woman who hired him three months ago.

"Sheriff?" he asked, crouching beside her.

"Yeah? Where...where am I?" she asked.

"Ma'am...you're a long way from home. Are you okay?"

It took some time for the deputy's question to register to her brain. She was in a state of confusion—she always was after a seizure. Deputy Logan grabbed his radio and called dispatch for backup and an ambulance. Whatever this was, was bad.

***

For the first week of October, Sheriff McMurphy stayed in the hospital for observation. They were treating her for her seizures as Dr. Cumbersome made hourly visits to see her. She had become a strange case for him. He upped her dosage on the meds he had prescribed for her citing that maybe he should have done that to begin with.

"When I give out medicine, I always like to give out the lowest dose to see if that works. Obviously, in your case, we need to go higher."

During her stay, she was sent tons of flowers, and her parents, her brother, and most of the department guys came for a visit. Stallings even spent the night with her in her hospital room the first night.

"What happened to me?" she asked Stallings that night in the hospital when it was late. It was the same night Max was killed by the werewolf.

Stallings was slumped in an uncomfortable chair, tired and worried about his boss and friend.

"You were naked sitting in the middle of the road at three in the morning. Do you remember anything?"

Dana sat in her bed looking around, trying to recall the events that had escaped her mind.

"All I remember was Logan had brought me home from the office because I was getting sick and couldn't drive. That's it. I remember taking my pills at the station. Everything else...just ain't there. It's like all the other times."

"You were fifteen miles from home. Fifteen. Naked as a jaybird," Stallings said in a voice that seemed far away to her.

"God. I bet I was a sight."

"You were. I got here as soon as they called me."

"Thanks for staying with me," she said after a few moments of silence between the two.

Stallings waved her off, "You don't have to thank me. It's what friends do. But we have to get you figured out because you might not be so lucky next time."

***

Stallings and some more of the sheriff's department were processing the newest crime scene at Max Miller's house out on CO. RD. 123. Max's body had been photographed and examined and was taken away.

Stallings checked out the busted window determining that someone had probably been thrown threw the window from the inside given that all the glass was on the outside.

But when he checked the front door it was locked. Then he wondered wildly if someone had pulled the old man through the window. Then there was the blood. A lot of it led to the western side of the house like a macabre bloody brick road.

This time, the newspaper was there snapping scenes of the house and the crime scene. The next day, they ran another front-page story with the headline: ANOTHER MONTH, ANOTHER VICTIM. Under the headline off to the right side of the front page was a smaller headline that read: SHERIFF MCMURPHY HOSPITALIZED.

Several people after finding out that she was put into the hospital began to talk about maybe she was having a breakdown trying to solve the murders in her county. A few of the chiefs of police in the county started that buzz because they were pretty open about not liking a woman sheriff in their county.

***

A few days later, Stallings was working in his office when he received a phone call. He answered, and a familiar voice was on the other end.

"Detective Stallings?" Dr. Hanson asked.

"Yes? How can I help you?"

"Dr. Hanson. I read the bad news about Sheriff McMurphy. I hope she is doing okay."

"Yeah, she's getting there. Her doctor thinks that she might've had a bad reaction to the medicine he prescribed to her. But these seizures have been pretty bad before then. I think she's getting worse if you want my personal opinion."

"I'm sorry to hear that, I truly am. When you see her, tell that I asked about her, would you?"

"Of course."

"I also read another spot of bad news. Another attack."

Stallings dropped his head. "Yeah, we had another one a week ago. It probably happened on September 30th or the first or second of this month. It's the best we can do with the timeline from the man who checks in on him."

"I hate to hear that. But I might have a theory I want to discuss with you."

"Listen, Dr. Hanson. I think after seeing the crime scenes at the old man's house and the scene with the mom and her kid that I'm thinking now we're dealing with a man, not a wolf."

"It might not be a wolf, per se. Listen, I need to speak with you one-on-one about this. When is a good time?" Dr. Hanson asked.

Stallings sat at his desk, phone to his ear looking around. He was too busy to deal with the doctor at the moment. With the open serial killer investigation that was going nowhere fast, and with Sheriff McMurphy's health, he wasn't much for dealing with a zoologist.

"I don't know. It might be awhile."

"It's very important. Can't be done over the phone," the doctor insisted.

He wanted to put the man off, but he knew the sooner the better to get him out of his hair.

"Can you give me a few weeks? Maybe around the 28th?"

Dr. Hanson sat silently and wondered if that would be enough time. Then he yielded, "Yes, that'll be fine. I'll drive to you. By then, I should have a plan or at least something we can work with."

The two got off the phone. Dr. Hanson then dialed another number. It was to his friend, Dr. Phillips. When Dr. Phllips picked up the phone, Dr. Hanson cleared his throat and said, "Well, you were right on the money. There was another attack on the full moon. Now...where can I get some silver bullets?"

October 31st, 1986. Halloween—Full Moon

In the weeks after her hospitalization, Sheriff McMurphy became stronger and was able to report back to her office on the 20th of October. She had been taking her meds like clockwork. She was asked by Stallings many times if she felt as though they were working.

"I don't know. I won't until I can go a full month without a seizure. Then I'll be able to tell you. But so far, I'm fit as a fiddle."

All was quiet around the town but the buzz was still thick in the air that one of them—could be any one of them—was a serial killer hiding in plain sight. That notion alone that there was a wolf in sheep's clothing caused panic in all the towns in the rural county in Tennessee. Something else that people were still discussing: whether Sheriff McMurphy was fit for the job she was elected to do.

Some of the old timers said that if it was a man in the sheriff's chair they wouldn't be getting all stressed and breaking down and have to stay in the hospital. It was the first time that the sheriff had been called out like that in public. Most of everyone in the county—those who voted— liked her and had usually good things to say about her. But some of the loud-mouthed men of the county, like the chiefs of police in the towns, began to question her leadership. Hell, they questioned her on just about everything way before all the murders began.

Stallings was working the murders—all of them—and there were no leads. Nothing. Zip. Zero. Nada. It was as if a ghost had killed those people. The families of the slain called and showed up to his office weekly asking if there was any progress being made. And when he said he was following some leads—which was a lie to placate them—they told him that he was a lazy bastard and he needed to go back to Florida. That just added to the frustration he had.

***

"In three days, there's going to be another attack," Dr. Hanson said, sitting in Det. Stalling's office that night when the station was nearly empty and quiet.

"And how do you know that? You see it in a fortune cookie?"

"What is killing people in your county, in these towns, is not a man. It's not a serial killer."

"That's right, it's a wolf," Det. Stallings said sarcastically.

"A version."

"What does that mean? A version?"

Dr. Hanson shifted around in his chair to get more comfortable.

"Before I tell you this, keep in mind that I didn't believe it at first either. Okay? I don't know if I do now. But in light of what I was told and what I know about your case, I think it's worth exploring. It's the best option you have."

Det. Stallings sat behind his desk for a few minutes looking at the doctor, trying to figure out what he was going to say. It was his job to figure things out, but he couldn't figure out what he was going to tell him.

"At this point, I'll keep an open mind to just about anything. So...go on."

"Good. That's good. Because you're going to need it when I tell you what I think you're dealing with down here."

"Okay...Lay it on me."

It took ten minutes for the doctor to tell the detective what was killing people, how becoming a werewolf started, and how they would have to dispose of it. He walked through each of the cases, discussing the wolf-like signatures of the victims and how even his own thoughts indicated that there was a wolf much bigger than what was earlier killed. He also remarked that the attacks were all done on the full moon of each month.

Det. Stallings sat and listened to the zoologist and didn't interrupt him not one time. He gave him his full attention and allowed the doctor to lay it out there. And lay it out there he did. Even Dr. Hanson was shocked that he had known so much about werewolves, something he emphasized that he didn't believe in much either.

After his passionate statements to the county detective, Dr. Hanson sat back and waited for him to say something or even laugh. Det. Stallings did neither. He sat there and looked at the doctor with no emotion. After a few minutes of digesting what the doctor had presented to him, the detective finally spoke.

"A werewolf?"

"Yeah," Dr. Hanson replied.

"I've heard some wild and crazy stories from the guys I've busted and interviewed over the years but this one is top shelf my friend. When I was a detective in Florida, we got some crazy people doing crazy things. I thought I had heard it all...but this...this is just out there."

"You don't believe it? I didn't either. I don't know if I really do. But it's worth checking into."

"I'm a man of the law and you're a man of science. We can't just make leaps to the fantastic like this."

"It's not much of a leap. When all other practical methods have been exhausted, there are only extreme possibilities left. We do know that it's not a traditional wolf. We also know it's not a man. Those two things we both know for sure. Right? So the only thing that is left is the possibility of a creature that turns from man to wolf and then back to man."

Det. Starlings began to laugh, not of a mocking kind to the doctor, but as a resignation to himself.

"A fucking werewolf. That's where I'm at in life now. I'm chasing werewolves."

"Trust me, it took me some convincing too by my friend and colleague who is a folklorist at the university. He's forgotten more about this type of stuff than I'd ever remember. And when you put all the stuff we know about the crime scenes together, it does fit."

"Yeah, yeah it does fit. But this ain't a Stephen King book."

"I agree wholeheartedly. But sometimes when logic can't be applied, then we have to go another route. Believe me, as a man of science, this is rubbing me the wrong way too."

There was silence between the two for several minutes before Det. Stallings spoke.

"So, if we know when it will attack, which is on Halloween, how would we even know where to look? The county is a big place."

"I don't know the answer to that. I don't think there is an answer really. It's the literal needle in the haystack I'm afraid."

"To stop the killings, we have to find it and kill it. But to kill it, we have to catch it on a full moon, which is in a few days. Perfect."

"But we have to look. At least try. Maybe the gods will give us some luck that night and we'll find it and destroy it," Dr. Hanson said.

Det. Stallings sat in his chair considering all that he was told. He didn't believe it, any of it, but what else did he have to work with? Nothing. Besides, it's not like he was going to run and tell the newspaper that the investigation had turned into a B-Movie about a werewolf. No, this was going to stay between him and the doctor.

"All right. What else have I got to go on? Nothing. Be here around sundown on Halloween and we'll go patrolling. All night until first light."

"Maybe we'll get lucky," Dr. Hanson replied.

"Just make sure you bring the silver bullets. Because if we run up on a werewolf, we'll need all the silver we can get," Det. Stallings said.

***

On the 30th, the day before Halloween, Sheriff McMurphy had to do an interview with the local radio station about the killings and where the investigations stood on them. She answered as honestly as she could but used the same verbiage that Det. Stallings always used: "We're following up on his leads."

It was a lie because there were no leads. The wolf theory was the best she had. She had no idea that her county detective was now looking into the supernatural. And then there was an interview with the newspaper. Her health was addressed and she assured not only the reporter but also those who would read the interview in the paper tomorrow that she was fine, just having seizures and she was currently under medication to keep everything in check.

By the time she wrapped that all up she was getting tired, getting that feeling that a seizure was coming on. It had been nearly thirty days since the last one and she thought the pills were doing what they were supposed to do. But feeling like she was in her office she knew that was false hope. She knew that it was only a matter of time before her head played dirty tricks on her.

Stallings was business as usual around the office. He had pretty much stopped looking into the killings. There was no evidence of anyone who could be responsible. The only break in the case would have to come with someone coming into the station and admitting to the attacks. But that was not going to happen. The world rarely worked that way.

And then there was Dr. Hanson's theory. Was it a theory or a probability? Det. Stallings took what the man of science had told him with a grain of salt. He wasn't sold on what he was looking for being a werewolf. He spent countless hours at home pacing the floor going over the killings and then what the doctor had told him. It didn't make any sense—none at all—but there he was. It was the only lead he had.

The truth was that he hated himself for even indulging the doctor's wild theory. He felt later after the man left his office that his skills as a detective had diminished. What had he truly accomplished since he made detective back in Florida? Nothing. Just a couple of closed investigations where he nabbed the crooks who stole some stuff from a school and a mom-and-pop grocery store. That was it—all he had done in his career.

The truth was, he was not good at being a detective. He had told his dad that he may be ready for a career change soon. And if he didn't catch the murderer, or more people died on his watch, he would turn it over to someone else—probably the state boys— and go into the family business back in Florida. A car dealership was the family business there.

***

Halloween.

Sheriff McMurphy stayed at home in bed. She was having a difficult time with her headaches, nausea, and now what seemed to be vertigo. Bed rest was the only thing she could manage. The pills were not working now—nothing was—-and all the sheriff could do was cry tears of fear and pain. All she wanted was to be better, to get rid of this curse. What had she done to deserve it?

She was a healthy woman in her early thirties, still had her looks, and still had plenty left in the tank. The thought crossed her mind—but only a few times when she was at her sickest—to put her service weapon into her mouth and pull the trigger. That would fix it all. That Halloween, Sheriff Dana McMurphy stayed home in bed in the constant fear of pain.

***

That evening, Det. Stallings and Dr. Hanson were riding around in Stallings' car, slowly around the city streets and about the county roads. They didn't talk much—both were focusing on the darkness around them, trying to see into it, hoping that they would see what had been killing people. The chatter on the radio in Stallings' car was the usual chatter from the police on Halloween. Stuff like firecrackers going off, houses getting egged, trees being TPd, the usual stuff. No call about a murder. At least not yet.

The moon in the sky was full and silver around six-thirty when the first call came in. There was a disturbance with a possible fatality on Oakdale Drive in Appletown, some ten minutes from where Stallings and Hanson were. Stallings hit the blue lights and hit the gas. Both knew—neither said it—that it was showtime. The werewolf was out and about that Halloween night.

When Det. Starlings arrived on the scene there was already a crowd of bystanders leering while police cars and an ambulance were blocking the street. Stallings slammed the car in PARK and he and Dr. Hanson got out and rushed over to the scene. Laying on the street under a white sheet was a teenager by the name of Geff Godfrey. The police had a few other teens off the side speaking with them and Det. Stallings figured—playing a hunch—that those kids were eyewitnesses to this attack.

"Excuse me, I'm Det. Stallings. Did you kids see what happened?" he asked making his way over to the three kids who were with a city police officer.

"Yeah," the one kid replied shakingly, "Geff was our friend. We were all walking on the sidewalk and this dude dressed up like a werewolf came at us and growled and shit. We took off but Geff thought it was a prank or something. The guy jumps in him and starts killing him."

Det. Stallings looked at the other two kids and they nodded, their faces ghostly pale. And why wouldn't they be? They had witnessed their buddy get killed by an honest-to-God werewolf.

"We ran to that house over there and called you guys," the other kid said, pointing to the brown and white split-level home.

"Which way did he go?" Det. Stallings asked.

"Down the street that way. But that was like fifteen minutes ago."

Det. Stallings and Dr. Hanson look at each other. "Well, at least we have a point of direction. Let's go," the detective said.

***

The sidewalks were brimming with trick-or-treaters going from house to house. At one such house, Dave Derrick was handing out candy at the front door. He had been doing it ever since five-thirty that evening. It was usually a job that his wife loved to do, but she was running behind at work and wouldn't be home for another hour or so. Dave wasn't much in the Halloween mood and hated getting up and down to answer the front door for all the ghosts and goblins holding out bags. He nearly just shut all the lights off but he would never hear the end of it from Jean, his wife, if he did that.

After the most recent trick or treaters visited his house: a vampire, a zombie, and a mummy, Dave was about ready to shut the door and retire back into his house when he saw down the end of his driveway his trash can had been knocked over and trash bags spilling out. He just knew that if he didn't get it cleaned up, the neighborhood dogs would be by later and tear it all to pieces for him to pick up in the morning.

Sitting the candy bowl on a table on the front porch, Dave left his front door open and walked down the driveway to pick up his trash can.

"Damn kids, knocking over shit and not picking it up. Hate this night. I really do," he grumbled the whole way there.

He bent over and lifted the trash can and stood it upright next to his mailbox. The trash pickup was coming tomorrow and hopefully, it wouldn't fall again. One thing Dave hated was picking up trash from the street. It happened once and never again. Making sure the trash can was stable, Dave walked back up to his driveway. He was hit from behind by something with so much force that it snapped his neck instantly. He was dead before he hit the concrete of the driveway face-first. The werewolf clawed and tore poor Dave Derrick—who hated Halloween and giving out candy—to bloody strips.

***

Det. Stallings and Dr. Hanson drove down the streets of Appletown slowly, watching all the kids dressed up, some with their parents, trick-or-treat houses while keeping sharp eyes out for their werewolf. They had been driving for about fifteen minutes since they left the last scene where the teenage boy had been attacked and killed. And in that time nothing, no police chatter on the radio about a fatality. It was just random Halloween stuff going on the radio.

"This thing could be all the way across town by now. Or even back in Charleston. Hell, maybe hiding out in the woods someplace across the county," Det. Stallings said.

Dr. Hanson kept his eyes looking through the passenger side window, looking at kids and houses as they drove slowly on the streets.

"Maybe. I don't know the habits of werewolves. Up until recently, I didn't think they existed."

"Well, that makes two of us. I can't necessarily put out an APB on a werewolf."

That made the doctor smile, almost making him laugh out loud.

"No, can't do that. Those kids back there are the only eyewitnesses of this thing. So we know the werewolf exists because others have seen it. Now, we just have to find it and kill it."

"I wonder who it is?" Det. Stallings asked, turning on Millroe Lane.

Dr. Hanson shook his head, still looking out his passenger-side window. "Who knows? Could be anyone."

"You know how lucky we're going to have to be tonight to find this?"

The doctor laughed this time, "Extremely. It's going to be astronomically difficult to find this creature. Accepting that such things are real is one thing entirely. But now finding it and killing it is a completely different issue."

"What if we don't?" Det. Stallings mused.

"Then we'll have to try again next month. We know two things here. One is that werewolves are seemingly real. I'm still struggling with that mind you. Two, we know it comes out on full moons. We have to be at the right place at the right time."

"I think we'll have better luck picking lottery numbers."

"Indeed," the doctor said.

***

At the Baker home, Annie, the sixteen-year-old babysitter who was hired by Betsy and Bill Baker, was sitting on the couch that evening talking to her friend on the phone. Danny was in the kitchen at the table going through all the candy he had gotten earlier when Annie had taken him trick or treating. It was creeping up towards ten that night and Annie figured that the Bakers would be home any minute. She and her friend were making plans to go to a Halloween party after she finished her job.

"You think your parents will be upset?" her friend asked on the phone.

"No," Annie said. "I'm just going to tell them that I'm spending the night at your house. They'll never know the difference."

"You're getting braver the older you get."

"Well, sixteen is the new twenty-one."

"I hear Mickey Thomas will be there tonight."

"Wow, I hope so. That would be totally rad if he were," Annie said.

"I think he likes you. I see how he looks over at you in biology."

Outside, peering into the front living room window unbeknownst to Annie, the werewolf was watching her talk on the phone sitting in a chair. The creature snarled and licked its blood-stained lips. It was hungry and the power that drove the werewolf to do horrible acts was growing stronger. It wanted to be inside the house, wanted to feed on her. And that's just what the werewolf did...

Annie giggled only like school girls can, "Yeah, I catch him sometimes too. I heard he dumped that bitch, Courtney. God, I hate her."

"Me too," her friend replied. "She thinks she's it. Just because you're on the cheerleading squad doesn't make you better than us."

Before Annie could say something else on the subject of Mickey or Courtney, someone was at the front door.

"Hey, I'm coming over. The Bakers are here. Bye." Annie hung the phone up on the table and called for Danny. "Danny! Your folks are back! Have a great night, kiddo and I'll see you next time!"

"Okay, bye, Annie!" Danny shouted, keeping his focus on the plunder on the kitchen table.

Annie grabbed her bag from the table and went to open the front door. She got the shock of her short life when standing before her was something out of a horror film. It was a hulking werewolf, growling and licking its chops. Before Annie could say anything, the creature flew into the house, landing on top of her, and knocking the kid to the hardwood floor. Annie tried to get away and began to finally scream. The werewolf started to take huge, bloody bites from her neck and chest while she tried to get out from under it.

Danny, hearing the commotion coming from the living room, got up to see what was going on. What he saw stole his very breath.

***

Det. Stallings and Dr. Hanson had been driving all over Appletown and had discussed going over into the country via the backroads to see if their subject of mythical lore was roaming around. After some pros and cons, they both decided to do it.

"I'm going to pull over and take a piss. I can't hold it anymore," Det. Stallings said.

"Right here in the middle of this neighborhood?"

"Yeah, they ain't nobody going to see. Relax. I do this all the time."

Det. Stallings stopped the car and put it into park. He got out and walked to the back. He looked around at all the houses making sure no one was outside or looking through their windows. Most of the lights were off in those houses on both sides of the street. The trick-or-treaters were gone for the night, safely at home going through their candy.

He unzipped his pants and was taking that piss when his eyes caught a house where the front door was standing wide open. He didn't think anything much of it until he heard a scream coming from that house. Up on the second story, someone—a kid—was screaming for help from a bedroom window. The detective zipped his pants and began to walk quickly across the street toward the house. Dr. Hanson rolled down his window, "Where are you going?"

"Get on the radio and call for backup. Crawroad Street!"

"What's going on?"

"Crawford Street! It's here! It's here!"

Det. Stallings drew his weapon that had a clip full of pure silver bullets thanks to Dr. Phillips who had gotten them from a guy he knew. The kid was screaming at the top of his lungs as loudly as he could while the detective raced across the lawn that cold night toward the house. He cautiously ran up the front porch, weapon at the ready and entered into the home ready to come face to face with the monster.

Back at the car, Dr. Hanson unhooked the CB and called for help. He told dispatch their location and that they needed backup for a possible homicide. He knew there would be a death or two by the time the night was finished. He hoped that his detective friend would make it out alive.

Just in case, he got out of the car, pulled his gun from his coat pocket, and gripped it sternly. He had never fired a gun before but the detective had given him a crash course in how to do it before their werewolf hunting began earlier that night. He was shaking as he walked quickly across the lawn while the kid screamed from the second-story window.

***

Det. Stallings walked through the open front door and saw the remains—what were left of them—of someone. He couldn't tell if it was a man or woman or the age of the victim. All he saw was a bloody figure of blood, guts, and what looked like hamburger meat. He could hear the kid still screaming. The detective exhaled deeply and rushed up the stairs. Just as he did that, the werewolf busted through the locked bedroom door where the kid was behind, standing at the window screaming for help.

Danny turned around from the window and saw the werewolf lurking closer and closer with each step it took. He ran over to his closet and got in, holding the doorknob with his small hands screaming and crying, telling the monster to go away. Just before the werewolf could reach the closet and pull the child out, Det. Stallings ran into the bedroom and stood before the werewolf. They both looked at each other.

In an instant, the detective couldn't believe what he was seeing. It should have been impossible and just a few days ago he didn't believe in such things. But there it was, standing before him.

The werewolf made a sudden move toward him and Det. Stallings raised his gun and fired seven shots of pure silver bullets into the werewolf, causing it to stagger backward toward the window. The werewolf tried to jump at the detective again, and again the detective shot it, emptying his clip this time. One of those silver bullets hit the heart and the monster crashed against the window with a furious growl, falling out and landing on the ground below.

The detective stood there in a state of bewilderment as Dr. Hanson came rushing up the stairs calling his name.

"Are you okay?!" he asked. "Are you okay?!"

"I'm fine," Det. Stallings said, shocked at what just occurred. Danny was still in the closet crying and screaming. "I emptied my clip into it...fell out of the window."

Dr. Hanson rushed over to the window and looked down. He stood in a state of confusion, not believing what he was seeing. Then he slowly turned to the detective and said, "You better come here."

Det. Stallings walked over to the window beside the doctor and looked out. He, too, was confused.

Two stories down, on the ground, lay the naked body of Sheriff Dana McMurphy.

AUTHOR'S NOTES

Writers, by nature, are pretty moody people. I think it's part of the trade we're in. I have never known a writer who wasn't moody when they wrote. A writer's mood will, for the most part, reflect in the story and the characters. The stories in this new collection were all written in various states of moodiness. The themes in here are of loss, death, and looking back. I didn't plan the stories to be mainly about that, but it certainly turned out that way. Was I happy with the final product? Yes. Even though some of these stories are depressing at times, they are, at their core, about the human condition.

Writing about the human condition is depressing because, for the most part, *life* is depressing. We find happiness when we can, where we can, and with who we can. Nothing about life is easy. My writing style reflects the human condition in terms of my characters' having to try to deal with something outside their comfort zone throughout my stories. What's more disruptive than something outside our comfort zone that can negatively impact our lives and our day-to-day?

Some writers use monsters, ghosts, and the supernatural to put fear into their audiences, and yes, I do that, too, to varying degrees. However, I think the scariest stuff is the everyday things that can happen to you. A car accident. The death of a child. The death of a parent. A job loss. A diagnosis of inoperable brain cancer. Any of those things can happen at any moment because one thing I know for sure about life is that it is very fragile. A literal second can alter your entire world. What's scarier than knowing your life can end or be changed for the worse at any moment in the day? Nothing.

I try my best to write characters that are relatable to my readers. I think, for the most part, I have over the years. At least, that's been the feedback I've received. Writing authentic characters with which the readers can empathize makes the story more believable, even if its plot is far-fetched. If I can believe these characters and have shared some of their experiences, I know my readers will connect with them. It's those authentic characters that can be any of us that make readers of books and watchers of films buy into what the writer, actor, or director is trying to achieve.

Let's be honest here: being a human is hard work, and not everything we try to do works. We fail more times than we are successful. Even in my writing, I can't tell you how often I failed at something. In the hard drive on this computer, there are many stories and parts of novels where I failed at capturing what I was trying to craft. Sometimes, you can't get it done in writing, much like in real life. I was thankful that the stories in this collection wanted to be told and written. Sometimes that's not the case. When it does work and all comes together, it's nothing but pure magic.

I want to tell you, the reader, who has been with me since my first book in 2020, that I truly appreciate you and the time we've spent together. We've come a long way, haven't we? Still, there are many miles left to go.

I'll see you in time!
July 3rd, 2024

Mathew McConkey

Waltisms

This opening story is about how we remember those we've lost along the way and how they impacted our lives. In this story a friend dies and the other has to give a eulogy at his funeral. I've given only one eulogy, and that was at my dad's funeral. I had sat for two days writing it out and thought I included everything I wanted to say about the man. But when I got up to the podium, I discovered that what I had written didn't sound right—it sounded rehearsed. So, I put the papers away and just spoke from the heart. I think it turned out better. This story came about because of my dad. The man had a saying for just about everything in life. I never knew where those sayings came from, but man, did they resonate with me as a kid, and more so as an adult. He's been gone for seven years now, but those nuggets of wisdom are still with me

At the Stars

This story is about the passage of time between five friends who gather when one of them dies. This story was based on several conversations I've held with my lifelong group of friends. I asked them, each separately, what things were going to be like when one of us finally died. How does that shape us going forward, knowing we can't speak to them anymore? When someone dies, they become just a memory of what was. Are those memories good or bad? I explored this in the story because I wanted to know how a group of friends deal with death when it's one of them.

Regular People

This story is about death and not being able to let go. Letting go is hard and not many people can do it. Would I ever be able to let go of someone who meant the world to me? No. I can answer that one. Everyone grieves at a different pace. Some get better, while others, like Eddie in this story, can't let go. Does this make Eddie and others like him in real life mentally warped? No, I don't think it does. It hurts me down to my core to see someone struggle like Eddie does in this story.

Signs and Wonders

The deer event happened to me in real life. I've told this story a lot over time; people either believe it or they don't. I don't care if they don't believe it. I was there when it happened. During my divorce, I was struggling mentally with how to life keep going. I had so much self-doubt and so much pain that I wasn't sure about anything in my life. At that point, everything was up in the air, even if I wanted to live or not. I asked God to give me a sign, something to let me know that things were going to get better. And out of the woods stepped a deer. I detail that event in this story with exceptional accuracy because it fundamentally changed my life at that point going forward.

Picking up the Dead

As much as writers write about haunted rooms, being buried alive, and ghostly hitchhikers on deserted highways, I wanted to add one more to the ever-popular horror trope. I don't think you call yourself a writer unless you have tackled this subject of the ghostly hitchhiker.

I'm the Man Who Kills the Monsters

Written for the anthology *Just About Sundown*, this short has a lot of H.P. Lovecraft influences in it. That was not intentional at all because I am not a Lovecraft fan. I've read his work, but not all of it. I read enough to know that I wasn't a fan. However, his influence did impact me, and you can see in this short where that is. I remember this story being an unintentional one, and it took me two days to write it. For whatever reason, I was on fire at my desk writing this. The end result was one of my oddest shorts if I do say so myself.

A Night in the Meadow

Originally written exclusively for an anthology called *Just About Sundown*, this short is about an odd painting that seemingly is alive as a killer is stalking the small cottage inside the painting. I've always thought haunted painting stories were unsettling. I've seen a few paintings in junk stores that had been long forgotten and wondered what the painting meant and what the person was like who painted it. Many writers have long written about the idea of a haunted painting over the years. I guess I'm just one more in the long line.

Like a Rocket

Another one of these stories that was mined from growing up. There was an old man named Bob Darnell who lived at the end of my street with his wife in a single-wide trailer. He was a retired man who collected cans and would take them to a place where he could get money from them. I met him back when I was like maybe ten years old, and I brought him some cans. He paid me, and I remember going to the drugstore to buy comic books with my five dollars. Over time, I would visit him and listen to his stories, and man, did he have a lot. He and his friends used to sit out on his front porch and tell all kinds of tales. I would sit there on the front porch steps, drinking a Pepsi and listening to them all. There was a draw for me to go there and hear the old men talk. I think back on those times, over three decades ago, and can still remember feeling like I was a part of something, even if I was just sitting there listening.

Horizon Hotel

I've wanted to write a story about a haunted hotel for a long time, and a few years ago, I was able to put one down. It's one of those stories where it could've been much longer, maybe even a novella or a full-blown novel, but I wanted to keep it compact. I think it works better this way. When writing a short, never overstay your welcome. That is one of the best pieces of advice I can ever give to those who write shorts. It's tempting to make the story longer, but sometimes you just got to know when to stop. Always leave them wanting more.

Messages

This was a tough story to write because it deals with the death of a spouse. I have never had to deal with this type of tragedy, but I know several people who have. I have seen the impact it has on them. It is a total heartbreak to lose the one you love. I couldn't imagine. In this story, I asked two questions: what if you could have one more conversation with them, and what would the two of you talk about? This remains the only story where, in the end, I had chicken skin after I finished it. There's something about that final scene that gets me emotional.

Halloween Movie Night

Written in 2023 as an exclusive for my website, this is one of the fun shorts that brings me back to two things: my love for Halloween and an author who was very influential in my writing, J.B. Stamper. She wrote these books called *Tales from the Midnight Hour*. They were spooky short stories geared towards kids my age, and man, did they have an impact on my writing. Had it not been for her work, I don't think I would have ever gotten into this writing gig. What happens when the person you love comes over for Halloween to watch scary movies and isn't who you think they are? A quick and spooky short right for the Halloween season.

Door to Door

Another website exclusive, this one from 2022, is another homage to J.B. Stamper's work. This short is about one kid's quest to trick-or-treat nearly every house in his town with one spooky side effect. This one is for her.

104

This short was an idea that I had for several years that takes place in that world I had started way back in my first collection, *Scarecrows and Shadows*. The global event was a dangerous flu called "Bumblebee Fever" and was the title of that first apocalyptic story. I wanted to revisit that world a little bit, focusing on one man who had caught it and how it was working on him. Plus, I think fever dreams are cool. I've had a few myself throughout my life that I still remember to this very day. This is a story of how one man's fever dream takes him to death's door.

The Wolf at the Door

This was the final short story I wrote for this book. I wanted to write a monster story that showcased a werewolf but had no idea where to start or how to do it. I'd never written about these things before. This story was new territory for me, but you know what? It was a truly fun experience writing it. I wrote it in January 2024 and finished the first draft in a few days. I let it sit for nearly a year before I went back to it to give it a polish. I'd say ninety-nine percent of the story remained after an edit, which is rare for me. It's a straight story; I don't try to make it what it's not. I don't try too hard to keep the werewolf's identity a secret. This short is just a good recipe of 1980s horror mixed with a dash of suspense.

THE AUTHOR

Matthew McConkey is a novelist, fiction writer, and playwright. He is the author of three novels and three collections of short fiction. His plays are forthcoming. He lives in Tennessee.